THE
LONG
GAME

CRESCENT CITY #2

CASSIE FLINCHUM

Copyright © 2023 by Cassie Flinchum

All rights reserved.

No part of this publication may be reproduced, distributed, or transmitted in any form or by any means, including photocopying, recording, or other methods, without the prior written permission of the publisher, except in the case of brief quotations embodied in critical reviews and certain other noncommercial uses permitted by copyright law.

This is a work of fiction. Any names, characters, places and incidents are the product of the author's imagination or are used fictitiously, and any resemblance to actual persons, living or dead, business establishments, events or locales is entirely coincidental.

The scanning, uploading, and distribution of this book via the Internet or via any other means without the permission of the publisher is illegal and punishable by law.

ISBN: 9798851591549

Spicy Cover Design: Jo, Dark Ink Designs

Discreet Cover Design: Aliyah, @kylahdesigns

Editor: Jenn Lockwood Editing

Proofreader: Sophie, Iris Peony Editing

First paperback edition July 2023

www.Cassie-Flinchum.com

AUTHOR'S NOTE

This is just a friendly reminder before you begin reading that while this is a contemporary romance, there are still potentially triggering topics for some readers. I hope I have handled these topics with the care and generosity they deserve. Please proceed with caution.

Triggers: Anxiety, depression, foster care, and abandonment issues.

This book is recommended for those 18+.

If you have any questions, please don't hesitate to reach out to my email, authorcassieflinchum@gmail.com or my Instagram, @authorcassieflinchum

DEDICATION

For anyone who has ever struggled with a mental illness.

You are not a burden, your feelings are valid, and you are not defined by your struggles.

You are a warrior.

PLAYLIST

Tattoo – **Loreen**
Till Forever Falls Apart – **Ashe and FINNEAS**
Girls Like Me Don't Cry – **Thuy**
Broken Promise – **Jon Dretto**
Wolves - **Lauren Jauregui feat. Ty Dolla $ign & Russ**
Girls Like Us – **Zoe Wees**
Give You Love – **Alex Warren**
Spark – **Ed Sheeran**
Arms – **Christina Perri**
Sweet Silver Lining – **Kate Voegele**
Carry On Wayward Son – **Kansas**
18 – **One Direction**
Nightmare – **Halsey**
Desire – **Meg Myers**
Oxygen – **Robin Schulz & Winona Oak**
Survive My Own Mind – **Ashley Kutcher**
All My Heart – **Sleeping With Sirens**

Bennie And The Jets – **Elton John**
The Heart Wants What It Wants – **Selena Gomez**
Honest – **Kodaline**
The Only Exception – **Paramore**
Stop And Stare – **OneRepublic**
Under Your Scars – **Godsmack**

CHAPTER 1
RILEY

I don't know how much fucking more I can take.

It doesn't matter who you believe in—God, spirits, or whichever—they say that they give the hardest battles to the strongest warriors.

Well, I'm no fucking warrior and I'm certainly not strong.

And to whoever cursed my ass or is currently sticking pins in a voodoo doll shaped like me—I'd love for you to quit because I'm tired of being life's proverbial punching bag.

It's the only explanation as to why I'm standing in my apartment looking at a pile of boxes full of my personal things that were clearly thrown haphazardly together, with no regard to their value. Not that they have much anyway.

"What the hell, Madison?" I ask in disbelief.

"Look, Riley. I'm sorry. Nolan was kicked out of his place and he's my boyfriend; I can't let him live on the street," she states, defending the situation.

"And how the hell does that translate into kicking me out?"

My entire world is falling apart and there's nothing I can do to stop it. I wish I'd never agreed to rent from her without my name on the lease.

"He's a musician. Your room has to be his studio or else he

won't be able to work. I hate to do this, especially since you've been a good tenant, but I'm sorry. And no guy wants to live with his girlfriend and a random roommate."

Hearing her refer to me as a 'random roommate' hurts, but not enough for me to carry the pain out of this room when I'm gone. We started working together a few years ago, and I've been living here for two of them.

"This is bullshit, and you know it, Madison." I shake my head. "This isn't right."

"We all have to do things that we don't want to," she says with a resigned tone.

She tells me like I don't already fucking know that, but she doesn't know my life. I don't think anyone truly does, even my best friend.

"I'll give you to the end of the day to get your things," Madison adds. "If you don't—"

"Don't finish that sentence," I grit. "I'll get my shit later."

As I'm turning to leave, her voice filters through the air, effectively stopping me in my tracks. "Riley."

I cast my eyes over my shoulder, refusing to face fully in her direction. "What?"

"Can you pay this month's rent? Nolan doesn't get his check for a couple weeks and I'm a few days late already."

"You're kidding me, right?" Her lack of an answer tells me all I need to know. A dark, humorless laugh escapes me before I have the chance to keep it inside. "You screw me over, then you want me to pay you? Funny." I laugh again.

I reach into my pocket, and relief pops into Madison's eyes. "Thank you, Riley. You don't know what this means to me."

"Don't be here when I come back for my shit," I demand. When I finally pull my hand out of my pocket, it isn't money that she's getting. Her relief quickly turns into a scowl.

"Fuck you and your shitty musician boyfriend, Madison. Have a nice life." Flipping her the bird, I turn around and leave the apartment, slamming the door behind me.

Not my building, not my problem anymore. Let the neighbors complain about it now.

I walk down the three flights of stairs at a languid pace, letting my new reality sink in. When I find my way outside, I drop down onto the stairs, feeling heavier than I have in a long time.

It feels exactly the same as it did when I was five, standing on the doorstep of a church with no idea what the hell was about to happen to me, nor what I was supposed to do.

Tears well in my eyes against my will, spilling over like a sink whose faucet was left on. Not very many people see my cry. I hate it. I spent the majority of my childhood doing it, and it made me a target.

I'm only vulnerable around very few people, and even then, it's not total transparency.

Because in the wrong hands, those vulnerabilities can be used as a weapon whose only intent is to maim or kill. And there's no worse pain than being wounded by your own making.

With my head tucked into my knees, quiet sobs wrack through my body. The realization that I'm out of a place to stay keeps the tears flowing, persisting to the point of becoming a blubbering mess.

I'm just... so tired.

So fucking tired of working my ass off. Killing myself slowly working multiple jobs and getting nothing in return.

Working to get by, living paycheck to paycheck with little money to use simply for myself—it's not enough anymore. I want things for myself. I deserve it.

But we don't always get the things that we want. I learned that early on.

Like the saying says, "Want in one hand, shit in the other. See which one fills up faster."

The weight of my current situation presses down on my shoulders, with each metaphorical pound cracking a part of my exterior, threatening to crush me into nothing.

But I've gotten through worse, and I can get through this.

I'm just worn out from always trying to 'get through it.'

The first person I want to talk to is my best friend, Blake. We've been best friends since middle school, and she's seen me in some of my worst moments. It wasn't easy letting her in, and I fully intended not to, but being the trailblazer that she is, I wasn't given much of a choice.

She found me sitting alone at lunch one day and asked why I was by myself. When she didn't like my answer, she said, "you don't have to sit alone anymore. I'm your friend now. My name is Blake."

As much as I want to call her, I'm hesitant. Today is her first day as head coach for the New Orleans Warhawks, our local NBA team. She's worked so hard for this, and I know she's on cloud nine after their first practice of the season.

But see… that's the sad reality of my life. Blake is all I have. And she'd beat my ass if I chose to keep this from her only to find out later.

Shakily, I pull my phone from my pocket and bring up her contact. It rings for so long I'm certain that she won't answer, but then the call connects.

"Hey, Ri. What's up?"

"Blake?" I sniffle, not managing to get out anything else.

"What's wrong?" she asks immediately, her tone full of concern.

"Everything," I all but yell.

I explain what happened through graceless weeping, questioning if I'm even coherent. I know right now that my emotions are overloaded, and my words tend not to work during that time.

When my words cease and the tears return in full, Blake offers a bit of hope.

"Riley, I have an idea."

"What is it?" I cough, my voice feeling like I've gargled jagged shark teeth.

"Go to Miles's house. He's got extra rooms and I know that he'll help."

I take back what I just said. That wasn't hope, that's a death sentence.

"No, he won't. Plus, I don't want to stay…"

I try to say that I don't want to stay with him, but I redirect instead.

"What about Asher or Caleb?" I ask. I don't mention her other brother, Hunter, because he's a pro baseball player out of state. "Don't they have space?"

"Ri, you know how Asher is. I love him to death but he's a grumpy asshole who doesn't like people in his space. That's not an option."

"And Caleb?" I ask, my hope dwindling away.

Blake instructs me to stay on the phone as she orders Kyler to try ringing Caleb. He tries once, twice, three times. Even sends a few texts but doesn't get any response.

"I'm sorry, Ri. We couldn't get a hold of Caleb. He's not one to answer his phone much anyway. Not unless he wants to."

"Are you sure?" I ask meekly.

"Riley," she says sternly but comfortingly. "Miles is the only option. My apartment is gone, and we don't have any available rooms here with all my storage. Plus, it's Miles. You've known him forever, we're family. Meet me there, okay?"

I want to say no. God, do I fucking want to say no. But she's right. This is the only option.

"Fine," I murmur, ending the call.

I hate that this is the only option I have. I can't afford a nightly hotel fee until I find a place of my own, and I don't have any other friends.

But living with Miles? My best friend's twin brother?

Yeah, we're more apt to kill each other before I can even get my stuff through the front door.

The sad thing is that we used to be friends and then things… changed. It hasn't been the same since.

But maybe since he's away for games the majority of the season, I can live peacefully—at least until I can find a place of my own.

The likelihood of that happening is slim, and so is finding a roommate. Because rent isn't cheap, and I do well enough to get by as it is.

Grabbing my bag, I stand and wipe the mascara from under my eyes, composing myself into an almost functional human being.

When I get into my car, I take a deep breath. Yet no matter how many times I inhale, I can't seem to get enough oxygen.

The tears prick my eyes again, but I blink them away. I'd like to not total my car today seeing as I'm already out of a home.

Checking my phone, I plug in the address that Blake gave me for Miles's house, feeling like I'm signing a piece of myself over to the old Riley—the lonely girl who wanted nothing but to be wanted by someone, yet was reminded that I never will be.

After all, he's the one who solidified that in my thoughts.

And except for the one day we interacted when Blake needed us both, we haven't spoken for years. Not really.

Now we'll be living together.

Fucking great.

CHAPTER 2
RILEY

It took me nearly thirty minutes to get here. And being parked here now, in the driveway, has my throat feeling like my stomach has risen and taken up new roots.

I don't even know what I'm doing here. Showing up on his doorstep with no context, forcing a favor on him.

And I know that's what this is. He is not going to want to help me, but he will—Blake will make sure of that. Because if there's anyone that he never says no to, it's his twin.

Pushing the nerves to the back of my mind, I shut and lock my car, then glance at the house before me. It's completely different from the house he was in before, and much further off the road.

Over the summer, it appears that Miles moved into a more permanent place, seeing as this is the house he's been working on for a year.

Blake talks about her brother often. And I listen… a lot.

This house is freaking huge. It has to be sitting on about one-hundred acres at least, and it's gorgeous.

It has a French country style architectural build, with gray, light red, and brown brick stones and flat front facades making up the exterior. The roof has overlapped beige clay tiles, and tall, rectangular windows in various locations adorned by baby blue shutters. There are also wrought iron structures decorating the house—stairs and balcony railings and nightlights.

What sticks out the most though is the iron statue of what looks to be a Cherokee War Chief, a representation of his family.

It's actually the thing I found most interesting about the Rainwaters when I first met them—their Cherokee heritage. Not that their dad, Sam, was a famous NBA coach or the fact that they were filthy rich, but because they had such a deep-rooted history, one that they're loyal to and proud of. It's something I've always been jealous of.

Tears prick my eyes, and instead of forcing them away, I let a few fall. I just may need them to convince Miles that I need him. The words make me gag. I hate needing anybody, much less *him*.

"What are you doing parked outside my house? And why are you staring?"

I jump at the sound of Miles's voice, letting out a squeal as my focus shifts to the front door.

"Your sister told me to come here," I say, watching as his brows furrow.

"Why would she tell you to come here?"

"Because I need your help," I say sheepishly, the words tasting like acid on my tongue.

Miles doesn't speak. Instead, he descends the stairs and starts walking toward where I'm standing at my car.

He stops a few feet in front of me and directs his gaze at me, trailing my body from head to toe. I hate the way it makes me feel, like he's assessing me. And being under the scrutiny of his stare thickens the lump in my throat and makes me question myself.

I've spent most of my life conforming myself into who I needed to be to get by, so much so that I've lost a lot of myself. But the Rainwaters… I've never had to pretend around them. They accepted me, took me in, and we were friends—all of us—until we weren't.

Case in point: the man in front of me.

And he is all man, even if I hate to admit it.

"You need my help." He repeats my words, and I feel so fucking small. I'm not above asking for help when I absolutely need it, but I'll move a mountain before I have to ask for it.

But this situation... I know I don't have any more options. This is all I have, and I have to own it.

"Yes," I finally respond.

"Convenient," he says, and turns to head back to the house.

His words cut deep, but it doesn't change the situation.

"Miles," I yell, but he continues walking. Refusing to accept his cold shoulder, I chase after him. He's in the middle of shutting the front door when I stick my foot between it, preventing him from closing it.

"What the hell, Riley?" he bellows.

"You don't have to be such an asshole."

"I'm not. I'm simply stating facts."

Miles backs further into the house, either tired of standing here or trying to ignore me.

Not fucking happening.

"Name one damn fact," I demand, following his retreating form into what seems to be the living room.

"You constantly asked me for lunch money in high school," he begins.

"Lunch money? Are you serious? I had to eat. And I always paid you back."

"What about the time you got busted for shoplifting at the mall and I had to come pretend to be your brother and talked the store out of pressing charges?"

That one was stupid, but I was a kid. And I... no, no need to bring up the past. Even for myself.

"You were one of my best friends. Of course I would call you, and it never happened again."

When Miles doesn't try to respond, I take a step closer to

him, and the reason why I'm here creeps back in, letting the tears form again.

"Miles, I haven't fucking needed you in years. I haven't needed *anyone* in years. I've worked my ass off for things to be this way. But like the rest of my life, it decided to fuck me again and not in the way that's fun."

"Then tell me what happened while I'm willing to listen."

"This isn't exactly willing," I say, pointing at his uncaring posture as he stands by the couch. He stands taller, crossing his corded forearms over his chest, and I hate the way I'm drawn to them.

"But if you're willing…" I continue, "my jackass of a roommate kicked me out with no notice so that her boyfriend could move in, and then had the audacity to ask me for rent money. In a place I'm not even staying."

"Your roommate sounds like a bitch," he says.

"Trust me. She is."

"So, why does that put you here? I'm lost."

"You really haven't talked to Blake?" He shakes his head. Taking a deep breath, I push back the nerves and go for it.

"Because I don't have anywhere to stay, Miles."

"I still don't see how that concerns me."

Liar. He's probably purposely acting dumb about it. Miles picks up the water sitting on the table beside us and opens it, placing it in his mouth to take a sip.

"Because she wants me to stay with you."

A splash of water hits me right in the neck and chest, trickling down my bra to in between my breasts.

"She fucking wants *what*?" he says, wiping the water from his lips.

Don't know how there could be any left when I'm wearing it all.

"She wants me to stay with you," I snap, angry that he's just wet my only pair of clothes for now and because I have to repeat myself.

As I'm trying to dab at the water between my tits using the

dry part of my shirt, a car door sounds from outside and Miles is out the door in a second, practically sprinting.

Instead of following him outside, I step to the window and pull back the curtains, watching a very animated conversation between Miles and Blake.

I can tell that he's speaking loudly, using his hands, and Blake is coming at him just as hard with a bit of what looks like confusion on her face until she steps forward and places her hand on his shoulder.

Everything shifts at her touch. The tension, the negatively charged energy in the air, it all dissipates when Blake uses that sisterly tone—the one I know she's using. It's what gets things done.

A few moments later, Miles stomps back into the house and disappears into one of the other rooms. Blake and Kyler, Blake's boyfriend and Miles's teammate, are still standing outside, so I take it upon myself to walk outside and meet her.

This whole living together thing… it's bound to turn into a disaster, especially with how much we dislike each other now. I have every reason to dislike him, but no clue why he returns the favor now.

She's still staring at where her brother walked to, but at my appearance, she directs her gaze to me.

"I love you, Blake. I really do. And if I had somewhere else to go, I would be there. Because as grateful as I am for this, you have no idea what you've just done by putting me here."

"I don't understand," Blake says, confusion furrowing her brows.

"Miles and I haven't been friends in years, Blake," I say.

"Which still doesn't make sense to me, but you've been fine around each other on the occasion that you're in the same proximity, so I figured this would be okay. And like I told my brother; we're gone a lot for the season. You'll barely be around each other."

One, she'll never know the reason why. Two, I'll still be in *his* space, and that's enough for me.

"Now that I'm here, I'm not sure how comfortable I feel with this."

"Come inside," she tells me. "We can talk about it."

Blake rests a gentle arm on my back and escorts me inside, straight to the couch. In the last few minutes, Miles has resurfaced from wherever he stormed off to and is holding an intense glare in my direction as Kyler speaks in a low tone to him.

"Miles," Blake says, grabbing his attention. His scowl only lessens at the sound of her voice. "Would you grab Riley something to drink? And a blanket, too."

"If she's going to be staying here, she'll have to figure out where everything is anyway. Let her get it."

"Miles," Blake scolds, glaring at her brother with an intensity that could start a fire from thin air. "Don't be so gvsgasdagi."

Rude. I've been around them enough to know that word.

I would call it more like being a dick, but the Cherokee don't have room for curse words in their language apparently.

What a shame.

"Just because you're older—" Miles begins.

"Exactly. I'm older," she says, cutting him off. Miles grumbles something about *'only two minutes,'* but Blake doesn't catch it. "Now stop being so fucking stubborn and just do what I asked. She's been through enough today."

A few minutes later, Miles places a glass of water on the table and practically throws a blanket at me. Blake glares at him again, but I'm not bothered by it. I'd hate for someone to invade my space too.

"Now, tell us what happened," Blake instructs, rubbing soothing circles between my shoulders.

She's one of two people that have shown me that kind of comfort in my life. The other is currently sitting across from me, but those eyes—the enticing, beautiful chocolate orbs—aren't the ones that used to show me sympathy, compassion... no.

These are full of detest and resentment.

"My roommate traded me in for cock, and not even good cock. I heard her moans through the wall at times, and they were fake." *I would know.*

"Traded you in?" Kyler questions.

"Yeah. Kicked me out so her boyfriend could move in and use my room to make the next worse hit." Sarcasm rolls off my tongue as easily as rain on a window, dripping into a puddle at my feet.

Over the years, I've learned to see life through fogged glass. You can see what's on the other side, though it may not be clear, and you know what to expect—for the most part.

But the fog provides a reminder that things aren't crystal clear, and what's on the other side of the window won't always be what you expect.

"I knew I didn't like her," Blake says. "What about your things?"

"Wants them out by the end of the day," I grumble. "And that was before she asked for rent money."

"Bitch," Blake laughs. "Don't worry. Kyler and I will go and get your things and bring them back here. You don't need to go back there. You should stay here and get situated."

"I can help. I don't mind. It's my shit anyway."

"No," Blake demands. "You can't be there. If I decide to punch her, which is highly likely, it's better if you're not a witness."

"You can't punch her," I nearly shriek.

"Yes the fuck I can," Blake laughs.

"But Kyler will be a witness," I remind her.

"What are you talking about?" Kyler asks. "I see nothing. If something goes down, I was loading the truck."

"You two are fucking perfect for each other," Miles grumbles from the couch.

"We know," the couple says in unison.

"Look," Blake starts, "we'll go get your things packed up and brought over, even if it takes more than one trip. On our way back, we'll grab food. Sound good?"

I nod, though the last thing on my mind right now is food.

After texting Blake a thorough list of my things—because that bitch is *not* keeping my Kellin Quinn signed *Sleeping With Sirens* poster in the living room—she and Kyler leave to head back to Hell, or my so-called ex-apartment.

Miles stays planted on the couch, staring at me with fire burning in those brown eyes that I hate that I love—*used* to love.

"Listen," I start, dropping my guard enough that my sincerity can be sufficiently convincing. "I know that you're not comfortable with this, and I know it physically pains you to have me here. Trust me, I know. But I want you to know I appreciate you doing this, even if it is just for your sister."

"Whatever," he groans, then stands, facing me with an angry glare. "Follow me."

Miles bolts out of the living room and then hustles up the stairs. He doesn't give me time to pay attention to where I'm going or what the rest of the house looks like, but I can't lose him either.

He stands at six-foot-five while I stand a solid foot below him at five-foot-five. Miles takes two steps at a time to my one, and I nearly lose him at the top of the stairs before following him to the end of the hall near a light brown door.

"I haven't furnished the house yet, so this is the only room besides mine that has furniture." Miles opens the door, and what's inside is breathtaking, even plain.

First off, the room is the size of the living room and my room combined back at the old apartment. I've never in my life had this much space of my own, even if it is temporary.

The walls are beige-gray, and in the middle of the back wall sits a deep, caramel colored King-sized bed.

This can't be just a guest room.

Small dressers stand on either side of the bed, with two

dressers—one with a mirror—on opposite walls and a huge walk-in closet that I can see just from the doorway.

"The TV is hooked up to all the streaming services, and the bathroom is just down the hall, but you have your own ensuite also. We can talk about other shit later but if you have questions, I guess you can ask. Or figure it out yourself. Doesn't matter to me either way."

"Thank you—"

"Don't. It's whatever."

When Miles steps away, he makes it just across the hall before twisting the handle on the room across from mine.

"Where are you going?" I rush out.

"To my room," he says in an obvious tone.

"Your room is across from mine? Don't you think that's something you should have mentioned?!"

"No, because it doesn't matter," he says, reaching for his handle again. "Let me know when they get here with your shit."

Then the door slams, and I'm left having a mini panic attack.

Not only will I be living here, in the same house with him, but now I'm in the room closest to his where he can hear every fucking thing that happens in this space.

If I have to listen to that shithead masturbate, I'll rip my ears off.

Or you'll like it, the voice of younger me says.

The me that was infatuated with my best friend's brother, but knew that no matter what happened, we'd never be more than friends.

After what happened near the end of senior year, I never thought I'd be here. Forced to rely on him.

But then again, I'm life's proverbial punching bag.

And I've landed in Miles' ring until further notice.

CHAPTER 3
RILEY

I'd like to say that I slept well last night, but that would be a lie.

Once Blake and Kyler finished bringing my things over, Blake helped me settle into the room Miles provided me.

And like I had predicted, she did charge at my ex-roommate before Kyler pulled her back. So, she used her words instead.

But trust me, those are just as lethal as her fists when she wants them to be.

I wish I could say that I felt bad about her treating Madison that way, given she was nice enough to share her place with me for a lower rent—at first—but then she threw me out, as if I had a backup plan.

I didn't, until Blake gave me one.

The Rainwaters, Blake in particular, are always saving me.

Once Blake and Kyler left late last night, I avoided Miles as much as possible. I waited until I heard his door shut to grab a drink from the kitchen, and I waited until his room was quiet before I even showered.

And I waited until I heard him leave for practice before I ventured outside this morning.

This place may be my temporary home, but it feels like anything but.

The walls in the hallway upstairs are bare, only the rhinestone-colored paint covering them.

An oak-wood banister trails the stairs as they descend into the downstairs hallway that leads into other rooms of the house and back to the living room.

I amble down the hallway, checking into all the doors first. Like a weirdo, he keeps them all shut—unless they're in use, I'm assuming.

The first door I come to happens to be a memorabilia room, filled to the brim with past awards, trophies, basketball paraphernalia and large, framed pictures of monumental moments from Miles' life.

Pictures from Senior Night in high school, the game where he scored his one-thousandth point, when he signed to play for college, and when he got drafted into the NBA.

All of those memories were great for him, and it set him up for his future. A successful one.

While I distanced myself from him years ago, I've never stopped keeping tabs on him.

Before the tightness in my throat shifts into tears, I step out of the room, shutting the past behind me before walking further down the hallway.

There's a smaller half bath, a storage closet, two more empty rooms—one bare and one decorated like an office space—and the hallway mirrors the one upstairs. Bare.

I venture through the house more, finding more random rooms—none of which are furnished, so at least I know that's not a lie—along with a door that leads to the basement.

I'm not sure why I was expecting something dark and dingy —I've watched too many horror movies, clearly. Sometimes I forget that this house is fairly new.

There's a den downstairs with a big sectional and two smaller couches and a big ass TV bolted to the wall, but the small hallway off to the side leads to another room. The only other one down here besides another bathroom, which turns out to be another empty room.

After finding nothing interesting, I retreat upstairs to make some breakfast with whatever Miles has in the fridge before heading to unpack more boxes.

I don't have many things, just what I've acquired over the years. When you move around as much as I did, you learn not to keep a lot. It makes it easier when you're forced to leave.

Although things have been more permanent since meeting the Rainwaters, I've still learned to not keep more than I need. I don't have a huge wardrobe like Blake, only using half of the one available for me, and none of it is fancy. Fishnet tights, black shorts, black jeans, and simple t-shirts.

Style isn't my thing though, comfort is.

I have a few knickknacks, but what I own the most is books.

Predominantly romance, but a few fantasy novels. Harry Potter was my saving grace as a child, allowing me to escape the real world and live in another full of wizards and magic.

That's what books are for me, an escape. One that I so desperately need most of the time.

Because why would I need to live my own shitty life every second of every day when I can live others for hours at a time?

Once my books are unpacked onto the shelves Blake and Kyler got from the old place, and my clothes are put away, I sit back and look at the space around me.

How little I have.

I want more for myself one day. I want to have a permanent home, one that I can fill with whatever my heart desires. Somewhere I can renovate to my liking, tear apart and put back together and decorate how I want.

Someplace I can truly call my home and not have to worry about leaving on short notices.

I want to feel secure in my life.

Maybe this is the blessing I need dressed in a hellish disguise.

Because even though this situation is the furthest from what I want, I can rest easily knowing I have a safe place to stay for the time being.

And I have Miles to thank for it.

Add it to the list of times the Rainwaters have come to my rescue. I just wish I was able to even the score.

I never will, but at least I'm used to the feeling of losing.

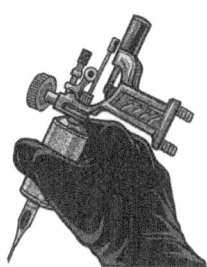

Miles is downstairs when I decide to journey out again hours later. I would have avoided coming down here if I knew he'd already gotten home, but maybe it's time that we talk about all this.

"How was practice?"

"Jesus fuck," Miles says as he drops veggies to the floor. He takes a deep breath as he bends to the floor to pick them up.

"I'm sorry if I scared you."

"You're a pipsqueak, you don't scare me. But next time, announce your presence first," he instructs. "I'll put a freaking bell around your neck if you don't," he mutters under his breath, but I still hear him. It's a direct contradiction from his anger yesterday, which only confuses me more.

"I thought we should talk," I add.

"About what?"

"About me staying here."

"What about it?"

Miles grabs the veggies and carries them to the sink. He starts washing each one, and when I think he isn't going to say anything, I begin to turn away. Until his smooth voice floats through the air in waves.

"You're staying here. That's all there is to it. Why do we need to talk about it?"

"Because I don't want you doing anything for me for free."

"We've always helped you for free," he states, walking from the sink to the island before beginning to chop the vegetables.

"Well, I don't want you to anymore," I snap, my voice raising. Realizing my overstep, I soften my voice and say, "help me for free, that is."

"What do you want to do then? Pay rent? Because I don't want your money. You obviously don't have a lot, or you wouldn't be here."

Okay, rude. But true. "Maybe I can contribute in some other way. I don't want to be another burden while I'm here."

"You're not..." Miles stops chopping, looking at me with an unreadable expression. "We can talk about it over dinner."

"You're cooking for me?" I ask incredulously.

"Are you expecting me to let you starve while you're here?" he asks, sarcasm lacing his tone.

"No, but... With how you were acting yesterday, I was expecting you to make me fend for myself."

"And have you burn down the house? Absolutely not. You don't cook."

"I've learned to make a few things over the years," I defend, crossing my arms.

"I don't care what it is. We're not having a repeat of the ramen incident."

"I forgot water. Big deal."

"Big deal?" he repeats, laughing lowly under his breath. "You nearly exploded the microwave, the kitchen wasn't visible due to the smoke, and all the fire alarms went off."

"It was an accident."

"Still, I rest my case."

"Surprised you remember," I grumble, not loud enough for him to hear, but as luck would have it, he does.

"That's the most agonizing part about this new situation, Riley. I remember every fucking memory I have of you, and it's fucking painful having to see you all the time. Because the memories I have of you and the version I see now, they're not the same."

I'm not sure how to react to that. It's the first time he's been genuine since I moved in, and the whirlwind moment only makes me defensive.

"We're not going there," I grit. "We're going to talk about the present, not the past. Got it?"

"No, I don't 'got it.' But that doesn't matter, huh?"

"No." My answer is firm. "We'll talk about the current living arrangements and what I can do to contribute. That's it."

"Fine."

"Fine."

"At least grab the damn plates and shit," he demands, and the force from his voice alone makes me plant my feet, never mind the actual demand.

"I will after you say please. I'm your guest, not your damn housekeeper."

"Are you kidding me?" he asks, staring at me with his knife suspended mid-air.

"No, Michael Myers. I'm not kidding. I have values."

"Just not morals," he mutters.

It angers me, and I would normally dish it right back to him, but I don't. Old Riley would have, but this me... I can't. Because then the past is brought back up, questions are asked, and tension is pulled so tightly that when answers aren't shared, people get hurt.

"Get your own fucking plates. I'll be in the living room until you're done."

I'm in the middle of watching *Stranger Things* when Miles waltzes into the living room carrying two plates of food that smell delicious. I wish he would have let me fix my own plate because I've always hated for my food to touch each—

"Don't worry. It isn't touching."

I hate that he keeps remembering things about me. It does something weird to me, sending little tingles in my chest.

I'm not sure if it's painful zaps of memories from the past trying to torture me or remind me of what happened so it doesn't repeat itself, or if it's my traitorous body falling for my best friend's brother—*again*.

Disregarding the fact that I've only been around him for a couple days again after over nine years apart.

But that's the effect Miles always had on me.

He always did the right things, like right now. Separating my food for me, helping me with homework I was capable of doing on my own, watching out for me at school with people who tried to bully me or get in my pants.

Miles always knew the right thing to say too. When they convinced me to stay with them permanently—having a famous coach for a father really helped with my social worker—and when I got stood up at my freshman dance.

The same thing happened sophomore year, and instead of letting me wallow in pity in the girl's locker room, Miles took me straight to the center of the floor and danced with me. He told me that my worth wasn't measured by a guy with a tiny dick that couldn't have enough respect for me to show up.

I shake the thought out of my head, forgetting those memories. They're too painful to relive anymore.

"Uh…" I swallow the growing lump in my throat at the thoughtfulness. "Thank you for that."

"It's whatever."

It isn't whatever, but I won't argue with him.

"We should talk," I add.

"Eat your food first."

"Why?" I snap in response. His tone is too demanding.

"Because if this conversation goes south, I don't want to wear your food."

My feelings immediately flip, and I giggle lowly under my breath. Basking in the moment for a minute, I let the nostalgia of past times consume me. But the familiarity of those times, much like this fleeting moment now, hurts.

I paint a mask of neutrality on and take a bite of chicken. I can't place the taste—all I know is that it's amazing, exploding my taste buds with each bite.

Realizing I never responded to Miles's joke, I finish my bite of food and swallow. Then again for good measure.

"I promise I won't throw my food at you."

"Pinky promise?" he says, startling me.

For as long as I've known the Rainwaters, one thing has always been clear…

Pinky promises are for Miles and his twin sister, Blake, only. They always have been. They've never been shared with anyone else, as silly as it is.

"We don't pinky promise, but you have my word," I say.

"Your word?" he grits, his tone rising. "Your word is…" he trails off. "Never mind. Continue."

Fucking backwards ass sour patch kid—acting sweet and then sour.

"I know that you hate this situation. The feeling is mutual given… well, you know. But I need to contribute while I'm here, for however long that is."

"You don't need to contribute. I make millions of dollars a year. House payments are chump change to me."

I'm tempted to throw my food at him, but I gave him my word. And this time, I'm keeping it, so I place the plate on the coffee table in front of us.

"Look, I don't care how much money you make. I've never known the luxury of chump change. So, if there's a way I can contribute otherwise, I'd like to do that."

"If it isn't monetary, how the hell do you expect to contribute?" he asks.

"I don't know! I could clean," I offer.

"I have a cleaning service."

"I could take the trash off."

"I have that handled."

"What about cooking?"

"Absolutely not," Miles blurts. "We've been over this."

"Then I don't know how the hell to contribute," I sigh in frustration.

Miles doesn't get it. From the moment he entered this world, he's been waited on hand and foot. From meals, to driving, and general care.

I had none of that.

"You can take care of my dog when I'm gone," he finally offers.

"You have a dog?"

"Yeah, but he's in obedience school right now. Couldn't have him pissing and chewing on all my new shit."

"When does he come back?" I ask.

"Soon."

"I can do that. It shouldn't be too hard. I love dogs," I tell Miles. He nods, so I quickly add, "what else?"

"On off days, or days that I go in late, don't wake me up before nine."

"Okay. What else?" I cross my legs and turn towards Miles, waiting for him to come up with something else. I don't feel right staying here if I can't bring something to the table, since money is the last thing he needs.

"I don't know," he says, staring at the TV. "Give me some time. I'm sure I'll figure out something."

"Make sure it's not something I wouldn't be comfortable doing."

It's unspoken, but the energy in the room shifts. I can feel Miles's body go rigid from across the couch, I can feel the temporary harmony of the moment snap like a torn thread.

"You know what…" he begins. "I don't why I thought things would be different. While you're here, we should just keep our distance. I'm going to eat in my room."

Miles grabs his plate and starts to trek up the stairs to his room. Normally, I would let it go. Not push him further. It's what I've done before.

But something about this moment right now, and the fact that we're going to be around each other for the foreseeable future, has me chasing after him.

Him and his stupidly long legs have already made it to his room by the time I reach the top of the stairs, and before he can shut the door, I race to it and place my hand on it to stop him.

"What do you want?" he gripes. "Did you not just hear me say we should avoid each other?"

"I heard you, and for the next thirty seconds, I don't fucking care," I respond. My heart is beating out of my chest from running up the stairs, my breathing is heavy.

As I'm waiting to catch my breath, I steal a look at Miles in his current form. Noting the way his deep brown eyes swirl with indifference, how his brows are furrowed, the way his lips are pulled into a taut line.

"Are you going to get on with it?" he grumbles.

"Why are you letting me stay here?"

"Let's get one thing straight," he says, pausing. "You're here because I'm doing a favor for my sister, and you need a place to stay. That's all."

Miles goes to shut the door again, but I put the weight of my entire body on it to halt him again.

"That's where you're wrong. You don't have to do shit if you don't want to. So why are you letting me stay if you hate it this damn much?"

Miles steps closer, brushing his chest against mine in the doorway. He looks down his nose at me, his nostrils flaring and teeth clenching while his hands flex closed.

"Because you're family, Riley. That's fucking why."

The proximity is suddenly too close, and I step away from him, breathing in oxygen that doesn't smell like him so that my senses aren't clouded.

The door shuts as soon as I'm out of the way, and I replay his words over in my head.

The way he said family… it wasn't right.

He said it like he despises the word, like it pains him in a way.

And that confuses me more than anything else because we've always been family.

Always.

But I guess I shouldn't be surprised.

People never stay in my life.

I guess the inevitable finally happened, dwindling what little family I have left by one.

Only a few left until I'm truly an orphan, and that pains me in a way that I've never felt before.

I head back downstairs and grab my food, then I disappear outside to finish the rest of my meal, listening to what Miles wants.

For me to stay away from him.

Well, wish granted, Miles.

Wish granted.

CHAPTER 4
MILES

Her shit is *everywhere*.

Shoes, random clothes, jackets, nail polishes, her hairbrush.

Everywhere I look is another reminder that she's here.

Don't even get me started on the fact that her laundry somehow ends up with mine. It's not like we wash them together.

Riley does so many things that get on my nerves too. She sings in the shower, even though she sounds like a dying... Well, like a dying something. She kicks her shoes off in the entryway and doesn't put them away, so I'm always tripping over them. And she plays her music so damn loudly. Granted, she does turn it down if she realizes I'm here, which isn't always immediate.

What irritates me the most is that she's always coming in late and sleeping most of her days away—at least some of them.

But that's what irritates me, not what *bothers* me. What bothers me is that I want to know where she is when she comes in late.

She's here because she needs to be safe, to have a roof over her head, and the thought of her doing things that compromise that...

It makes me angry at *her* and angry at *myself* for caring.

I stopped caring about her nine years ago.

Or so I thought.

But now... I don't even know where to begin.

Pushing all thoughts of Riley aside, I finish getting my things ready for practice. I brush my teeth, throw whatever I need into my gym bag, and make a protein shake and bagel to eat on the way.

Getting out of the house, away from her presence, is my only time to breathe these days. Having her there and being forced to relive all the memories of our past every time I see her drives me up the wall.

It just... drives me insane to have her around. And now that she's back, it drives me crazy to *not* have her around.

I wish things were simple but then that would be too easy.

As soon as I'm in the locker room, things change. My mood immediately lifts, and my muscles relax. Because while I don't get Riley or the way she makes me crazy, I *do* get basketball. And within these walls, it's my main focus.

"Are you ready for this?" Kyler asks from beside me.

"Ready for what?"

"Practice."

Confusion washes over me. "I'm always ready. Why are you asking?"

"Because your sister is in a mood today and it's probably not going to work out for us as a team."

"What did you do to piss her off?"

"I'm going to save your ears by not answering that question," he says with a cocky smile. "But she also had a meeting yesterday and the pressure for her to perform as a first-time coach is weighing on her a bit."

"My pit bull of a sister who takes no shit is letting something get to her? I'm shocked."

"Your sister isn't as pit bull as you think. At least, not all the time." He hesitates. "Just don't give her that normal twin sass you usually give her today, okay?"

"I wish I knew what you were talking about." I smirk.

"It's not just *your* funeral if you don't listen." Kyler shakes his head. "Let's go then."

Thoughts are plaguing me. Many, many, many thoughts.

Thoughts like, how long does it take a pig to eat a dead body? Will burying a body in acid and lye completely dispose of it? If I drop it in the ocean, can I guarantee sharks will dispose of it all?

That's what goes through my head as my sister—my coach—makes us run the fiftieth sprint in a row.

I think I could do it.

"Rainwater!" Coach yells. "What the fuck are you doing? Your times are shit."

"My times are shit because you've ran us until we fucking can't anymore."

"Do you want to get smart with me?"

Kyler goes to step in, but I wave him off and make my way toward my sister. "Blake, you're crossing a line. I get that you're under pressure but taking it out on us like this will not get you results," I say, trying to reason with her.

Blake runs her hands over her face, sighing into them. "I will not repeat this, but you're right. I'm sorry. I just… I have to do well, or I could lose the very thing I worked so hard for."

"Blake, you excel at everything you do. Your determination to exceed is unmatched. But you need to breathe." She does. "Now, stop working us like mules and actually coach us."

"Yeah. Yeah. I will." Blake smiles before grabbing my arm. "Thank you for always calling me out on my bullshit."

"What else are siblings for?"

Two hours of intense drills and plays later, and we're back in the locker room. My lungs are overworked, my muscles are shredded, and I need a fifteen-hour nap—which I'll do the minute I get home.

But my exit is quickly halted by my sister.

"Miles, wait up."

"What do you need, BOGO?"

"That damn nickname," she mumbles with a smile. "I wanted to ask you how Riley is settling in."

"I don't know. I didn't give her a survey on my hospitality." Something about her bringing up Riley makes me turn... hostile.

"Yeah, because you'd fail it. She's my best friend, Miles. She needs this. Do not make things hard for her. She's been dealt a shit enough hand as is."

"She's still there, so I guess she's fine." I grip my bag tighter in my hand. "Is that all?"

"Yeah. I guess that's all."

I'm nearly down the hall when Blake yells at me again.

"If you hurt her in any way or make her feel bad, I'll kick your ass."

She doesn't know it, but the only one who has ever done the hurting in that scenario is Riley, and I won't put myself in that position again.

Over my dead body.

An hour ago, I was sleeping. Now, I'm surrounded in a club by booze, women, and the guys from the team. Couple that with music that could bust my eardrums and you've got a good time.

Except, this isn't a good time. Not one that I'm used to.

Dean Russell, the Warhawks' resident playboy and post-player, came up with the not-so-genius idea for each of us to pick women for each other tonight.

A regular guy probably wouldn't care, but I do. I'm particular with my taste, and very rarely do I venture from it. But that idea flew out the window the minute Dean brought up the idea.

Kyler and Jackson chose their women over coming out, which probably isn't a bad thing considering how the night has developed. We make light conversation as we scope out prospects for the others.

"Dude, I hate to break it to you…" Dean begins, "but your sister is a ball buster."

"I contemplated murder today because of that practice. And if you don't want to have another one like it, don't say that to her face."

"I still can't believe the coach is your sister," Silas says, taking a sip of his beer.

"Don't get me wrong, I'm happy as hell for her. But it's weird having your twin as your authority figure."

"It could be worse," Silas adds.

"Like having two siblings as authority figures?" Dean adds.

Silence. "You're joking, right?" Silas says, in shock.

"I wish I was," I mutter.

"You know the General Manager for the team? Asher?" Silas nods. "It's Miles' older brother."

"Does your entire family have ties to the organization?"

"Yep," I say, popping the P. "All but one. Dad started the team. My sister coaches while my brother manages. And my oldest brother, Caleb, is an agent for a few of us. I have another brother, Hunter, who took the baseball route."

"Sounds like an intense family affair," he says in response.

"Intense is when you really piss off Coach," Dmitry adds in his thick, Russian accent. "Now are we going to shoot the shit, or are we going to find pretty girls?"

"Pretty girls," we all say, damn near in unison.

"Okay, okay," Dmitry says, rubbing his hands together. "Silas. You get the red head by the bar. Green dress."

"Red heads aren't usually my thing, but I can roll with it," he agrees.

Something about the way he says that—so disrespectful and laced with misogyny—rubs me the wrong way. Strikes me like he thinks he's God's gift to women or some shit.

Am I a saint? Hell no. But do I respect women? Abso-fuck-ing-lutely.

"Your turn, Rainwater," Dean says, scanning the area behind me. "Your lovely lady is that sinful looking blonde dancing in the middle of the crowd like she's the only one in the room."

Dean's pearly whites dig into his lower lip, his eyes roaming up and down the so-called blonde behind me. Following his gaze and my curiosity, I find the woman he's pointed out for me.

Long, flowy blonde hair that glistens like a diamond in the light of the club, touching the top of a round, pert ass. Tone, slender legs covered in tattoos along with her arms.

She's the kind of girl that gets blood rushing to my dick.

Until she lifts the blonde hair cascading down her back to the top of her head, displaying the back of her neck and the purple calla lily tattoo that resides there.

The blood that rushed to my dick. It's gone now. Along with the simmering attraction I was feeling at the sight of the stranger.

Because this is no stranger.

This is Riley fucking Davis.

My new roommate and the resident pain in my ass.

"You look like you've seen a ghost," Dmitry points out. "What is wrong?"

"Uh... I can't flirt with that girl. You need to give me someone else."

"No, no, no. The whole point of this was that we don't get to choose. You take what you've been handed."

Cutting a glare at Silas, I chug the last bit of beer in my bottle. "No way. I'll streak naked down Bourbon Street before flirting with her."

"Come on, Miles. What's the big deal?" Dean taunts.

"The big deal is that she's my current roommate who just so happens to be my sister's best friend that I've known for over fifteen years. She's off limits. I don't think of her that way."

"Shit, *that's* Riley?" Dean's eyes widen, looking over my shoulder to blatantly check her out. "I didn't even recognize her."

"Come on, man," Silas butts in. "You can't tell me you've never thought about fucking her."

"I... no. No. It isn't like that."

"You're such a liar," Silas laughs. "You've definitely thought about tapping that."

One more word. One more word and I might lay this motherfucker out for speaking about Riley—I mean, women this way.

"We've got history, but nothing like that. But I meant what I said. It's not happening."

"I'll pick someone new then," Dean says.

"No," Silas interrupts. "No new blood. We'll switch."

"What?" The word flies out of my mouth as a deep growl. Given the vibes this guy puts off, I don't want his measly hands around Riley.

"You don't want her, and redheads aren't my thing. We should just switch. Riley is fine as fuck, and blondes are more my poison. Seems like a win-win to me."

No. Not a win-win. Either way, I'll lose. I can't explain that though.

Not to them, and definitely not to myself.

"Works for me," Dean voices.

"Me too," Silas says before throwing back the rest of his drink. "If I don't see you again, have a nice night." With a wink, he's gone, sauntering to the floor where Riley is still dancing like she's the only girl in the room.

My eyes meet the table as my grip on the empty beer bottle tightens. I hear Dean voice that he's going to get another round, but it's like he's submerged underwater when he speaks.

"Rainwater," Dmitry's baritone voice booms, pulling me back to reality.

"What?" I grit, still gripping the beer bottle.

"I'd rather you not commit murder tonight, but if you do, I can help you get away with it."

"No murder. I'm good."

Dmitry chuckles. "If you're good, then I'm American. But we can both pretend." He rolls his eyes, a sly grin spreading on his face.

I'm not commenting on whatever that was, but it is fucked. Dmitry can clearly see the strain between Riley and me, but no one will ever understand the severity of that tension.

I hate how it all makes me feel. I hate that seeing her out, seeing her things in my place, and seeing her flirt with other guys bothers me in ways that it shouldn't.

She came into my life like a storm, left me with the wreckage, only to enter again like an unhinged tornado.

I know that I don't have a say in Riley's life—and I don't have the right—but I can't fucking stand seeing her with the new guy.

That guy… He just rubs me the wrong way, and if he does anything to hurt her, I'll jeopardize my entire contract to make him pay.

Fuck.

I sound like high school Miles, the one who was willing to throw it all away for her.

I thought things had changed, but clearly, they haven't.

It still doesn't change what happened.

But I care about her, deep down underneath the hatred I feel.

For an hour, I watch Silas touch every bit of her exposed body.

Blinding rage flows through my veins, and I can't do a fucking thing about it.

And when Silas convinces Riley to leave with him with a smile on her face, those feelings of rage, anger, and something else I can't describe, cease to exist. I become numb.

So, I turn to what I do best.

"Point me to the new girl, Dmitry."

Then I grab his glass of whiskey, down it, and begin my new mission to try and forget.

Just like I have for the last nine years.

CHAPTER 5
RILEY

When I was a child, birthdays were never something that was celebrated.

I never had the animal-shaped Piñata, the fun color schemes, the big cake designed for my favorite show. And gifts? No, I never received those. And those are just the vague memories from before my birth mother tossed me away like trash.

After that, things didn't change much in the birthday department. The majority of my foster families didn't even acknowledge the day.

I never truly knew what a birthday could be like until I met the Rainwaters. They were the first people to give me a birthday cake in my favorite color, black and my first ever gift.

Their family made up for everything that I had never had before. Love, loyalty, and dependability. Every year since, they've always made sure it was something to remember.

But it isn't my birthday, it's theirs. Blake and Miles turn twenty-eight tomorrow, and to say they're throwing a little party is an understatement.

I'm talking catering, a DJ, dancers, and a guest list that is way too big in my opinion but that's just me.

I want to put on a happy face, to celebrate my best friend's birthday, but it's fucking hard.

Since I was an early teen, I've struggled with both anxiety and depression. And today, the day before this big party, is not one of my good days.

I feel the knot inside me thickening. The tighter it gets, the heavier I feel. Waking up today was a task, and getting out of bed tomorrow will be a miracle.

But I have to. I've been a burden enough to the Rainwaters, and I refuse to shit on their day because I don't feel good.

"Riley," Blake says, pulling my attention back to her and the laundry she's helping me fold. "Are you sure you're okay with this party?"

"Why wouldn't I be?" I ask, plastering on a smile.

"Because you don't look it," she states. "Is everything okay?" Blake asks, laced with concern and sincerity.

"Everything is fine, promise. I've just been really tired lately. Looking for places, balancing work schedules. It's been hard to juggle it all."

"You know you don't have to work two jobs, right? It's not costing you anything to live here and if you need to cut back on something for your sanity, it would be that."

"No," I say too quickly, then slow myself down. "No, I like to work. And the people I work with there are great."

"You're never going to tell me where you work at night, are you?"

"Nope. Plus, I need all the money I can get to save up so that I can get out of here."

Those were not the right words, but it's too late when I finally try.

"Get out of here? What do you mean? Is Miles making your stay here uncomfortable? I fucking told him…" she says, beginning to stand, but I yank her back down by the wrist.

"It's not Miles."

"Then what is it?" she demands.

From the minute Blake said that we were friends, she's always been the one to come to bat for me. Whether that be sticking up to a bully, punching a guy in the face for me, or making sure that I always had a place to feel safe.

She knows when something isn't right, for the most part, so I've only been able to keep very few things a secret from her. Miles—our history—is one of those things.

"You know I don't like to leech off other people. It makes me feel icky. I've been taking care of myself my entire life, so when I can't, I feel like a fucking failure. I need to do this for myself."

"We're family, Riley. Maybe not by blood, but we're family. So don't you ever think that you're leeching off any of us. We take care of our own, and that includes you."

"I know," I say, but I'm not totally convinced.

Even though the Rainwaters have never said it, I've always felt pitied. Like they do it because I have no one else. And as much as I don't want to feel that way, I can't help it. It's so deeply rooted that I can't pull it free.

"Good. Because I love you, and I'd never think you were leeching off me or anyone else. Your character is too pure for that."

I laugh internally at that one. My character is anything but pure.

"Sure," I huff, but Blake continues to stare.

"I'd stay and try to convince you, but we have team lifting and tape in about an hour, so I've gotta get over to the gym." She tosses the pile of clothes she was fake folding back onto the bed. "Have fun folding clothes. I love you."

"Love you too."

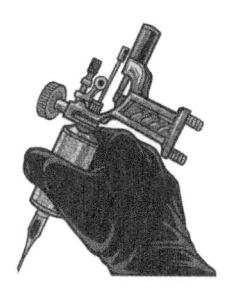

After I finished my laundry and put in another load, I couldn't physically bring myself to do anymore. I went straight to bed, where I've been for the last four hours.

It's all the energy I've got. I've been reading since Blake left, wrapped up in a cocoon of blankets in my room. I don't have to be at work until ten, so I'm relishing the calm and quiet until I have to put a fake face on—again.

I hear the door slam downstairs but make no move to get up. That is until the door to my room slams against the wall, and Miles walks in, seething.

"What the fuck did you say to my sister?"

"What are you talking about?" I ask, sitting up in bed. I'm braless in a tank top, and I quickly pull the blanket back up to cover me.

"She accused me of making it hard for you to live here. And while I've not been Mrs.-Freaking-Doubtfire, I haven't been the damn devil either. I don't like you spreading lies, Ri."

"First off, knock before you come in. This may be your house, but I could have been naked. Have some respect."

"Nothing that would impress me," he quips.

"Second," I say with conviction, ignoring his comment, "I haven't said a damn thing. I told her it was personal. I defended your ass, actually. You're welcome."

"I'm welcome?" he snorts, coming to stand at the edge of the bed. "What the hell does that mean?"

"You're right. You haven't been Mrs. Doubtfire when it comes to the welcome department, but it's nothing I can't handle. I know I'm the last person you want to share your space with, but I'll get out as soon as I can."

Miles begins to leave, but I have one more thing to add. "And for your party tomorrow, please make sure people stay out of this room."

He pauses in the doorway. "Pissed about my party invading your new space? Don't worry. I'll put a big 'Do Not Enter' sign on your door. I'm sure your new friend Silas will know it doesn't apply to him."

"Is that what you're really pissed about? Me sleeping with your teammate. How did you even know? Are you stalking me now?"

"Saw you leave with him at the club last week. And I'm not pissed. Didn't expect you to sell yourself out to guys like him, but I guess things don't change with you, do they?" he spits.

"I know you're fucking kidding me." He doesn't say a word. Not giving a shit how I look anymore, I throw the covers off and meet Miles at the door. "Speak to me like I'm a whore again and I swear to God I'll cut your balls off and feed them to you for breakfast."

"I didn't—" he begins to say, but I cut him off.

"Go fuck a cactus, Miles." Then I slam the door in his face, lock it, and get back to bed. Back in my safe space with my warmth and my book.

Hours later, I put on a fake face, sneak out of the house and head to work.

"Please tell me there's more booze," Blake pleads as she brings the last of the bags into the kitchen.

"Beer, wine coolers and mixers are all out back in coolers of ice. Liquor is set up on a table."

I couldn't sound more detached if I tried. I didn't get home until nearly three, but the party starts around noon since the pool is still open and it's weirdly nice outside.

It doesn't help that I only got a few hours of sleep, but I feel even worse today than I did yesterday. Miles and Kyler are setting up outside while we work on things inside, so it's been easy to avoid him.

What he said yesterday… Fuck, I wanted to punch him. He has no say in who I sleep with, but he said it with such vitriol that it made me feel disgusting. He hasn't looked at me like that since senior year of high school. Graduation, to be specific. The last time we saw each other.

It doesn't matter. He had no right. And as much as I don't want it to affect me, it does. I cried in silence until I fell asleep last night. Because as much as his words hurt, it's true.

Maybe I am a whore. I know he didn't call me that specifically, but I understood what he meant. I thought I'd changed since high school, from the Riley he knew, but maybe I haven't.

Like teenage Riley, I'm still finding temporary content in the arms of random men, searching for something I know deep down I'll never find.

It's not a daily occurrence, nor is it that often, but when it's times like this. When my mental health is wearing me down. I look for companionship, for time to pass…

For happiness.

Even if it's fake.

"Are you okay?" Blake asks.

"Yeah," I say, snapping out of the intrusive thoughts in my head. "Yeah, I'm fine. Just spaced out. What were you saying?"

Hours have passed and I still feel numb, taking shots and

staring at the people around me who are enjoying themselves to the fullest extent with their booze and food.

I've lost count of the number of shots I've tossed back. The goal being to quiet the voice in my head and lower my inhibitions. I've been successful on the latter. But the former? I'm admitting defeat on that one.

"So, Riley, what do you do?" asks Makenna, Jackson's wife.

Blake pulled me out of the comfort of the house and made me join a circle of people. Some I know, some I don't. I remember meeting Dmitry, Jackson, and Silas before—obviously—but I've been introduced to Dean Russell and now, Jackson's wife.

"I'm a tattoo artist," I say with confidence. No matter how shitty my life has been, I've always been able to lose myself in art. It's why I'm obsessed with tattoos. There is a power in expressing oneself without ever having to say a word.

"That's so cool!" Makenna beams. "Do you have any favorite pieces?"

"I put part of myself into each piece I do while trying to capture exactly what the client wants, but I do have some personal favorites."

I use Blake's canvas to show a few of my favorites, then a couple on my legs that I was able to do, but the one I'm most proud of is on my back.

"I wasn't able to tattoo this one myself, but I drew it up and a friend of mine at the parlor did it for me. It took six months to complete the entire piece."

I slip off my top, leaving me in just a bikini, then turn around for the group to see the piece.

"Oh my God," Makenna gasps behind me. "It's beautiful."

This particular tattoo begins at the base of my back, a graveyard full of empty skulls that pose as the floor. On top of those skulls sits the silhouette of a woman, hugging her knees to her chest as she stares into the abyss.

The only color on the girl is the presence of a blue tear

trailing down her face and the bloody, red heart dripping from her hand in front of her knees.

Behind the girl is a Gothic castle—like a twisted version of Rapunzel—towering over her with the night sky above to represent the loneliness that I—that *she*—has felt her whole life.

I see Makenna stand from over my shoulder and crouch down behind me, getting a closer look at the details.

"The details in this are breathtaking," she gushes.

"Thank you," I say with a tear in my eye. No one knows the story behind this tattoo, not even Blake, because it's too raw.

"Let me take a look. I didn't get a good look last time," I hear Silas say, right before hands grip my waist and pull me backwards. I feel the calluses on his fingertips as he traces from the top of my tattoo to the bottom, coming too close to the swell of my ass.

Hair rises on the back of my neck, but they're not from Silas's touch. I look up, not knowing what I'll find. I'm met with radiant heat coming from Miles, and not the good kind.

His chiseled jaw is clenched tight, and I can practically hear his teeth grinding together. The veins in his forearms are protruding from the skin, evidence of the way his fists are grasping his shorts to the point of nearly ripping them.

But what confuses and scares me the most is the look in his eyes. Those deep brown irises of his, normally dark and brooding, are lit with burnt orange flecks. They're a flame that is burning deeper with each trace of Silas's fingers along my skin, preparing to explode.

But he shouldn't be burning that way, and I shouldn't be feeling the effect of his flames. Especially on a day where I haven't been feeling at all.

Miles stands, and the way he towers over, even from feet away, makes my breath hitch. I'm expecting him to stomp over—unbeknownst to why I think that—and pull me from Silas's hold. Maybe because of the way he spoke to me the other day, I'm not sure why.

But he doesn't do it. Instead, he stares at me. It feels like he's assessing me.

For a second, I wonder if he sees it. The stiffness in my body from the way I'm being touched, the catch in my breath at the way he looks at me, or if behind it all, he sees the darkness in my eyes.

The loneliness I feel and the way I'm screaming to get away from all the prying eyes, but that I'm holding on by a thread just to not ruin their day.

Those flames keep flickering, boring into my soul. But as quick as I see them, only a few seconds, they're gone as if the rain came down and extinguished the remaining embers.

"Kyler," Miles announces. "Let's go grab something stronger than beer. I think I need it."

I step away from Silas, excusing myself from the circle, and grab an airplane bottle of something from the table before finding my way to the basement bathroom and locking myself in.

My head is swimming. What happened up there doesn't make any sense.

The way Miles looked at me...

When we were teenagers, he had that look all the time. It was the kind that dared anyone to try and touch me.

That same look was his expression just a few minutes ago toward Silas, and the way his hands were on me. Which doesn't make any fucking sense.

Since I've moved in here, we've had a love-hate relationship, with a big emphasis on hate. We fight over my stuff being everywhere and him being loud when I'm trying to sleep. He spits hateful words at me, I slam the door in his face.

But the way he looked at Silas, like he could see himself strangling his teammate to death in his head, proves otherwise. It makes me think he cares, even if it was temporary.

Back when we were teenagers, I would have believed that.

All the Rainwaters cared for me, but Miles was one of my fiercest protectors, in every way.

Until I screwed it up.

Maybe being here has helped lessen some of the anger he has toward me, and the hatred. His disdain has largely dissipated since I've moved in.

I'd like to think things have changed. I'd like to think that maybe, someday, we can be friends again. It's all we'll ever be able to be.

What the fuck is happening?

My head is still swimming even as I down the airplane bottle of vodka. The alcohol sends a warmth through my veins, accompanied by a diminutive sense of calm which is just enough to have me standing and making my way upstairs.

Voices from the kitchen stop me in my place, my back hitting the wall a millisecond later to keep from being seen.

"You should really watch your facial expressions," the thick Russian voice says. *Dmitry.*

"I don't know what you're talking about," another voice responds, one that I know all too well.

"If you're going to pretend that you don't like her, you need to wipe the desire off your face."

"The only desire I have for Riley is for her to get her shit together and get out of my place. Having her here is driving me crazy. That's all."

My chest feels heavy, like the weight of an elephant is sitting on it. My skin stings, like the initial feeling of a tattoo gun making contact. The worst part is the wetness pooling in my eyes hearing the harsh words come from him.

It's exactly like what happened in high school when I overheard him say…

No, I can't go back there. I know that I'm the reason for them, but hearing the truth hurts too much.

Agreeing to stay here, allowing him to save me, took a part out of me. A part of myself I give to no one, and that's my vulnerability. Because that's exactly what I felt when my life blew up—vulnerable, and very angry.

At myself, for getting myself in that position, and my piece-of-shit ex-roommate for being, well, a piece of shit.

For the past few days, I've been putting on a brave face, pretending to be okay. Smiling like nothing was wrong, like I was excited to celebrate this day.

When the reality is... I'd love nothing more than to stay in bed, under the covers, listening to anything to drown out the noise outside *and* in my head.

And I've been strong, to an extent. Holding it all together so that Blake could have a good birthday, for all the times she's held it together for me.

But now... I'm done. I'm done holding it together, I'm done putting on a smile, and I'm done acting like I'm okay.

I wipe the welling tears from my eyes, remove any facial expression I have, and walk past Dmitry in the kitchen to find Blake.

I find her sitting in the same spot as earlier, except she's on Kyler's lap now. When she sees me coming toward her, dragging my feet, she snaps up straight.

"What's going on?"

I know my eyes are bloodshot and empty looking, my body weak on its feet. "I'm not feeling too well. I think all the alcohol is getting to me," I lie.

"What can I do? Do you need anything?"

"I think I just need to lie down."

"Okay," she says, her voice softer. "If you want, I can bring you some food later."

"That's, uh, fine. Yeah. Thanks."

As I turn to walk away, Blake's hand grabs my wrist, halting any further movement. "Are you sure you're okay?"

Blake knows my history, but after the first time she found me crying on the floor in the bathroom at her house, I've hidden those darker feelings deep inside. Only the minorly dark ones available at the surface.

"I'm fine. Some sleep will do me good," I ensure. In a softer tone, I say, "I'm sorry to skip out on your birthday. I feel like a bad friend."

"Never." She stands quickly, pulling me into a suffocating hug that only Blake can do, given she towers over me like a freaking giant and folds my small frame into her bigger one. "You're the best friend. No matter what."

I know she's telling the truth. Blake doesn't lie and if she didn't think it, she wouldn't say it. Doesn't stop the voice in my head from calling me a shitty friend though.

"I know. I'll see you later, okay?"

"Okay," she says, reluctantly releasing my body from hers.

I find the least populated route to get to my room, momentarily dodging Miles in a closet before finding myself in my room.

When I get inside, I shut the door behind me. Stripping myself out of the bikini, I find myself in a too-big t-shirt, baggy shorts, and cocooned underneath my covers.

Scrolling through my phone, I find my usual playlist for when my mood drops, hook it up to the Bluetooth speaker, and play it loud enough so that it drowns out the noise downstairs.

Unfortunately, it isn't loud enough to drown out the hateful thoughts in my head.

The one that tells me that I'm a burden, a charity case, that no one cares about me. That I'm only here because I was dealt a shit hand early on and the Rainwaters pity me.

I know Blake cares about me and so does the rest of her family. She wouldn't bother wasting time on me if she didn't, but I still can't keep these thoughts at bay.

Maybe it's because these pack a bigger punch. These thoughts are tied to the weight I've been carrying around for far too long, the weight that nearly caused irreparable destruction to a person that I care about a lot.

Being here, around him, is causing my brain to want to shut down. I'm battling my head enough as it is, and now my heart has entered the ring, begging me to make things right again.

But I'm afraid that there's no making things right in the eyes of someone who only sees you as the villain. After all, it's better me than someone he trusts and loves.

Those thoughts flood my head until the tears fall, and the darkness sweeps me under its spell.

It's a good thing the darkness and I are old friends.

CHAPTER 6
MILES

I THOUGHT I WOULD HAVE LEARNED MY LESSON AFTER MY TWENTY-first birthday, when my oldest brother, Caleb, told me that 'those shots sneak up on you.'

He said, "first one makes you feel warm, the second makes you feel good. The third one gets your blood pumping, the fourth one gets your mouth running. But that fifth one... that's the one that knocks you on your ass. Unless you're a bitch that can't handle shots."

It's been seven years and I can say with certainty that I have not learned my lesson.

Knocking down one and two was easy, then I took a break to let it settle. Three went down even easier after I saw those fucking hands running all over her skin, and I followed right after with number four after realizing I shouldn't be so affected by what I saw.

I don't remember shot number five, but it remembers me because I'm now feeling the full effects of it. Not even the hair of the dog could help me now.

"Dude, I think something is severely wrong with me," I say to whoever is listening.

Kyler, Dmitry, and Jackson pulled me onto the court at my house for a game of two-on-two. Not sure when it went from a competition to a pour-my-fucking-heart-out moment.

"Because you have a thing for your sister's best friend?" Jackson answers nonchalantly.

"What? Pshhh," I blow out a breath. "You're not talking sense... Wait, that's not right. You're. Talking. Nonsense. Yeah," I smile, proud of myself for getting it right this time.

I knew that fifth shot wasn't a smart idea, but I've never played smart when it comes to Riley.

"You're such an idiot," Jackson laughs, looking to Kyler. "Tell him, Kyler."

"No, I can't," he responds quickly. "If I acknowledge that I see something—which I'm not saying that I do—then that means I'd have to keep something from Blake, and I refuse to do that. That woman is scary, and I'd like to keep my balls attached to my body. So, I'm pleading the fifth."

"Smart move," I say, pointing the ball at him.

"However," he begins. "Let's pretend like I do see something. Like the way he's inwardly possessive, refusing not to show it but not doing a great job. Because we can all see the way he is when other guys are around with his clenched jaw and fists of fury. Or the way he looks at her like she's the only person in the room."

That'll sober me up. Real damn quick.

"No." The game has paused, but I take the shot from where I'm standing. Even intoxicated, I can still make it. "You don't see anything. There's nothing to see. Not now, and not when she broke my heart."

"Hold up," Kyler says. "What? Blake didn't tell me about this."

"She doesn't know. Please don't tell her," I rush out. "Nothing happened. It almost happened. I wanted it to. But she hurt me so bad, and I lashed out. I told her I'd never forgive her and avoided her like the plague until I left for college."

"Why not say anything?" Dmitry questions. "As they say, honesty is the best policy."

"Because it was our little secret," I whisper, but it comes out louder than it should. "I pinky promised my sister when she first met her that I wouldn't 'use my playboy ways on her'—*I say using air quotes*—and you don't break pinky promises. It's a twin thing. Like blood brothers or some shit. It's basically signing a contract."

"Did you seriously just say pinky promise?" Jackson laughs, again.

"Yes. It's a sacred thing. You don't break them," I say sternly.

"He's right," Kyler says. "Blake is fiercely loyal, and that includes keeping promises, however childish they may seem."

"Wado, Kyler."

"Dude, I know like three words in the Cherokee language, and they are *I love you*. You need to translate."

"It means thank you, dipshit."

"Back to the point of this conversation," Jackson says, interrupting our bro moment. Wait… broment! I'm a genius when I'm drunk, thinking of new words and shit.

"What about the conversation? There is no conversation. I don't like Riley, I will never like Riley, and being around her sucks donkey dick. I want her gone."

I flop into the grass beside the court, looking up at the clouds that look weirdly like a dog running. My vision of the funky cloud dog goes away as Kyler, Jackson and Dmitry tower over me.

"Admit it," Jackson says. "If she left today, you'd feel empty without her around."

"Nope. Can't admit something that isn't true. I hate her. She hurt me."

It's true. Oh, is it true. But I can't admit it out loud because that'll make it real, and I can't make it real.

"Fucking liar," Kyler says. "You don't hate her."

"You're right, I am lying… lying down." I laugh at my joke,

but the three serious looks pinning me down have the laughter halting as quickly as it began.

"Here's the final test then," Dmitry says, gathering my attention. "She may not be here much longer. She overheard our earlier conversation in the kitchen about how you wanted her to leave. And if I've gathered anything about her from our few encounters, it's that she'll do anything she can to get away from you now."

I sit up, my veins flooding with ice. "Yeah? And what makes you think you know Riley so well?"

"I don't, but I do know her eyes. She puts on a good front, but those eyes hide something deeper. I won't step on toes but pay attention to her eyes. They speak volumes when her voice fails to do so."

The thought is like a punch in the gut, and I quickly stand, immediately regretting the movement as my stomach swims. "Do you really think she'd leave? I want her safe, and that's here. For now."

"I think she will if you don't pull the stick out of your ass."

"Exactly," Kyler and Jackson say in unison.

"Hey boys," a voice yells from the door to the house. It's Blake. "I'm ready for some damn cake. Are y'all coming sometime today or what?"

"We're coming, baby!" Kyler says in response. Once he steadies me on my feet, he keeps my hand tightly squeezed in his and drops his voice. "If this conversation ever becomes known, I will deny everything. We clear?"

"Crystal."

The stern look breaks as we both begin laughing. I know he's only giving me shit, but I respect that he doesn't want to keep secrets from my sister. He's one of the best guys I know.

"Word of advice, off the record," he says, stopping me just before walking inside. I nod. "Whatever you're questioning, don't drag it out. It'll hurt you more than it will her, but it will hurt her. And if you hurt her, you hurt Blake. And I can't protect you when she comes to beat your ass, and that's after kicking you in the balls for not telling her that something is going on with you and her best friend."

"Nothing is going on."

"Yet," he responds quickly.

It won't happen.

It can't happen.

I still hate her... right?

"Ulihelisdi udetiyisgv, Blake." *Happy birthday.*

"'Ulihelisdi udetiyisgv, Miles."

"Okay, what kind of cake did you even get?" I ask my sister.

"The only real kind. Red velvet. But that's just for us, everyone else has vanilla or chocolate to choose from."

"I knew I loved you for a reason."

"I wasn't aware that you needed a reason to love me, being your twin and all." She laughs. "But we've got to save a piece of ours for Riley because that's the flavor she likes."

"What do you mean save her a piece? Where is she?"

"She came to me a bit ago and said she didn't feel good, that she may have drank too much. Not sure I believe it, but I've learned not to push Riley when she gets like this."

"Like what?"

"I can't say," she states in a lower tone, like she's hiding something. "Let's get through the cake and then I'll take her some along with food."

Hearing my sister say that she doesn't believe alcohol is why

Riley doesn't feel good has a sour feeling settling in my belly. Dmitry may be right about her overhearing our conversation, and that makes me feel like I could puke.

"When did she come to you?" I ask, hoping the answer isn't what I think.

"Not long after she showed off her tattoos."

Fuck. Fuck. Fuck.

She heard and now she thinks I don't want her here when in reality, it's the opposite. As angry as I am about what happened when we were seniors, I could never directly hurt her, and I know I have.

God, I'm such an asshole.

"Hey, BOGO."

"Yeah?"

"Do you mind if I take it up to her instead? I want to check in on her."

"Sure." A smile peeks onto her face. "I knew it would be a good idea for her to stay here."

"Why do you say that?"

"Because you've always watched out for her."

That makes the sour feeling in my stomach twist itself around like tumbleweeds.

She came to me for help when it was the last thing she wanted to do. She refused to stay here unless she contributed. She hasn't been hard to live with either, if you take away the fact that she throws her shit everywhere.

And I have been the most insensitive piece of shit I could possibly be.

I don't think I can ever forget what she did to me, because it was the worst betrayal possible. Especially when she knew how I felt…

But maybe I can put it past me and not make things harder than they should be for her.

As soon as we're through with the cake cutting, I make a

plate of food and dessert to take up to Riley. I can only hope she doesn't slam the door in my face again, but I deserve it if she does.

The closer I get, the better I can hear voices coming from her room. I know Riley's voice as well as I know mine, and the other one must be that fucker on the team who raises my defenses.

"I'm not in the mood," Riley says. "Please leave."

"Come on. We had fun last time, right? I couldn't stop thinking about fucking you again, especially after you showed off your ink outside and let me feel you up."

"That wasn't an invitation," she says, but something's off about her voice. There's no feeling or emotion.

"I bet if I slipped my hand inside your shorts," Silas pauses, "you would be wet for me," he finishes saying, almost in a whisper.

I'm about to step away, refusing to listen to Riley fuck this guy—because not even that is something I can handle—when I hear a grunt, followed by a crash and some groans.

"What the fuck?" Silas shouts. "What's wrong with you?"

"I said no," Riley responds, anger in her tone.

And that's my cue.

Stepping into the room, I see Silas propped against her dresser, guarding his junk, glaring at Riley who's still seated in bed. I sit the plate on the first hard surface I find.

"Party's over for you, Capetti. Get the fuck out."

"Are you serious? She's the one who elbowed me in the dick."

I look at Riley, expecting her to throw out one of her little quips like she normally does, but her expression is empty, her eyes vacant.

Pay attention to her eyes. They speak volumes when her voice fails to do so.

"She said no. It's not a question, not a fun little phrase—it's a fucking sentence."

I walk over to a fuming Silas. Grabbing him by the collar of his shirt, I lift him off the floor and pull him close enough that I can smell the alcohol on his breath.

"I said the party's over for you, Capetti. Get your shit and get out of my house. You're not welcome here."

"Fine," he says, pulling my fists from the collar of his shirt. When he starts to walk past, I turn and physically kick him in the ass, sending him through the door and into the wall.

He turns to stare at me with shock and anger written all over his face. In return, I give him my best smile and slam the door in his face.

I know why Riley likes to do that so much. It makes you feel good.

I grab the plates I set down and turn back to Riley, who's taken her place back in bed and is now staring at the ceiling.

"Riley." She doesn't respond. "Riley," I say again, louder this time. No response again. "Riley!" Her name comes out of my mouth like a growl, rumbling my chest and the air around me.

She doesn't even look in my direction. "What do you want?" The monotone nature of her voice has me concerned.

"Did he hurt you?" I ask.

Riley continues to stare at the ceiling, not answering me. Each second of silence that passes by adds to the fire burning in me, each second more leading us closer to an explosion.

"Riley," I grit, losing my sense of resolve. "Did he hurt you?"

The desolate look in her eyes, the tenseness in her posture, the paleness to her skin. It's fucking terrifying. If he did something to her, fuck my contract and fuck an assault charge. I will destroy him beyond repair.

Grabbing Riley's chin, I gently pull it toward me. Wanting to be gentle but needing to see her face more.

"Did he fucking hurt you, Ri?" She finally looks at me, but nothing passes over her. "If he hurt you, you have to tell me."

Only then does something happen. It's so minuscule that I almost don't see it, but I do. Her eyes glisten with unshed tears, but then she blinks and they're back to being vacant.

"I don't get hurt, Miles. I do the hurting. Remember?" The words slice me in the chest like a knife. "Now remove your hands from me."

I do so quickly, not wanting to push her further than she already has been. But I don't leave. Instead, I scoot closer, nearly brushing her leg with mine.

"Riley. Are you okay?"

"I'm fine."

"Fine like you're really okay, or 'girl fine' where you're not actually fine at all? And don't choose the first one, because being fine doesn't look like this."

"I get like this sometimes. It's no big deal. Go back to your party."

"No."

"No?"

"Yep. No. It's a sentence." That doesn't even spark a hint of a smile. "I think we should talk."

"About what?"

"The conversation you heard earlier."

"I'll be out of here as soon as possible, okay?" Riley turns the opposite way, taking the cover with her. I don't let that slide.

I grab her hip, feeling the warmth of her skin against mine, ignoring the way electricity shoots up my arm at contact.

"You're misunderstanding it," I tell her.

"'The only desire I have for Riley is for her to get her shit together and get out of my place. Having her here is driving me crazy. That's all,'" she says, repeating my own words back to me. "How is that misunderstanding?"

"I didn't actually mean it," I tell her.

"Sure sounded like it," she mumbles.

"I know it did. And having you here… it's driving me crazy. That part isn't a lie. But it's driving me crazy because of our history."

"Our history," she repeats.

"Yes. When I look at you, I forget about the Riley that was my best friend, that was always there for me. I just see the version of her that hurt me. Badly." She doesn't say a word.

"But then if I stare too long, I see beneath that version of her. To the one that stayed up all night talking with me about our fears, our likes, watched copious amounts of *Supernatural* with me. The one who was my best friend, who I loved."

"Maybe this isn't the time to talk about this," she says instead.

"Maybe not." I look at Riley, who's looking away from me. "Take away all the shit that's happened, what almost happened. You're important to Blake, to my family, and to me. No matter what. And that means I want you to be safe. If safe is here, then that's where you should be."

"You can stop now," she says in a definitive tone. "I'll stay. But I need you to promise me something."

"Sure."

"Keep hating me for what I did. Because the minute you stop hating me, every feeling I had about you will come back in full force, and I can't take it," she finishes on a whisper. "So please. Hate me."

"Riley," I croak, wondering why my voice sounds like this. "What…"

"I really want to be alone right now, Miles. I'll be okay."

This time when she turns over, I let her. Riley pulls the covers over her head, shielding herself the rest of the way from me.

Before I leave, I grab the food and place it closer to her in case she wants it. Once I'm back in the hallway, I walk into my room, shut the door, and slide down until my ass hits the floor.

I'm so fucking confused.

I can understand hating yourself. I've made mistakes before that have made me feel a similar way.

It's the other thing she said that has my mind reeling.

Because the minute you stop hating me, every feeling I had about you will come back in full force, and I can't take it.

I always knew how I felt about her back then.
It was never a question, even though I couldn't act on it.
But why did she mention feelings?
She didn't have them too…
Right?

CHAPTER 7
MILES

When I pull into my driveway, a pang of disappointment hits my chest at the sight of Riley's car not in it. It's been this way for the past week, ever since our weird conversation in her room on the day of the party.

When she's around, she drives me up the wall. When she's not around, I want her around—even if she's holed up in her room—and that drives me just as crazy as her not being here.

But then it just makes me wonder. Where is she if she's not here?

That just confuses me more, and I hate feeling confused.

It's like this constant feeling of something crawling underneath your skin. And no matter how much you scratch it, rub it, or treat it, it doesn't go away.

There's a solution though: pretend that the problem causing the confusion doesn't exist.

I just need to forget the words that Riley told me last week. Forget that she may have had feelings for me in the past.

Because that's exactly what it is—the past.

It has nothing to do with the future, and I have to remember that.

Yeah, that's it. Pretend the conversation didn't happen and then I don't have to analyze her words. Poof! Confusion gone.

That is until I walk inside, and her shoes are in the doorway, signaling that she's home.

But if she's here, where's her car? And how did she get home?

Music from upstairs grabs my attention, so I make my way to the stairs. The music gets louder as I draw closer, and it's some of her music she listens to normally.

I would know. The shit stays on the loop most days.

Opening the door to my room, I toss my bag down. It's earlier than I normally get home, but Blake let us out of practice for some R&R—rest and relaxation—since we have another press day tomorrow.

Figuring I should be nice and see if Riley has eaten before I order takeout, I walk across the hall grab the handle, but I stop myself. Respect can go a long way and seeing as she was angry that I didn't knock last time, I decide to listen now.

My knuckles rap against the wood three times, but after a minute, there's still no answer. I do it again, much louder this time.

When she doesn't answer again, I start to worry. What if she's having another day like she did at the party? What if she's not okay?

I knock again, yelling over the music, "Riley, I'm coming in!" Opening the door slightly, it pushes against something heavy and when I look down, I find a large combat boot at the door—a size that can't be Riley's.

Upon a closer look, I see the trail of clothes that lead to the bed, and what I see there has acid pushing its way up my throat, my blood feeling like cement, and a dizzy feeling that makes hitting the floor seem appealing.

The bare ass of some tattooed fucker with a big dragon piece on his back is pounding into Riley, followed by the sound of her moans and whimpers, equivalenting to the sound of nails on a chalkboard in my mind.

His hands run over her inked flesh, memorizing the soft skin in ways I thought I would someday. But seeing them fucking in her bed, in *my* house, reminds me exactly why it will *never* happen.

It doesn't stop my body from flooding with rage or the parts of my brain filled with hatred for her from firing all their synapses.

The minute I hear, "I'm so close, Zeke," I gently close the door, race to my own room, and collapse onto the bed, screaming into the pillow.

After my throat has turned raw, I turn on my back, letting the music from the hall silence the running thoughts in my head.

All that's left now is the aching in my chest that mimics the feeling of having your heart ripped out, the tingling in my skin that buzzes so furiously it feels numb, or the hollow feeling in my mind.

For a brief second, I thought maybe things could change. I thought maybe the choices Riley made as a teenager were simply because she was young. Because we both were.

I thought maybe, just maybe, I could grow to forgive her for what she did.

But seeing her say those things to me—the ones I'm pretending to forget—and then turn around and fucking another guy ten feet from my damn room makes me realize she hasn't changed.

And that makes it easier to continue to hate her.

Because hate is much easier to cover the pain of how things used to be.

A sudden crash outside has me shooting up in bed, rubbing the sleep from my eyes. Looking over at the clock, I realize it's already two in the morning.

"I told you to be quiet," I hear Riley say.

Fuck. They woke me up to listen to round two. Hell no.

"Why do you care if this dude hears? I don't mind," the guy, Zeke—the name I'll never fucking forget apparently—responds.

I press my ear to the door, waiting to see what she says.

"I just... I don't have to explain anything to you. It's casual. Now would you get out before you wake him up?"

That's my cue.

"Too late," I say, just as I open the door.

Leaning against the door with my arms crossed—may or may not be flexing my muscles—I stare down the guy across from me, only giving partial glances to Riley.

Douchewad in the cut-out tank and jeans with holes in them speaks first.

"Hey, man. I'm Zeke." He reaches his hand out to shake mine, but I don't move. Instead, I stare at Riley.

"I heard," I deadpan, raising my brows at her.

"What time did you get home?" she asks in a hurry.

"Early enough to hear the encore."

"Fuck," she mutters.

"Plenty of that happening tonight, I don't think there needs to be anymore," I joke.

"Boy's got jokes," Zeke laughs, but again, I don't move. The air is stagnant, so quiet you could hear a pin drop. "Maybe I should go," he adds.

"Best idea you've had all night."

The Billie Joe Armstrong wannabe leaves without another word, and Riley and I continue to stand there.

I'm looking at her, she's looking at me, neither of us speaking.

I don't want to notice the tank top that she's wearing, or how her nipples peek through it. I don't want to notice the skimpy underwear she's wearing, or how her legs tremble slightly. I don't want to notice the dip in her chest, or the slightly panicked but still lustful look in her indigo eyes.

But I do. I fucking notice.

I'm about to shut the door back to my room when she speaks. "How much did you hear?" she asks, voice barely above a whisper.

"Too much," I snarl, slamming the door.

I've been sitting on it all day. Letting it fester, letting the anger turn from an ember to a full-blown flame.

In fact, I'm fuming.

How dare she bring some fucking guy into *my* house, fuck him, and then parade his ass in front of me on the way out?

That may not have been her intention, but she made a choice —a shitty one.

It shouldn't bother me as much as it does. I'm no Virgin Mary

—or whatever the male equivalent for that is—because I do sleep around, but something about this rubs me the wrong way.

It's probably because of our past, the way she hurt me. How gut-wrenching her betrayal was.

Seeing a situation similar to it must be bringing those memories back to the front of my mind, letting the nasty monster of heartbreak rear its ugly head.

I won't be reminded of those demons in my own fucking house, my safe place. Hell no.

Pulling out my phone, I click on Riley's number and shoot her a text message.

> Miles: We need to talk. I'll be home around seven.

The most I get in reply is a thumbs up emoji. Cool.

A few hours later when I pull into my driveway, I stay in my car instead of heading inside. I'm so angry at her, and I don't want to push her away—for reasons I'm not sure of—and if I go in too hot, I'll do just that.

And regardless of how much I dislike her, she's still Riley. My ex-best friend/whatever we were. I want her safe, even if that means living in her orbit again.

God. What the hell is wrong with me? How can I be so angry with her yet intensely protective at the same time?

Taking a deep breath, I get out of my car and head inside, immediately knowing that the conversation I planned to have is about to do a one-eighty.

Riley is sitting on the couch, hands forming a steeple at her chin. Looking lower, I see a duffle bag at her feet. I begin to panic but don't show it.

The thought of her leaving again... it does something to me that I can't explain.

"What are you doing?" I ask, curious.

"You said we needed to talk," she says, looking at the ground.

"Yeah. Talk. What's with the bags?"

I drop down to the couch across from Riley, and I'm immediately drawn to her. The circles under her eyes, the sadness lingering in her gaze. Her body is slumped, skin pale and ashen. She looks like a shell of the Riley I'm used to.

"You said that we needed to talk, and after what you saw last night, I thought that you'd want me gone."

"And what made you think that?"

"You're you," she responds instantly.

"You say that as if you know me."

"I do. I know all about you."

"No," I grit. "You *knew* me. Past tense."

"I don't think you've changed."

"You're not changing the subject. Tell me the real reason you thought I'd want you gone." I lean forward, propping my elbows on my knees as I look deeper into her, trying to will the truth to the surface, only out of curiosity.

"Considering our history, I assume you seeing me getting railed seven ways to Sunday would piss you off enough that you'd kick me out."

I take a minute to really absorb her words. She says it in a way that seems calculated, rehearsed. Dare I say, purposeful, like there's a reason behind it.

Almost as if she wants me to kick her out.

Holy shit. That's what she's doing.

"You want me to kick you out."

"What?" Her voice rises, bewildered.

"You thought if I saw you fucking that guy that I would be so angry at you because of what happened when we were teenagers that I'd kick you out."

"That's not it," she says, but it isn't convincing.

"It isn't? Hmm. Before you go and audition for Broadway, you may want to work on your acting skills." She doesn't respond, but her leg begins to bounce and she picks at her fingernails—a telltale nervous Riley sign. "Now that we've established that's a lie, want to tell me why?"

"I wanted to give you a reason to keep hating me," she mutters, so lowly that I almost don't hear her. But it seems that even when I'm mad at her, I tune out everything around me so that she can be my full focus.

"Why?"

"Because of what I did!" Her voice is through the roof now, but her expression hasn't changed. She still looks like an angry shell of a person.

Like a pissed off Casper the friendly ghost, without the friendly part.

"What you did back then doesn't matter."

"Like hell it doesn't," she spits, standing from the couch and pacing the floor. "You haven't let me live it down from the minute I moved in here. You don't acknowledge me, we keep enough room for an entire galaxy to fit between us, and you look at me like I'm scum underneath your expensive ass shoes."

"I don't hate you," I finally say after waiting enough time that my silence has Riley full-on shaking.

"Who's lying now?"

"I'm serious, Riley. I don't hate you." I wipe my hand across my jaw, then run it through my hair. Consumed by confusion and pent-up feelings and something much worse. "Trust me, I tried to."

"How'd that work out for you?"

"It didn't."

"Because you hate me."

Riley stops pacing and comes to a halt in front of me. The girl may be a foot shorter than me, but she's standing as if she's twice my size.

"I don't hate you." I stand, towering over her. Riley's breath hitches, her chest heaving beneath the ripped band tee as she looks into my eyes, her own filled with unshed tears. "I just hate what you did to me, to us."

And the first tear falls. My stomach rolls, and I look away to keep from having to see it.

"I did it for your own good," she says, backing away.

"That's bullshit and you know it," I respond, following her step.

Riley stops behind the couch, grasping the back and taking a deep breath. "It isn't bullshit. What's done is done. Are you kicking me out or what?"

When she looks back at me, the slight vulnerability that was there not even a minute ago is gone, and her mask is back in place.

"No. I'm sorry you didn't get what you wanted from this."

I'm not sorry, though.

Fuck, stay on topic.

"I didn't want any of this," she mutters. I don't think she intended for me to hear it, but I did. And the ticking time bomb that is my emotions explodes.

"You could have prevented all of this shit!" I bellow. "What you did… It was the ultimate fucking betrayal, and it was your goddamn choice! I wanted things to be so different, Riley," I confess. "Things were good until they weren't. I thought you'd have my back."

"I did have your back whether you believe me or not," she forces out through gritted teeth. Riley walks around to grab the duffle bag, but before she gets to the stairs, I snap.

"You know what I think?"

"I don't care what you think," she quips.

"I think you ruin everything you have, however small it may be, because you've never had a true thing in your life. You were abandoned, shuffled around, and now, the minute that you meet people who give a damn about you, you sabotage it."

I keep walking until we're nearly chest to chest, until we can feel the body heat emanating from each other. "You can't stand to be happy because you've never experienced it. And instead of filling that void with the people who give a shit, you turn your back on them and fill that void with random dick instead. Am I wrong?"

"You're a dick," she growls, another tear slipping. "I don't have the energy to fight you anymore. I'm headed to work, away from you before I say some shit you don't want to hear."

Riley takes off up the stairs toward her room, but I realize the point I intended to make was never made.

"And Riley?" She turns to me, not speaking. "Don't you ever bring another guy into this house to fuck again. Do you understand?" She doesn't say anything. "Because if you do, he won't leave here walking, and he'll never be able to dissatisfy another person again."

I turn to leave, but her response catches me by surprise.

"And how do you know I was dissatisfied?" she questions, baiting me.

"Because I remember the sound of your fucking moans, and they were nothing like the act I heard last night."

And goddamn me to hell, I *do* still remember them.

Even if I don't want to.

CHAPTER 8
RILEY

Ever since I was a little kid, I've loved to draw, sketch, doodle—anything that involved putting different colors to paper.

Making art come to life, creating my own worlds to escape in, turning ordinary objects and beings into something extraordinary.

Something magical.

It's the reason I decided to become a tattoo artist.

I knew that I didn't want a regular nine-to-five, or a job where I had to be up at the ass crack of dawn. Because let's face it, I'm not a morning person.

If you are… are you even human?

The reason I chose tattooing instead of other forms of art, is because of the power and creativity that tattooing can give you, and the amount of healing it can do.

Tattooing in its original definition, at least in Tahitian, is *to mark oneself*, but for me, it's *so* much more.

It tells a story of one's life—the dark moments, the light and fluffy memories, the shadowed areas that are a combination of both.

And for some, me included, it can highlight moments that

you never want to forget, or reminders of all that you've overcome.

The birth of a child. The death of a loved one. The moment you decided to keep living.

Choosing to get a tattoo is empowering, creative, brave, and courageous. And I get high off providing that for other people.

Creating those forms of escape, putting a picture to those life-altering moments, and bringing creativity to something so deep.

It's been a dream of mine since I was a kid to own my own parlor, but considering my inconsistent finances, that isn't something tangible—at least for the time being.

Which is why I'm currently working for someone who doesn't appreciate me in a place that I love but doesn't feel like home.

When I was an apprentice, I found this place and its owner and immediately fell in love. My mentor, Rhett, made me feel like I was a part of the family, taught me everything to know about tattooing, running a business, and he encouraged me to follow my dreams.

That is until his heart gave out, and he passed, leaving his business to his son, Zeke.

I know, I'm sleeping with the boss's son who is now the boss. How professional of me.

But so much changed after Rhett died. Where he mentored me, treated me with respect, and gave me exactly what I earned through my work; Zeke doesn't.

He has most of the appointments and takes fifty percent of the walk-ins, leaving me with only those who specifically schedule with me and whichever walk-ins I can get to first that he tosses aside.

I didn't expect it to go on for so long. It happened right after his dad passed and considering how much of a fatherly figure he was to me, I was devastated.

Zeke preyed on that devastation and my grief. Got me in bed

with him. Promised me things—like more clients and a lesser chair fee—as long as we kept things casual.

Four years later and nothing has changed. If I thought for a second that I could get out of this place and open my own, I would. But that isn't in the cards for me now.

Instead, I go to work in hopes of one day having that for myself, saving up every penny I have to put a down payment on a place of my own and a studio.

I'm not used to getting what I want, so for now, I'll be looking for a place to stay instead of a studio. Which is why I'm going with Blake after work to look at a few places.

When I walk into the studio for the day, my mood goes from barely feeling to totally keyed up. I have a scheduled piece coming in around an hour from now, and it's the third session on a horror sleeve for a guy I met in the square. He saw my ink, asked where I got it from, and then after telling him and showing him my portfolio, he came in the next day and scheduled an appointment with me.

Zeke nearly shit his pants at it, and I know it pissed him off that he wasn't getting the commission. He's a narcissist in all its definitions, but it makes things bearable around here. Soothes the loneliness, temporarily.

City & Sin Ink is an equal distance from the local university and zoo; I'm here for the better part of the day.

Regardless of the ownership, this place is actually pretty cool. The old brick structure is classic, a whitish, tan colored brick forming the architecture. Arched openings are on either side of the building with full windows, though you can't see in them, and the front entrance is a lion iron door with flower patterns throughout.

Upon entering, four black leather couches occupy the space at the front, with coffee tables, magazines, pre-drawn design books, and frames of art covering the wall.

It's a comfortable place overall, and I'm glad I can still do what I love.

Getting settled at my station, I begin going through my daily routine.

The horror sleeve we're working on is badass, and we may have only two or three more sessions until it's fully complete. I'm really fucking proud of myself for what I did today.

On my way out, Zeke stops me at the reception desk.

"I need to talk with you before you leave."

"What do you need?"

"About your cut," he begins, and my stomach drops. "I've gotta raise your cut to sixty percent."

"What?" I bark.

"Sorry."

"Is everyone's cut getting raised?"

"You're not serious," he huffs. "You know the drill. They're raising to sixty-five, so be glad I'm being generous." The patronizing tone has me wanting to gouge out his eyeballs, but I hold back.

So much for a riverfront apartment. There's no way I'm affording one now.

"Whatever. I've gotta cut out, so I guess I'll see you later."

Zeke reaches down, wrapping his hand around my hip and pulling me close. "You know I take care of you, right?" I nod, trying to end the conversation. "I can pick you up at nine if you want to come back to my place."

"That won't be necessary," a voice cuts in from behind. "She's with me tonight."

Fuck, I know that voice.

"It's nice to see you again, man," Zeke says, stepping forward.

"Wish I could say the same," Miles responds, and I note the disinterest in his tone.

"What are you doing here?"

"I came to pick you up, obviously."

"Why?" I ask in a panic. We haven't spoken since he told me that I ruin everything and that he remembers my moans. I shiver at the thought. "Where's Blake? She's supposed to pick me up and go with me."

"She got dragged into a last-minute meeting and couldn't make it. I'm here to take you."

I shouldn't have let Blake drop me off today. I should have just driven myself.

Fuck. "Okay."

We're in the truck for all of two minutes before I'm snapping. "Why did you come?"

"Because you needed me."

"I'm a big girl, I could have gone by myself."

"I was free," he responds nonchalantly like the act doesn't matter.

Crickets. I have nothing to say. And that leaves room for thoughts. Thoughts like why the hell is he so damn hot and cold with me? I'd rather him stay cold. I know what to expect then.

"Can I turn on the radio?" He nods.

Grabbing the auxiliary cord, I hook my phone up and immediately begin to play my favorite playlist. Minutes go by with Miles not saying a word, but I can see the tenseness in his shoulders, how his nose is scrunched up, and the way his eyebrows are furrowed.

He always hated my taste in music.

"How much longer are you planning to torture me?"

I hold back a grin, no matter how badly I want to show that I'm quite enjoying this.

"This isn't torture, Miles. *Sleeping with Sirens* is like listening to freaking angels sing."

"He sounds girly."

"You sound annoying," I quip.

"He looks weird," he continues.

"You look…" I pause. His hands grip the steering wheel, causing the veins to pop out in his forearms. Straight-arm porn is what it is. And his biceps, so muscular and toned… they represent so much strength, and my thoughts trail to dirtier places.

"Good. I look good. It's okay, you can say it."

"That wasn't what I was going to say."

"Then what were you going to say?"

Fucker. He knows I'm stumped. "I was going to say…" A thought hits me. "You look like you have a small dick. You drive a big truck. That's what that means, right?"

"I can pull it out right here and prove you wrong, or you can continue thinking about the size of my cock. Your choice."

"Option three—neither."

"Guess I missed that option," he says with a sarcastic tone.

"You did," I speak with conviction. "But are we going to keep this shit up, or will you drive me to my first viewing?"

"Don't have to. We're here."

This is only one of four places I'm looking at today, and it isn't in the worst area. Again, not something I'd choose for myself, but it's in the budget.

The realtor showing off the apartment, Gina, is a ridiculously sweet middle-aged woman who seems great at her job. She walks us through the place, explaining details about the amenities. One bedroom, one bathroom, small kitchen, but that's the better part of it.

It needs a paint job, badly. The rugs in the bedroom need to be replaced, the place itself is dingy, and I'm not even going to mention the rat droppings I saw in the bathroom.

The visit itself lasts less than thirty minutes, and Miles is practically dragging me out of there by the end of it.

Once we're in the truck, he levels me with a look that has me cowering in my seat.

"What?" I ask.

"Show me the rest of your listings for the day. I know they've got pictures."

I pull out my phone, click on the listings, and hand it over to Miles. He swipes through each one, focusing on all the little details as he stares intently. The right side of his mouth is raised, lips pursed, eyebrows lowered, glowering at the pictures.

"No." His tone is final.

"What?"

"No. No more viewings."

"Why not?"

"These places, they aren't safe. The buildings are ancient, they're in shitty locations not even close to where you work, and one even looks like someone was murdered there. Because that is not paint on the brick, it's blood."

"Those are my only options right now."

"No, the fuck it isn't. You're staying with me where you're fed, taken care of, and where I know you're safe. Got it? Cool."

He takes off, not in the direction of my next viewing but back toward his house. "And I don't have a say in this?"

"No. Because inside, I know it's what you want."

"What I want?" My voice squeaks as it rises. "What makes you think that what I want is to stay in the house of someone that used to be my best fucking friend but now only cares about slut-shaming me, making me miserable, and saying things that are meant to cut deep because you're hurt?"

"I was over the line the other day," he starts.

"There was no line because you obliterated it," I snarl.

"I felt bad after I said it," he sighs.

"That's not the point. It's the fact that you said it to begin with." A pained expression appears. And weirdly, I'm the one that feels bad. "This is why I've been looking so hard for a place. You don't really want me around, Miles."

"Yes, I do," he rushes out.

"No, you don't. The Miles that I know—that I *knew*—would have never said such heinous things to someone he cared about. And although I know you hate me, you do care, or you wouldn't be doing this."

"I told you I didn't hate you," he says, but I still don't believe it.

"You avoid me as much as possible, you can barely look me in the eye when we're in the same room, and you say some awful things about me, Miles. If that isn't hate, I don't know what is."

"It's not hate." I level him with an incredulous look. "It's close to it though."

"What I thought," I grumble.

"It isn't what you think."

"Then, please. Tell me what it is. Because I don't know how much more of this I can take."

"You were my best friend, Riley. For most of my adolescence. I shared everything with you, trusted you…"

I know where this is going, and my chest begins to tighten, my palms sweat, legs shake.

"When you did what you did, I felt like I'd been sucker punched in the face at the same time my heart was ripped out of my chest and thrown into a wood chipper. Because I thought…" Miles takes a deep breath, blowing it out through pursed lips. "I thought we had something brewing. And when you… did what you did, I took that as the most considerable betrayal possible."

"I know," I admit.

"You hurt me, Riley," he tells me, his voice trembling. "I guess that's why it's easier to be angry. Because then I don't have to feel my heart breaking all over again when I see you or remember how close we were."

"People heal from broken hearts every day, Miles. And your life turned out fine without me in it."

"You say that so easily, but a broken heart is only a small price to pay when you're not the one who has to pay it."

His words rock me to the core, and I immediately want to feel guilty for what I did to him. But then I think about what he's accomplished, how successful he is, how happy he seems, and that feeling vanishes.

"I paid in my own way," I mutter to myself.

"I'm sorry for saying those cruel things to you the other day. It's… how I protect myself."

"I'm not saying it's okay, but I do understand."

Miles pulls into the driveway and when we reach the house, he cuts the truck off. His hands rub at his thighs, huffing air. Then he begins to tap the steering wheel. After a minute of neither of us speaking or moving, I turn to face him.

"Is there any way we can get back to a neutral place?" He opens his mouth, but I continue. "I'm not saying that you can't be angry, because you have every right to be. I know I hurt you. But I am asking that if you want me here, truly, please stop treating me like you don't."

"I can try," he says, and fuck me if I'm wrong, but I believe him.

Once I nod my acceptance, Miles exits the truck and heads inside.

I really hope things begin to change around here, that we can be somewhat friendly—maybe even similar to how it used to be.

And I hope he never says anything like that to me again because it fucking hurt. And the reason it hurt so damn much—the reason it *still* hurts—is because it's true.

I do ruin things, and I ruined them for us back then.

But not because I wanted to.

Because I had to.

CHAPTER 9
MILES

Do you ever get the feeling that you need to think, but you're not sure what you need to think about? So instead, you start thinking about everything, and eventually, you're having a full-on conversation with yourself about all your life choices.

Just me?

Because right now, I'm thinking about one thing, and one thing only.

And it isn't basketball like so much of my life has been consumed with.

It's Riley.

Something about her is different now. Obviously, people change. It happens as you grow older, even if you throw things in the way to keep it from progressing. It's inevitable.

When we were younger, I was absolutely mesmerized by her. She was focused on art and staying out of the limelight. During her lunch period, you could find her in the art room sketching or painting or tucked away in a corner of the library sketching scenes from the books she read, or sketching random people spread out across campus doing the most random things.

One day, we were sitting outside at one of the picnic tables and I caught her drawing a trash can, but it wasn't typical. This one had lights shining from it, and the garbage inside was made to seem cool. I remember asking her, "Why'd you make the trash can look so pretty? It's not meant to be that way."

Her reply is still clear in my mind. "Everything is beautiful, Miles. Sometimes, all the shit just covers it up."

That's what I think about the version of Riley that I see now. She's beautiful—*so* damn beautiful—but I think all the shit that's happened to her makes her feel like she's covered up.

Something else has me feeling... off.

I know I haven't made things easy for her. But even when we were younger and I was tough on her, she was always quick-witted and full of sarcasm.

Not saying that she isn't now, but it's more acidic; her responses aren't as playful as they used to be.

That fire is still there though. I just want to know what put her fire *out*.

And the day of our birthday party where she shut herself in her room. The way she looked... Her eyes were empty, haunted. Her skin was pale and cold. It's like she wasn't even there, and I don't understand it at all.

Why is she so sad? Have I done something to her? Did... oh God, did something happen to her? To make her so sad?

The thought causes an uncomfortable churning in my stomach. Looking over at the clock, I see it's past two in the morning. Deciding that I need some water, I begin to head downstairs.

Just as I'm near the bottom, the front door opens, and Riley comes in. She comes into view, and my jaw drops.

She's wearing combat boots with red fishnet tights, skin-tight shorts with the lowest part of her ass cheek hanging out, and a solid white halter top that I can see her nipples—wait, are those piercings? Fuck me, I can't think about that—poking through, standing on alert. Her face is caked thick in makeup as well, whereas daily Riley is more on the simple side.

A protective feeling washes over me at the thought of her

going out, doing whatever, in that outfit, past midnight. It's New Orleans—you can never be too safe.

"Where have you been?" I ask, a bit too aggressively.

"Work. What does it matter to you?" Her tone is dejected, and instantly, I know something is wrong.

"It matters because you're out late, dressed unlike yourself and you look... like that," I say, pointing my hand at her and waving from head to toe.

"Like what?" she asks, barely a bite to her tone. Not like Riley.

"Like your favorite band broke up."

"Those are fighting words, Miles."

"What's wrong, Riley?"

She drops her bag to the floor, untying her shoes before kicking them to the side—not caring to pick them up. *Typical.* Her bag is in her hand again as she rises, and she walks into the kitchen.

I speak again, "what's going on, Ri? Tell me."

"I'm fine," she murmurs.

"You're not."

"You say that like you care, like you know me."

"I do care, Riley. Because only someone who genuinely cares about you can hear you even when you're quiet, and you're completely mute."

"I'm talking. That's the opposite of quiet."

"Words can just be noise, Riley. It's the pleading beneath the noise that truly speaks, and I can hear it. Please talk to me."

"I can't talk to you, Miles." Riley rummages through the kitchen, grabbing some chips, an apple, and a couple of bottled drinks. "I have an early doctor's appointment before work tomorrow. I need to get some sleep."

"Riley..." I beg. I want her to talk to me. I want to know everything there is to know about her. Maybe if I know, I can figure out why the hell she did what she did. And the other part of me, the non-angry and confused side, selfishly just wants to know her.

Because through all the anger, I've missed her.

She was my best friend, and I lost that for years. My partner in crime, my confidant, my *everything*—at one point. And now she just looks so… lost.

"Stop, Miles. I'm tired. Maybe I'll explain someday but for now… I just can't."

Riley escapes to her room, and I hear the lock click as I move closer to both our rooms. Retreating to my own, I fall back in bed and will my mind to let me sleep, but it doesn't.

It's too consumed by empty looks, saddened voices, and brick walls.

Why won't she let me in?

Riley was gone before I left this morning. It's a way to avoid me, I know. I want to push her so damn badly, but I feel like she'll completely shut down if I do.

There's only one person who can give me even a semblance of clarity, which is why I find myself in her office after practice is finished.

"Hey, BOGO," I say, shutting the door behind me and taking a seat in front of her desk.

"Hey, shithead. What's up?"

"I need to talk to you about something."

"Team related or personal?" she asks, eyes peering at me from over her laptop.

"Personal."

"Seems ominous." Blake shuffles around, closing her laptop before resting her arms on the desk, palms clasped together. "What's going on?"

"Is Riley okay?"

Blake's guard immediately goes up. "What do you mean?"

"You don't seem surprised. Is there something you know that I don't?"

"I'll disclose that if necessary. Tell me what's been going on."

Taking a deep breath, I run my hands through my hair and sink further into the chair. "It started with our party. When she disappeared to her room, I went up and pulled Capetti off her because I could see she wasn't into it, and God, she was so distant.

"She had this look in her eyes that was so empty and she didn't want to talk. Since then, I've started noticing little things. She's not as sparky as she was before, you know, with her witty comebacks and her attitude. Even though Riley has always been on the darker side, she was always light around us."

Something passes across Blake's face. Her posture droops, her eyes close, and her mouth straightens into a line. "I need you to know that before I say this, I will not tell her story without her permission. If you genuinely want to know, you'll have to wait until Riley is ready to confide in you."

"Tell me what you can disclose then."

"Riley has never had it easy; we know that. I know more than you do because she wanted it that way. She was light with us, but not with me. She spared you that."

"I'm not sure what you're talking about."

"We all have demons, Miles. Most people can't defeat the demons of the people they love without becoming collateral damage, but Riley, she became her *own* collateral damage. It's more than just having a tough life."

"Is she dangerous? To herself?" Panic simmers through my insides, worry clenching in my chest.

"No, it's never been that severe." I go to open my mouth, but she stops me. "Don't ask me any more questions. Anything else you want to know you'll have to ask Riley about."

"She won't talk to me," I sigh.

"Then you'll have to suck it up like a big boy and wait until she does *if* she does."

"You suck."

"I'm your sister, Miles, but I'm also her friend. I won't pick and choose." She levels me with a look, and I nod. "Now, I've got a meeting in a few minutes that you can't be here for. So, I love you, see you later."

"Damn. Kick me out, why don't you." I know I have to go, but I wouldn't be myself if I didn't give her a little shit.

"I can kick you in the ass if that will make you move faster," she suggests. I immediately laugh, then say my goodbye and leave the room.

I still don't have any more clarity than what I went in with.

It sucks.

A few days later, I come in from an early morning practice to see Riley sitting on the couch, crying into a bowl of popcorn, while *Stranger Things* plays on TV.

"Is everything okay?" I ask.

"Life sucks. My day keeps getting shit on, and Bob fucking died. He died!"

"Who's Bob?"

"He's Joyce's boyfriend," she blubbers through tears.

"Who is Joyce?" My voice rises. I'm slightly irritated because I have no clue who she's talking about.

"On the show, Miles. It's on the damn show!"

"How am I supposed to know that?" I yell back.

"Do you live under a rock?" She sniffles. "Do you not know what *Stranger Things* is?"

"No. I haven't watched it."

"Holy shit. You're a unicorn," Riley whispers.

"I'm a unicorn?" I can't help it. I begin to laugh.

"Yes. You're one of the very few people I've met that hasn't seen this show. How?"

"When I'm not practicing or playing basketball, I'm thinking about practicing or playing basketball. I don't watch many new shows."

"Sit down. Now. We're starting over."

"We are?"

"Absolutely. Now sit."

Hours later, I've been introduced to Demogorgons, the Upside Down, this weird doctor—who is a total dick—and a girl who can move shit with her mind.

It's fucking cool.

I'm smiling like an idiot as I turn to face Riley on the couch, but the minute I see the hollow look back on her face, I stop.

"What's wrong? Still sad about that Bob guy?"

"No, this isn't my first watch. I knew it was coming, but he didn't deserve it. I want Joyce with Hopper, no question. But Bob deserved to live."

"Then what's up?"

"Just, um… just a bunch of shit going on in my head, I guess."

"Do you want to talk about it, or do you want to be distracted?"

Her eyes widen. "I'm not fucking you, Miles."

I laugh at the thought. "That's not what I was insinuating.

I'm talking about something that would actually make you happy."

"Which would be?"

Turning the rest of the way toward her, I ask, "want to go pick up my baby from obedience camp with me?"

"You know, I was beginning to believe you having a dog was a myth."

"Why would you think that?"

We've been driving for about thirty minutes, and we still have that many to go. Riley is staring out the window, the sun reflecting in her eyes, making those cerulean blues appear even brighter, if possible.

"Because I haven't seen a dog, and I've been here like two months."

"He's been at obedience camp. He should have been back earlier, but he wanted to be a bit stubborn."

"Sounds perfect for you," she mumbles, but I hear it anyway. "What's his name?"

"Chief. He's a German Shepherd. He's such a big baby when he's not being a little shit."

"Yep. Definitely sounds like you." She laughs and it hits me square in the chest.

"What is that supposed to mean?" My jaw drops slightly, my mouth tilting to the side.

"You may act all tough shit, but I remember the Miles that

would haze younger players during the day yet cry watching *10 Things I Hate About You* with me at night."

"Hey, that poem near the end hurt my heart, okay? Anybody with one would do the same."

"Sure, they would," she smirks, and the sight makes my heart smile if that's a thing.

After twenty-some more minutes of driving, we pull into the parking lot of Pawsitively Perfect Pups Canine Services. I dropped Chief off right before Riley moved in.

Normally, they'd do daily sessions for a set number of weeks, but a friend of mine told me about this place that boards the animals while training them. Apparently, they had better outcomes since they spent more time being around other dogs, and people and can totally focus on training. Since the alternative is the dog coming home each day and ruining what learning they were taught during the day.

It pained the hell out of me to leave him for so long, but with my schedule the way it is, I wanted the sitter to have it as easy as possible with Chief while I'm on the road. I was able to make as many visits as I liked though.

"This place is… bright," Riley says with distaste in her mouth.

"You would say that." I smile.

Riley has never had an affinity for bright colors, but she isn't lying about this place. Pretty sure every color of the rainbow is plastered on the walls.

"Miles!" Deena, the middle-aged, brunette that runs the place, skips over to me from the front desk. "It's so good to see you! We weren't expecting pick-up until tomorrow."

"I know. I hope it's okay that I showed up a day early. My friend here…" I pause, realizing my word vomit, "she needed a pick me up, and nothing does that better than a puppy."

"You've got that right. And who's your friend?"

Riley steps out from behind me, hesitantly reaching her hand out. "I'm Riley. It's nice to meet you."

"It's nice to meet you too, sweetheart." Deena glances back at me. "Sarah here will finalize your paperwork and payment, and I'll grab Chief for you myself."

I hear him before I see him. The minute I place the pen on the counter, a big ball of fluff runs at me, jumping halfway up my body.

"Hey, buddy," I say, scratching behind his ears—which he loves—but the moment ends as quickly as it began when Chief sets his sights on the pretty lady behind me.

He takes off toward her, sniffing at her heels before climbing up her body. And with her height, he doesn't have to try so hard to reach her face.

"Oh my gosh, you're so cute!" she states, squeaking the last couple of words. "And so fluffy!" she adds.

Chief goes back on four legs with Riley squatting to the floor to continue giving him pets. He's clearly happy to see someone new—tongue hanging out, panting, tail wagging—but that's not the best sight.

No, the pure happiness on Riley's face is what stalls me. How her blue eyes are normally hollow but are now filled with a sparkle that I haven't seen since our reconnection. And her smile, *fuck*.

A smile like hers, all toothy and wide and radiant, could give inner peace to anyone who entered her orbit right now.

I know a little part of myself sees peace at this, at seeing her what I think is genuinely happy.

It makes everything I'm feeling worth it, to know I'm providing a place that brings that part of her back. Because before she moved in, I don't believe she'd felt real happiness in, well, a long time if I had to guess.

After Deena hands us a goody bag for Chief, we head back to the truck. I open the back door for him to get in, but he looks up at me with literal puppy dog eyes and whimpers.

When Chief sees my defeat, he perks up and jumps into the

front seat. And you guessed it, snuggling directly into Riley. My heart flutters at the sight.

Back in the truck, I take in the sight of Riley holding onto Chief, the way he's snuggled into her neck with paws on either shoulder, hugging her.

"I think he likes you."

She grins, but there's something hidden behind it. "I like him too. I've never had a pet before. Even if he's not mine."

"As long as you're here, he's yours. We can share him. Especially since you'll be taking care of him." The words fly out of me, and I thought I would regret them, but I don't.

Riley doesn't say a word, but she grins, and I know I've done the right thing.

I'm not sure when it happened, but I think I stopped hating Riley.

Forgiving her? Yeah, I'm not there yet. I'd have to know what I'm forgiving, and until she talks, I won't.

But at the same time... this is Riley. The person who used to cheer for me endlessly, even though she hated the sport. The person who never missed a game. The person who sat up with me, late at night, and let me vent about things my family wouldn't understand.

The person who was *my person*.

Okay. Maybe I do still hate her a little bit, but I think it's because she ruined our friendship, ruined us. And that stings worse than anything.

And also, maybe a little bit, I think I hate myself. Because if I hadn't been so hard on her, truly listened to her, then maybe she wouldn't be where she is now—so sad, so unhappy, struggling.

I think I'm hating her a little less...

Because I should hate myself more.

CHAPTER 10
MILES

When it comes to away games, I've never been antsy or nervous about leaving for days on end. I didn't get Chief until the postseason, so I haven't worried about him. I had no one to come home to. Other than making sure I had all the shit I needed for the game, I didn't worry about anything else.

That's not the case now for some reason.

I find myself stocking the fridge with enough food to feed an entire team, checking all the security cameras, and making sure the thermostat is working fine.

I make sure that Chief's water and food are both easily accessible, so she doesn't have to lift anything heavy, load the dishwasher, and arrange for Caleb to come to take out the trash while I'm gone.

We're heading out straight after our morning shoot, so I grab breakfast to eat on the way over. Breakfast sandwich and protein shake in hand, I turn toward the fridge to grab a drink when Chief flies past me, taking out my legs, and causing everything in my hands to catapult elsewhere.

And by elsewhere, I mean Riley.

The protein shake—a very, very dark chocolate color—makes

contact with her shirt, splattering everywhere, her face, her arms, the floor.

We both stay frozen. I'm zeroed in on the huge ass stain on her solid white shirt, and she's staring at the floor while shake continues to drip from her.

"You've got to be fucking kidding me," she finally grumbles. Her voice is hoarse yet quiet as if she just woke up.

"I'm so sorry."

"It's… it's whatever." She walks to the sink, grabs a few wet paper towels, and begins to scrub at her shirt. When she lifts it, I see a glimpse of toned, inked skin and taut muscle.

And seeing her, like that, makes me want to rewind and accidentally pour the entire shake on her so she'd have to remove her shirt instead, not just scrub at it.

The thought passes quickly when I realize the somber expression on her face.

"Are you okay?"

"Nope," she says, popping the p. "But does it matter?"

The answer throws me off. "Whoever told you it doesn't matter is callous and apathetic and should be punched in the face."

She looks up at me, and her eyes flicker with something I don't recognize. Riley releases her breath, places the towel on the counter, and slides down to the floor.

Chief finds her immediately, laying his head over her legs but licking her shirt while he does so. I sit down as well, not wanting to tower over her.

"This is my favorite shirt."

The shirt in question is a bright white—or it was—with a skeleton surrounded by flowers in the middle, but the words 'dead inside' stands out perfectly. "Shirts can be replaced."

With the way she looks at me, she doesn't like that answer. "Maybe for someone with money. It's easy to replace something that doesn't mean something to you. But this is so much more than a shirt."

"How?"

"Don't laugh at me."

"I won't. I promise."

Riley gently runs her fingers through Chief's fur, and the amount of love in his eyes is unmatched, even though he's only known her for a couple of days.

"Growing up, I had nothing. I got hand-me-down clothes—some fit, some didn't—and shoes. The only meals I was guaranteed were those I got at school, meaning that I couldn't ditch like other kids. I didn't know what it was like to have something that was truly mine, other than the heirloom I was left with. But even then, it wasn't mine.

"The first money I ever made was from Caleb. He paid me, and I did his laundry for a week. It was only twenty dollars, but it was mine, you know?" She looks at me, her eyes glistening with unshed tears. "I found this shirt at the French Market one day, and I didn't question it. It fit me perfectly, but it took every bit of the twenty dollars that I had. I didn't care, though. Because this thing, this shirt made of only cotton, was one thing that was rightfully mine. It wasn't given to me, it wasn't used. It was the first thing I bought for myself; it founded my independence. So no, Miles, it can't be replaced."

I know it was an accident, but I can't help it, I feel like total shit. This shirt meant something to her, and I took that away. That feeling summons a part of me that I haven't felt in a while—the part that wants to comfort her in whatever way she needs.

My hand reaches toward her, and I find myself holding her hand—it's shaky—and running my thumb gently over the vein that sticks out of it. I hear her intake of breath at our connection.

"Are you going to be okay?" I ask, my voice raspy.

"I hope so," she says, but I can tell she isn't convinced. She pulls her hand from mine, rubbing absentmindedly at the place we were just touching. Riley stands, swiping at her eyes. "Have fun at your game. Break some records or some shit. We'll, uh, see you in a few days," she rushes out.

Riley disappears into her room before I have the chance to say anything else, leaving me with a sour taste in my mouth.

Hours later, as I board the plane, that sour taste is still present, burning its way from my mouth all the way to my gut.

"Where was your head at tonight, Rainwater?"

"On the court, with the rest of my body."

"No, it wasn't," Dmitry tells me. "Ever since you've been here, you've scored a triple-double and had no less than five assists per game. That wasn't you out there. What's up?"

"Nothing. Just feeling off, I guess."

I don't guess, I know. For the first time since I started playing the sport, I hate that I'm away. Because Riley is at home, she is not okay—regardless of if she says so—and I don't like that I've left her there. All alone.

There's something up, and I haven't had a chance to really ask her about it. If I ask her, I could make her angry. If I don't ask, I seem like I don't care.

I hate dancing the line between wondering if I'm doing too much or not enough.

"It's about little blondie, isn't it?" Dmitry pins me with an all-knowing glare.

"You're freakishly inside my head, all the time, and it scares me."

A deep laugh escapes him. "I have special skills, my friend."

That doesn't surprise me.

"I don't want to talk about it here."

"Good thing we're roomies tonight. Let's go. I need tea." He grabs his bag.

"We'll stop by somewhere on the way out and get you some."

"Funny guy. I meant *the* tea."

Laughter escapes me at the mix-up. "Later. I promised the guys I'd go to this club with them, get some drinks."

"That sounds like a bad idea. I'll go with."

At the club, we find our way to the VIP section, and we're immediately flocked by fans and waiters with drinks. A Steamroller is put in my hand, and a blonde quickly takes a seat on my lap.

"Hi," she yells over the music, smiling from ear to ear. I can smell the alcohol in her breath.

"Hello. Goodbye."

Her hand flies to her chest. "What?"

"You're not my type." She stumbles off my lap with a huff, instantly finding another player to find a seat on.

"Dude, she's gorgeous," Dean states. "How is she not your type?"

"I'm not into blondes." I lie, but only a small one.

Dmitry scoots in closer on the other side of me. "It's okay. You don't have to lie. Your secret is safe with me."

"I don't have secrets."

"We all have secrets," he says. "And yours is that you do like blondes, but you only have feelings for one."

His insinuation isn't lost on me. "Now you're the liar."

Dmitry retreats with a smirk. The dude is still in my head, and it truly is freakishly scary. Either he's a psychic, or I'm not as mysterious as I thought.

By the end of my second drink, the guys with girls have migrated to the dance floor with only a few of us left in the VIP section. To my left, Dean and Silas are talking about their latest hook-ups. Just before I tune out, I hear *her* name, and my cool, relaxed demeanor changes into one of rage.

"You're not picking up anyone tonight?" Dean asks Silas.

"Nah, man. I'm planning to hit Riley again once I'm back. She accepted my apology."

The alcohol already has my body warm, but hearing his words makes my blood turn scorching, flooded with absolute rage. How dare he speak about her like that when he doesn't respect her wishes?

I stand calmly, finishing the rest of my drink before placing the empty glass on the table. My hands tingle as I flex and unflex my hands, taking measured steps across the small room to where Silas is sitting.

"Capetti."

He stops mid-drink, looking above his glass at me. "What can I do for you, Rainwater?"

"What are you drinking?" I'm itching to sucker-punch this guy in the face.

"Local draft. Why?" *Because I don't need to slip in the rest of your beer while I'm threatening you.*

"I thought I'd get you another. I'll take your glass for a new one."

Before he can answer, I gently snatch the glass from his hand. As I turn around, Dmitry takes the glass from me with a smile.

I knew I liked that dude.

Silas has gone back to laughing with Dean when I face him again. I crack my neck.

Reaching down, I grab Silas by the collar of his shirt, lift, and spin him around until he's pinned against the adjacent wall.

"What the fuck?" he bellows.

In my peripheral, I see club security start to rush over, but Dmitry steps between us, placing a hand against them. "I'll pay for any damages. You don't step in."

Yep. Definitely like that guy.

Focusing back on Silas, I pin my arm at the top of his chest, applying pressure and pushing him further to the wall.

"You're not hitting *anything* when you get back. She is not a piece of ass you can hit and quit when you want, and she certainly isn't someone you disrespect the way that you did. She's worth much more than that.

"So, when you get back, you're going to take your phone and delete her number. If you so much as speak about her again, reference her in any way or attempt to see her, I will ruin your entire career. If you choose not to listen, then I'll have to threaten you in another way. Understood?" I force my words through gritted teeth, but I make them loud and clear.

The cheeky grin and jeering expression he's wearing pisses me off. "How long have you been fucking your roommate?" A pause. "Because if you don't want me in your territory, just say so."

"I don't have to say so. Saying so would be admitting to your shit, and I'm not doing that. I'm giving an order. That's what I'm doing. And you will follow it. Do you hear me? Because I won't tell you again."

"You're heard," he says with a wolfish grin. I release him with a huff, and he straightens out his shirt. But then my threats prove futile when he opens his mouth. "It's not like her pussy is that great. I won't be missing anything."

"You fucking—"

"Nope," Dmitry says, cutting in. The big guy, who stands about six to seven inches taller than me, braces his arm across my chest from behind and drags me back across the room, turning and pushing me down the stairs. "You need to get some air, and you need to keep your hand for our next game. The point guard can't point if his fingers are useless."

CHAPTER 11
MILES

Back at the hotel, Dmitry grabs the room key from his wallet and lets us in. The first thing I think of when we enter the room is that I didn't trip on anyone's shoes, and a small part of me misses that.

Because at least when I trip on them, I know she's home.

Home. It's an unusual word to use in the same sentence as Riley's name, but I guess she's always been a part of my home.

Even when we were estranged, even when she betrayed me.

Because a small part of her has always lived within me, and it always will.

"I'm taking a shower. I expect the tea when I'm out," Dmitry announces.

I try to distract myself from her, but my mind is consumed with thoughts of the little blonde-headed girl with sad eyes who snuck into my room at night, put away her own shit, just to listen to me complain about the imperfect parts of my seemingly perfect life.

I should have listened to her more. Maybe she thought I took advantage of her, and doing what she did was payback.

I push away the thought, realizing the only answer I'll ever get that's the truth, will be the one from her perfect lips if she ever chooses to disclose it with me.

Maybe I'm dwelling too much on the past. We were stupid kids, making stupid decisions.

But *fuck* if those decisions didn't cause a lot of pain.

Even with all the swirling emotions going around in my head —which I blame on the alcohol consumed earlier—I still pull my phone out and open a text thread with her.

> Miles: How's Chief?

Because I'm too much of a pussy to ask her directly how she is, afraid that she'll answer honestly, and I won't be there to do something about it—or at least try to do something to help.

> Riley: He's a freaking angel, that's how he is. We had a nice walk, I got him a special bone after work, and there were no accidents in the house.

The image of her in my house, probably in something skimpy that shows the outline of her nipples again, has a familiar feeling shooting straight to my dick.

> Miles: You're spoiling my dog, huh?

> Riley: You said as long as I'm here, he's half mine. And I think he deserved a treat.

> Riley: Chief agrees. He says he's been exceptionally good today.

A smile immediately spreads on my face. I could be totally wrong, but she seems happy in her texts.

An image comes through of her and Chief on the couch, but I can only see his head laying in her lap, and so much bare leg, plus a sliver of abdomen.

That didn't help the picture I already had in my head of what she looked like at home alone. I knew she was in something skimpy, teasing me without even knowing it.

> Miles: He won't even like me once I get back.

> Riley: They do say dogs are smart.

> Miles: Ha-ha.

> Riley: Congrats on the win.

> Miles: Thanks. But the stretch isn't over yet.

I'm not sure what else to say right now. I want to keep talking to her, pry into her mind a bit, but she doesn't let me.

> Riley: Chief is ready for a bathroom break. Talk later.

My heart instantly aches, like it's missing something. She's still so closed off, and I don't know how to knock down those walls. I guess I'm hoping if the bricks come down, the truth will come out.

"If you don't watch it, you're going to trip over that lip of yours. Since it's stuck out so far."

I place my phone on my chest and put my arms behind my head, glaring at Dmitry while I do. "You're an ass."

"You just don't like my honesty. It keeps you from believing the lie in your head because it reminds you of the truth."

Stupid dude is stupid right.

"The truth hurts dude." My eyes find the ceiling, trying to find answers in the spiral designs making up the artwork.

"I want my tea now," Dmitry prods.

I knew he wouldn't forget it, but I wish I knew where to begin. There's so much to our history, but just as much unknown.

"Riley and I met in middle school. Blake found her one day

by herself eating, declared her as her new best friend, and then brought her home with us. She was a foster kid whose foster parents cared less about where she was, so eventually, my dad became her new foster dad. It helped that he had a big name. It allowed him to jump through some hoops.

"Being Blake's twin, and both of us being into the same sport, put me and Riley in the same place most of the time. She was always different from the people I knew. Whereas they were extroverted and acted like your typical ridiculous teenagers, she was introverted and preferred more intimate things, like art or reading. But she wasn't introverted around us. When she finally broke out of her shell, she was one of us—a Rainwater."

"I want the juicy tea, Miles. Cough it up."

"It started in high school. That's when my dad started riding my ass the hardest about the game. When I wasn't in school, I was at the gym or on the court. The pressure was a lot, and it affected me mentally. I couldn't talk to my dad because he wouldn't understand, and if I talked to Blake, I know she would have convinced me to give it up if that's what I wanted. But it wasn't.

"Riley began noticing something was wrong. One night, she snuck into my room, and she didn't leave until I aired it all out for her. She soothed my mind and then said that whenever she was around, she didn't want to hear about basketball. Not because she didn't care about my love for it, but because she wanted to remind me that I was more than the game."

"So, you were friends first?"

"Yeah," I say, smiling. Remembering the late nights, the inside jokes about random shit. "She became my best friend. Spent most late nights in my room talking, watching movies, and talking shit. And when I tweaked my shooting arm my junior year, things shifted. She heard my concerns, assured me it would all be okay, and took care of me. I saw her differently then."

Dmitry nods. "She became more than your best friend."

"Not in the way you would think, but you're right. I saw her as more than my friend, but as someone who I felt something for. But then as I felt that, I realized I'd been feeling it since I met her but couldn't understand what it was. We toed the line a lot, where comforting became cuddling, innocent forehead kisses, and embraces that were more than friendly. It worked us both up, and one night, we nearly crossed that line by touching in ways that weren't friendly. But I pulled away last minute because I don't break promises."

"What promise would you have to break?" he interrupts, asking at a raised volume. "You liked the girl, you had the girl, you let the girl go. What is wrong with you?"

"Because I made a promise to my sister, okay?" I yell, then swipe my hands down my face. I sit up and face Dmitry, finally. "When she noticed Riley and I spending more time together, she told me that I couldn't have feelings for her. Because when I inevitably broke her heart—because I was a playboy back then pretty badly—she wasn't going to choose, and she didn't want to be put in that position. And with Riley's family life, she didn't want my dumbass decisions to cost Riley the only family she'd ever known. We made a pinky promise, which to us is the most iron-clad contract possible. Twin thing and all."

"You were pretty upset when she came here. That's what I want to know about."

Talking about that... it's something I don't do. I can still remember the sight of the two of them as clear as day. The anger that flooded through me, the betrayal that pierced my heart, the sadness.

"I don't want to drag it out because it still stings, but I got into some legal trouble with a guy who got handsy with Riley at a party. I could have lost my scholarship and hurt my chances with the NBA draft. The guy dropped the charges, but that's after I found out that he was involved with Riley.

"I was so close to saying 'fuck the promise I made with my sister' because I thought Riley and I had something special, but I was wrong. I was hurt, I was betrayed. I managed to ignore her until we graduated, and then I didn't see her again until she moved in, save for one more time. She and Blake stayed as close as ever, but I wasn't involved. And that's the tea."

"That tea is bitter."

I laugh at the comment. I never said the tea was sweet.

Dmitry sits across from me, elbows resting on his knees, his fingers forming a steeple on his chin. His brows are furrowed, his gaze one of contemplation.

"Have you ever thought about what happened?"

"More often than not. Why?"

"Something is off to me. If something was really happening between you two, whether you admitted it or not, I don't think she'd hurt you on purpose."

"You didn't see her man," my voice cracks. The raw emotions from that day creep back up, making my chest feel tight. "She looked like she was really into him."

"Do you remember what I said? About paying attention to the eyes?"

"Yeah."

"Do you remember them from that day?"

"No." I think back to the moment. "I was too far away to see her eyes, just her body language."

"Then maybe you didn't see the whole truth, but just what was visible to the eye. Things may be a lot different than they seem. But this frigid thing you have going on with her won't get you the truth."

"It's never been the right time to ask. Not then, when I was angry. And not now, when things are so different and unstable."

Dmitry leans forward, piercing me with an honest gaze. "Just because it wasn't the right time *then*, doesn't mean there will *never* be a right time," he offers, his thought changing my entire stance on the situation.

CHAPTER 12
RILEY

Loneliness is a feeling I know all too well. The only time I haven't been is when I was a true part of the Rainwater family. But all the other years before and after them, I was by myself, in more ways than one.

It was only a shirt, but fuck, it *meant* something to me. I miss it. It symbolized the first thing I ever truly did for myself. Twenty bucks spent on a shirt, but it gave me much more than the satisfaction of actually owning something.

It gave me the confidence that I could actually do something for myself because as someone who never had anyone, it solidified that I didn't *need* anyone. That I could be truly independent.

To others, it may just be a shirt, but to me, it was a turning point in my life.

I know there's no getting it back, but I'm still allowed to be sad. So, I'm going to grieve, and then I'm moving on.

Maybe it's a sign anyway. That we shouldn't hold onto material things. Or maybe Miles and I shouldn't hold onto past resentment and anger.

That line of thought has me thinking about Miles.

I didn't think I'd ever say this again, but I miss Miles. He may be angry, spiteful, and generally grumpy, but the old him I knew is still in there somewhere. And at least when he's here, whether we're avoiding each other or watching TV, I *know* he's here, and that I'm not alone.

I don't know what changed, but ever since we went and got Chief, we've moved into more neutral territory. An almost friendly one. I'm not sure we'll ever get back to how we used to be, but maybe this time around, things can be better.

He's only been gone for two days now, but I feel like it's been at least a week. I don't hear his blender early in the morning fixing his stupid protein shakes, I don't hear him yelling at old film tape from the living room, and I don't smell anything amazing coming from the kitchen.

It's a tragedy, really. I'm forced to use the microwave. I was going to try pasta, but when I put the pot on the stove, there was a note taped to the temperature knob that said, "Don't even think about it. I made you meals, they're in the fridge. Heat them in the microwave ONLY."

It made me smile, genuinely. It wasn't forced, it wasn't fake. It was real. I'm surprised that he's the reason behind it as much as I don't want it to be.

I'm surprised because things with us have been so rocky since I moved in nearly three months ago, but also not surprised because if I ever felt bad when we were younger, he'd Google the darkest of jokes to make me feel better.

His white soul knew how to infiltrate my black one, and I'll never be able to explain how that makes me feel. Weirdly, I feel seen. And that makes happiness flutter in my chest.

Barking from the foyer has my attention drawn, and as I follow the sound, the security app that Miles downloaded on my phone dings, alerting me that someone is outside.

They place a box on the steps, then proceed to leave. From the camera, the package doesn't look that big, but I didn't order anything, so this must be for Miles. I pull my phone out to text him.

> Riley: You've got a package. Where do you want it?

> Miles: It's not mine. It's for you.

For me? What the hell is in it? I didn't ask for anything.

The box isn't heavy, which is oddly relieving. Heavy most of the time means it costs more, and I don't like the idea of someone wasting money on me.

Finding my way into the kitchen with Chief hot on my heels, I place the box on the counter and grab a knife from the drawer. I'm careful cutting into it, not wanting to damage what may be in there, when my phone buzzes again.

> Miles: I'm sorry. I hope you like it.

The impatience takes over, and I rip the lid off the box and turn it over. Packaging bubbles spill out, and the contents in plastic drop to the table.

Whatever it is, is individually wrapped in small bags. Unzipping the bag, I pull the item out, immediately realizing it's a t-shirt. It falls open, and my jaw drops.

The first thing that catches my eye is the design on the front, the silhouette of a female skeleton with her hand over her mouth, and an array of flowers sprouting from her head. It's gorgeous, but it isn't the most important part.

No, that would be the words scrawled across the bottom in a beautiful Gothic font.

Dead inside but forced to be here.

It's... God, it's fucking perfect.

I take the time to check each shirt, finding that each one has some version of a skeletal woman or skeleton hands with flowers in the design and the words *dead inside, dead inside but still here*, or *dead inside but caffeinated for your benefit*.

There's seven in total, and the realization hits that there's one for each day... My stomach hits the floor. A tightness works its way into my chest, my heart beating so fast that it could penetrate through the wall of my chest and catapult to the floor.

This gesture... it makes me think he genuinely cares. He ruined my shirt—by accident, but still—and replaced it, even though he knew it would never be the original.

But the fact that he wanted to makes my heart spin like an uncontrolled tumbleweed across an open plain.

He cares, and the thought alone has my brain on overdrive. I was convinced he hated me, and I wanted to keep that hatred going because it was easier to know he hated me than to know he felt nothing. Because hatred is *still* a feeling.

I wanted him to care about me as much as I wanted him not to because the selfish part of me *wanted* him to still care, even though I was the one that hurt him.

Miles makes me want to be selfish, and that's the exact reason that I can't. Being selfish with your own feelings and others only ever leads to heartbreak. I've experienced it before, and I vowed at a *very* young age to never do it again.

But I can't help feeling it. This gesture, his change of heart, the glimpses of our old friendship that poke out every little bit.

All of it makes me think that getting kicked out of my place, moving in with Miles, and pushing each other's boundaries was exactly what was supposed to happen.

Throughout all the plastic wrappings, a small piece of paper sits folded up. My name is written across the front.

Riley,

I know that I'll never be able to replace the original, but I hope this makes up for my carelessness the other morning. I did some research and found the business that was there when you went and had them fast-track seven different shirts for you.

Your independence isn't measured by what you have or what you own. It's about how you live. Whether you worked for it or were given it, you deserve it.

I'm proud of you for what you've done for yourself and how independent you've been. You should be too.

Miles

Butterflies erupt in my belly, multiplying by the second. The palms of my hands grow slick, my body tightening as my heart races. My body flushes with heat.

Did the air stop working? Is there a weird late-November heat wave?

I'd strip if I thought it would help.

These feelings though... I haven't felt them since I was fourteen, and ironically, it's for the same guy.

The one with hypnotizing brown eyes, a million-dollar smile, and a heart much bigger than he lets on.

Those feelings completely screwed me over as a teenager, forcing me to make decisions I didn't want to, but *had* to for the sake of people I cared about.

People I still care about.

I can't let those feelings cause me to act rashly again. So, whatever it is, I have to get rid of it, no matter how friendly Miles and I become again.

No matter how badly I want more like I always have.

Against my desires, I slowly rebuild those bricks, reinforcing the wall I put up ten years ago after shattering my heart.

I won't let myself feel that level of hope again, just for something to come between it and knock it down. Because I have to face the truth. With Miles's status, and his level of fame, there will always be something else, another sacrifice needing to be made.

I've sacrificed enough in my life, and I won't do it again.

My feelings be damned.

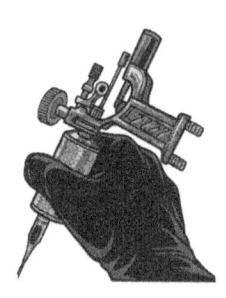

Thoughts of Miles are pushed far into the back of my mind as I head into work later that night.

Bodacious Beauties is a strip club I've been working at *officially* since I was eighteen. I worked under the table for two years prior to that, only because my boss knew my papers were fake, but he needed help and swore that if anyone came asking, he knew nothing.

I wasn't going to say shit, he knew I needed the money. I still do, so I'm still here ten years later.

I'd love to be sufficient enough to live my dream of being solely a tattoo artist, one where I'd own my own business, but that isn't in the cards for me. Not anytime soon, maybe not ever.

Even before I lost my place, I was living paycheck to paycheck working two jobs. Not having to pay rent helps that a lot, but I dread the day when I'm no longer living with Miles, and I have to start factoring rent and utilities into my expenses again.

Adulting. Gag.

Normally, I'm a bartender and waitress. I sling drinks behind the bar and deliver orders to tables, sometimes the VIP rooms, and occasionally, I'll dance.

It's not something I like to do, mainly because I'm not particularly good at it, but I oblige when the boss is short-handed. It's great extra pay.

"Wednesday," my boss, Rambo, yells as I walk by his office.

Stepping in, I say, "what's up?"

"I need you as a dancer tonight. Bunny called in. Alright with you?"

Friday night as a dancer? That's a guaranteed grand, so I quickly respond with, "damn straight."

Rambo nods, and I head back to the dressing room to find an outfit. Most of the girls bring their own, but there's always a variety of unclaimed outfits that belong to the club, and anyone can use them.

Rummaging through the pieces, I find something that speaks to my stage name—Wednesday, because of my not-so-bright personality and all—a running joke between Rambo and me because he thinks I'm always unhappy—because there's no way I'm giving my real name out, and everyone can see the darkness in me. Hence, Wednesday.

Putting my things into a locker, I find an empty mirror and begin to apply a bit more makeup than what I had on, making my lips a solid black and adding a dark burgundy to the lids of my eyes.

Aurora walks up behind me, another dancer, and takes the straightener from my hand, finishing the rest of my hair.

"I see he pulled you out with the dancers tonight. Are you okay with that?"

"Absolutely."

"Well, if you need to tap out, just yell for Oscar or Duke. They've got our backs."

Oscar and Duke are two of the security guards that monitor the floors for us and follow us to the VIP rooms if needed. Oscar has a vicious smile and could break you in half with his look alone, and Duke has dreamy blue eyes but is silent in his violence. The point is you don't fuck with either of them *or* their girls unless you want to leave here without the full package, if you get my drift.

"Thank you for looking out for me."

"Us girls have to stick together," she says with a smile, placing her hand on my shoulder.

Aurora finishes my hair, bids me with a "see you out there," and heads to her station to get ready with a few of the other girls, Coco, Lux, Monique, and Roxy—all stage names, of course.

The way our club works, each girl gets a ten-minute stint on stage, switching out with the others at the end. While one of our dancers is on stage, the others work the floor and VIP room.

By the time our group number is up—which isn't even really a routine at all, just all the girls on stage—I've made nine hundred bucks, and I still have hours left of my shift.

After the girls split the tips from our group number, bringing my nightly earnings to around thirteen hundred, Rambo tells me that Aurora and I have been requested in the Gold Room, our most prestigious VIP room, usually reserved for bigger groups.

The room itself has a small bar cart in the corner with a variety of top-shelf liquor, decorated in red leather couches, a small, one-pole stage in the center, and low lighting with a spotlight shining toward the pole.

These guys look like rich, entitled assholes. They're attractive, I'll give them that. But not even that matters. Rich, entitled assholes usually equal fat wallets, and that's what I'm aiming for.

Aurora and I begin at the pole, using each other's bodies to draw the attention of the customers. A brush of our breasts here, a swipe of our lips there, and then a giggle as we sway our bodies toward the men.

One's head is looking down at his phone—which he isn't supposed to have in here, but whatever—and I take it upon myself to sway his focus to something else.

I step until my knees contact his, then turn and drop to his lap. My hands travel up my sides, spending extra time at the sides of my breasts, until my hands intertwine in my hair, lifting it from my neck to reveal my almost bareback.

Calloused hands grip my hips, pulling me back until I'm flush with his chest.

"Funny running into you here," his deep voice speaks into my ear, one that's familiar. "You look hot as hell, Riley. This outfit on you... *Damn*."

Fuck. Shit. Damn.

I know that voice. I've *fucked* that voice.

Well, not the voice, obviously. The guy behind the voice.

I flip around in his lap, coming face to face with Silas. I've only spoken to him once since he tried having sex when I didn't want to at Blake and Miles's birthday party, and it was for him to apologize for being a dickhead.

"What are you doing here, Silas?" I whisper-yell over the low music playing.

"I'm here to have a good time with a few friends, but yours wasn't a face I was expecting."

"Ditto. I keep this part of my life private."

"I won't say a word," he says, raising his hand to zip his lips. "I did pay for a good time though," he says, a smirk growing on his face, showcasing blinding white teeth.

"Sure, you did," I laugh, beginning to slowly grind on his lap.

"I'm sorry for being a dick, though. I really am."

"It's all good now. Just be glad that Miles didn't do worse to you. And learn that no means fucking no, 'kay?"

"I don't know what came over me, but I'll do better." He

says it so genuinely that I want to believe him, but it isn't my problem. I continue to slide across his legs, swaying over his body enough that I'm touching him but not pressing down too hard.

"Speaking of Miles..." he begins, and my movements slow. "What does he think about you working here?"

"He doesn't know," I quickly reply.

"Interesting," he smiles, and I can see the ego boost it gives him to know that he's got something over Miles. Those two definitely don't get along, for good reason, I guess.

"He doesn't have control over me anyway. I do what I want."

"I don't doubt that, but I have to ask. Is there something going on between you two?"

"What?" I guffaw. "Absolutely not. What the hell makes you think that?"

"The way he threw me out of your room, that's being overprotective. The way he looks at you is like you're the sunshine on a rainy day. And the way he had me pinned to the wall of a bar a few days ago threatening me over you? That's something else entirely, like love."

What the... "He threatened you. Why?"

"He doesn't like how I treat you. He thinks you're worth more."

Warmth invades my chest, seeping into the healing cracks of the brick I reinforced earlier. But then confusion comes because Miles has openly shown his distaste for me, then he goes and fixes me prepared meals, has his brother take out the trash while he's gone, and tracks down the seller for where my favorite shirt came from.

He's been so hot and cold, granted he's been more on the warm side lately. I don't know what to even make of this; the hamster wheel in my brain is spinning too fast, jumbling everything around.

"Did he say anything else?" Part of me wants to know, while another part of me is... thankful? Angry? Turned on?

I don't need anyone to protect me, but the fact that he cares enough to do so…

"No, he didn't. Other than he'd ruin my career and if I chose not to listen, he'd take it to another level."

"Jesus," I huff.

"If you're not together, then what's up with you two? I can sense something is there. Pretty sure everyone who looks at you two can."

There's no way that's true. "We have history."

I'm no longer moving, just sitting on his lap. His hands rest gently on my hips, not attempting anything further.

"History implies that something is in the past. And although you two clearly aren't on the same page, whatever you've got is *not* in the past." His words pierce me in a way that they shouldn't, but they do, damn it.

We'll always have unfinished business as long as I'm keeping secrets from him.

But unfinished business is better than shattering the idea someone has of a person. I'd rather bear the burden myself. I'm good at it.

"You really don't see how he is about you, do you?"

Honestly, no. I try not to analyze things because that leaves an opportunity for them to be misconstrued, and then I'm the idiot who thought that way in the first place. "It's more complicated than it seems, but he doesn't know that."

Wonder passes over him, I suspect. "What are you hiding from him, Wednesday?" He grins.

"Nothing I'll ever admit to you, or to him. If I don't have to."

"As much as I hate this, we can't have any more… naked encounters." We both laugh. "I have another year and a half guaranteed with the Warhawks, and I don't want it to be tense. I had a lot of fun, but you two have some things to figure out."

"We don't. The past is better left in the past."

"Not when it's affecting your future," he responds with conviction. "Take it from me. Your secrets will eat you alive until the only part left of you is the shame that comes with not telling him. And that's a shit thing to live with."

"You're supposed to be a dick. Not a wise man."

"I can be a wise dick," he smiles, and I follow with laughter.

Silas's words still sit heavy with me as I leave the club later, and in that moment, I realize he's right.

I need to talk to Miles, to keep myself from succumbing to the secrets I've kept.

CHAPTER 13
RILEY

Anxiety is an incomprehensible thing. It's a constant nagging in your own mind, a fickle nuisance that changes based on the struggles going on in your life.

Varying depending on the day, the minute, and the situation. People say it like it's a joke when they ask if you woke up on the wrong side of the bed, but for some, it's not a joke. What's small to someone else is life-altering for others.

And this morning, I woke up on the wrong side of the bed. Literally.

I tossed and turned all night, consumed with thoughts of Miles. How Silas said he pinned him to the wall, threatened him, and all to defend my honor.

It makes my head swim, my thoughts constantly caught in their own tidal wave, pulling themselves under.

I don't think anyone can ever truly understand what it's like to have a constant battle going on in your own head, over everything, anything—nothing at all, even.

You're your own worst enemy, but at the same time, you're the only person that can resolve your inner turmoil. But how can you resolve something when that face in the mirror, the voice in your own head, is the one that's drilling everything that's wrong in the world, and with you, into your head?

Right now, my only thought is… why would Miles do that?

When we were teenagers, he was my everything. I have an inkling that the feeling was mutual, as well. Neither of us ever said anything, but it was there.

It was in the stolen glances, the unspoken words, and the silent nights of sharing a bed while we talked about anything we wanted to. It was in the way he protected me from things he thought may hurt me, how he made sure I ate, made sure I was included, and always told me that I mattered when he had no idea the mental struggles that I was facing.

It just makes the reality that I'm living in now that much more confusing.

Whatever trust Miles had in me, I broke it. Shattered it like glass, the pieces spreading all over, never to be repaired again. Or so I thought.

The way he's acting now makes me think that things are different. Will we be friends again? The way we were before.

Or is he doing it out of obligation because I'm his sister's best friend, and he's defending me on a purely platonic level?

And the other thoughts in my head… the impure ones. Well, they're wondering if there's something more to Miles' actions. Something that would be crossing the invisible line that was made the minute our feelings matured into something more than friends, simply because we happened to be connected by the person we loved most.

Somewhere deep in the back of my mind, my imagination starts creating something. A reality where I didn't hurt Miles, and we're able to be something more than friendly.

It's scary to think this way. It's *selfish*. And I'm not selfish anymore.

Yet again, he makes me *want* to be, and I hate him for it as much as I'm appreciative of it.

I know that my life isn't glamorous. It hasn't been since I was abandoned by the person who was supposed to care for me.

The action of one person, one inconsiderate, uncaring asshole caused my entire life to shift without my control. Now, I'm more cautious of people. Do they want to hurt me? Do they really care? Are the words they're saying actually what they mean?

I hate that I've had to live life on the edge, but past trauma set the ball rolling for my lack of trust in the human race. It's why I don't let myself be selfish.

You get settled, you're adjusting, and then the rug is swept from under your feet. It's selfish to want something… because when you don't get what you want, that pain you feel is the equivalent of a boulder sitting on your chest.

That's how I feel about Miles right now. These uncertainties, not knowing why he's been acting sweet and protective.

It's driving me fucking crazy, and the anxiety that it's causing is detrimental to my health. The rapid heartbeat, the constant buzzing under my skin, the lack of focus, the pit in my stomach, and the persistent unease make me feel sick.

I may have constant anxiety in my life, but I manage it. But when it's this loud, this consuming, I have to address it, or it'll continue to get worse.

Thankfully, I have the night off. After doing some laundry and going on a walk with Chief, I find myself on the couch watching reruns of *Criminal Minds*, enjoying the moment that someone's mind is more fucked up than my own.

I'm fully invested in the gloriousness of Derek Morgan and Spencer Reid when Miles comes down the stairs. It's nearing six, so I assume he's going out for the night with the guys. But the minute I see him, I know that's not possible.

Miles is wearing a tuxedo—probably one of the fancy brands like *Hugo Boss* or *Tom Ford*—and the breath leaves my body.

The color is the blackest black I've ever seen, making the golden tone of his skin stick out tremendously. The *tip-tap* of his shoes sounds as he descends the last few stairs, the burgundy Oxford's being the only color on his person.

He seemingly walks in slow motion toward me, and up close, everything about his look is much more intense.

His normally unruly hair is now styled with a low fade, the thickness intensifying as it ascends to the top of his head, where the silky waves are perfectly placed.

The tuxedo hugs his body like a second skin, outlining every ripple and swell of muscle on his arms, thighs, chest—that ass, too.

The way I can picture it flexing as he drives into me…

No. Save the dirty mind for your book boyfriends.

I finally meet his gaze, those mocha brown eyes drinking me in the same way I am him. His mouth stretches into a flirtatious smile, his tongue peeking out to wet his lips.

"Are you checking me out, usdi danuwaanalihi?"

You looked like you walked off the cover of GQ Magazine, of course, I'm checking you out! But I can't say that.

"Not at all," I squeak out. Not obvious at all. "What did you just call me?"

"That's for me to know and you to find out…when I feel like telling you," he answers with finality.

"What's with the fancy outfit? Big date?" I ask, switching back to my original thought.

He huffs. "If you call a fancy date schmoozing older rich men out of their money, then yes. Huge date."

My brows furrow in confusion. "Our yearly fundraiser," he

continues. "Same shit every year. Try to get more money from people who already donate or convince others that you're worth spending their money on." He pauses. "I thought you'd be going with Blake."

"Not my scene. I don't fit in with the likes of those people."

"Those people?"

"People with status and money," I say with distaste. "I went with Blake to a gala a few years back when she was still in Phoenix, and although I was dressed up like everyone else, people still asked me for drink refills, assuming I was the help. It reinforced to me that I didn't belong there."

Miles moves quickly to sit on the coffee table, nudging my knees apart so that his legs can rest between mine. His thumb and forefinger grip my chin, pulling my face to look at him.

The gaze he pins me with has shivers running down my spine, my heartbeat slowing yet thumping harder.

"It wouldn't be like that if you were my date. No one would ever believe you're the help. I would show you off, and everyone would gawk and wonder how the hell I ended up with a date as amazing as you." His hand moves from my chin to frame my cheek, his thumb wiping tenderly just below my eye. "You're right. You don't belong with those people. Because those people wouldn't appreciate you for the person that you are. You're right where you're supposed to be, with us. The people who love you for just being you. Okay?"

The words pierce me in a way I don't expect, releasing rampant thoughts in my head. Thoughts of what things would be like now if I hadn't ruined them in the first place. Of what it would be like if we could be more.

"How long will you be gone?"

Miles pulls back at my words, his brows furrowing. Like he's snapping out of whatever just happened.

The selfish part of me wants to keep him here, wants him to embrace me the way he once did. But once we break the contact barrier, it opens the door for all hell to break loose.

Because I know the minute that we touch, even if it's platonic, I'll never be able to *stop* touching him.

It nearly killed me once before. I won't be able to resist again.

"I should be back in a few hours. Why?"

My fingers find the hem of my shorts, tweaking at a loose string that's barely detached from the seam. "I think we should talk when you get back. That's all." I don't mean for my voice to come out shaky, but it does.

"Is everything okay? Are *you* okay? I can stay here if you want me to."

Sentiment consumes his words. "Absolutely not. You need to go schmooze. Me and Chief are good here, aren't we buddy?" He followed Miles down the stairs, taking his place beside me on the couch.

He likes it here. *I* like it here. And that scares me. Because when I'm starting to enjoy where I am, I usually have to leave.

"If you need me, I'm here." He says it in a way that makes me believe him, and I want to say I need him because I do. But how do you admit that you need someone when you've spent your whole life not needing *anyone,* and the one person you finally want is the one person you can't have?

"Go schmooze, Miles. We can talk later."

He pulls away reluctantly, letting his hand linger on my skin until the distance forces him to let go. The shivers he leaves behind don't ease up, even after he's gone.

My stomach sits heavy in my abdomen the more that time

passes, and I've been unconsciously shaking since he left. Evidenced by the way my hand trembles when I pick up my phone to check the time.

The time that's edging by too slowly.

Knowing that I have to talk to Miles has my chest squeezing tight, and I feel out of my body in an unpleasant way. I'm about to tell someone that I care deeply for—that I've never stopped caring deeply for—that I purposely ruined whatever could be for his success.

He says he doesn't hate me, that he never could, but that's about to be put to the test by what I tell him.

Shortly after ten, Miles arrives home, but he's not as empty-handed as he was when he left.

"I brought something for you," he says with a wide smile. He walks over, placing a plate of something on the table in front of me, taking a seat beside me.

"What is this?"

"If I still know you, you don't take care of yourself like you should. And considering I don't see any signs of a proper dinner, I'm assuming you didn't eat tonight. I brought you some food."

"What is it?" I ask as he pulls the wrapping off the plate.

"Fancy foods that I have no idea what it is, nor could I pronounce the name," he laughs.

Butterflies erupt in my stomach. Few people have done nice things for me, which is why this small act of kindness has my heart tumbling over itself inside my chest.

"Thank you."

"You're welcome."

He smiles, and the pit in my stomach increases in size.

"Miles, we need to talk."

"About what?"

"About how you threatened Silas not to come near me again."

The smile he had only a few minutes ago is long gone, and he whips his body toward mine at rapid speed. "How the hell do you know about that?" he growls out.

"I ran into him at my second job, and we had a nice little chat. But that doesn't answer my question."

"Considering Silas only goes to bars and strip clubs; I'm going to assume it was one of those. Am I right?"

"I don't need to tell you that."

Miles' hands, rested upon his knees, flex and unflex until his eyes—that are flashing with fire beneath them—pin me in a way that makes me think he knows all my secrets.

"Are you still working at that fucking club with that creepy ass boss? The one you were at when you were eighteen. I thought you left that place."

"I never left. I've been working there for ten years. I needed money, and it's a good job with some really nice people who work alongside me. But that is not the damn point." My voice gets higher on the last word.

"You want to know why I threatened him?" His face is rigid, eyebrows hiked high, jaw clenched tight.

"I asked the question, so yeah."

Miles stands and begins to pace the living room. He unbuttons his suit jacket, draping it across the chair on the opposite side of the room.

"Tell me."

He continues to stall. He even disappears into the kitchen, coming back with a beer in hand. Miles takes a seat across from me, putting distance between us.

Maybe that's a good thing.

"Why can't you just tell me?"

"Because I thought it was obvious!" he blurts in a hurried tone.

"Thought what was obvious?" I respond breathlessly. I haven't been able to take a breath since the words left his mouth.

"That I fucking care about you!"

CHAPTER 14
RILEY

Laughter spills out of me. "Miles, no you don't. You can say that you do all you want, but you always see me as the girl who hurt you. You won't get over that."

"Listen to me clearly," he demands in an eerily calm tone. "If I say something, I mean it. I don't say what you want to hear, and I don't lie. So, understand me when I say that I care about you. More than any other person in this world alongside my family." He draws closer to me. "You, Riley," he says, pointing his finger at me. "You. No one else."

My heart beats faster at his words. Words that cut so deeply that I want nothing more than to wrap my arms around him and believe what he says.

But there's one part of his statement that makes me uneasy. When he said he means what he says. Because if that's the case, either he's telling the truth and he thinks those things about me —the things he said in high school—or he's lying through his perfect teeth.

"Does that mean that you meant what you said in the locker room at Senior Prom?" His brows furrow in confusion. "One of the guys asked if we had something going on, and you laughed.

Said that I was a worthless slut, just like my addict mother, and if my own mother couldn't even want me, then neither would you."

Miles' body turns to stone. I feel like if I poked him, he'd crumble to the ground in pieces. He's staring over my head, jaw taut and mouth in a flat line. Something is happening behind those eyes.

I can't bear to look at him, to hear him say that it wasn't a lie. That he really does think those things about me. The person that laid up at night and convinced me that I wasn't what people said I was.

Distracting myself, I take a step back and look to the ground, breaking the bubble we were in where we breathed the same air. Being close to him like this… it hurts. Especially when it's the person you've shared the most with in life. Even if it was years ago.

My entire body begins to tremble, wracked with every emotion in the book—anger, sadness, defeat. I hate that we ended up here, I'm sad that yet another thing in my life didn't work out, I feel defeated by the circumstances.

I hadn't even realized I was crying until a tear hits the top of my foot. It's the sign I need to get out of here. I can't tell him the truth, not when I feel this destroyed. But it's what I deserve.

I destroyed him first.

Throwing myself into gear, I turn to run to the stairs, prepared to lock myself in my room for the foreseeable future, when a strong hand grips my arm, halting any further movement.

My body collides with his chest, his arms wrapping around me in a tight hold. His scent is the first thing that I notice, embracing me like a warm memory. The strong aroma of patchouli mixed with the slight sweetness of sandalwood smells like coming home.

I could never leave his embrace and be fine, but that's not in my reality. He doesn't know how I feel, how I've always felt, and his lack of response means that what he said is the truth.

I can't stay here. I can't. I have to go.

"Don't pull away from me," he finally says, a rasp to his voice that wasn't there before.

Miles' hands pull away from my back, sliding agonizingly slow up my body, waking every active nerve ending on his ascent. His hands come to frame my face, holding me with a ferocity that isn't painful, but firm like he's begging me to stay, to listen.

"I need to know how you heard it."

He wipes a tear from under my eye. "I came to find you," I admit, voice just above a whisper. "Prom. We hadn't spoken all day, and I knew you were upset about what was going on, and one of your friends told me you were in the locker room. I had barely opened the door, but when I heard you say that..."

Miles pulls back, and the grip on my face becomes firmer as he tilts my head up, his face level with mine. "Riley, I need you to know that I did not mean one fucking word that I said. Okay? Not a single one." His eyes, the brown beauties that are nearly black, filled with anguish and longing and sincerity, are staring so deeply into me that I feel it in the very pit of my soul.

"Then why did you say it?" I nearly scream the words out, but he holds me still.

"Because hurt people, *hurt* people. And you hurt me, Riley. Worse than I'd ever been hurt before."

Do you know how a hose pipe gets when you kink the wire, and the water gets backed up, creating immense amounts of pressure that only continues to get worse? And then it explodes.

I'm the explosion.

With all the strength I have, I grab Miles' arms, yanking at them until his hands leave my face and I put space between us.

"It was for your own fucking good, okay!"

I collapse onto the couch behind me, covering my face with

my hands, taking deep breaths. No matter how much I expand my lungs, I feel like I don't get enough air in.

All those years I've kept this secret, all the times I seen the rest of his family and managed to keep it in, and now it's out there. Maybe not all of it, yet, but by opening this door, it's bound to come out sooner rather than later.

When I finally take the chance to look at Miles, he's standing closer to me again. His hands are clenched tightly by his side, an angry redness is touching his neck, and those eyes that were so deep with pain moments ago are now ablaze with fire, anger.

"What the fuck is that supposed to mean?" he asks in a demanding tone.

"Can you sit down?" I ask calmly.

"Sit down. You want me to sit down? How the hell can I do that when you just said you hurt me for my own good, and I feel like sitting down is going to change my life forever!" he yells, arms flailing in every direction.

"I need you to sit down because I want to tell you the truth! And having you stand above me, making me feel small, is not how it's going to be. I need to have a semblance that we're on the same level."

Miles runs his fingers through his hair, tousling the black strands. He ambles over to the couch, collapsing with a sigh. Running his hands over his pants a few times, he takes a deep breath and turns to face me.

"This is going to hurt, isn't it?" he asks warily.

"Maybe, but not more than it will hurt me. I've been keeping this secret for years, but things just feel... different now. Between us. Am I right?"

"Yes," he says confidently, igniting a bit of hope in me. "But—"

"Hold on. I need to explain myself first, and then we can talk more about this. Okay?"

He nods. Both of us are staring at each other, the current in the air making it feel electric. My skin is buzzing. My heart is beating rapidly against my chest. The pit in my stomach weighs like a boulder.

Either way this goes, I'm fucked.

"What do you remember about back then?"

"I know that I punched a guy out for disrespecting you, I know he pressed charges, and I know that he dropped the charges." I nod. "I also know that you got with him after he tried to ruin my life."

"How'd, uh... how'd you know about that?"

"I saw you. You were in the middle of Jackson Square. His fucking arms were around you and his face was in your neck."

Sure. That happened. But he missed me pushing the guy off and kicking him in the balls. It's what got him sucker punched in the first place—not understanding the word no.

"Can I ask you something that will put things into clarity for you?"

"Sure."

"When did you see me with him? Before or after the charges were dropped?"

"After," he responds. "Why?"

"The reason he dropped the charges is because I paid him off, Miles. If he had gone through with it, you could have lost your scholarship and your NBA prospects. I wasn't going to let you lose your dream for someone like me. So, I took care of it."

All the tension I was holding—well, most of it—dissipates from my body as the truth comes out. The only noise in the room is the sound of Chief lapping from his water bowl. And while no words are being spoken, Miles' body language speaks for him.

He's pissed. Evident in the way he finally growls out, "you did *what*?"

"I. Paid. Him. Off," I say, enunciating each word. It's as simple as that.

"Not to sound like a dick, Riley, but you didn't have any money. The only thing you had of value is..." he trails off, as if he's realized something. And he must have because eventually, he softly says, "Riley."

In a split second, his hands are wrapped around my arms, and he's pulling me toward him on the couch. So much so that one of my legs is folded under me while the other is draped across his body. His hands make a featherlight trail down to my wrists, where his thumb rubs little circles on the bare skin there.

"Your birth mom's bracelet... it's gone," he mutters. "It was Cartier; worth like ten or fifteen thousand. Why would you sell it? You never took it off when you were younger. You said it was the only thing she was good for, leaving you something nice."

"My mom threw me away like trash, Miles. I don't care about her in the slightest, or what she left me. But you? You meant so much more to me, and it was my fault in the first place that you punched that guy. It was only right that I fix it."

"No. No, it wasn't. He chose to get handsy with you, he chose to not listen to you saying no, and I chose to hit him. It wasn't your responsibility to take care of me."

"It's who I am, Miles."

"What is who you are?" His hand moves to frame my cheek, and the way he's looking at me right now makes me think he could reach into my soul and magically repair every damaged part of me.

"My mom didn't want me, she tossed me out. I had to put my feelings aside. I found a foster family that wanted to adopt me, then they got pregnant and decided that they didn't anymore. I had to put my feelings aside too. Then I was moved from foster home to foster home, forced to fend for myself. Do things I wasn't proud of just so that I could eat every day.

"But then I found your family." My voice cracks at the end. "You gave me a home, food, security, safety. You supported me in every way. You became my family. But you know that losing your chance to play basketball professionally would have put a fracture in that family, and I couldn't allow that to happen. Not because of me," I say, aggressively poking my chest. "I'm not worth it."

"Tell me why you did it." His hand mindlessly strokes my thigh, sparking goosebumps all over.

"It's like you said. I thought it was obvious." The hint of a smile tilts my lips, but it's gone almost instantly at the weight of what I'm about to say.

"What was obvious?" Miles asks just above a whisper, lacing his fingers through mine while putting our foreheads together.

"I fucking cared about you, Miles. I've never known the feeling of love, but I'd like to think what I felt for you was pretty close."

His thumb sweeps across my bottom lip, pulling down slightly. Driving me insane.

"I know, Ri. I know."

Miles wraps his arm around me, pulling us into a half-lying position on the couch. He holds me tightly, kisses me on the forehead, and makes gentle strokes up and down my back, comforting me.

"What are we doing, Miles?" I ask, my eyelids growing heavy.

"We're finally getting the chance to explore what we couldn't when we were eighteen. And I'm finally getting to hold you the way that you deserve to be, the way I've always wanted to."

"We still have so much to talk about."

"Not now," he insists. "But I do need you to make me a promise. Promise me that you'll never do something to directly affect my life, at the expense of yourself, without talking to me first, okay? I don't want to lose you again."

"I promise."

We lay there in silence for a few minutes, until I'm almost asleep. Then Miles speaks again.

"Can I tell you something, Ri?" His fingers are tracing up and down my arm, my thigh, making cartwheels flip in my belly.

"Of course."

"I don't think you will ever realize, but you changed everything for me the minute you walked into my life. And whether you believe it or not, you belong here. Okay?"

For the first time in a*n exceptionally long* time, I have hope. Hope that things will be okay, and hope that the only family I've ever known will be mine forever.

CHAPTER 15
MILES

WHEN I WAS ELEVEN, I MET A GIRL.

She had long blonde hair, tangled but with a windswept look to it, like she woke up and came to school that way. Her baby pink lips were chapped, her skin pale and ashen. There was a small dusting of freckles across her nose and cheeks, and her eyes were the bluest I'd ever seen.

The backpack she wore looked like it had been ripped to shreds on a train track, and her clothes were two sizes too big, a little dirty, and even had a few holes in them.

I remember thinking, "why does she look like that?" I know it's a shitty thing to think, but I was eleven. My dad always took care of us, but it wasn't until a couple years later that I found out the truth.

She never knew her dad. Her mom dropped her at a safe haven when she was five. Then she shuffled around from home to home until she found us.

It was half of the reason I never pursued her. In the time she became my sister's best friend, she had also become mine. I wanted her around, and I didn't want to jeopardize it with a childish crush. I mean… that's all it can be at fifteen, right?

The second half is my sister. The minute she saw my eyes

linger toward Riley a little too long, she dragged me to my room, sat me down, towered over me and threatened me. I remember it clearly.

She'd said, "I swear to God, Miles. If you so much as go within ten feet of her with your dick, I will castrate you and feed it to the pigs. Do you hear me? She has been through too much for you to ruin it with your inability to commit. Got it?"

I had joked around with her, pretending that it meant nothing. But deep down, I knew it did. My usual conquests—what my sister called them—only had the ability to make my dick feel things. But Riley—she made other parts of my body feel. It was a weird thing to comprehend, something I wasn't used to.

So, I easily pushed it away. Even made a pinky promise to my sister.

I know what you're thinking. You were a teenager, and now you're a grown man, so why the hell are you giving your word in the form of a childish gesture?

Because with us, it's like law. Promises between siblings are intense but promises between twins are ironclad, unbreakable. It's nearly a criminal offense to go against one another.

It's why I never acted on my feelings. I may have toed the line—a lot—but never truly crossed it.

Now, all I want is to say, 'fuck the line' and obliterate it to smithereens. Forget that it was ever there and do what I really want.

Then again, I'm still so angry. Angry that she felt the need to go behind my back, hurt me, betray me—or so I thought.

But then I look at her, her long blonde hair fanning across my chest as her breath warms my skin, her arms wrapped tightly around me, and that anger goes away.

Because she's *here*.

She fell asleep on me last night, and I didn't have it in me to move her. Selfishly, I didn't want to let her go.

Because deep down, underneath the story I once thought was true but is now a lie, is the girl that I fell for over ten years ago.

The one that let me bitch about the downsides to being an athlete, the pressure of living up to expectations, the future I envisioned for myself. With her, I wasn't a Rainwater or a legacy or a basketball prodigy.

I was just me.

And now as I think about it, she sacrificed the only family she knew to allow me to be that guy, the one she always told me I could be.

It doesn't erase my anger though. Why the hell did she think it was okay to do that? If paying that guy off was an option, my dad would have handled it. To put it simply, we're rich. You're not an icon, or a G.O.A.T, like Sam Rainwater and not get paid. So, why didn't he take care of it? I know he knew. He's the first person I told.

My brain feels like it's made up of strings being pulled in multiple directions yet only ending up a tangled mess.

Deciding to take a step away, I gently remove myself from beneath Riley, lying her head back down onto the pillow I placed below her.

She looks so peaceful in her sleep, and I find myself wanting to stay and watch her forever, protect her from anything that could hurt her in such a vulnerable state.

But instead, I head to the kitchen and start making her breakfast.

When we were younger, she was obsessed with cinnamon French toast, so I want to make it for her. Reminisce in the good parts of the past, incorporate it into now so we can remember how things used to be.

I start a pot of coffee, grab my ingredients and begin fixing food. By the time I've finished the French toast, warmed the syrup and the coffee is done, Riley comes dragging into the kitchen, hoisting herself onto the seat at the island before plopping her head against the table.

"Morning, sleepyhead," I say.

Something between a grumble and a moan comes out, but it's

muffled by the way she's holding her arms around her head.

"Do you want some coffee?" The only response I get is a thumbs up, making me laugh under my breath.

Once I'm finished with her coffee, putting enough cream and sugar in it that would make a diabetic cringe, I slide it over the counter to her. I nudge her hand so she can sit up, feeling the electricity that passes through us at the contact.

When she doesn't move, I say, "you know you have to actually sit up to drink that, right?"

"I know," she sighs as she lifts her head. "I'm just not a morning person. I need time to come to the land of the living."

"I'm used to early mornings. It's part of my routine now."

"I feel for you," she says, perking up a little.

Silence spreads between us until it cracks. "Please tell me that last night was a dream and we didn't have a knock down drag out fight that ended in me telling one of my darkest secrets and falling asleep on you and probably drooling," she pleads.

"You're really adorable when you sleep."

"Fuck," she says. "I thought I dreamt it."

"Dreaming about me, Ri?" I ask, unable to dismiss the opportunity to mess with her.

"Sometimes," she responds so honestly that it takes me aback. I was expecting her usual level of sass or sarcasm, but not this time.

"That just makes me more confused, Riley," I sigh.

"I, uh… I'll answer any questions you have."

"That's just it… I don't know what the fuck I'm thinking. All my shit is jumbled right now," I admit.

"Then explain your shit to me. Tell me what you're thinking."

This is going to sound like word vomit, I know it already.

"What I'm thinking is that I'm so angry at you for sabotaging what we were building. Angry that you gave up the only thing you had from your past. Angry that you went behind my back, even if it was for my own good. I'm so thankful that I found out the truth, but I'm still angry." She nods.

"We lost so much time, Riley. Because even if we had never tried a relationship, I'd still have my best friend."

She nods again, but when I look at her, I note that her eyes are glassy. "I want to say that I'm sorry for my actions, but I'm not. Because had he gone through with it, you wouldn't have the success that you have now. I won't apologize for giving you the opportunity to have everything you ever wanted."

The look she spears me with tells me that there's no changing her mind, that she'll always stand by her decision. A part of me is mad at her for doing it, but the other part of me is immensely proud. Because there have been so many times in her life where she didn't have the opportunity to make her own decisions, and she did this one so selflessly.

"Riley, you've done enough sacrificing in your life. You shouldn't have felt like you needed to do more. I could have handled things just fine. You spent years away. You sacrificed the only family you had ever known and while I'm angry at you, I'm also angry at myself."

"What?" she asks, eyes wide. "Why?"

"Because I should have known something was wrong. I should have just handled it myself. It was my violent hands that started it in the first place."

"You guys took me in, gave me everything I could ever want. I felt like I owed you and since I'm not rich or connected or anything, I did the only thing I knew I could."

"Riley." My voice quavers. "You never owe anybody anything for the kindness they choose to show you. The minute you came home with Blake, you became a part of our family, and family takes care of family."

When she doesn't respond, I choose to get up and fix her plate. French toast, side of eggs and some fresh fruit. I also pour her a glass of orange juice to go with her coffee.

I slide the plate to her before sitting back down, and when she sees it, she lets out a barely audible gasp.

"Are these new plates?" I nod. "Miles, why the hell did you

buy sectioned plates?" she laughs.

"You don't like your food to touch."

For a moment, she freezes. Then, a slow grin stretches across her face, and she begins to eat her breakfast. I gather my plate too.

"I've never been taken care of—not really. I was kept alive out of obligation by foster families. I've never known what being taken care of means from a familial, or even loving, stance. In my foster homes, I was given hand-me-downs and fed poorly, but they did it to keep receiving a paycheck. It's hard to accept as anything but a transaction, you know?"

Every time she talks about her upbringing, a part of me cracks inside. I want to rage on the person who gave her up and those who mistreated her. And then I want to steal the little girl with the fake smile and broken eyes and show her all the ways that love should be.

"Love will never be a transaction with us, Riley. It's an extraordinary gift, to be loved by someone. And I'm going to make sure you get to experience that, okay? I want you here not because I'm getting something out of it, but because I *want* you here."

She takes a bite of fruit, chewing slowly, avoiding eye contact. "You really want me here? Because you weren't so accepting about it at first."

"I want you here more than anything, Ri. And I wasn't accepting at first because I was angry, yes, but also because I was angry at myself for not hating you as much as I thought I would. I'm starting to question now if I ever hated you at all."

Before she can speak, I add, "and I like coming home to you."

The weight of the words hangs in the air, and just when I think it'll go unanswered, she surprises me. "I like being here for you to come home to."

It's just above a whisper, spoken so softly that I almost miss it, but the way it makes my heart skip a beat makes me glad that I heard it.

CHAPTER 16
MILES

LEAVING FOR ANOTHER AWAY STRETCH WAS LIKE TAKING A GUT punch when you're already down. Riley and I, we're in this weird sort of limbo. Ever since we hashed out the past, we've been toeing around each other, stuck in this cycle of existing while simultaneously playing with the idea of something more, though neither of us has brought it up.

The unspoken elephant in the room is the same for both of us, I'm sure—my sister, Blake. Her best friend. My twin. The person I promised that I'd stay away from Riley.

I'm different from when I was a teenager though. I don't feel the same about commitment as I once did. The hormonal, teenage version of me cared about two things, basketball and getting laid.

The adult version of me, though? He's not that person. He's searching for more. Someone to share the dream with—both the ups and downs—and someone to share *myself* with.

Me, not the famous athlete.

I've only ever had that with Riley.

And sure, there's always been an attraction there, but is it more than that?

If there's something, is it worth hurting the relationship I have with my sister?

Because if she were to be okay with it, which I highly doubt, and it ended badly, things would never be the same. I'm not sure either of us are prepared for the downfall of that.

More so Riley since we're all she has.

The thought of ruining that for her makes me sick, but the other part of me craves to find out. To see if she feels for me what I've always felt for her—a deeper connection, something beyond normal caring.

I'm itching to get into the hotel room so I can talk to Riley. We had a tough loss tonight, and talking to her will make me feel better, I know it. But Dmitry is moving at a snail's pace with scanning the room key.

"Dude, if you don't hurry the hell up, I'm busting this door down."

"Calm down," he chides, finally opening the door. I run and claim the bed closest to the window, pulling out my phone to see if I have a text. "What's got your panties in a twist?" Dmitry asks.

"Nothing. Just wanted to be back here. Get a good night's rest before leaving tomorrow."

"No. Something is different. You kept the ball from Capetti all night, you didn't want to go out, and you're staring at your phone like sunshine will shoot out of it if you stare hard enough."

Dmitry furrows his brows, squinting in my direction. He must be channeling some freaky telepathic capabilities because he finally says, "something changed with Riley. Did you finally tell her how you feel? Or did she?"

"It's not like that," I defend immediately, mainly because I don't know what the hell to even say. "We got a lot of shit off our chest, but I'm not sure that we made any progress in other areas."

Dmitry strolls over to the second bed, takes a seat, and leans forward with his elbows propped on his knees, hands together. "I'm going to need the full story before I offer advice."

Going over this again is going to suck, because I'm trying to move past it, but I can't ignore that Dmitry's advice is always useful. I haven't been on this team for long, but we immediately became good friends, and I trust him more than most people.

I fill him in on everything. The past, the new information, and even some context into what our friendship used to look like, and who she was to me.

"And you don't want your sister to find out, yes?"

"Not that there's anything to find out, but yeah."

Dmitry sits silently, contemplating. "Is that what you're really afraid of? Coach finding out about you two. Or is it something else you haven't voiced out loud yet?"

The truth in that is alarming. "I'm convinced you have psychic powers."

"Very observant," he responds.

"Yeah, Asher is the same way."

My brother is one of those people that is the silent type around most, only choosing to engage when he needs to. He prefers to watch, to observe, to get inside people's heads. It's part of his charm. Works well for him too when he's not being his grumpy dickhead self.

"You know what I think? I think you're more afraid of it not working out than your sister finding out. Because you know no matter what happens, your sister isn't going anywhere. You're bonded for life. But with Riley... if things go wrong, you could lose her forever."

There's a tightening feeling in my chest. A pressure that expands until my entire body feels locked. Because he's right.

Too fucking right.

"It makes me sick to think that if we acted on these feelings—which could still be totally one-sided—that shit would blow up and I'd be responsible for stripping her of the only family she knows. I feel like I'd orphan her all over again, and fuck, I *can't* do that."

"But what if you gave her something permanent?"

The thought makes me excited and terrified at the same time. So, yeah.

What if?

As ready as I am to get home, I can't sleep. It's barely ten, but I know it's around eleven in New Orleans. There's no guarantee if she's home or working, or even awake, but I try anyway.

> Miles: Hey, are you up?

Those three dots pop up instantly.

> Riley: Please tell me that wasn't an attempt at a booty call.

> Miles: It wasn't, but would it have worked if it had been?

> Riley: Absolutely... not. That was awful and cringy. But since it wasn't, what warranted the late-night text?

> Miles: I just wanted to talk to you.

And I do. A call feels too intimate now, and I know that's not what she would want. Texting allows a level of anonymity that speaking doesn't. And I think it's good for what we need right now—a bridge of some sort.

> Riley: Ditto.

Miles: What are you doing?

> Riley: Snuggling...

Miles: What did I tell you about bringing men into my house?

> Riley: You know damn well I didn't because you'd know by the cameras outside. The man in question though is the one that you brought in.

The text follows with a picture of her and Chief snuggled under the covers in her bed, his body fully splayed across hers in the way I wish mine was, like we used to. Connecting with a friend is one thing, but connecting with someone you care about? It's a comfort like no other.

The picture makes me homesick. I wish I was with them instead of alone on the road. I have my teammates, yeah, but it isn't the same.

> Riley: Jealous yet? If so, it's your own fault. Didn't know you were into bringing men to me. Like being a cuckold, Miles?

Miles: What's a cuckold?

The only response I get is a winky face, so I quickly Google it. The hell?

Miles: Absolutely fucking not.

She replies with multiple laughing crying faces.

> Miles: You may not know this now, but what's mine is mine. I don't fucking share.

> Riley: Understood. Too bad I like sharing.

Rage floods through my body, tingling at every nerve ending. My phone buzzes again.

> Riley: I'm just kidding. Boy, do I wish I could see your face right now.

I'm glad she thinks it's funny because I do *not*. If we ever cross that line, a man won't even be able to look at her incorrectly without me wanting to go David and Goliath on their ass.

> Miles: You wouldn't like it.

> Riley: I've missed messing with you...

> Miles: I've just missed you.

> Riley: Me too. So much.

I begin to type one more thing, afraid of the answer but also wanting to use this anonymity to my advantage.

> Miles: Riley, is there something between us?

Those three dots go on and on and on. So much so that I think she fell asleep with our text thread open. Until a message pops up.

> Riley: Miles, there's always been something between us, even if it was under the surface. It has always felt like more with you. I wouldn't have done what I did if you didn't mean that much to me. But we both know why nothing ever happened back then.

Miles: And now?

> Riley: The issue is still the same now. But I've started not to care. Because I may not have security or fame or a fat wallet in my life, but I should at least get to experience love, right? Not that I'm saying it's what this is. But it could… it could lead there, right? I don't even know what love is, I've never experienced it. But if anyone can show me, I feel like it would be you.

Miles: If we do this, I don't want to jeopardize the family you have.

> Riley: Can we just vibe with this new territory first? Feel things out a bit? If not, we're just gonna freak ourselves out.

Miles: I'd really like that.

> Riley: I'd like that too.

> Riley: Now come home soon. Your puppy is hogging my bed.

Miles: I could hog it instead. I smell much nicer.

> Riley: GOODNIGHT MILES.

I laugh.

Miles: Goodnight Riley.

Coming home has never felt so good.

It's been a shit few days on the road. Ever since I threw Silas out of Riley's room, I can barely stand to look at the guy. It's affecting my game. I know I should leave shit off the court, but all I can think about is what may have happened if I hadn't intervened.

It's not like he's a starter anyway, but we've lost the last two out of three on the road and that isn't acceptable. For any of us. I need to get my shit together.

But the minute I step through the house, all thoughts of basketball are gone for the rest of the day.

We weren't supposed to be home until around midnight, but Blake was able to get the jet to leave earlier, putting us here around dinnertime.

When I shut the door, all I can hear is the deafening sound of music flooding the speakers throughout the house. It's so loud that I don't think she even heard me come inside.

I drop my bags at the door and walk around the corner towards the living room, and I stop in my tracks at the sight before me.

In the middle of the living room, Riley dances in circles. The coffee table has been pushed to the side, and she's wearing a severely oversized long-sleeve shirt that when she turns around, I realize belongs to me; it's our practice jersey from last year.

A part of me goes feral at seeing her with my last name on her back, but I tamper that down because it's too early for me to go all possessive caveman on her.

But if she were mine, which I hope she will be because I've wanted it for so long, then a possessive caveman is all she's going to get.

Bennie and the Jets by Elton John blasts throughout the house, and Riley continues dancing in circles, singing to the lyrics as she jumps around. Her long blonde hair is in a loose, messy braid trailing down her back.

The kicker is that Chief is standing on his hind legs, being held by his paws. His tongue hangs out the side of his mouth, and when he shakes his head in a circle to the music, the laugh that she lets out makes my skin raise with goosebumps.

I think that's the first authentic laugh that I've heard from her since she moved in here over three months ago. And I can't help but feel like it's the environment she's in—here with me—that's slowly bringing back the light in Riley.

When she turns around and finally sees me, she screams *Fuck!* and puts her hand to her chest, laughing as she does.

"You scared the hell out of me," she yells, trying to catch her breath.

Chief comes trotting over to me, jumping up my leg excitedly. I bend down to scratch him behind the ears, then I quickly stand and look at Riley.

"I'm about to hug the hell out of you so if this is something you don't want, tell me now."

"What are you still standing there for?" she asks with a cheeky grin.

In a few quick strides, I'm wrapping my arms around Riley and lifting her up. Without asking, she circles her legs around my waist, hugging me like I've been gone for far longer than just a few days.

Hugging her makes me forget all the bad things in the world, makes me forget that we were ever apart, and makes coming home worth it.

"I've missed you, Ri."

"I've missed you too, Miles," she whispers into my neck.

My hand lightly runs up and down her back, holding her to me so that she doesn't let go too early.

"I'm glad that I'm able to miss you again. That we're okay."

"Thank you for not kicking me out."

"Here is the only place I want you to be, Ri."

At this moment, I know I was misguided in my earlier thoughts. Because I don't *like* coming home to her.

I love it.

CHAPTER 17
RILEY

I'VE MISSED BEING AROUND PEOPLE THAT CARE. PEOPLE THAT ARE genuinely concerned about my well-being—if I have a safe place to live, if I have food, transportation.

They're family.

I've never known what it was like to have a family. I have vague memories of my birth mom, but I don't spend too often trying to remember anymore. She gave me up and that's all I care to know.

But being around the Rainwaters? I know it's like having a family. I've seen the way they treat each other. Sure, everyone has some kind of strain with their parents, but it's usually all out of love. The way they support each other, fight for each other, love each other… it's unmatched.

And although I still feel like an outsider, I know they're my family. At least, Blake and Miles are. Even the other shithead brothers, but I don't see them enough. It's why the offer Miles presents me with is tempting, but it'll take more than that to get me back there.

"So, uh… we're celebrating Christmas later this week, and I wanted to know if you wanted to come." I freeze. "I know you weren't there last year, and I know you missed every year before that. And it's okay if you don't want to come, but…"

Fuck. There's a reason I haven't been back in years. The last time I was at that house, I was eighteen and packing to move out. Their dad, Sam, stared me down as I took all my belongings to my car, and I could feel the judgment there.

Again, I don't regret the decision I made because it helped Miles to be where he is now, but damn do I wish things could have been different back then.

I miss having the sense of family, a huge one that will go to battle for you, if necessary. But is it worth going back there and facing the criticizing eyes of the remaining Rainwaters?

I have no doubt that Miles told them what happened, but they don't have the full story. Will they hate me? Will they tell me I don't belong there?

The uncertainty of facing them again is nearly suffocating…

"I'm not sure, Miles. I don't want to intrude on your family time."

"Intrude. How can you intrude when you're a part of the family? You always have been. And if you ask me, Riley Rainwater sounds way better than Riley Davis," he states with a cheeky grin.

The thought has my stomach flipping but for different reasons entirely.

"Funny. But seriously, Miles. I don't want to impose; I haven't been there in years."

"Fine then," he says. "I'm done asking."

A weird twinge settles in my chest. I've got to admit, it stings a little that he's given up on asking me to celebrate with him.

"Because I'm done asking," he adds. "You're too stubborn to say yes, and I'm too stubborn to take no for an answer. Therefore, no asking. Because you're coming."

"I'm also too stubborn to be bossed around," I quip.

"I can't be bossing you around when it's what you really want and won't admit." He's got me there. "Plus, I want you there. I don't care what anyone else thinks if you're worried about that." He pauses. "It wouldn't be the same without you, okay," he says so sincerely that my stomach begins fluttering.

"Then I'm there," I say before realizing what I just agreed to. But the smile he gives me in return… it makes it worth it.

Sleep. Everything about it is a total lie.
Get eight hours of sleep and you'll feel better.
I don't.
Close your eyes and you'll fall asleep.
It doesn't work that way.
Want to know how I know?

Because I went to bed early last night, kept my phone away so I'd fall asleep, and I still ended up only getting four hours of sleep.

I tossed and turned, counted sheep, and woke up with the same damn nightmare that I've had since I agreed to celebrate the holidays with the Rainwaters.

Everyone's surprised to see me there, yet overly welcoming. We get drinks, we sit at the table, and then begin eating. I'm chewing my food, but something didn't taste right about it. I asked, "what's in this?"

Then Sam Rainwater, stern face and nearly black eyes, looked at me and said with no expression, "don't you already know? It's you."

Next thing I know I'm looking up at the people from the surface of the table, without a body, and an apple in my mouth. I spit out the apple and yell, "what's going on? Why did you hurt me?"

"Isn't it obvious?" Miles asks from beside me. "You hurt me first. It's only fair."

Then I woke up. Sweating, gasping, heart racing. I've had my fair share of nightmares growing up—who hasn't? —but this is something totally different.

I can't tell if it's my nerves or a bad omen, warning me that I'm walking into the wolf's den.

But it doesn't matter now since we're leaving in ten minutes. Miles told me to wear semi-nice casual clothes, whatever the hell that means, and I had to go out and actually buy an outfit.

I never shop. I've had some of the clothes I own for years. But I feel like I need to make a re-impression, especially coming off the drama of our last encounter, so I bought something new.

It's nothing too over the top, but it is a step out of my comfort zone. And by that, I mean it's not black.

Well, the pants are still black but… semantics.

It's a burgundy wrap cross-drop shoulder cable knit jumper, super soft, and still on the edge of sexy with the lower V-neck. Paired with black skinny jeans, a black belt with a gold emblem, and my signature combat boots, it's as nice as this is going to get.

Deciding to go with a full face of makeup—bold eyes, dark lips, enough under-eye concealer to hide the raccoon look, and highlighter—I feel confident enough to face the potential judgment.

Caleb and Asher won't give a shit. Hunter will make a joke out of it. Miles knows most of the truth, and Blake knows even less than that. It's their dad I'm worried about though.

He's a force, Sam Rainwater. Big, bulky, intimidating as hell. The only father figure I ever knew, but not in a comforting, emotional way. More like he made sure I was fed, clothed, and alive—just enough to make his kids happy.

I always felt like he looked down on me. Like my filth from the way I came up would infect his kids or something.

But it doesn't matter. I'll have to face them one day or another if Kyler ever pops the question to Blake. It'll be a family affair.

My phone buzzes from the bathroom counter.

> Miles: Why does it always take girls six hours to get ready?

> Riley: It hasn't been six hours, you ass. I'm coming down.

Here goes nothing, I guess.

MILES

I feel like I've been waiting an hour for Riley to get ready. Sure, I told her what time we were leaving, but I also said if she was ready earlier that we could leave ahead of time.

But alas, she's used every available minute.

We can't be late. If Sam Rainwater is anything, it's punctual.

Finally, I hear footsteps hitting the stairs, so I meet her there. What I find when I do nearly takes my breath away.

I've always thought Riley was attractive. I'd be out of my mind if I didn't.

But there's something about this moment that makes everything much more… amplified.

Her legs are covered in simple black skinny jeans that show off just how toned her legs are, and the little rip at the knee shows a hint of a tattoo there.

She's paired it with an almost red-wine-colored sweater that hangs dangerously low to her chest, so much so that I can see a hint of cleavage and the dagger tattooed between her breasts.

Her tits look amazing, and I stare longer than I should, but I don't regret it. She's a fucking beauty, and beauty deserves to be admired.

Her long blonde hair is wavy, hanging down over her shoulders in a way that makes it look like Ariel's from *The Little Mermaid*, with a small chunk of it pinned to the top in a small ponytail.

The darkness of her eye makeup makes the bright blue irises radiate to the point it makes you feel like her look could pierce you in the chest, right where it matters.

Her lips are also painted dark—the bottom being slightly bigger than the top—something I find myself wanting to bite—a color that nearly matches her top.

I briefly picture myself smearing that lipstick across her mouth as I trace my thumb across her bottom lip, right before I claim her mouth with mine.

I want it. God, do I want it. But there's some kind of mental block going on between us that is keeping both of us from making a move.

I want to learn what she's like now without discouraging the part of her I used to know. Because it turns out, she wasn't the devil I thought she was.

In fact, she was more like an angel.

My angel.

"Fuck, Ri," I rasp, really taking her in. I admired her beauty at first, but now all I can see is her.

"Is this okay?" she asks, running her hands from beneath her breasts down to her thighs.

"More than okay." I swallow. "You look stunning, Riley."

I realize then I'd wait as long as she needed me to if that's the way she looks at the end of it. Six hours, sixty hours, sixty days. I know it's an exaggeration, but damn.

"Thanks. I wanted to try something different, unlike my normal attire. I don't want them to remember me the way I was."

Stepping forward, I grab her by the base of her neck and tilt her head up to meet mine. My thumb traces a line along her pulse, noting how hard it's thumping against my touch.

"There is nothing wrong with the way you were or the way

you are. I want you to be exactly like this, Riley. Fuck them if they don't agree. Whatever happened between us, happened between *us*. They don't get a say in that, we do. And we've moved past it."

"You sound so sure."

"I am," I say with utmost confidence. "In my world, you're a Rainwater. There's nowhere else I'd rather you be."

Because here with me… yeah.

It's where she belongs. I just need her to realize it.

CHAPTER 18
MILES

The drive to my dad's house doesn't take long. And the entire drive over, Riley was tapping her leg against the floor, drumming her fingers against her thighs. She also chewed on the inside of her lip, and I wanted so badly to reach over and pull it from in between her teeth.

I haven't though because I can sense her nerves. She's worried she's not welcome here anymore. Blake always gave us an excuse for why she couldn't come back, but I just figured it was out of shame.

But this isn't a shameful thing. No, she has real fear in her eyes. And for what? Rejection? Fear of loneliness? Fear of failure?

All things I can relate to. So, when she began to twitch and tap more frantically, I reached over and grabbed her hand, squeezing it between mine as I rested it on her thigh.

Little sparks flew through me, but the real kicker is when Riley calmed down, tapping just a couple of times a minute rather than seconds.

Because I comforted her. I did that. And the fact that I can make that kind of difference, means that maybe this is real, this visceral feeling deep down that has seated itself inside me for so long.

When we pull up to my dad's, I park and get out, walking over to Riley's side and opening the door for her. She swivels in her seat, letting her legs hang off the side. Her eyes look like a deer in headlights, and even with the makeup on her face, I can see the paleness lying underneath it.

"Are you really that scared to face them?" I ask, a voice full of concern. "Because if you are, I'll turn around and we'll go home right now. If it makes you that uncomfortable—"

"If you want me here, I'm here," she says, but I know that something is still off. She's always wanted others to be happy, but I want *her* to be happy.

"But what do you want?" I ask, gripping her legs slightly tighter than I was.

The deer in headlights look in her eyes slowly disappears, and her eyes glass over as they pierce me. "You really want to know what I want?"

"Of course I do," I assure her. "Your feelings matter, Ri," I say, dipping down to eye level.

A hint of a grin tilts her lips, but it doesn't last long. Her hand comes to frame my jaw, her thumb gently tracing my cheekbone. "You're a good man, Miles Rainwater. Thank you."

I smile. "You should never have to thank me for considering your feelings. But that isn't an answer."

"I'm good, Miles. Really. I can handle it."

"Okay. If you need to leave, send the bat signal."

"The bat signal," she repeats, laughing. "And what's the bat signal?"

"Humuhumunukunukuapuaa."

"What the hell is that?" she asks, eyes widening at having to repeat it.

Understandable. It's a mouthful.

"It's the state fish of Hawaii. It's cool."

"And you know this because?" she asks, a full-blown grin showing itself now.

My heart beats faster in my chest knowing that her mood is lightening, and I smile in return.

"Found it out as a kid. It felt cool as hell when I figured out how to pronounce it. I haven't forgotten it since."

"Then that's the bat signal," she says with a smile.

Nerves forgotten, we make the trek to the front door and without even knocking, I push my way inside. I know that the rest of the family is already here given the slew of vehicles outside.

Noise is coming from either direction—the kitchen and the living room. Riley and I begin to head in the direction that we hear Blake, but the deep timber of my father's voice stops us in our tracks.

"Miles."

I can feel Riley tense up beside me, and it immediately puts me on edge. "Edoda." *Dad.*

"You're late…" he begins, "and not alone."

"I'm not. Dad, you remember Riley."

"How could I forget," he states in a monotone voice, and the pure disdain shining from my dad's eyes has my skin simmering, smoke practically billowing from the pores.

I don't get his dislike for her. Ever since we were teenagers, I've gotten that vibe from him. The only reason he agreed to foster her is because he wanted to keep his little girl happy, and he did. But that all flew out the window once we graduated and went off to college. She stopped coming around altogether.

And now it makes sense why. Being in an environment as toxic as this would make anyone avoid it like the plague.

"It's nice to see you again, Mr. Rainwater," Riley says with a timid strain to her voice.

My dad just groans his response.

"Your siblings are in the living area. I'm finishing the last few dishes. Dinner will be ready soon." He cuts a glare at Riley, then turns in the direction of the kitchen. We head in the opposite direction to my siblings.

When we walk into the room, everyone stops their conversation and looks our way.

"Well, I'll be damned…" Caleb begins. "Little bro finally bagged the sister's best friend. It's about damn time."

"Oh no," Riley defends, "we're just friends. I'm his roommate now. We tried calling you first, but you wouldn't answer your damn phone," she chastises him jokingly.

"Could've fooled me," he responds. "And I only answer my phone if I feel like it. Plus, it seems to have worked out. You haven't killed each other yet," he notes. Caleb rises from the couch, meeting us near the entrance of the room. "It's good to see you again, little Davis. We've missed you this last year."

"Year?" I ask. The question leaves me without thought.

"Uh… yeah." Riley begins to tap her fingers against her leg. "I may not have celebrated here, but we celebrated nonetheless at different houses."

She thought of everyone else before me, and she celebrated the holidays with my family, but without me there. I want to be angry—because it sucks to feel left out—but I know that I shouldn't be because of the way I treated her. Anyone would avoid that.

Her coming to me for help months ago seems like a miracle now, and not the burden I thought it would be.

Maybe the saying is true. Some of the worst things in life can be a blessing in disguise.

"That sounds nice," I say, coming back to the conversation.

Just as we're about to settle in, Dad's voice booms through the house saying that dinner is ready.

We gather around the dining table, and before any utensils are touched, we recite a Native American prayer for our thanks.

"Why don't you lead us this year, Miles?"

I nod and clear my throat. "May the warm winds of Heaven blow softly upon your house. May the Great Spirit bless all who enter there. May your moccasins make happy tracks in many snows. And may the Rainbow always touch your shoulder. May the sun bring you new energy by day. May the moon softly restore you by night. May the rain wash away your worries. May the breeze blow new strength into your being. May you walk gently through the world and know its beauty all the days of your life."

"Very well," Dad says. "Please dig in."

Finally. One of my favorite parts.

As a Cherokee Indian, a lot of our foods are based on our culture and the way that we tend to the land. From a young age, my grandfather taught me that the food that we grow is like having good karma. You do the right things and be a nice person, and then the karma will be good to you.

Our gardening, tending to the land, it's our good karma. We're good to it, and the Earth is good to us in return. And while planting this time of year isn't the most plentiful, we still honor those foods.

My edoda has been preparing food for us all day, focusing most of the dishes on the main vegetables: corn, beans, and squash. Our main dish is turkey with roasted vegetables, also with grilled salmon and trout, but I'm more interested in the side dishes.

Succotash, a mixture of corn, zucchini, lima beans, and bacon, roasted butternut squash, fried cornbread topped with butter and honey, harvest chicken casserole made up of chicken, Brussel sprouts, sweet potatoes and cranberries, and pinto bean bread, and fried green tomatoes.

We also make more modern dishes such as pumpkin pie, dressing, collard greens, and stuffed mushrooms, and you can guarantee that I eat all of it.

And the sweets… my mouth waters thinking about them. Cherokee grape dumplings are amazing, but my favorite is the wild rice pudding. Consisting of wild rice, maple syrup, vanilla, toasted nuts, jasmine, and berries such as blackberries, strawberries, raspberries, and blueberries, it's one of my favorite dishes of the holidays.

"How has the game been, son?" Dad asks, pointing his stare at me.

"Fine, other than the last two losses. We're always a little distracted around the holidays with everyone wanting to see their families and such."

"Are you sure that's the reason you're distracted?" he asks, cutting his eyes toward Riley.

"Yeah." I pause, then continue as I think about what he asked. "Why do you say that?"

"The only other time you've been distracted is when she was in your life," he states, and this time his gaze is directly on Riley and she's staring back at him with her eyes wide, her skin pale, looking nearly catatonic.

"Edoda, alewisdodi."

Father, stop. At least my sister has my back.

Riley pushes her seat back, clearing her throat as she stands. "Excuse me," she whispers, her voice wavering before she retreats from the kitchen.

I move to go after her, but Blake is out of her seat before I can even put my fork down.

When they return, Riley is distant from the evening—like she's in her own world. And maybe she is.

And a part of me would rather be in her world than in this one because of the hostility my dad has toward her... it's unbearable.

No matter how many times I tell him that the assault wasn't her fault, he still doesn't believe me. A guy got handsy, but *I'm* the one that chose to put my fist in his face. Ergo, my fault.

Riley sticks by Blake's side for a while, hanging back every time we do something tradition related. The hanging of the Cherokee flag, the woodcarving, storytelling, and the music.

Our last tradition of the night is the sunset bonfire. We gather around the fire and talk about our history and how we still honor it today, all while wearing our shawls made by my ulisi. My grandmother, Snowbird.

Caleb and Asher disappeared earlier to light the fire, while Blake and Kyler went to grab the shawls. We're halfway out the door when I realize we forgot something.

"Damn it. I didn't grab the marshmallows."

Just then, my brother yells from the backyard asking for help gathering wood.

"Help him. I can grab the marshmallows," Riley offers.

"Okay," I say, then follow my brother's call of my name. We bring firewood to the barely sparked fire, settle around, and everyone falls into their chairs, the last being my father.

The chair next to me is empty, the seat saved for Riley.

Where did she go?

CHAPTER 19
RILEY

Being back in my old room... gosh, it feels so weird. Granted, it's not my room anymore. It's plain and minimally decorated, the perfect guest bedroom for people to stay in, where they can fill it with their own shit and not remember that they're in someone else's home.

Since the minute I got here, I've had this thick feeling in my throat, a weight in my chest. Nerves scratch at my throat, and I get this intense feeling to scream, but I can't. Nothing is more of a tell-tale sign that things are not okay than hearing someone let out a blood-curdling scream, the kind that silences a room filled with a thousand people.

When I made the choices that I did, I knew that I wouldn't have to worry about coming back here again because I wouldn't be welcome. And by the interaction I just had, I'm definitely *not*.

I was just getting marshmallows. Minding my own business, as one does in a hostile environment. Then the room chilled over, and tingles ran up my spine. Not the ones of anticipation, but the ones of fear.

Sam Rainwater is an intimidating man, rightfully so. He's the kind of man with power that can make or break a person because of all the connections he's made over the years and the status he has, even retired.

He was so angry. The things he said...

"What the hell do you think you're doing here?" he had asked.

I was stupid and responded with, "because I was invited."

"This is *my* house, and *I* didn't invite you. You should leave before you find a way to cause more issues for my son. You've done enough damage once before, don't you think?"

It cut me. Miles and I are learning to move forward with it, putting the past behind us, but the man in front of me just won't let it go. I mean, everything worked out and Miles got his dream. So why the fuck is he still holding onto it?

It didn't stop there though. No. Things don't work like that for me.

"Are you too stubborn to get the damn message? You don't belong here. You need to leave before you cause any more trouble to this family. You may not be able to get him out of it this time."

I know I was lucky. Not everyone would have taken a bribe. They would have taken pleasure in exploiting a family like Miles' and placing him in a bad light. He would have lost his dream, and it would have been all my fault. I feel responsible enough that it nearly happened, but it's in the past.

I'm not sure why I decided to come to my old room though. It's not like I could leave, so I guess this was the next best thing. But being here is an equal shock of nostalgia and what could have been.

The 'what could have been' is what stings the most.

If I had told Miles and Blake about what was going on, they would have handled it. They were eighteen, they got their trust funds already. I know they would have helped. But I needed to do it myself.

I've had so many people help me out of obligation over the years—that's just how it is being a foster kid. Some foster parents are in it for a good reason, to give love to a child, but others are in it for not-so-good ones. Maybe a paycheck, a feeding ground for abuse, to use for their own reasons.

It wasn't so bad here. Sam took care of me, kept me fed and clothed, and helped me when I needed it. But then as I got older, things changed. He looked at me like I was becoming a problem, and he was just waiting for the day he could kick me out. And even though he changed a lot, I still felt like I owed him.

That's what you do when someone does something for you… right? You pay them back however you can.

Well, I've paid my dues. I just want to move forward. With the Rainwaters who matter.

The room is devoid of anything that used to be mine, but there's one thing that may have been left behind. A little memento of my past in this house and the man I came here with, though he doesn't know it.

The closet that once held so many things of mine is now empty, stripped down to only the cream-colored walls and empty racks. I take a seat on the floor, sitting against the wall as I trace just above the baseboard. Noting the divots there, I begin to remember the reason that they're there.

I sit and trace, remembering simpler times. Times where I didn't worry about bills, what career I'd have, how I'd afford lunch next week. Times when all I worried about was the new season of a show I loved coming out, going to parties, and drawing.

A knock on the bedroom door has me holding my breath, stilling my movements to keep my hiding place hidden.

"Riley?" The soft, caring tone of Miles' voice has me releasing my breath and sagging against the wall. "Are you in here?"

"In here," I sigh, wishing I could escape without facing anyone. Escape into a book, into a new world. One where the problems aren't my own.

Miles steps into the closet doorway, leaning against it with his hands in his pockets. "What are you doing in here?"

"Hiding. Escaping. Avoiding. All of it."

"Why is that?"

"Because your dad so graciously reminded me that I'm the reason for nearly blowing up your life and I don't belong here. I'm just waiting until you're ready to leave."

"With the way he's treated you, I'm ready to leave right now. Let's go," he says, reaching down for me.

"Hold on. I want you to sit down with me for a minute." His brows furrow, showing me that he'd rather leave than stay. "Please," I add, and I see the submission in his eyes when he hears the pleading in my tone.

Miles takes a seat on the floor beside me, his arm brushing against mine with his legs bent up. Mine aren't even touching the wall ahead of me, but we're not going to talk about that.

"What brought you to your old room?" he asks.

"To reminisce about old times, I think. I don't regret the decisions I made when I was eighteen, because I've only ever wanted the people around me to be happy, and you got your happiness when you made it to the league."

"At the expense of your own happiness?"

The words shake me to my core, and my heart rate increases at the intrusion.

"My happiness has never been the priority, Miles. Not in a long time. And I think it's why I'm back here. Remembering when it was."

"You were happy back then?"

"In a lot of ways, yes. In some, no."

Miles' hand slips from his thigh to mine. His calloused fingers intertwine with mine, his thumb tracing across my knuckles. My head falls to his shoulder as if it had been waiting all day to do so.

"Tell me about it," he prods in a gentle tone.

"I was never happy growing up," I begin. "I had no semblance of family, no kids wanted to befriend the weird foster kid at any school I went to. Foster parents didn't care what happened to me. Unhappiness was something I was used to."

"I wish I could have changed that for you," he speaks wistfully.

"You did," I say, lifting to look him in his eyes. "Meeting your family was one of the best things to ever happen to me in my life. Those were years of true happiness for me, something I'd never had before. Then it got dark again."

"But you still had my family. Even when I wasn't there, they still kept you a part of everything. Why did it get dark?"

I let out a sigh, dropping my head back to his shoulder as I grip his hand tighter.

"Because you were a big part of my happiness Miles—one of the biggest parts—and you weren't there. I know it was of my own doing, but… I never stopped missing you."

Miles lifts my head, our eyes meeting instantly. "I never stopped missing you either," he whispers.

Something sparks in the air between us. My skin tingles where his hand holds my face. A kaleidoscope of butterflies erupts in my stomach, but it's as if I can feel them all over my body. My breath ceases to exist with the way he's looking at me like his soul would cease to exist if he let go of me right now.

A part of me wants him to make the next move, but there's another part of me that feels like I need to get one smaller thing off my chest.

His mouth opens, but I stop him before he's able to say anything.

"Can I show you something?"

Miles closes his mouth and clears his throat. "Of course."

Arranging my body so that he can see the wall I was against, I grab his hand and lead it to the divots in the wall, tracing his thick fingers over the lines.

"What is this?" he asks when I'm finished.

"When we were younger, there were so many times that I wanted to cross that line of friendship with you. Movie nights, times we'd lay awake talking about things no one else knew... the night that douche I dated the summer before senior year decided to try and film us before I stopped him, and he called me some bad things.

"That night comes to mind more often than not, because that night, you made me feel more beautiful than I had ever felt in my life. I wanted to kiss you so damn bad... but you only saw me as a friend. And I never forgot the way you saw me then, even if it was platonic."

Miles's hand travels to my hip, framing it with his palm as his fingers dip into the meat of skin there. "I don't think I ever saw you as a friend. I thought that was the only way *you* saw me. We may have been friends, that's true. But I don't think a true friend would ever imagine the things I used to dream about doing to you..."

I don't miss the innuendo in his words, and heat begins to settle in my body.

"But I don't understand how any of this relates to the markings on the wall," he adds.

"Well... you may have thought I saw you as a friend, but I didn't. And these lines are my proof of that."

"I don't understand," he says, his brows creasing in the middle.

"Whenever I wanted to cross that line, I'd come in here and mark a line into that wall. I couldn't risk the family I had, so I would mark a line into this wall and imagine what it would be like to have more with you."

Miles goes back to the wall, tracing over the lines that are engraved along the length of the baseboard.

"There's so many of them," he admires. But I can see the wheels turning in his head. "If you made this many marks, then you must have been going crazy not acting on your feelings."

"You can say that," I say with a small grin.

"Are you still feeling crazy?" he asks.

Miles leans away from the wall, rising to his knees as he

swings his legs behind him. My limbs feel like cement, and I'm unable to move.

"I'm... not sure. Maybe? I mean, crazy is a sensitive word so I'm not sure that I'd use that in terms of admission of feelings."

I continue to ramble, knowing what's coming next. I've imagined kissing Miles so many times, but now that it's about to happen, I'm not sure I even know how to function anymore.

What if it sucks? What if I don't know how to kiss anymore? What if we've built all this tension, crossed all these invisible lines, and there's nothing there between us?

People talk about the spark when kissing someone you care about. What if there isn't a spark?

I may cry if there's no spark.

Miles' hand cradles my face gently, tipping my chin up. "I never want you to feel crazy or make another mark on that wall —or any wall—ever again," he speaks softly.

My hands are sweaty, my heart is pounding against my chest. My throat feels drier than it ever has, and there's a thumping in my stomach as the butterflies flutter at maximum speed in there.

"Okay, but I—"

"No more talking," he demands, so close that I feel the heat of his body consume me.

Then his lips are on mine.

For a moment—a singular moment—I'm stunned, frozen in the heat of his kiss. Then emotion kicks in, and I begin to kiss him back.

Electricity sparks between us each time our lips collide, and I feel them race through my entire body.

Thank fuck, there's a spark.

Miles' lips feel soft and pillowy against my own, and I can taste the beer lingering on his breath from earlier, a crisp peach flavor with a hint of bitterness on the end.

As our lips continue to move, I can note the tickle of his breath above my nose, his hands moving from the curve of my jaw to the nape of my neck.

His fingers tangle in my hair, and I rise to my knees to meet his kiss better. His hard cock presses into my abdomen, and the hand on my hip slips back to palm my ass, gently squeezing.

My head is spinning, and the minute that his tongue peeks its way through my lips, making soft swipes against my own, I feel eerily calm.

He completely consumes me. All the years of wondering how things could have been, all the time since we've reconnected that I wondered if it was all worth it… it led us to this moment, in my teenage closet, where I feel we truly are connecting on another level beyond the uncertainty of what we were before we stepped into this house earlier tonight.

This is more than just a kiss. It's a union, a pair of mutual feelings fusing together to create something more, something special.

And now that I know what it's like to kiss Miles, I don't think I could ever go back to the way it was before. To the illusion we were living in that things were simply platonic.

They've never been platonic, and I know that now. I can feel it in my chest. The Miles-sized hole that's been in my heart since I was eighteen isn't there anymore. The muscles fused back together, my heart beating at full function again, the minute his lips touched mine.

Miles's fingers, which are tangled in my hair, loosen at the same time his lips slow against my own.

I don't want him to pull away. When he does, the moment is over. And I want to live in this little bubble we've created for as long as we can.

Miles' kisses slow to small pecks against my own, but his forehead never leaves mine. He pushes my hair away, keeping his hand wrapped around the side of my throat as he keeps us close together.

"That was…"

"Yeah," he responds. "It was."

Our eyes meet, and the smallest of smiles tip the corners of both our lips as we soak in the meaning of what we just did.

"You kissed me," I state.

"I did. I couldn't let another minute go by without claiming you as mine. I've been wanting to do that for so long, but after seeing what you did in here... I craved it."

He's saying all the right things, but I only registered one word—*mine*.

"I'm yours, huh?" I ask, a somewhat cocky grin growing with each word.

"Riley Davis, you have been mine for longer than I even knew, and I want to make it clear to you that this is something special. Before now, we were in this weird limbo between friends and more, and I know without a doubt that what we have is beyond what we could have ever dreamed of as teenagers."

"What are you saying, Miles?" I ask, the pit in my stomach growing in anticipation.

"I'm saying that we have real feelings for each other, and we can't deny them any longer. I want to give this a go, Riley. I want to give *us* a go, to have the shot that we didn't have before."

"Are you asking me to be your girlfriend Miles Rainwater?"

"I am, but if you don't quit avoiding the question" —he pauses to laugh— "then I'm not going to ask, and I'm just going to tell you that you are."

"I want to be your girlfriend, Miles... but I have one condition."

"Okay." Miles sits back on his legs, focusing on the serious hint in my tone.

"We can't tell Blake. Not yet, anyway. I want it to just be us for a while, and then we can discuss it."

His lips purse, his eyebrows inch up his forehead, and then he smiles. "Deal."

His hands grip my face, pulling my lips back to his as he consumes me once again. This kiss is filled with more urgency and want than the first, but the feeling is all the same.

"Are you ready to go home and watch some TV? I think I'm ready to get out of here."

"You took the words right out of my mouth."

Then we sneak out of the house where no one can see and spend the rest of the night wrapped up in each other, and Chief, on the couch watching *Stranger Things*.

And it's better than anything I could have ever imagined.

CHAPTER 20
MILES

Game days have been the thing that I look forward to the most ever since I picked up a basketball. The squeak of my shoes as I run down the court, the way my jersey sticks to my skin, the feel of leather against my callused fingertips, the power I feel when I'm holding the ball in my hands.

It's an electric feeling. The echo of the ball against the polished wood, the adrenaline of competition, the surge of confidence from the skills you possess, and the cheering crowd.

I've never felt another feeling like it.

But I can't deny that something about this game is different. Maybe it's the dynamic of the crowd, the competition of the team we're against…

Or maybe it's the breathtaking blonde sitting behind the team wearing a Warhawks jersey that, I would bet this game against, has my name on the back.

Beautiful, she is. Inconspicuous about our relationship, she is not.

Blake calls a timeout—fuck, I forget I can only call her Coach right now—pulling us to the sideline. We're tied and looking to pull out another win so we're a shoo-in for the playoffs in a few months, but we're down to the last minute of playtime.

"What's the plan, babe?" Kyler asks, and the death glare, my sister, sends him has the rest of us taking an extra step back in the huddle.

"The plan is for you to not call me babe at work. I'm your coach right now," she says in a stern voice. She takes another step before pinning her gaze on me. "What's the plan 23?"

Last name and jersey numbers. Regular identifiers in the world of sports.

"Best bet is to hit Rhodes or Aldridge on the opposite wing."

"Why?" she asks, even though she already knows the answer.

"Because the more the ball is passed around, the more jumbled their defense gets to the point where they fall more to one side than the other."

"Still get the honor of being called my brother. It's what I would have suggested." She looks at her watch, counting down the last few seconds.

The referees come over to give the final call, and then the whistle blows.

"Go add another win to the record," Coach orders.

The Lions have possession of the ball, and when they bring it down the court, Dmitry fouls their big guy under the basket. Some may think it's stupid because of the dwindling time, but it's smart. It puts the final possession in our hands, and it means we have a better chance of winning—since their big guy can't shoot free throws for shit.

My ulisi could shoot better than that with a blindfold on. And she's in her early eighties.

As suspected, the big guy misses both his free throws. Dmitry rebounds the ball, immediately finding me. The first thing I do is check the shot clock, noting there's only twenty seconds left to shoot. Plenty of time to execute the play.

As soon as I cross half-court, I nod to Kyler and take off to the left. Kyler sets a screen as I pass by, and when he rolls off the screen, I put the ball in his hands.

Kyler repeats the same motion over on the right wing, and I make a lap around the post before catching the ball again at the key. Only twelve seconds left, so we run the same play again. Then, when the defense is jumbled, Dmitry steps to the top of the key, setting a screen for me.

I crash down the middle, pulling the defense with me. The guard defending Jackson pulls back toward me, allowing him to sneak to the corner for an open shot. With three seconds left, Jackson pulls up, sinking the baseline shot with not enough time left on the clock for the opposing team to score.

Fuck yes.

No one other than athletes can really understand the feeling of a win. The adrenaline rush, the ego boost, the jolt of self-confidence and self-accomplishment knowing your hard work is paying off. It's indescribable.

We've got a few days' break coming up, so Coach is letting us have tomorrow off from practice. I'm grateful for it because my body needs a break.

Once I've done my due diligence with the media and showered, I find myself in the hallway heading to the back exit when I see my blonde-haired tattooed beauty leaning against the wall with no one around.

"What are you doing by yourself my usdi danuwaanalihi?"

"Waiting for your sister." She looks around, and once she realizes we're truly alone, she stretches up and pecks me on the lips before quickly retreating back to her position on the wall.

"What was that?" A crooked grin appears as I stare at her lips, noting how the bottom one juts out a bit from the other.

She looks around again then whispers, "it's a congratulations kiss, obviously."

She's cute when she's sneaky.

"That was like a high school congratulations kiss. For players with stats like mine, we deserve much better," I say, goading her.

Checking that the hallway is still empty, I find the first empty room—a storage closet—and drag Riley inside.

The minute the door is shut, I press her against it, immediately finding her lips with my own. They're soft and welcoming, so I push my tongue past them, relishing the lingering taste of stadium popcorn and beer.

The kiss goes from zero to one hundred quickly, and before either of us knows it, Riley's leg is wrapped around my back, and I'm grinding my hips into hers like a sex-starved teenage boy desperate for friction.

My hands run fervently over her body, appreciating the dips and curves and change in body heat as I move my hands from her hips to the space between her thighs. She moans when I rub her clit through her jeans, and then she's pulling back.

"Miles, wait."

I stop immediately. "What is it?"

"We can't do this here. We're in a freaking closet not even twenty feet from Blake's office, in the place you work, and we haven't even discussed anything past that we have feelings for each other, but we haven't figured out what those feelings are, and I guess I'm just—" she rambles on almost incoherently.

"Hey, hey, hey. First, I wasn't planning to fuck you here. You deserve more than a few minutes in a closet full of cleaning supplies with a questionable musty smell. I respect you more than that, but I got carried away."

"Me too. And I appreciate that," she says, as she runs her fingers gently down my torso, stopping to hook them in the loops of my jeans. "But I'm second guessing ever taking this to the next step if you can only offer me a few minutes."

The teasing in her voice brings a smile out of me, and I find myself pressing her against the door even harder than before as I grab her chin between my fingers, tilting it so that we share the same breath.

"If you think for a second that I can only give you a few minutes of pleasure, then you have no idea the measures I'd take to make sure you came until I felt you couldn't walk the next day. And then when you did, you'd come again at the thought of what happened to put you in the position of feeling the ache of me still inside you."

I feel her swallow against my thumb, and I know if I slipped past the painted-on jeans she's wearing, she'd be wet for me the same way that I'm rock hard for her.

"I'm supposed to be meeting Blake for lunch, I need to get back out there."

My lips find hers again, this time much gentler, really focusing on their softness, the way they fit perfectly with mine like they were made from a mold and hers are the only ones sculpted to fit perfectly.

"Let me check and make sure it's clear," I whisper, briefly pressing my lips to hers again before doing so.

When I open the door and see that the coast is clear, I slip Riley out behind me and continue our conversation. "Thanks for the congratulations. I guess you're proud of me the way you're sporting around in my jersey."

"Oh, this old thing?" She grabs the collar, lifts it, then drops it back down. "No, this isn't for you. This is for the superior Rainwater—the coach."

"It has my number on the back," I add.

"Yeah, I had to have the number to get the name. Not my first choice but…" She shrugs her shoulders, her lips pursing out to hide the smile I know threatens to expose itself.

"You're such a little shit." I take a step forward to grab her again but stop in my tracks when I see the door to Blake's office open.

"I didn't think I'd ever get off the phone," she says, blowing out a breath. "You ready to go grab food, Ri?"

"Absolutely." As Blake locks her office door, Riley adds with a wink, "I'm starving."

Me too. But not for food with the way she's looking at me.

After grabbing my things from the locker room, I take the back exit out into the private lot. I've pushed the door halfway open when I see my edoda leaning against the building, but he rights himself quickly when he sees that it's me exiting.

"What are you doing here, Dad?"

"Waiting for you to finish flirting with the run-down ragdoll so I could speak with you."

The minute the words leave his mouth, I picture myself pinning him to the wall by his throat, watching his face turn beet red as he struggles for air.

I'm sick and fucking tired of the way he talks about her, but if I react, our secret is as good as exposed.

"I wasn't flirting with her, and don't talk about her that way. There's a lot more to Riley than you think."

"Doesn't matter. I want us to have lunch tomorrow to discuss your playing. Twelve, at the café on Market Street."

"I can't make it until one." I stand my ground, keeping my chest out and shoulders squared. These little meetings are what he expects when I play in a way that isn't up to standard for him, no matter if we get our ass kicked or blow the opposing team out of the water.

"Busy with the ragdoll?" he asks with a voice full of disdain.

"Keep referring to her that way and you won't see me at all."

His jaw tightens, and his hands ball into fists at his side before straightening. "One is fine. I'll see you then."

CHAPTER 21
MILES

I'VE ALWAYS HAD RESPECT FOR MY FATHER. HE CONTINUED TO RAISE us when my mother stepped out, provided us with everything we needed, and gave us opportunities that most kids wouldn't dream of getting.

That respect has never wavered. Not until now.

I'm not sure where his feelings are coming from, but it's like he has a vendetta toward Riley, and wants to make her life absolutely miserable whenever he can. As if she hasn't been through enough already.

I won't be able to tolerate much more if he continues to degrade her the way he does. She's in our lives for good, and that will never change. Not if I have any say in the matter.

When I arrive at the restaurant, I can see that he already has a table for us in the outside seating area. He's dressed in black slacks with a navy-blue button-up, his hair is pulled back into a low-lying braid.

"Edoda," I greet him as I stop by the table. He doesn't stand, doesn't move, just motions to the chair across from him.

"Miles."

Just as I've sat down, a young girl—probably still in her teens—approaches the table.

"Good afternoon. My name is Rayna, and I'll be your server today. What can I get you fellas to drink?"

My father and I both order water and when the waitress returns, we order lunch as well.

"Your game yesterday was good," he states.

"Thank you."

"But—" There's always a but with him. "Your free throw percentage dropped, you favor the right side, and you're not seeing enough of the court."

It doesn't matter that our team won. It doesn't matter that I put up thirty-two of the one-hundred-and-seven total points. It doesn't matter that I had eleven assists either.

Because with a man like Sam Rainwater, he'll always point out that you could do better, and work harder. It's never enough.

"Last time I checked, you weren't my coach. My free throw percentage was off by one shot, I favor the right side because it's my dominant side and our shooting guards shoot better on that side. As for seeing the court, I do. I see it so fucking clearly. But I listen to my coach and trust that what she calls is best."

A pause, silence creeping in. I continue.

"Why are you still acting like an asshole? I thought you were coming around after what happened with Blake a few months ago."

"My relationship with Blake is nothing like the one I have with the rest of my children. If you, or your brothers, wanted a better relationship with me, you could have it. It's a two-way street, Miles."

A comical laugh escapes me in return. "It can't be a two-way street when one side is permanently blocked, edoda. You did that. Not us."

The waitress chooses that time to come over with our food, and when everything is settled, my father leans forward in his seat. He rests his forearms against the table, interlocking his fingers above his food.

"I suggest you think long and hard about how you speak to me. You owe me some respect."

I stab my fork into my food, then level my father with an intense glare. "Respect isn't owed, it's earned. And you haven't earned mine yet—father or not," I say with conviction.

We continue by eating our lunch and discussing the next line of games after the New Year holiday tomorrow, which we're lucky to have off.

Once we've finished our meal, we continue talking about the organization. How Blake is as a coach, how Asher is managing the team and upcoming events he thinks I should attend.

"There's a charity gala for local youth to participate in sports that you should attend next month. Your schedule is free, I checked."

"You're joking, right?" My father's eyes trail over my shoulder, zoning out as I continue to talk. "I'm not against attending but don't just assume I'm free. Speak with my agent."

"I did. Your brother said you're free."

Remind me to gut punch my brother next time I see him. "I'll consider it."

My father continues to look past my shoulder, so much so that he doesn't respond to anything I'm saying now.

"What the hell are you looking at that's so important?"

A menacing smile appears on his face. "Nothing. Just a ragdoll being exactly who I thought she'd be."

Any other time, I'd disregard him. But when he used that word—ragdoll—I know with utmost certainty that he was talking about Riley.

I twist in my chair, following his line of sight. We're a few blocks away from Riley's shop where she works, but for some reason, she and her boss—Zack, I think his name was, the guy whose bare ass I'd love to forget—are walking out of another place down the street.

In one hand, Riley has a bag of what I assume is food. But the other hand is currently gripped into a fist as the emo asshat possessively holds onto her forearm. He's too close for my liking, and his other hand is resting dangerously close to her ass.

It takes everything in me to not get out of my seat and charge over there, but my father's next words have me cemented to the spot.

"Guess the girl still likes to rub all over strange men on the street."

The audacity. "If you think for a second that what you just saw was consensual, then you're more delusional than I thought. And what the hell do you mean by *still*?"

My father's mouth goes into a firm line as he wipes with a napkin. He takes a sip of water, then promptly moves his empty dishes to the side.

"She's the reason you got into the situation you did before college. That girl nearly cost you your career. And even though she practically mauled the guy on the street, you still want to protect her. I thought after what she did, you'd learn your lesson."

"That girl has a name, Dad. It's Riley." But something else is off. "Wait, how do you know what happened? Not even Blake knows the extent of it."

My father stays silent, and I scoot to the edge of my seat. My skin is burning like the fire of a thousand suns, my heart is racing, and my blood begins to boil.

"What the fuck did you do, Dad?" I growl.

"I'm the one who told her exactly how to fix her mess and made sure that she went through with her promise—get the guy to drop the charges and disappear from your life. No woman is worth your career, and I didn't want you learning the hard way like I did."

"Un-fucking-believable," I say a little too loudly, grabbing the attention of nearby customers. I stand from the seat and tower over my father. "You had no right to do what you did, and until you accept that Riley is a part of my life permanently, stay away from her. And mark my words… this is the last time you interfere with my life. I'm not going to end up miserable like you."

I toss down a few twenties and leave the café without another thought. Because after the bombshell he just dropped on what I thought was the truth, I have somewhere more important to be.

Traffic makes the drive to City & Sin Ink much longer than I'd like it to be, but maybe that's a good thing.

Riley told me the truth, yes, but she left out the part about my dad. The biggest part. And while I've let go of that anger for her and what she did, she should never have had to do it that way.

I would have given up the game for her to not have to carry the burden of tearing us apart. Especially since that blame should go to someone else—my selfish, conniving father.

Why wouldn't she tell me? I would have forgiven her much quicker had she told me that he didn't give her a choice. I wouldn't have even hated her at all…

Someone is definitely looking out for me because as I pull up to the tattoo parlor, there's an empty spot waiting directly in front of the door.

I've barely turned the ignition off before I step out of the car and move frantically toward where I know she is. I can't even remember taking my seatbelt off.

Upon entering the place, I see Riley near the back cleaning off what I assume is her workstation. It shouldn't turn me on the way she looks right now—hair in a bun, toned arms wiping down the seat, tight tank top and shirts with a flannel hanging around her, teeth bit down on her bottom lip in concentration—but I can't deny how effortlessly uwoduhi, or beautiful, she is.

The sagonige, or blue, of her eyes, like the clearest of skies. The soft curve of her cheeks as they slope down to her soft lips. Or the way she smiles, truly smiles, and how it's an immediate dose of happiness because you know you're one of the very few she shows it to.

I walk past the front desk, ignoring the way the woman there calls for me, and make a beeline toward Riley. The receptionist's antics grab her attention, and a small gasp escapes her when she sees me striding toward her.

"Miles, what are—what are you doing here?"

"We need to talk," I rush out.

"What about?" she asks in a questioning tone, but I see the lift in her brows as she runs over what this could be about.

"You lied to me about what happened when we were younger."

"I didn't," she defends. "I handled it. That's the truth."

I step closer to Riley so that we're not overheard, and her breath hitches at our closeness.

"Well, I just left an interesting lunch with my father, and he had something different to say."

If I thought she was pale-skinned before, that has nothing on the way she looks now. She looks like she saw a ghost. Her pupils are dilated, goosebumps dot her arms, and I can practically see the hairs standing up on the back of her neck.

"Let's step outside and talk."

Riley leads me through the rest of the parlor, and we exit on the backside of the building in the alleyway where their cars are parked.

She leans against the brick wall, head hanging low as she stares at the ground.

"What did he say to you?" she asks, her voice barely above a murmur.

"That he was the one who told you what to do and made sure that you went through with it. Unless there's more that he left out."

She shakes her head. "No, it's that simple. But with a few more words."

I press my hand beside her head on the wall and lean in, joining our heads together.

"Then tell me what he said…"

I feel the minute she relaxes into me, and her hand falls to her side as she places it in mine.

"You were at practice one day when he came to my room. He started picking over the things I'd gotten while I was living there, asking if I appreciated it. Of course, I said yes. I've always been grateful for the few years I didn't have to worry about my safety, when I could eat, or if I'd be clothed.

"Then he basically told me I owed him, and your family, for what you'd done for me. That it would be disrespectful and a disgrace to disregard who you were about to be."

My free hand traces the slope of her cheek, trailing the path of a stray tear.

"I would have done it anyway. Because there's nothing, I wouldn't have done for you to live out your dreams."

"My dream was you, Riley. Even if I didn't have it right now, my dream would still be *you*."

Her free hand reaches to palm my cheek, and she brings her lips to mine in a chaste kiss that tingles through my entire body.

"You still haven't asked me why I did it. Why I didn't come to you for another way."

"Why?"

She brings our joined hands to her chest, cupping them both with the hand that was previously cupping my cheek.

"This thing in my chest… it's always belonged to you, Miles. I wanted you to have everything you've ever wanted in life, so when I pushed you away, it was so you could have it. I was okay without it because I've gone my whole life not getting things I want. But I never left, not really... because I gave my heart to you unknowingly a long time ago, and I knew you'd keep it safe. You've always had a part of me, Miles; a part I was okay living without because I hoped that one day, you'd come back and fill that missing piece of me again like you did when we were seventeen, and you never even knew."

My blood is white hot, my entire body races with electricity like an uncontrolled live wire, and all I want to do is consume her the way she's consumed me and protect her the way that she's protected me.

Because it's the same for me. She took a piece of me a long time ago, and it took what happened for us to find our way back to each other again, those missing pieces pulling us back together like magnets.

"I knew, Riley. I knew. Because I felt the exact same way about you. I always have. The hate that wasn't really hate; the anger that wasn't really anger... I've never felt so consumed or so infatuated with someone as I am with you. Even more so with the way you sacrificed the only happiness, you knew to make sure I was happy. I'm fucking crazy about you, Riley Davis. And all I've ever wanted was you, in every way you'll have me."

"I want you in every way, Miles. The good, the bad, the ugly. I don't care if this thing between us goes up in flames, as long as you're by my side while the fire consumes us."

"Every way has always been how I've wanted you. Your smart mouth, your inability to cook, your insane amount of talent, your darkness. But I want nothing more right now than to take you home, strip you down, and worship you the way I've wanted to do for ten years so that you know I mean what I say when I tell you that you own me, Riley—body, mind, and soul."

Her lips crash into mine in a kiss so fierce that I feel the heat between us rising in temperature.

"Riley, if I wait another minute to have you, I'm gonna lose my mind."

"We've waited ten years. There's no reason to wait any

longer." She presses her lips to mine with an intensity that is overflowing with promise, and my cock hardens at the feeling. "Let's go home, Miles."

And with the way she says home, like she's finally accepting that she has one with me, has me dragging her back through the parlor at a speed that barely lets her announce her departure from work, or grab her things before I'm shoving her into the car —thanking whoever that she didn't drive hers today—and speeding off, desperate to finish fusing this connection we have between us by claiming her in every way possible.

CHAPTER 22
RILEY

Miles keeps turning to look at me as we drive back home. The way that his gaze feels on my skin as if he's summoning each goosebump individually, makes it seem like he could devour me right here, right now, and still not feel full.

Miles reaches over and grips my bare thigh, sending a rush of heat to the spot between my legs. His fingers begin to make little patterns, and each time he brushes the edge of my shorts with his hand, my stomach clenches with anticipation that he'll go further, and move past the denim barrier.

Electricity buzzes in the air, increasing in voltage as we speed down the gravel driveway to the house. I grip Miles' hand in mine as he slows to a stop by the front door. He cuts the ignition off and turns to face me.

"Are you sure you want this?" he asks with such concern.

"Of course I do," I reply honestly. I let out a breath and drop my head to the seat, then turn to face him again. "But what if this changes everything? What if the bubble we've been in pops, and you realize that this isn't what you want?"

Miles' hand frames my face gently, and his gaze—full of comfort, care, and pure want—bores into me so intensely that I forget to breathe.

"Riley, there's nothing more that I want than you, and nothing can change that. I just want to show you how much I appreciate and care about you by giving you everything you deserve."

I nod, but fear still lingers. "I'm just scared…" I admit.

"Hey, that's normal. To be scared of something is to care about it, at least in some way. But you never have to be scared around me, Riley. I will always keep you safe."

His words soothe me in ways I can't comprehend. "I know that. There's just no going back once we cross this line."

"I don't want to go back," he says gently but directly. "I only want to go forward with you."

"I want that too." He smiles, and it's like an epinephrine-style shot of happiness straight to my soul. "I'm ready. I need to learn to take what I want, even though I think I don't deserve it. I want you to claim me, Miles—claim me in all the ways you haven't before."

"Fucking finally," he growls, claiming my lips in a fiery kiss that doesn't last nearly long enough.

He pulls away, and we both stumble as we exit the car. When he reaches my side, I expect him to kiss me again. But to my surprise, he wraps his arm around my thighs and tosses me over his shoulder, causing a laugh—the loud, boisterous kind that comes from deep within—to escape me.

I hear the deep gravel of his laugh intertwine with mine, and then I'm cackling uncontrollably as he pushes the door open and drops me in the foyer. He presses me against the nearest wall, and my laughing ceases as our eyes connect.

His chestnut brown eyes darken to a chocolate color when our eyes meet, and the kidding around turns serious as the weight of what we're about to do mushrooms over the top of us.

My stomach tightens as his hardness presses into me, and the heat between my legs burns hotter as his hands begin to roam my body, paying special attention to my backside where he squeezes and pulls me harder against him, leaving no space between us.

With two small taps, I jump to wrap my legs around his waist. My fingers find their way into the hair at the nape of his neck, tugging on the strands as he devours my mouth.

The way we're moving together—it's intense but sensual, passionate but aflame, all-consuming yet I still crave more.

"God, you're beautiful," he admires, and it makes the butterflies in my stomach take flight, but something else sparks as well.

Pure carnal desire.

"Take me to bed, Miles," I demand.

He wastes no time taking us upstairs to his bedroom. The thought of all the girls before me plagues my mind, and I hate the intrusion.

"What's wrong?" he asks when we reach his doorway.

"Maybe we should go to my room. I'm not fond of the idea of having sex on a bed where other girls have been."

A wrinkle forms between his brows. "I'm not having sex with you on the same bed that fucker was in. And no one has ever been in my bed, Riley. Only you. It will only ever be you."

The thought has me sliding down his body, brushing against his hardness as it reignites the fire in my body from downstairs. I grab onto the front of his shirt, pulling him into the room. He catches on quickly and walks us over to the bed where he lays me down gently.

Miles hovers over me and reclaims my lips in a searing kiss—teeth clashing, tongues tangling, hands wandering. My hands find their way under his shirt, tracing the divots of his abs, and the lines of lean muscle across his back.

He pulls away from me long enough to pull his shirt over his head, discarding it somewhere on the floor. I rise to meet him, reaching for the hem of my shirt before he stops me.

"Let me," Miles insists.

He removes my hands from my shirt, then begins to slowly

roll it up over my torso, hands brushing the exposed skin and ink, making my breath increase at the torturous pace he's set.

"You're trying to kill me with how slow you're being."

Miles discards my shirt with his, leaving me in my bra and shorts. I lean back on my hands as he kneels before me.

"Riley, I've wanted this for a long time. I'm going slow because I want to savor every bit of this moment with you so when I replay it in my mind years down the road, I'll remember every single detail."

He's saying all the right things, and I'm eating up every word like the most delicious candy.

"We'll remember. I'm sure of it."

"And why's that?" he questions.

"Because this is the moment things change for us. Something of that much importance isn't something we'll ever forget."

Miles smiles, collapsing on top of me again as he begins unzipping my jean shorts. He pulls them slowly off my legs, rubbing his calloused hands up and down the inked skin there.

Every brush of his fingers feels like I'm being zapped by an electric fence, a taser, hell, even jumper cables. I may make no sense to anyone else in the world, but it makes sense to me; it's the only way I can explain the intensity in the way he makes me feel.

Instead of bringing him back to the bed with me, I crawl forward to straddle his waist. His hands form a bruising grip on my hips, pressing me against his hardened cock. I instinctively begin to rub up and down his length, feeling the slickness grow between my legs.

Miles's hand travels up my spine, causing my entire body to tense. He reaches the clasp of my bra, releasing it with a snap. The straps fall off, and I finish removing it for him.

When his gaze drops to my chest, an animalistic groan escapes him.

"Fuck, you've got your nipples pierced," he says, licking his lips.

"Yeah, got them done years ago."

"Please tell me they're sensitive," he practically begs.

"Very," I answer breathlessly.

Miles grins like the Cheshire cat, and then his hands descend on my breasts. He palms both in his hands—just enough for a handful—and tests the weight of them, his thumbs barely brushing over my nipple.

They pucker under his gaze, and then his mouth descends on me. One hand is fully pinching one nipple, tugging and twisting it, while his mouth occupies the other.

His tongue swirls around my nipple, causing me to drip with arousal. A moan escapes me as heat shoots directly to my core, which only encourages Miles as his teeth begin to nip the rosy peak.

My skin buzzes more intensely with each swipe of his tongue, the way his warm mouth embraces it and how he makes them tighter by blowing cool air on them, making me crave him even more.

Both hands squeeze my breasts as he brings his mouth to my neck, starting at my collarbone and moving up. His lips are smooth against my skin, and his hot breath against mine warms the chill on my body in each place he isn't touching me.

Miles begins to suck the sensitive skin on my neck into his mouth, marking me in a way that only the two of us will understand.

As his mouth comes back to mine and his hands fall to my breast and backside, I find myself getting lost in my thoughts.

There were so many times I imagined this very moment. What it would be like to be with Miles in this way. If it would be awkward or life changing. If he'd be rough or gentle, selfish or giving.

For so long, I thought of him as a brother-figure, and then a friend. And even though it changed into something more, I still had to treat him as a friend and brother.

The nerves from before are still there, and I'm not sure they'll ever really go away. I'll always wonder if this was the right decision, if it's worth cracking the façade of friendship—and if Blake ever finds out, will she hate me and kick me out of her life, or will she be okay with it?

"Don't pull away from me, baby. Please," he begs, continuing to lock our lips together.

"I'm still so scared."

Miles pulls away instantly but wraps his arms around me and embraces me tighter.

"Riley, it's okay to be scared. I'm not faulting you for that. But would you rather be scared to experience something life-changing and realize that fear was playing tricks on your mind, or never experience it at all and let that fear have control over you?"

"I don't want anything or anyone to have control of my life, especially fear. But my anxiety... my anxiety doesn't make that easy. I'm always having intrusive thoughts and playing things out in my head that aren't real but could be."

"We'll work through it together, Riley. Whatever it is. So, when you have those thoughts or visions, talk them out to me so I can reassure you of reality and try to settle your nerves some. Okay?"

His words settle me for the moment, and I let his promise course through me and bring me back to the moment—this vast, monumental moment in time where the only things that matter are me and him and *this*.

"Okay." I smile, ready to welcome this next step in our relationship.

CHAPTER 23
RILEY

THINGS PICK UP FROM THERE, AND INSTEAD OF CONTINUING WITH ME on his lap, he lays me back down and strips himself of his pants. He slides down the bed until his knees hit the floor, his hands circle my ankles, and then he pulls my panty-covered pussy straight into his mouth.

He nips at the wet cotton, and my legs tremble at the feeling.

"Relax your legs for me, baby. Let me see just how wet this pussy is for me."

Miles nips at my clit, and then proceeds to lower my panties, inch by inch, until I'm free from the last thing separating the two of us. He drops them to the floor, and I watch as he rolls his boxers down to the floor with them.

"Tell me, Riley... is this something special, or are you always this soaked for me?" His finger brushes lightly down my slit, causing a shiver to run down my spine.

I swear more arousal gushes out of me at his words. We're only getting started and I'm already a puddle. Who the hell knew he'd talk like this?

I want more.

"I asked you a question, Riley," he says in a gravelly tone, hovering over me, so that his voice vibrates against my clit.

"Something special *and* because it's you."

"Mmm, love that."

I feel the warmth of his breath against my clit, and then his lips are wrapping around it, sucking it into his mouth. It's not a sudden intrusion at all, but after the teasing, my reaction feels that way.

My back bows off the bed, my fingers gripping the sheets as he drives me wild with his tongue. I've been with many guys who have no idea how to give head, swiping their tongue around like a slobbering dog, but not Miles.

Miles laps at my clit with slow strokes, like licking an ice cream cone in slow motion. It's gentle, like a caress, but with enough pressure to drive me absolutely mad.

"Fuck, I knew your pussy would taste good, but goddamn, I didn't think one hit would make me so addicted. I could stay here all night."

"Please don't," I rush out. "It feels amazing, but I'll combust before long if you're not inside me."

"You can rush me all you want, Riley Davis, but I'll stay down here and worship you all night long and you won't say a word because you've been aching for this as badly as I have."

I go to speak, but words cease to exist in my brain. All I can do is whimper, "uh huh."

He lets out a low laugh, and then his mouth is on me again. My abdomen clenches with each stroke. The oxygen in the room must be depleted because I'm trying to inhale, and nothing. My mouth is severely dry, so I swipe my tongue over my lips to help and stop when I feel Miles's finger press at my entrance.

Miles's head pops up from between my legs and catches my eyes, and the visual of my arousal over his mouth and chin has me metaphorically drooling.

"I'm about to finger fuck you into your first orgasm, and when I do that, I want you to watch me. Watch my fingers disappear into you, watch the slickness coat them," he demands, then adds in a growly tone, "watch what I do to you."

I follow his order, loving the way it feels to submit to what he wants. I've never experienced true intimacy, not like this, but now that I have, I never want to go back—and I only want to experience it with him.

Miles wraps his lips around my clit again as his finger circles the wetness around my entrance, and when he sucks it into his mouth, releasing it with a pop, he slides his finger inside me.

My vision turns hazy, and my eyes close against my will at the intensity.

The callused skin of his fingers scrapes against every inch of my walls, intensifying the feeling of him stretching me, and suddenly I'm thanking whoever is in charge for his hands feelings this way.

"I remember telling you to look at me," Miles reminds me as he draws his finger out to the tip.

I open my eyes to look at him, and when I do, I nearly orgasm on the spot. While I can't see his cock with our current position, I can see the motion of his arm and imagine the way he's stroking it.

Is he working himself up, or is he painfully hard? Is he barely touching himself, or is he gripping it hard to combat the animosity of his desire?

This time, when he enters me, he adds a second finger, then curves them into a place that not even *I* can hit.

Miles increases his speed, and I wonder how his fingers aren't cramping with the rapid pace he's set. His thumb reaches up to rub my clit with a pressure that is anything but gentle yet not painful either, alternating with the swipes of his tongue.

My legs begin to tighten against his head, and my stomach contracts until it's rock hard. The buzzing in my body starts in my chest, gaining speed and intensity as it shoots downward to my core. The pressure moves down, down, and just as I feel my clit begin to throb under his tongue, Miles groans. "Come for me, baby."

The pressure detonates between my legs, and my body curls

over Miles as he continues to lick me through my orgasm. The hand stroking his cock is now pressing down on my abdomen, prolonging my orgasm. My hands tangle in the strands of his hair, unintentionally pressing his face harder against my pussy.

When the feeling subsides, my body gives out and I collapse against the bed. Miles licks me through the aftershocks, my body continuing to spasm mildly as I come back down from the most intense high I've ever felt. No amount of adrenaline or drugs could ever compare to this feeling, and I never want it to.

I only want to experience this with Miles.

"Fuck," I sigh. "That was…"

"The best thing to ever happen to me," Miles finishes my sentence for me as he moves to hover over me, his cock—which I now know is painfully hard—presses against my mound, causing my clit to begin throbbing again. "I've imagined so many different ways over the years of how I'd have you in my bed, but none of those could ever surpass how it feels for this to be real and not a figment of my imagination."

"What do you mean?"

"I may sound cheesy here…"

"Never. I read romance books, remember? Cheesy shit is romantic, even if it makes me cringe at times," I admit, a slight grin tilting my lips.

"Okay. It may be cheesy, but I've never felt anything like this before. It's like my birthday and Christmas and the NBA draft day all happened on the same day, yet so much better. We haven't even had sex yet and I already feel so consumed by every piece of you."

"You consume me too," I admit. "Mind if I'm cheesy now?"

He shakes his head, alerting me to go on.

"I've never had a home. Even when I stayed with your family, it all felt temporary. But right here, right now, what this is… I feel like if I lost everything in the world to me—this house, my jobs, my car—I'd always have a home in you," I admit. "You make me feel safe."

"You'll always have a home with me, Riley Davis. I'd live in a cardboard box if it meant I never had to separate from you."

"I guess we need to stick together in every possible way then, huh." A cheeky grin on my face meets the shit-eating one on Miles,' and he takes that for the invitation it is.

To claim me in all the ways he hasn't.

Our lips clash together, and I feel the moment that he swipes the head of his cock through the slickness between my legs, tapping it against my clit to make my entire body gear up for the pleasure that he loves to give.

"Last question, I promise," he says between kisses. "Are you on birth control? Have an IUD? Or would you like me to wear a condom? I want to do what you're comfortable with."

"I have an IUD, and I'm clean. I've waited many years to feel you this way, to have absolutely no barriers between us. And while that's what I want, I want you to be okay with it too."

I don't want to be selfish with my decision if it's going to make him uncomfortable.

"I'm clean too, so I'm more than okay with it." With the final breath of his words, his cock breaches my entrance, and the entire world explodes in color, making me realize just how in the dark I've been.

He enters me at a tortuously slow pace, dragging out the painfully pleasurable feel of his cock stretching me.

I bite down hard on my bottom lip, and Miles lets out a hiss between his teeth as he burrows his face in the crook of my neck. When he's finally to the hilt, he lifts his head to lock eyes with me, and I see the restraint and desire flooding his beautiful brown eyes.

"Fuck, Riley," he groans, like being inside me is too much but not enough. A shock to his system.

He begins to move slowly inside me, absorbing the feel of our bodies connecting in the most raw and vulnerable way. While his thrusts remain slow, his pressure doesn't reflect that. He pulls out, leaving just the tip in, before he thrusts back inside against the resistance of my walls as I adjust around him.

His thrusts become easier each time he re-enters me, until finally, there's no resistance at all. Miles places his hand on my thigh, running it down to my knee as he wraps it further around his back.

Then his hand comes down over my hip, gripping my ass, and pulls me so tightly to him that his pelvic bone brushes my clit with each stroke, coiling the rope tighter in my stomach.

He kisses the edge of my jawline just below my ear, sending a shiver down my spine.

"So good," he whispers. "So tight. You're taking my cock like such a good girl, Riley," he praises.

The pressure in my abdomen increases, and my heart begins to rattle around my ribcage. Sweat gathers on my skin the more we glide together, and everything begins to tighten.

"I can feel you squeezing my cock, Riley. Are you about to come?"

Looking up at him with wide eyes and my teeth sunk into my bottom lip, I whimper, "yes," in a tone that is more like a squeak.

Miles reaches a hand up, pushing his thumb into my mouth.

"Suck it," he demands, and I follow his order, getting it extra wet.

When he pulls his thumb from my mouth, he reaches between us and begins to rub his wet thumb against my clit with merciless precision, using just enough pressure that the use of his thumb and the angle of his cock against my g-spot put me on the fast track to coming.

"I'm close," I admit breathlessly, my words simply a gust of air from my lips since he's fucked all the rest out of me.

"Come for me, baby," he orders in a deep, gravelly tone. "I want you coming so hard on my cock that you're dripping off me."

The tightness in my belly moves south, my legs tense up, and my chest is on the verge of caving in when I dig my fingernails into Miles's back, running them down the taut muscles there.

"That's it, baby. Mark me. Mark me so everyone knows who owns me. Fucking come for me, usdi danuwaanalihi. You can do it," he encourages.

His thumb presses harder against my clit, increasing in pace until the tightening shoots straight to my pussy, and I'm exploding around his cock.

Miles continues to fuck me through my orgasm, and my hand falls to his ass. His pace increases, hitting that sensitive spot in me again, and his ass clenches tightly the minute he lets out a groan, emptying himself inside me.

His thrusts slow monumentally until he's no longer moving inside me, and he drops his head against my chest.

"Goddamn," he sighs.

"Ditto."

"Riley, that..." He lifts his head up, locking eyes with me. There's so much compassion, content, and satisfaction in his eyes that I reach up and brush my lips over his again.

"That was everything I ever thought it'd be and more," he continues. "I've never felt anything like that before. And if you weren't under my skin before, you're fucking embedded in my damn soul now."

The way he talks about the way he feels for me, has my heart squeezing in my chest, and those little butterflies flutter rapidly in my belly.

"We're really doing this, huh?" I ask, needing the words spoken out loud. I don't want to assume anything and get let down because of it.

"Yeah baby," he says, running his fingers down the length of my face, landing on the back of my neck. "We're doing this. You and me."

"You and me."

Miles smiles, summoning one from me as well, and he kisses me until we both fall asleep, where he instinctively wraps his body around mine, holding me tight throughout the night.

And for the first night in a long time, anxiety and rampant thoughts don't wear me down to sleep. The comfort of him around me is what does.

CHAPTER 24
MILES

For as long as I can remember, since I was a little kid, I'd wake up first thing in the morning and only have one thought on my mind.

Basketball.

I'd think... when can I get on the court? When can I feel the grip of leather in my hand? How can I train harder today than I did yesterday?

But not today.

No. Today, the first thought I had when I woke up was Riley.

I turn my head to the side, and I'm immediately overwhelmed with the scent of grapefruit, something like jasmine, and a faint hint of vanilla as well. It's feminine, it's citrusy, it's elegant.

I'm not sure where it's from or what it's called, but all I know is that it's perfectly *her*.

Riley's long blond hair trails down her back in tangled wisps, dancing against the dimples on her lower back. Her arm drapes over my stomach, squeezing tightly like she's afraid I won't be here when she lets go.

She's sleeping so soundly, and I don't want to wake her. But I can't help myself when I reach to brush a stray strand of hair away from her face, tucking it behind her ear. And I can't help myself when I linger there, tracing the soft features of her face.

Her porcelain skin, her prominent cheekbones. The way her thick lashes rest gently against rosy cheeks. Her luscious lips are parted slightly, dry from sleeping that way, and the warmth of her breath tickles my chest, summoning goosebumps on every inch of my skin.

Riley must feel my gentle caresses because her tongue peeks out to lick her lips, and her eyelashes begin to flutter against her cheeks.

"Morning," she grumbles, eyes still closed. She begins to lift off the bed, pulling herself up, but I reach out and immediately bring her back to my chest.

"Stop," I gently demand.

"But I have to pee," she whines, and it's the cutest thing ever to see her half-asleep with pouty lips.

"Okay, and you can. I just want you to lie back down for a few minutes, okay?"

"Fine." She surrenders, lying directly on top of me, propping her chin up with her hands. "But why?"

"Isn't it obvious?" She shakes her head. "You're the most gorgeous woman in the world to me, Riley. I'd be crazy not to spend every free moment I have looking at you."

The pink on her cheeks turns from a soft rose to a bright magenta, and a thought enters my mind.

"You do know you're beautiful Riley. Right?"

She averts her eyes, and a whisper of an answer falls off her tongue. "Sometimes. Sometimes not. It's, uh, complicated…"

"We've got time."

"We do," she says. "So, what's for breakfast?" she asks, switching the conversation.

"Whatever you want, Riley."

"As long as I'm not making it, right?" she asks with a smile.

"Oh 100%. I really love my house and I'd like to keep it," I say, pinching her hips.

A sound similar to a screeching pterodactyl escapes her as she flinches on my body.

"Are you ticklish?" I ask, gripping my hands tighter.

"What? No," she rushes out.

"I've known you for over fifteen years and I never knew you were ticklish."

"Because I'm not—"

The sound comes out of her again when I start pinching her hips, her sides, under her arms. She kicks and thrashes until she lands off the side of the bed.

"Don't make one more move mister," she tsks.

"And what are you planning to do about it if I don't listen?"

I stand by the bed, barely a foot from her, and I see the wheels turn in her head and she looks around the room with a panicked look in her eyes.

"I'm gonna… run!"

Her takeoff isn't as fast as she expected it to be, I presume, since I'm able to pinch her again before she makes a run for the bathroom.

"I told you to quit!" she yells while laughing as she locks herself in the ensuite bathroom.

"I'm sorry, I just wanted cake for breakfast!"

"Oh my gosh," she mutters through the door, but I know that she's smiling, and that's what keeps the smile on my face as I throw on sweats and head downstairs to make breakfast.

By the time Riley comes downstairs, I've got pancakes, eggs, bacon and coffee sitting on the table.

"This is a spread," she notes.

"What else do you expect for the birthday girl?" I ask with a smile.

She stops in her tracks, an ashen look washing over her face.

"You remember my birthday?"

"As well as I know my own."

She meanders over to the island, hopping onto the stool before grabbing her coffee.

"Thank you," she murmurs into her cup.

"You're welcome."

She places her cup beside her plate, then proceeds to grab a pancake off the stack before drizzling it in heated maple syrup.

"What's wrong? Do you not like it?" I ask, worried I overstepped.

"No, not at all. I love it." She plays around with a piece of egg on her sectioned plate. "I've just never made a big deal out of my birthday."

"What do you mean? We always used to do things for your birthday. Bowling alley, restaurants, paintball…"

"The keyword is used to, Miles," she speaks in a sharp tone, hitting something deep inside me.

"I'm sorry," Riley adds, her tone much softer now. "After we graduated, birthdays weren't the same for me anymore. Blake was playing college ball, we weren't talking… Blake would always celebrate with me whenever we saw each other, but I haven't spent a birthday that wasn't alone until today. It's just… I'm not used to it, I guess."

I've moved on from the past, but it's times like these I want to give a swift kick in the ass to eighteen-year-old me for harboring my anger against Riley without even letting her get a word in.

"I'm sorry we lost all those years."

"No, you're not allowed to apologize," she says, swatting at my hand. "I'm perfectly content with just this. Spending time with you."

I smile, a content and comfortable feeling settling deep within me knowing she's okay just being with me, but I'm not.

Because she deserves more.

"Too bad, because Blake and Kyler will be here soon and we're going out today."

"We are?" she asks to clarify, and I smile and nod.

Riley jumps from the stool straight into me, knocking me off balance. We crash into the refrigerator, magnets hit the floor, and a crashing noise sounds from inside.

"Ow." The sound falls from my lips, caused by multiple protruding magnets stabbing me in the back right now.

Riley gasps. "I'm so sorry."

"Don't be. I haven't seen you this excited since we got Chief from his camp."

"That's totally a lie," she states as she yanks her head back to look at me. "I was definitely excited last night."

"What was last night?" a feminine voice, one that I've known my entire life, speaks from the kitchen doorway.

Riley pulls away from me so fast that she leaves smoke in her wake.

"Last night…" Riley begins but nothing else follows.

Beautiful girl needs to become a better liar if she plans to keep this from Blake for the foreseeable future.

"She's referring to last night when I made her dinner and surprised her with her mini-birthday cake at midnight."

"Where's this cake then? I love cake," Blake says with excitement.

"It's so gone," Riley says, finally catching on to the ruse. "I ate it all last night."

"Did you at least get a piece of cake, man?" Kyler adds, but with the imploring nature of his expression, there's some insinuation in there.

"She gave me a little piece."

Riley cuts her gaze at me. "I gave you a big piece, thank you very much."

There's a playfulness in her tone that I see right through.

I think she's enjoying this a little too much.

"Okay, talking about cake is making me hungry. I need sustenance." Blake walks over to the island, pointing at the spread in front of her. "What's all this?"

"Birthday breakfast of champions," I respond.

"Nice," she says, popping a piece of bacon in her mouth. "Because I'm gonna need the energy for the day I have planned for you."

Once Blake finishes fixing her coffee, she takes a seat at the island across from us beside Kyler.

"It's nice to see you two being cordial with each other. I feel like for the longest time there was so much tension there."

A small smile etches its way over my face. "Something about living in someone's space forces you to get close. Right, Riley?" I ask, nudging her elbow beside me.

"So close," she says, holding in a laugh.

"Good. I like it when you two get along," Blake comments.

Oh, Blake if you only knew just *how well* we're getting along…

CHAPTER 25
MILES

Riley's birthday has been full of fun activities. Some planned by me, some planned by Blake.

We spent the majority of the day on a tour of the bayous and swamps of New Orleans, a combined tour that also included a tour of the famous Oak Alley plantation.

Blake brought up the idea of a tour, but I'm the one that suggested this one. I had my reasons.

When Riley was in high school, she never thought much about school. It was more of a stepping stone to what she wanted to do with her actual life.

But she always loved history. Seeing the way the world was, how it's changed, what and who started some of the most significant movements in history.

The thing about the Oak Alley Plantation is the rich history of slavery. Riley's big heart and simple human nature had her heart breaking for the mistreatment of those involved in slavery. She cried during her homework one night—I remember it vividly now that I'm thinking of it—because she was tired of people being punished for their race, their gender, their upbringing…

It's one of the things I love most about her. While she hides from so many things, her big heart is still underneath it all. She wants to give love to so many things, but I'm not sure she knows how to fully accept it.

I want to spend every day reminding her she's worthy of it.

After the plantation tour, we spent a few hours on the boat watching alligators, turtles, water birds, and other local wildlife. We learn about the people who live in the bayous, some New Orleans history—not that it matters since we grew up here. But we've never done many touristy things.

Nothing was better than watching the look on her face as she admired the wonders of New Orleans, or the gleam in her eye every time she looked at me and smiled.

I can't go back and change the past, but I can make sure she never spends another birthday alone, and that I spoil her more and more every year.

But now that we've finished with the nighttime haunted cemetery tour and have broken up from the group—Kyler and Blake had a dinner to get to with his mama and stepmom—I get to spend the rest of the night with the birthday girl, and it's easily the best part of my day.

"What's the birthday girl want to do for the rest of the night?" I ask as we walk through the front door of the house.

The question is barely out of my mouth when Riley turns and wraps her arms around me, a warmth rushing over me at the first intimate contact we've had since we left this morning.

"I think this is the best birthday I've ever had," she mumbles into my t-shirt.

My heart swells at the confession, and I'm thankful to have made this day special for her.

"I'm happy that you had a good time."

"A great time," she counters, pulling back to look at me. Her hands run up the length of my back, sending shivers down my spine. "I haven't spent a birthday with someone in years, and I forgot what it was like to have people care about you."

"I'm not letting you spend another birthday alone. Ever."

"Promise?" she asks, a hopeful look in her eyes that I want to snatch away and replace with utter certainty.

"I promise."

Her lips brush against mine, and I reach to grab her cheeks, pressing my lips firmer to her mouth to deepen our kiss.

Every time I kiss Riley is different. The feel of her isn't the same, the response I feel isn't the same. I know it's crazy to say, especially since there aren't many different ways to kiss someone.

But it's like saying that all stars are the same, when in reality, each differs from the others in a variety of ways. The same way that kissing Riley is.

Because no kiss can ever be ordinary when the woman you're kissing is *extraordinary*.

This kiss isn't hurried, like so many of our others have been. This one is slow and explorative. Sweet and electric as we memorize the makeup of each other. Underneath the sincerity of it, I feel the words Riley isn't saying.

When our kiss slows to a stop, I pull back and push a stray blonde strand behind her ear. Unable to resist, I press featherlight kisses to her lips, her cheeks, the tip of her nose and her forehead.

Riley nuzzles into my hand, looking up at me like I've hung the moon and the sun, and an overwhelming feeling of admiration and attraction and need washes through me.

"You know I'd do everything I could to make you happy, right?" The words come without warning, but the resulting look in her eyes—the one that mimics the feelings in mine—keeps me from regretting saying it.

"Of course, I do," she smiles. "You haven't failed me yet on the matter."

"Good," I smile, tapping my finger on her nose. "Now what can I do in this moment to make the birthday girl happy?"

"I've had a long, draining day, and all I want right now is a low-key, quiet night with you."

"I'd love nothing more."

Riley's version of a low-key, quiet night is wrapped up in a blanket on the couch wearing pajamas, her lying on my lap while Chief lies in hers, watching *Stranger Things* from where we last stopped.

We've reached the end of Season 2 where Eleven closed the gate, and now everyone is at the Snowball. The exact scene is when everyone is dancing with their partner, but Dustin is left by himself on the bleachers.

When I feel wetness drip against my leg, I try to turn Riley to face me, but she doesn't come. I immediately pause the TV.

"Baby, what's wrong?"

"No one wants to dance with him," she sobs.

"Hey, Nancy went over to him. It's okay."

"No, it isn't." Riley rolls to her back. "There's no telling how long he had to sit there, watching his friends get to dance, and question why he wasn't good enough for anyone to ask him to dance." A tear rolls down her cheek.

"Why do I feel like this is more than just a TV show?"

"Because it is," she says with a sigh.

"Talk to me, then."

Riley rises from my lap, scooting around in the space beside me to cross her legs while still facing me.

"Seeing him alone, wondering why he wasn't enough... it brought up some really shitty emotions for me. It always does on my birthday, one way or another."

"How so?"

"Did I ever tell you that when my... birth giver abandoned me, she did it on my birthday?"

"No." I swallow. "You didn't."

My heart aches something awful for young Riley.

"Yeah. I remember it vividly. She gave me pizza, a stuffed animal, and then dropped me off at some church like I was trash. I don't like talking about it, but it's this damn day that always elicits the reaction. That I'm not good enough. It sends me down a dark path of self-loathing and some other shit I'll never be able to understand."

I rub my hand on her leg in a comforting manner, wanting to be present but not overbearing.

"My emotions will always be this way," she continues. "I'll cry at things others won't understand because things affect me differently. I'll see or hear something that will trigger a memory that is totally unrelated to what I saw or heard, or eerily similar, and I will react. I've been called a baby for reacting emotionally. I've been called overly dramatic. But I can't help the way that I feel, and I can't control the way that I need to react," she says in near panic.

"Feeling is not dramatic, in any way. Fuck whoever said that to you."

"Isn't it, though? Dramatic?"

"No," I say with finality. "But why do you think that way?"

"I was not this way when you met me. I've always held in my emotions—bottled them up until it was full and instead of letting go of it, I just started another bottle. But when I was eighteen, right after everything happened, a flip switched in me."

"Explain it to me," I say, urging her forward.

"I suspect it was happening years before, but losing the semblance of family that I'd had for years living with y'all... it fucked me up. I couldn't fill any more bottles and I kind of shut down. It started small, worrying about my job, how I'd pay rent, but in a way that was obsessive. I pictured everything that could go wrong but at a level that was on steroids. It spread into other things. Obsessing over things that didn't even affect me, losing my trust in people, indulging in things I thought would make me feel better. A doctor is someone I never really saw, but a girl in one of my art classes in college suggested it to me."

"I'm glad they did," I comment.

"They diagnosed me with severe anxiety, gave me a small dose of medication to manage it. But it got worse. Getting out of bed each day was a struggle. Drawing was the last thing I wanted to do, which was taxing since I was finishing my degree and beginning my apprenticeship. I didn't want to eat, or shower. Hell, most days I didn't want to exist.

"I was diagnosed with depression about six months after my first diagnosis. And it was... God, it was a struggle at first. I struggled with nausea, insomnia, stomach pain, headaches, and a few other things I'll save you the grossness of hearing regarding medication side effects," she says with a slight laugh, but it's forced. "After it finally got settled into my system, I tried some different things to try and cope along with medication, but it didn't work for me. I've been taking medication ever since."

This feels like a lot to understand at once. I can't even imagine what it felt like going through all that alone. God, I wish I was there back then. But I'm thankful that I can be here now.

"Is there anything I can do? I don't know much about your struggles, but I want to. I want to help in whatever way I can."

"I appreciate that." She grabs the hand I have on her thigh and embraces it between hers. "You know, that's what happened on yours and Blake's birthday this year. When I heard you talking to Dmitry, it triggered me. All I wanted was to shut down, and I did."

"I'm so sorry." I spring forward on the couch, pulling her to my side immediately. "I promise that I'll never be the reason you're triggered again."

"I know you were going through your own things—" she begins.

"No. Don't try and defend what I did. I was an asshole, no matter what I was feeling at the time. I promise not to let you struggle through this alone, okay? Tell me what I can do to help, and I'll do it."

"You're already doing it." Riley looks at me, and I see so much appreciation and fulfillment in her eyes. "Being here, holding me, comforting me… caring for me the way you do. It'll never be a cure, but it'll help heal me in ways that medication never will. Please trust me on this."

"I do. I trust you."

"Good." She snuggles further into me, and for a reason I know has everything to do with what she just confided in me, I hold her tighter. "But I need you to promise me something."

"Anything," I whisper into the top of her head.

"Don't treat me any differently. Don't treat me like I'm delicate or breakable because I'm not. Blake tried to do that when I first told her, but she learned really quickly that while she's bigger, I'm not scared to try and kick her ass."

The end of her sentence has me deeply chuckling. "Noted. But I want you to know that nothing you say could change the way I feel about you. Your quirks, your interests, your inability to cook"—she laughs— "and even your struggles, make up who you are. And I'm totally smitten with every part of you, Riley Davis." I turn her head up to face me. "Every single part."

Riley smiles, then drops her head to the skin over my heart. She falls asleep to the chaotic rhythm beating in my chest, the one that occurs only when she's in the vicinity.

Because my heart knows as well as I do.

That I'm crazy for this girl.

CHAPTER 26
RILEY

IN MY ENTIRE LIFE, I'VE NEVER FELT SUCH PURE BLISS FOR AN extended period of time. The type of feeling that nothing could fracture or shatter.

It's been a bit over a month since Miles and I became an official—secret—couple, and in that time, I've never felt more appreciated or cared for than I have in my entire existence.

Miles is constantly putting my needs first. He sends me messages during the day asking how I'm doing, makes sure I'm fed—even if he's on the road, he'll send me takeout—and never fails to make me smile at least once a day.

Usually by attempting to tickle me, which never goes well since I always thrash and end up kicking him in the shin unintentionally.

I mean… he knows the risks.

And while I'm completely basking in the happiness of the way he makes me feel and what I can see for us in the future, there are still things looming over my head about our relationship.

Will Blake hate me—hate us—for going behind her back? Will Miles feel obligated to keep his father out of his life the way he has because of his preposterous opinions of me? Will he still want to be with me when push comes to shove, or will he toss me to the side the way that my mother—I cringe at the term—did to me as a child?

"What are you thinking about?" Miles asks from beside me on the couch.

We just had breakfast, but the caterers will be here soon for the Valentine's Day party Miles is throwing at the house. Silly boy lost at rock, paper, scissors and got stuck with hosting.

"Nothing."

"Liar," he laughs. "I can see the wheel turning in your head so fast it's leaving dust in its wake. Tell me."

"I'm just worried someone will figure out we're together. It's so easy when we're at home because we don't have to worry about things like that, but when people are invading our space, the risk is higher."

"You can't think about that, baby," he says, brushing a loose hair out of my face while I stare up at him from his lap.

"Yes, I can. If someone finds out about us and tells Blake before we can, the damage may be irreparable."

He gazes back at me with a creatively optimistic look. "We could tell her, you know."

"What?" I huff out. "You're crazy."

"I'm not crazy. I just want to be able to care about you in the open."

The normally confident demeanor he has fades away at the blatant ignoring of the conversation that I'm doing.

"You can care about me all you want, as long as you don't cross the line of friendship in front of people we know. I'm not ready to tell her yet, okay?"

I can tell he wants to say no, can tell he wants to say fuck it and not have to hide it anymore, but I'm not ready for Blake to know. Not yet. She needs to warm up to the potential idea of it...

I wouldn't know what to do with myself if she took it the wrong way and I lost the only family I've ever known. And from someone who never had that, who doesn't know what it's like... I don't want to risk it.

"Okay," he relents, kissing my forehead as he pulls me further into his arms.

I like being in his embrace too much to risk losing it so early on in our relationship. But I don't want the weight of the secret to make him resent me eventually.

Fuck, I need to figure out how to tell her.

Before this secret comes back to bite me in the ass.

Hours later, the house has transformed into Cupid's Wonderland. That's what the decorator called it, at least. The entire place is draped in red, pink, and whites with hearts, little arrows, and all the love-related paraphernalia that you can possibly think of... and then more.

Most of the Warhawks organization is under Miles' roof right now, and the effect it's having on my anxiety is overwhelming. I feel like all eyes are on me even though when I look up, I see that they're not.

But the paranoia that accompanies my perturbed mind thinks that people can see past the friendly front Miles and I have put on since people began flooding our safe space.

"What's up with you, Ri?" Blake asks.

Not long after everyone had passed through the food area, I busied myself in the kitchen by replacing some of the empty food with what the caterers left to keep it replenished. I don't know many of the people here, so I was beginning to feel like the walls were closing in on me.

"Nothing." The lie rolls off easily.

"There's no way. You're glancing around the room with wide eyes like the walls are about to come alive," she laughs.

"No," I laugh. "There's just a lot of people I don't know, and it's got me all scatterbrained. It's a lot to take in at once."

"I can introduce you to some people," Blake offers as she grabs a beer from one of the coolers against the wall.

"No, I promise I'm fine. I have people I do know. I'll find some of them and talk a bit. I'm just working on this and taking a step away from the suffocation of others." I laugh again.

"Oh, I know that feeling. I tap out after being around people for so long too."

"Makes us great friends," I say.

"Yes, it does."

The minute she agrees, a wave of nausea washes over me. Blake is the sister I never had, who stood up for me with bullies, brought me into her home, listened to me rant and cry… and here I am betraying her like she means nothing to me.

I feel like I'm going to be sick.

Just as I'm opening my mouth to say something—though I don't know what the hell to actually say—one of the guys on the team comes into the kitchen. I don't know his name, but I remember seeing him on the sideline.

"Coach," he interrupts us.

"Yes, Long?"

"Some of the guys are starting a pick-up game out back and they proposed a bet."

"And what was the bet?" Blake props her hip against the island while she takes a swig of her beer. I know my best friend, and the minute a challenge is propositioned, she's in.

"They want you to play with us. But, if any of the guys on the team outscore you, we get tomorrow off practice."

"And when I win?" she questions.

Not *if* but *when*. It's amazing to see her confidence shine like this. I'm nothing like her in that way, but I wish I could be. For anyone who has ever thought I was... well, I'm great at hiding things by cloaking them with others.

"You win, nothing changes. We report to practice as normal."

"Ha," Blake guffaws. "No. When I win, you report to practice and have an extra hour in the weight room because of your assumption that I'd ever lose, and whatever else I can think of. I'll be there in a minute."

The guy leaves the kitchen shortly after, probably wishing that he never came in here in the first place because they're for sure getting punished at their next practice. Blake places her beer down.

"Are you good, Ri?" Her meaningful gaze is quizzical but grave.

"I'm good. I promise. Go wipe the floor with those guys," I say with a smile.

"They are seriously going to regret this shit when I'm through with them," Blake says as she exits the kitchen.

Although I wish I didn't, I sigh in relief when she's gone, like I don't have to hide anymore.

I finish refilling the food trays and grab a bag of garbage to take out—keeping busy and all that—but on my way to the door, a warm hand wraps around my wrist and the garbage hits the floor.

"What the—"

"Shh, baby, it's just me," Miles' smooth, husky voice washes over me like a warm blanket, immediately putting me at ease. He begins to drag us upstairs.

"What are you doing? Anyone can see us."

This is it. This is how we get caught. I just know it.

"No, they won't." He presses his lips to the space between my neck and shoulder, and goosebumps rise on every inch of my body in rapid succession. "Everyone is outside, and we're going upstairs," he whispers, "where no one can hear us."

Where no one can hear us?

Oh shit. No. No, no, no.

"Miles, this is a horrible idea," I whisper-yell, as he pulls us into the hallway bathroom on the second floor, just a few doors down from our bedrooms.

"Insinuating this is a bad idea is like saying I wasn't born to play basketball. Because I was, and this is a great idea."

He locks the door right before his mouth descends on my neck again. I won't deny that his touch isn't eliciting a visceral response of arousal in my body, but Blake is right outside and the shaky feeling I have is not from his touch.

"Miles, we can't do this. If we get caught…"

"Riley," he kisses underneath my jaw. "I'm trying to get you to relax and take a damn minute to breathe. You've had this deer in headlights look going on since Blake walked through the door. And when you're anxious, I'm anxious."

"I'm sorry that I'm putting you in this position." My throat feels tight as regret settles in there.

"If I didn't want to be in this position, I wouldn't be." His gaze is serious. "But if we're talking about positions, there's one I'm thinking about that's much more enticing than this one."

Miles ghosts his hands down my sides, the touch so gentle that it sends a shot of heat straight to my core. His hands wrap around my backside, and in one swift moment, he's got my ass planted on the edge of the sink and his lips against mine.

I pull away from his kiss, giving into the feelings that are consuming my body right now. "We have to be quiet."

"Oh, I can be quiet. It's you that has the sweet moans and the addictive whimpers that I'm always wanting to hear on repeat," he informs me with a coy grin.

"I'll be quiet, I promise."

I'm terrified, but with the pure lust and need shining in Miles' brown orbs, there's no way I can say no to this. Because beneath all the fear and anxiety of getting caught, I want him more than anything.

His thumb presses against the seam of my shorts, rubbing

tiny, pressured circles against my clit. "Good. Now get these sexy fucking shorts off."

I fumble with the button as Miles rips at my shirt. He takes a break between removing my shirt and unclasping my bra to discard my shorts and panties in one go.

I've never met a man who can strip me of my clothes in a hurry yet still maintain a delicate, sensual touch that drives me absolutely insane.

"I've been staring at your ass in these jean shorts all night, the way you move in them, and all I've been able to think about is your ass bent over for me while I watch my cock sink inside you."

"There are worse things to think about," I say breathily, unable to breathe correctly with the way his thick fingers are trailing my slit.

"There are," he agrees. "But I'd like to focus on what's in front of me, rather than imagining it."

Miles runs his hands up the length of my legs, pressing his thumbs into my thighs twice. "Spread these legs wider for me, baby. Remind me how pretty this pussy is."

Arousal zaps to my core, and I comply instantly. A shiver runs through me at the first languid swipe of Miles' tongue.

"You taste so fucking good, Riley. So sweet, so addictive."

Miles' tongue circles my clit as he reaches up to cup my breasts. The sensation makes my stomach clinch, but when he tugs at my nipples, at my piercings, my legs quiver and clamp around his head. I release my hold as quickly as I can out of fear of hurting him.

"Don't stop on my account," he says, pulling away from my pussy. "Squeeze my head, pull my face to your pussy. Encourages me to drive you even crazier," he tells me with a wink.

When Miles returns to my pussy, he suctions my clit into his mouth, swirls his finger around my arousal, then uses that to help him slide two thick fingers into me.

"I love how you're always ready for me." Another tug at my clit. "Such a needy girl, my baby is."

"Needy for you," I add.

"Mmm," he moans against me, causing me to clench. "I'll never get over hearing that."

Miles works his fingers in me mercilessly, hitting every nerve ending as he rocks his fingers in and out of me, flooding my entire body with an insane amount of pleasure.

The way he touches me is both ravishing and tender, animalistic and savoring. Like he'll die if he doesn't have me right now but wishes he could prolong the moment at the same time.

I've always wanted someone to crave me the way he seems to, and I'm over the moon that it's him worshiping at my altar. He's the one I always pictured being there. It's like a dream come true.

Miles snakes an arm around my waist to grab a handful of my ass, then pulls me further to the edge so that he can nuzzle himself even closer to my pussy.

His hand moves to my right breast, his thumb and forefinger squeezing, tugging and twisting at my sensitive nipples. Each tweak of my nipple sends a surge of heat to my core, and it's as if Miles can feel it because his movements become more hurried, more ruthless.

"This pussy is fucking addictive, Riley. The sweetest dessert I've ever tasted," he mumbles, the vibrations of his husky voice making my clit throb painfully with pent up pleasure. "You clench my fingers so beautifully baby. I'd love to see how tight it squeezes them while you come for me."

Miles' filthy encouragement lights the fuse, and his tongue wraps around my clit the minute that the heat travels rapidly south. My stomach clenches, my legs tighten, and the charge detonates as my vision hazes, and I collapse against the mirror.

"Fuck," I yell, overwhelmed by the orgasm coursing through my body at the talented hands of the man below me.

The high starts to dwindle down, and Miles continues to lick my clit as I return to the land of the living.

"God, you have a wicked tongue," I tell Miles. He's still on his knees, his tongue continuing to make languid swipes of my slit.

His eyes connect with mine, his tongue still making lazy swipes and circles on the most sensitive part of me. "Can't risk wasting a drop either," he says in that heated, gravelly tone of his.

"Fuck," I repeat. He says the hottest things to me, and it makes me want to continue this moment.

I sit taller, about to hop off the counter, when there's a knock at the door.

"Riley?" Blake's voice booms like thunder.

Fuck. Fuck, fuck, fuck.

"That's my sister," Miles whispers into my leg.

"No shit," I mouth back to him.

I can't breathe. I can't think. My hands are shaking, my heart is rattling around uncontrollably in my chest.

"Yeah, it's me," I yell back.

"Are you okay? I came back in and couldn't find you."

"I'm good." So good, considering my current position.

"Okay, good. I was coming to find you and heard you say fuck, so I thought I'd check in."

"Just stubbed my toe on the cabinet," I lie. Miles starts to laugh, and I slap my hand over his mouth to keep him from giving us away.

"Okay. I'll see you back downstairs," she says. I feel some relief at her departure, but it's short lived. Another knock. "Hey, have you seen Miles? There's someone from one of the sponsorship organizations here and they want to talk to him."

"Uh." *Think fast, Riley. Think fast.* "Yeah, I'm pretty sure he went down—downstairs somewhere. For more beer."

"Cool. I'll go find him. Thanks babe."

After waiting on bated breath for a solid minute, I assume Blake is gone and release the breath I was holding.

Miles runs his hand up my thigh gently, comforting me. "Are you okay?"

"Not at all," I say, my voice shaking.

"What can I do?"

"I don't know," I answer honestly.

Miles stands and wraps his arms around me. I don't miss the way that he's still fully clothed and I'm as naked as the day I was born.

There's something about the moment that has me apprehensive about keeping this a secret. Would it really be that bad? Would she really hate me so badly?

"Penny for your thoughts," Miles says, his voice filled with concern.

"I'm thinking that this was a stupid idea. That we should never have kept it a secret. That *I* should never have kept it a secret."

"Why?"

"Because I don't like this feeling," I say through gritted teeth. "I hate the regret for not saying anything, the burden, the anger, the anxiety and worry. It makes me sick, yet it makes me even sicker when I think about having to tell her."

I've never felt more vulnerable than I am right now. I'm naked in many ways; physically, emotionally, mentally.

"Can I share something with you?" he asks and I nod. "When Blake and I were teenagers, not long after I first met you, she made me pinky promise something. She made me promise that I wouldn't pursue you in any way."

"Are you serious?"

"Yeah," he responds. "Granted, I was a complete fuckboy back then, and my only focus was basketball. Like the majority of teens, I didn't have the capacity for anything serious and she knew that. I knew that."

"It doesn't give her the right to tell you who to lo—who to care for. That's messed up."

"Maybe," he says, pushing a strand of blonde hair behind my

ear. "But I don't blame her for doing it. I wasn't good for you back then."

"But you're good for me now," I defend.

"She doesn't know that." His forehead rests against mine. "To her, basketball is still my only focus, and she thinks I'd choose it over anything."

"Would you?" I ask, afraid of his answer but unable to hold it in.

"If it came down to it, no. I wouldn't. I've learned there are more important things in life that are more certain than a temporary game."

This is huge for him. To say he'd choose something else, maybe even someone else, over basketball is... well, it's mindblowing. It'd be like giving away your only dream, not knowing what's to come in the future.

"What do we do?" I ask.

"I think you were right to keep this a secret," he says, and time freezes.

"What? Since when do you agree with me?"

I could have sworn that he was only holding off on telling her because I asked him to. Now, I'm not so sure.

"Since right now." Miles grabs my hands in his own, squeezing lightly as he places them between our chests. "I can see now that I need my own time to prove myself to Blake. To prove that who I am now can be good for you. More serious, less about the game and more about people, that I can be reliable."

"Is this what you really want? I don't want to put you in the same position where you have to lie to your sister, your best friend, every day. I can't do it anymore. I won't..."

"You won't what?" he asks in an angry tone.

"I won't ruin your family again. I've already caused a strain with you and your dad, and I won't do it with Blake. I love her, and I care about you, and I won't do it." My voice is firm.

"This is what I want, Riley. Nothing will be ruined if we can just give it some time. Build up to it. I promise it will be okay."

Miles presses a kiss to my forehead, and though I'm scared, his words settle me in the moment.

Maybe things will really be okay…

"We should get back downstairs," I finally say. "We've been gone far too long."

"You mean you don't want to finish what we started?" Miles rears back in shock, a playful glint in his sultry eyes.

"Absolutely not. Save that shit for later." He laughs at me, but my patience is so thin. "Babe, give me my freaking clothes! We have to get back!"

Miles laughs as he grabs my clothes off the floor, placing them haphazardly on the sink beside me.

I dress in record time, and Miles reaches for the door, but I swat his arm away.

"What are you thinking, Miles? I need to go out first since I'm the person actually supposed to be in here," I berate.

"You're cute when you're like this."

"If you want a continuation of what just happened once everyone is gone, you'll rethink your words." My stare is stone cold serious.

"Okay."

I reach for the door to leave, cracking it open just a tad to check the hallway when Miles pulls me back into him.

"Are you crazy? The door is open!"

"Only crazy for you." He wraps his arms around me, skating his hands down to cup my ass. "Just wanted to kiss you before we have to go back to pretending like we don't fuck every night."

I roll my eyes at him but can't resist laughing. "Okay, one kiss. Then we leave."

"Deal," he smiles big.

Miles' lips connect with mine, and I get a heady rush through my body when I taste the remnants of myself on his lips. His tongue slips past my lips, tangling with my own as he makes smooth swipes inside my mouth.

Sparks reignite with the feverish way he kisses me, and I know that if I don't pull away, we'll get lost in the moment.

"Miles, you're playing dirty. I said one kiss."

"I didn't pull away, so that is one," he says proudly. "Thought I could change your mind."

"Not happening," I laugh. "Now shoo. I'm sneaking out, you come down in a few."

I check the hallway, noting its emptiness, then I slip away from the bathroom and hurry toward the stairs, hoping I'm put together enough.

"Your ass is mine later," Miles whisper-yells from the bathroom.

"Be quiet," I mouth back to him.

His quiet laughter follows me down the staircase, and I make a mental note to make him work extra for it later for nearly giving me a heart attack and getting us caught.

And now that the moment has passed, and the high is gone, I can't seem to get the thought out of my head that Blake made Miles promise to stay away from me.

Why would Blake do that? Does she not think I'm good enough for him? Is there another reason why she wouldn't want us to be together?

Is she worried that I'd make her choose? Because I'd never do that.

I would like to think none of what I'm imagining is true, but until I talk to her—which I can't do unless I'm ready to let out our secret—I'll have to assume otherwise.

And assuming for someone with my struggle, my anxiety… it only leads me down a dark path of self-doubt and possible self-sabotage.

Maybe there's a way I can ask her without giving us a way.

If only I could figure out how.

In a way that won't backfire.

Yeah… I may just be totally fucked.

CHAPTER 27
MILES

"You've been playing a lot better lately," Blake says, catching me just outside the locker room. "Got a minute?"

"Sure."

I follow Blake to her office, wondering why she's pulling me in here. I'm assuming game strategy, but I could be wrong.

She sits down across from me before planting her arms on the desk between us. There's a look in her eyes, one that I can't decipher—which speaks for itself considering we're twins, and normally, I know her better than myself.

"What's going on with you and Dad?" she asks.

"Nothing you need to worry about."

"Come on, Miles. It's me. All of us are aware of the shit show that Dad is, and we all have our own issues with him. You can tell me what's up."

I don't think I'm making it out of here alive.

"How did you know I wasn't speaking to him?"

"He made some passive aggressive comment about his kids not listening to him because hanging out with the wrong people would get them hurt. And considering you were the only Rainwater not present at dinner the other night besides Hunter, I'm assuming it's you."

Of course, it's me. I know that. But how much can I tell her without letting on that my defensiveness is more than friendly?

"How long has Dad hated Riley?"

Blake's brows immediately furrow, and her lips form into a straight line. "What are you talking about? Dad doesn't hate Riley."

"You're joking, right?" I sit forward in my seat, as if the closer proximity makes a difference in jogging my sister's memory.

"Blake, are you forgetting the verbal beating he gave her at Christmas dinner? The way he's always saying mean things to her. Or how a few weeks ago, he called her a run-down ragdoll and insinuated that she was trying to ruin my career back in high school?"

"He called her what?" Blake asks in shock. "And she didn't ruin shit. You punched the guy because he was man-handling her, and she never asked you to."

"I know that," I say in frustration. "But Dad said something about how he knew someone like that and learned the hard way. He's putting his own experience on Riley, and it isn't fair."

"Okay, he can be a dick and we know that. But what was so bad that made you shut him out completely?"

"I can't tell you that, Blake." My head is throbbing. "Your relationship with Dad has gotten better since last season and I don't want what's happening between the two of us to affect that."

"Last time I checked, I don't need anyone protecting me, and I certainly can make my own decisions when it comes to him. If it involves my best friend, you better fucking spill."

The anger is written clearly all over Blake. Her eyes are nearly black in color, her jaw is clenched firmly. Her fists are balled so tightly that her knuckles are visibly white. And with the red tint of rage peeking through her complexion, she looks murderous.

"Do you know the reason why Riley and I stopped being friends all those years ago?"

"No," she answers. "She refused to tell me what happened, and then refused to talk about you at all until I convinced her to come stay with you. Why?"

"Dad made her take care of the guy that pressed charges. She used the bracelet her birth mom gave her to pay him off and drop the charges. He told her that it was her fault that I was in that situation, and that she had to take care of it. Instead of helping like a father should—regardless of his relationship to her—he made her fend for herself."

"Nahnai winiduyugodvna," Blake says in disbelief. *There's no way.*

"Yes, there is a way. I don't know what he's doing, or why, but I'm not putting up with his blatant mistreatment of her. Until he apologizes to her, gets his shit straight, and explains himself, he can stay away from me."

"Yeah, I don't blame you now. But why didn't you tell me? Hell, why didn't *she* tell me? I'm her best friend."

"I can't speak for Riley," I begin, "but I can say that she loves you so much. More than I think you'll ever understand. But I think she's just afraid." I know that for a fact. It's the focus of all our conversations in relation to telling Blake about what we are.

"What could she be afraid of?"

"Losing more people she loves."

"She could never lose me though."

"Really? There's nothing she could do that would make you think otherwise?"

"No. Never." She's certain.

"Then why did you swear me off seeing her?"

Blake's eyebrows raise, and her tongue pokes her cheek as she concentrates. "Are you talking about the promise I made you make me as a kid?"

"Exactly that."

"Miles, that was years ago." She shakes her head. "Plus, I never have to worry about that. You're not exactly each other's types."

"And if we were?" I challenge.

I'm on thin ice right now, and I know that.

"Miles, what don't I know? Is there something going on that you're not telling me?" Her voice rises with each word.

"Humor me," I say, ignoring her question.

"Fine. You two aren't right for each other. Riley has her own demons, and you're not serious enough to handle it. You care about basketball and basketball only, and you always have."

"That's what you think," I defend. "But would it really be so bad?"

"Yes," she responds with no hesitation. "It would be a disaster. If things went south… Things would never be the same."

I want so badly to stand up and scream, "it wouldn't be a disaster because I care about her!"

But I can't do that. I now understand why Riley is so put off to tell Blake about us.

Right now, she can't see that we're not the kids we used to be. She doesn't see all the ways that we can be good for each other—the ways that we *are* good for each other.

I'm going to have to prove myself to my sister, and I never thought I'd have to do that. She should have faith in me for this. And that hurts more than I care to admit.

Does she not think I can change? Or is there some other reason why she's so against the two of us?

I'm not ready to find out if so.

"You can't predict that, but it doesn't matter." I stand and grab my bag from the floor where I dropped it earlier. "Is that all you wanted to talk about?"

"Yeah," she says, voice devoid of any emotion.

"See you tomorrow then."

When I get to my truck, I give myself five minutes to dwell on Blake's words before leaving the practice facility. Did they hurt? Yes. Can I change them? Not without some serious work.

Instead, I focus on ordering groceries for pick-up because I have better plans tonight than dwelling on things that can wait for another day.

Riley doesn't know it yet, but I have a surprise waiting for her when she gets home later. It's something I've been wanting to do for a while, but I've only made time for it now.

When I get home, I let Chief outside to run and do his business. I take a seat in one of the rockers out back while he runs around and pull out my phone to text Riley.

> Miles: When do you get off work tonight?

I've thrown Chief's ball with him for at least ten minutes before I get a reply back.

> Riley: Now, actually. Night was slow as hell, so Rambo let me and Aurora out early. I'll be home soon.

Home.

There was a point in time where I couldn't picture saying *Riley* and *home* in the same sentence, and now I wouldn't want it any other way.

She may refer to this place as her home, but when I think of the word, I only see her.

> Miles: I'll be waiting.

Twenty minutes later, Riley walks in and I hear her as she

drops her bag by the front door. The clunking sound is so loud—makes me wonder if she's got half a wardrobe in that thing.

"Miles," she calls out.

"In the kitchen," I respond.

After Riley texted, I spent the next bit of time pulling out all the necessary ingredients and utensils needed to make the meal I've planned.

"What's all this?" Riley asks as she enters the kitchen.

For a moment, all I can do is stare at her. She's so unlike herself when she's dressed for work, but she's still beautiful even when she's dressed as her alias.

Wednesday really is the perfect name for my baby.

Dressed in these skimpy black shorts, fishnet lacing that connects to a leather bralette with gold beads around the triangles, and bold makeup that highlights the cerulean blue of her eyes, she's still as much of a dream as she is when she's stripped naked and bare.

But I've learned over the past few months that true beauty isn't about appearances but the composition of what makes up a person's heart and soul.

"Why are you looking at me like that?" she asks, an almost shy grin appearing on her porcelain skin.

"Why not?"

"Because I'm not me," she says, gesturing to her work outfit.

"It doesn't matter how you dress or paint your face or act because underneath it all, you're still my Riley."

Warmth and happiness washes over Riley as she takes quick strides toward me, wrapping her arms around my neck as she looks into my eyes.

"I'm yours, huh?"

"Of course, you are. I thought you knew that already."

"It's just nice to hear," she speaks gently.

"Well, let me make it loud and clear for you. You're mine. This ass is mine." I grab her behind. "This pussy is mine." I cup her over her shorts. "And most importantly, this right here is mine." I place my hand over her chest, and her resulting smile fills me with an immense amount of pride.

"And because you're mine," I continue, "I've got to make sure my baby's okay when I'm gone."

"How so?"

"By teaching you how to cook."

CHAPTER 28
MILES

"You're teaching me how to cook?" Riley rears back with wide eyes and disconnects from me. "Are you crazy? I could burn the house down!" she screams.

I laugh. "You're not going to do that because I'm going to teach you everything you need to know."

"I can't do it—" she starts to shake her head.

"Not with that attitude, you won't." I grab Riley's hands, linking our fingers together. "You're more capable than you allow yourself to think. For just a bit, can you humor me enough to have confidence in yourself to do this like I do?"

"You're confident I can do it?" she questions.

"I'm confident that you can do anything you set your mind to, baby."

I can tell that she's thinking it over, battling her inner thoughts about whether to give this a try and achieve success, or risk failure. Something flashes through her eyes, and then she stands taller.

"Okay. I can do this," she says with determination in her tone.

"Yes, you can, baby." Pure joy floods my system at her agreeing to take a chance on herself. "Yes, you can."

Riley walks over to the island where the items are prepped and leans down on it, drawing my attention to how well her ass looks in those shorts I just said were too short.

"You gonna stand there and ogle me all night, or are you planning to show me what the hell to do with all this?"

"I can do both. Don't underestimate my ability to multitask, Riley." I join her at the island and instinct has me wrapping my arm around her waist and pulling her to me. "What do you think is the first thing you need to do?"

"I don't even know what we're making," she laughs, but I hear the nerves woven in.

"I'm teaching you to make spaghetti."

"Really?" she asks. "Isn't that like the easiest meal in the world to make?"

"If it is, then why can't you make it already?"

Riley drops her jaw and begins blinking her eyes slowly at me, and it takes everything in me to not start laughing. I'm biting my tongue to hold it in.

"That was totally uncalled for." She glowers.

"Walked right into that one, babe."

"I can't help it," she defends, but her voice is a bit squeaky when she does. "You forget the water one time and then you never live it down," she murmurs. Riley shakes her head, and it's then that the laughter finally leaves me.

"We'll make sure that doesn't happen again," I say, swiping my thumb over her bottom lip, coming away with a dark lipstick stain. "Now go wash your hands and we'll get started."

Riley and I clean up and meet back at the island where all the ingredients are placed.

"Okay, we're making the sauce from scratch so there's a lot of prep work to be done. Veggie cutting, measuring, all that jazz. And while I'd normally do everything at once, I want learning to cook to be a positive experience for you—no absent water trauma—so we're going to go step by step. How does that sound?"

"Sounds perfect. I don't want to be overwhelmed," she expresses.

"And that's exactly why I'm doing it this way. Now…" I walk over to the counter by the sink and grab a few knives from the block. I walk back to Riley and hold out one to her. "Can I trust you with one of these? Or should I be wary?"

Riley smiles and rolls her eyes, and I pocket the expression for later. "Considering I'm terrified and clumsy—a not ideal combination—I'm probably more dangerous to myself than you."

"We'll be keeping limbs attached today, thank you."

I wash off all the vegetables before placing them back in front of Riley.

"Watch me cut and then repeat my motions." Riley nods. "We'll be dicing the onions, but the tomatoes don't matter because they'll be cooked down. Then we'll measure the seasonings afterward."

I proceed with showing Riley the best cutting technique, making sure to protect my clumsy girl's fingers, but I notice after a bit that she still hasn't made any cuts.

"What's wrong?" I ask.

Riley sinks her teeth into her bottom lip as she looks at the floor. When she lifts her head and locks eyes with me, there's an unwavering amount of vulnerability shining in her beautiful eyes.

"Can you show me?" she asks, her voice barely above a whisper.

"Absolutely."

Stepping behind Riley, I place my hands on her waist to steady her body. When I place my hands on her arms, gently running the length of them, I can sense her slight tremble.

My hand finds her wrist, steadying both her hand and the blade. "Take a deep breath, baby," I instruct her.

When she's finally ready, she nods, and I begin to move my hand with hers. "You want to make sure the knuckles on your left hand are tucked and start with gentle movements. Feel the way your body moves, go with the knife. It's an extension of you, nothing to be scared of."

"I think every final girl in any horror movie would beg to differ," she says, summoning a deep laugh from within me.

"Never change, baby."

She laughs in return, and the warmth that it fills me with is fiercer than any flame could provide.

We continue our movements, and once she starts to chase the cut, I back away from her.

"Where are you going?" she asks, mild panic in her tone.

"Letting you spread your wings. You've got this," I tell her, hoping that the intensity in which I speak encourages her to absorb the words more efficiently.

After a few free cuts, Riley's confidence increases and she reaches for the tomatoes all on her own, repeating the same technique with them though she doesn't need to.

"Look at you go," I tell her.

She tries to hide it, but I see the smile she lets herself have behind the shield of her blonde hair. It's fulfilling in ways I could never explain with words.

Riley proceeds to follow instructions impeccably, hanging on to my every word for something she should have learned, but wasn't fortunate enough to have, when she was younger.

A part of me aches for everything she missed out on growing up, but another part of me is filled with pride that I get to be the one sharing this moment with her.

I want to share so many more.

"How do I break this meat up in the frying pan?"

"Where I'm from, we call it a skillet." I grin. "But you use the black thing there to your right."

"The thing that looks like a star on the bottom?" She grabs the utensil and stares at it like it's a foreign object. "What's it even called?"

"It's a meat masher, or a meat chopper, but we just call it a meat beater."

A boisterous laugh leaves Riley. "The way that you say meat beater…" She continues laughing, unable to control herself. "I can't even."

She waves me off and continues chopping the meat in the pan, asking me every minute whether it's cooked enough or not. It's cute to see her like this.

My freaking face hurts from the constant smiling I do around her, but I'd take the pain over not seeing it each time it graces her beautiful face.

Not long after, both the meat and the sauce are done, so I tell Riley to combine the two and set the stove eye on low to simmer.

The next step is to boil the noodles, and after telling Riley how to do it, I watch as she frustratingly struts over to the sink, staring at the water like it's her worst enemy as it's filling up the pot, before bringing it to the stove.

She smiles big once she turns it on. "I didn't forget the fucking water this time. Take that."

"You're so damn adorable," I say, reaching up to pinch her cheek.

Not sure how that leads to Riley and I lying on the kitchen floor making out, but I don't say anything.

At least until Riley swats my chest and flies from the floor faster than I can grab her and pull her back down to me.

"You're gonna make me burn dinner," she chastises. "Some teacher you are," she says, grabbing the spoon to return to stirring the sauce so it doesn't stick.

Riley refuses to let me distract her again, much to my dismay. She only acknowledges me again once she checks the clock and realizes how long the noodles have been on.

I show her how to strain the noodles but stop her when she reaches for one.

"What?"

"That's not how we check to see if they're done."

"It's what everyone else does. How do you do it, then?"

"Like this."

I grab a noodle and take a step back, turning toward the refrigerator. Pulling my arm back, I toss it at the fridge with rapid speed.

When the spaghetti noodle stays stuck to the stainless-steel refrigerator, I turn back to Riley, her wide eyes on me. "That's how you do it."

"Did you just throw a noodle?" she asks, dumbfounded.

"I did." I grab a noodle from the strainer and hand it to her. "And now you're going to."

Astonishment shines brightly in her eyes, her smile reaching the widest it can be.

"Okay," she says cheerily.

Riley pulls her arm back, but instead of throwing it, she flings it toward the refrigerator with no strategy, and somehow, it sticks.

"That's so cool!" she squeals.

I'm amazed that something as small as throwing noodles in the kitchen could bring so much happiness to my girl.

That's one of the most beautiful things about Riley. It doesn't take much to make her happy. I could buy her all the gifts she could ever want, and she'd choose to cuddle on the couch and watch TV over all of it.

I didn't pay attention to it when we were younger, but now that we're living together—and my feelings for Riley are so intense—I'm picking up on even the smallest things about her.

Walking over to the fridge, I grab both our noodles and hold them out to Riley. "Now we have a taste test."

"Absolutely not. Do you know what has touched that thing? There's no telling what kind of germs are on there."

I take a few steps toward Riley, dangling the noodle in her face like a taunt. "It's not like it's gonna kill us," I say, right before I pop the noodle in my mouth.

"Tell me that after you're dead," she laughs, cringing away from the noodle I'm pushing toward her.

"Come on, baby. You're gonna let me risk death on my own?"

"Now my food is so bad that you'll die?"

"Not at all," I laugh, throwing my hands up. "But you'll only know for yourself if you try it."

"Nope!" she yells, then she takes off running.

Riley bumps her hip against the island trying to make her turn too short, and she laughs off the pain as she goes, me hot on her heels.

She runs straight to the living room, putting the couch and coffee table between us.

"Keep that thing away from me," she says sternly, but there's humor and playfulness to it that only comes when someone's being as stupid as I am.

I do it to see her smile.

Backing off a bit, I wait for Riley to relax, but it's then that I get her. In a moment of weakness, I wrap my arms around her and hold the noodle to her face. She thrashes around in my arms, and when her belly laughter makes it so she can't breathe, I toss it to the floor and wrap myself around her.

I turn her around in my arms and hold her to me, and when the laughter finally ceases, Riley reaches up and brings our gaze together.

Her hands frame my cheeks, and the seriousness in her eyes has my entire body stiffening in response that something may be wrong.

"Are you okay?"

"Miles, I've never felt better," she replies earnestly. "Can you tell me exactly why you wanted to teach me to cook?"

"Easy. I'm on the road a lot, and while I enjoy prepping meals for you before I leave, I know how independent you are, and I know that it probably kills you to not conquer something. And while spaghetti is small, it's something you can feel confident to do for yourself. I wanted you to be able to have that feeling."

Riley smiles, and the sentiment of it hits me square in the chest.

"You don't know how much this means to me," she says, tears in her eyes. "Everyone makes fun of me for burning the ramen—"

"I'm sorry."

"Let me finish." She continues. "Everyone makes fun of me for it, but none of them have ever taken the time to ask why, or to show me how. Not until you. Taking time out of your day to teach me, to spend time with me... it's worth its weight in gold in my eyes. Actions mean more than words to me, Miles."

"I'm happy that I can make you happy," I whisper, finally pulling her in to kiss me.

"So happy," she murmurs.

When we pull away, I hear lapping and turn to find Chief eating the noodle off of the floor.

"I mean... at least it's good enough that a dog will eat it."

Riley laughs in my shirt. "Ow," she continues to laugh.

Once our emotions simmer down, we fix our plates and find ourselves in our favorite place, on the couch with each other watching TV.

And when she asks me after dinner what my thoughts on her first independent meal was...

I tell her it's the best damn spaghetti I've ever had.

CHAPTER 29
RILEY

"Riley, are you sure you don't need my help?" Miles asks from the dining room, where I've asked him to set the table.

"No!" I yell in response. "I can do this. I've done this enough lately that I've nearly perfected it."

"I know." Miles' voice comes closer as he enters the kitchen. "We've only had spaghetti—what, like eight times in the last two weeks?"

"I'm trying to make it perfect."

"It's perfect because you make it, baby." Miles bends down to place a kiss on my cheek, little jolts of electricity shooting through me once he steps away.

Miles props his hip on the counter beside me where I'm stirring sauce on the stove. "Is there anything else I can do to help?"

"Not really. I'm just..." I don't even know what. "I'm nervous about tonight."

"I know you are." Miles places a hand on my back and begins to make gentle, comforting circles. "But we wanted to do this, right? We want to show Blake that we've both changed. I think this is a way to do it, but we won't know that until it's over."

"I'm not ready to face the consequences of my actions, Miles.

I want you more than anything, but I don't want to lose Blake in the process. She's my best friend, the sister I never had. And if she really doesn't want us together, what do you think will happen when she finds out about us?

"You're her blood, I'm not. I'm easily disposable compared to you."

There it is. Just like I expected. My mother disposed of me for some unknown reason, and now I'm worried that anyone in my life will do the same if I become too much for them.

Past trauma can rear its ugly head at any time, and mine has been sitting under the surface ever since Miles and I became a thing. And with Blake and Kyler arriving soon, for no other reason than a normal dinner—though there are ulterior motives —the real reasoning behind my wanting to keep a secret is exposed.

"You think you're disposable?" Miles repeats. His voice is full of anguish and pain and fuck... the tears in his eyes have my knees nearly buckling.

"Riley," he continues, stepping forward to grab my arms with gentle firmness. "You are so far from disposable. You're funny, snarky, hard-working, determined, beautiful, and selfless as hell. The way you help people, the way you see the world, and the way you support and sacrifice for the people you love..."

Miles' hands travel up my arm to frame my face, gripping my chin with unyielding intent, bringing us so close together that the warmth of his breath ghosts against me, warming me from head to toe.

"You are a damn unicorn, Riley. There is no one like you, and there *never* will be. Anyone who chooses to miss out on your life by disposing of you was never worthy of your time in the first place. And I consider myself the luckiest man in the world each day I get to spend with you."

His words do something. They solidify a small, jagged piece of me, slipping it back in place. It's an unfamiliar feeling, but my body feels more whole the longer I stand here with my eyes locked on the man who has taken better care of me than anyone else ever has.

"I think we're both equally lucky," I whisper, ending the conversation there but returning the sentiment.

Pulling back from Miles, I voice the question on my mind. "Is this dinner gonna be okay?" More so. "Are we gonna be okay?"

"Treat this dinner like any other, and everything should be okay. And for us," he kisses my forehead. "We're gonna be more than okay."

And for the first time, my anxiety doesn't infiltrate my thoughts, and I believe exactly what Miles is saying.

We *will* be okay.

"I'm really glad that y'all could come over for dinner tonight," Miles says to my right. "I know it's hard to nail down time together that isn't on the court."

"I thought being an athlete was hard, but I think coaching is worse at times," Blake states.

"It seems stressful," I add.

"It is. More responsibilities, more people pleasing, and a lot more ass-kissing," she laughs. "Not a fan of that but it's part of the politics."

Miles and Kyler hassle Blake about today's practice for a bit, and when the conversation quiets down, Blake speaks up.

"This sauce is amazing, Miles. Is it homemade?"

I freeze. I'm not sure why but I just do.

"Uh." Miles sets his fork down. "I'm not sure. You'd have to ask the chef," he says, turning to look at me.

Blake's fork clinks against her plate as she looks at me with astonishment and disbelief. "You made this?" she questions.

"Yeah, uh." I cough. "I actually did make this. Is it okay?"

"Hold up. There's no way you made this. You can't cook," she says matter of fact.

"I've learned a few things."

"This is more than a few things," Blake points to the table. "This is a full ass meal. The last time I saw you in a kitchen attempting to cook, we nearly had to call the fire department. I smelt burnt ramen for a week," she laughs.

"I remembered the water in the noodles this time," I say, a heavy dose of sarcasm in my tone as I smile at her.

I mean... I made a freaking meal, and that's a big deal for me. I'm immensely proud of myself for accomplishing it since there was a time I thought I'd never learn how. But I freaking did it, and I'm really proud right now.

"Funny," she adds with a quick laugh. "How did you even learn how to cook?"

"Well, I've—" Miles begins.

"I've just been watching Miles cook, and a few videos online. Guess they've rubbed off on me."

"Hey, it's pretty tasty. You did a good job."

"Thank you," I say. "I'm no Gordon Ramsay though."

"Riley, this is huge," Blake says. "This is the first meal you've cooked and didn't burn. It doesn't matter how you learned or what skills you have. You did this, and you got past your fear of cooking. It's a big step," she acknowledges.

"It is," I respond, happy that she can see how big of a moment this is for me.

"I'm really proud of you," she adds, grabbing another forkfull of spaghetti, moaning when the sauce hits her tongue again. "Still can't believe you made this sauce," she says, and I smile.

I'm happy to see how proud she is of me, but not as happy as when I turn to see Miles smirking behind his fork, his eyes full of admiration and pride as he watches me light up with self-accomplishment.

I wouldn't have been able to do it without him, so I smile back in return.

Once we're through with eating dinner, I slide back in my chair and begin to gather the dirty dishes.

Miles reaches out and grabs my wrist gently. "You cooked, let me clean," he insists.

"If that's what you want," I concede.

While I've never cooked like this before, I've used plenty of utensils with my takeout. I've washed enough forks and spoons in my life that I'd be okay to never have to wash another again. Those things are annoying as hell to wash, and they never feel clean.

At least Miles has a dishwasher.

"Tonight would be an amazing night for the hot tub," Blake speaks aloud, and immediately the thought of hot water against my muscles makes my knees weak.

"I love that idea. Why don't we do it?" I ask.

"Kyler and I didn't bring anything to wear," she says like that makes a difference.

"Babe, we're best friends. You know I've got you. And I'm sure Miles has something for Kyler as well."

"I do," Miles adds.

"Oh," Blake says, perking up. "Do you still have that dark blue bikini that fits me really well?"

"Yeah, I wore it the other day actually. It's been washed; it's upstairs in my room."

"You know what," Miles begins, "you two go upstairs and get ready while Kyler and I clean up. By the time we've put it all away, we'll be ready to join you outside."

"Sounds good to me. Let's go."

Blake takes my hand and starts pulling me up the stairs toward my room. The minute we're inside, she shuts the door and walks over to the bed, collapsing on top of it.

"Is something wrong?" I ask, wary of the question but asking as her best friend.

"We're in desperate need of a best friend date. I feel like I haven't talked to you at all lately and I miss you. We need to rant about random shit to each other and give shitty advice to make ourselves feel better."

I laugh. "I'll never say no to a best friend date. But you can rant now if you want," I offer.

"No, I don't want the guys to have to wait so long for us. How about lunch? Do you have any free time this week?"

"I don't have to go into the parlor tomorrow until the afternoon, so I can go for lunch around noon if that works for you."

"I'll make it work," she states. "Just shoot me a text tomorrow and tell me where you want to eat. I know how much of a mood eater you are."

I laugh. She knows me so well. And because she does, a pit forms in my stomach, but I push away the knowledge of the feeling.

"Works for me."

"Okay." Blake sits up, clapping her hands in front of her. "Show me where this suit is."

"It's in the laundry basket by the bathroom door."

After telling Blake where to find the bikini, I walk over to my dresser and rummage through my drawers to find one for myself. I want to find one that will drive Miles crazy without it being obvious that I wore it for that reason.

"Found it," I hear Blake call over my shoulder.

I hold up my black and deep purple bikini side by side, debating on which one is best. After quick deliberation, I decide on the deep purple one that makes my boobs look great.

"Riley," I hear Blake say.

"Yeah."

"Why are my brother's boxers in your laundry basket?"

Oh no.

No, no, no.

Yeah, Riley. Why the hell are his boxers in there?

Did he toss them in there after we had sex one night? Is it a mistake?

I have no words.

This is it. If I don't come up with an excuse that's convincing enough for Blake, my life as I know it will cease to exist.

And if we make it through this, I may kick his ass for leaving his obvious undergarments in my supposed Miles-free space.

My chest begins to feel tight and my hands tingle as I finish picking the bikini up out of its drawer. For a moment, my vision hazes, but I blink away the blurriness.

Think quickly. *You've pretended around others your entire life; you can do it with your best friend too.*

"Miles's housekeeper does his laundry, but I do my own. I told him I wouldn't use her while I was here because I couldn't pay her. He throws his laundry in with mine sometimes if he needs it. Something about game day rituals or something."

"Athletes are crazy for rituals," she tags on. "Thank God, though."

"What do you mean?"

"I thought for a second that you might be hooking up with my brother," she laughs, her tone laced with impossibility at the idea that could ever be true.

Making sure that I don't respond too quickly, I say, "I'm not hooking up with your brother."

It's not a total lie.

Are we sleeping together? Yes. But what we have is so much more than a casual hookup.

I just can't tell her that.

"Good," she says. "That would be awful."

"Why do you say that?"

"It's like I told him earlier, y'all would be so bad for each other."

"Your brother isn't a bad guy," I offer up. "I know he was tough when I first moved in, but we've since reconciled."

"I know he isn't bad. I'm just saying you'd be bad together."

"Wow. Tell me how you really feel."

"It's nothing personal against either of you," she says, walking over so that she can look at me. "I know how my brother is, and I know what you struggle with, and I know that the combination of the two would only end in disaster. I promise, it really isn't personal."

Too bad, Blake. Because it feels fucking personal.

I understand now why Miles jumped on the bandwagon of keeping us a secret.

The timing just isn't right.

"I know," I say anyway, turning back to my dresser. "Now I don't know about you, but that warm water is calling my name."

"Same," she sighs. "Give me a few and I'll be dressed and ready."

Once Blake heads into the bathroom to change, I sit down on the bed and release the breath I've been holding since she held Miles' boxers up to me.

I want so badly to talk to someone about this. About the happiness I feel with Miles, about the strides I'm taking to better myself and my quality of life. But the only person I want to talk to about all these life changes is my best friend.

And she's the last person that I can ever speak to about it.

The bitterness of that reality...

Yeah, it fucking sucks.

CHAPTER 30
RILEY

MEETING BLAKE FOR LUNCH TODAY IN A NEUTRAL ZONE IS PROBABLY the best idea I've had in a while. Especially after the laundry mishap last night. Not sure if I can survive in a room alone with her right now without short-circuiting.

I'm still waiting for Blake when my phone buzzes in my pocket.

> Miles: We just got out of practice. Blake should be there soon.

> Riley: Good.

> Riley: I forgot earlier but remind me to kick your ass later.

> Miles: Okay...

> Miles: But why are you kicking my ass?

> Riley: Because Blake found your boxers in my laundry basket last night and my heart nearly fell out of my ass!! I thought it would be the end of me.

> Miles: Fine. I'll just leave all the clothes in my room and walk around the house naked. If she hasn't figured out that we're together yet, she'll know then.

> Riley: ...You can keep your clothes on.

> Miles: You won't be saying that later (;

"Riley."

I jump at the sound of my name, glancing up to see Blake towering over me.

"Holy shit, you scared me," I say, slapping a hand to my chest as I try to calm my breathing.

"I said your name like three times," she laughs. Blake drops her keys and wallet onto the table and slides into the chair across from mine. "You seemed pretty distracted."

"Just responding to some texts."

"I don't think 'some texts' normally turn your cheeks all red."

Fairly sure my cheeks go from a normal red to a scarlet red when she says that.

"Riley Davis, are you talking to someone?" Blake gushes. I'm speechless. "You are! Damn girl. I know I've barely seen you since the season started, but you could have told me you met someone."

"I, uh, wanted to keep it to myself for a bit. Feel it out."

The waitress chooses that time to come over and grab our drink and appetizer order. Blake orders us both a beer on tap and grabs us the burrata bread with heirloom tomatoes and cochon de lait debris fries—basically bruschetta and cheese and pork-covered fries.

I had hoped that the conversation would be dropped with the interruption, but I turn out to be not so lucky.

"I thought that you were hooking up with the guy from the parlor?" she questions. My stomach drops at the mention of his name.

"No, we haven't hooked up in a while." *Since I'm sleeping with your brother instead.* "He's a dick. It started with raising my commission fee, taking away workdays and just being a general ass."

"That guy has always given me a weird vibe," she says, grabbing a bite of food. "So, how serious is it? With this new guy."

I wonder how honest I can be without giving anything away. Because I'm dying to talk to my best friend, but she can't know that the man in question is the person she shared the freaking womb with.

That would be crossing so many lines. Because even if she were okay with this, I think talking about our sex life would be on the hard-no list of potential discussions.

But I think there's a way to meet her in the middle.

A way to clue in my best friend in an inconspicuous way while also keeping our relationship a secret.

Worth a try anyway.

"It's still the beginning, honestly. But we're keeping it on the low while we work some things out."

"Like what?"

The waitress drops the food and our drinks, and I begin to stress eat my fries. *Fuck, they're good though.*

"His family is up in the air. I'm not so sure that they'll accept me, and he doesn't want to hurt anyone."

"How could you hurt anyone?" she asks, engaging.

Wow. Maybe this could *work.*

"I met his sister a while back in school, while I was getting my art degree." Only half a lie. "I'm worried that she won't approve. Or that she'll think we're not right for each other. You know better than I do how families can be," I offer up.

"Don't I know it," she says, grabbing fries for herself. "Why doesn't she think you'd be good together? You're one of the best people I know."

If so, then why don't you think we'd be good together? Pushing away my inner thoughts, I continue.

"This guy doesn't have the best past. He was a bit of a playboy. And he's still at that stage in life where he's responsible but also playful. She doesn't seem to take him seriously. But she also hasn't been able to see how we've changed since being together."

"People can change," Blake agrees. "Why not just show her the ways in which you have?"

"I think she's got these goggles on or something because we're showing her, she's just not seeing it." I pause. "Or maybe she's so against it because she'd rather not have the images of a friend sleeping with her brother," I laugh, adding it for humorous effect.

"I can imagine how that would scar a person," she laughs, cringing at the sound of her own words.

"I could imagine it as well." I pause before pushing forward. "Got any advice for me? I don't want to hurt a friend."

"Oh, um, let me think." Blake takes a sip of beer. "Well, you never want to hurt anyone. Anybody that has met you can see that. But if I'm being honest, unless you were upfront in the beginning, I don't think there's a way you can go about it that won't hurt her, at least in some way. It's a huge secret to keep."

"Helpful," I say, shaking my head.

"I pride myself on being the wiser sibling," she winks. "And hey, you said advice, not that it had to be good."

I laugh at her honesty.

"But whenever you plan to tell her, don't back down. Sometimes you forget the level of sass and strength that you possess," she adds.

"You're right about that," I say. "But I'm working to do better about that. Miles has helped a lot in that department."

Blake's eyes widen over her glass of beer. "Yeah, I can definitely see some changes. But how so?"

"We had a lot of shit to work out when I moved in, and it was a big adjustment. He told me the arrangement would never work if I didn't speak up for myself and my needs and feelings."

"He's right," she says, taking another bite and swallowing. "For the record, Ri,"—she reaches to lay her hand on mine in a sincere gesture— "I'm really proud of you. You look really good this way," she smiles.

"What way?"

"Happy," she says, and I feel full, but not because of the food.

She continues to eat but eventually adds, "Maybe Miles isn't such a bad influence on you after all."

And for the first time—I think ever—I have hope that this thing won't blow up when we decide to tell her.

Her response is what drives that hope all the way through our lunch, where heavy conversations are forgotten, and we spend time just being best friends as we've always been.

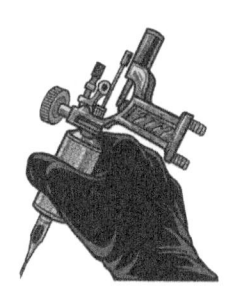

It felt really nice to catch up with Blake, but every moment I spend lying to her adds another pound of guilt to the weight I'm already carrying.

But after our lunch today, I'm hopeful that we won't have to wait forever to tell her about us. It's like she said, it doesn't matter if we tell her now or later, there's still going to be some level of hurt that'll need to be addressed.

I'm not allowed to think about it too long before walking into City & Sin for work. On the days that I'm here, I'm always earlier than I need to be, so I have time to prepare, clean, and study any pre-made appointment pieces for the day.

Although, on my way to my chair, I catch the patient I'm

supposed to be tattooing in an hour coming out of Zeke's room, a brand-new bandage wrapped around her forearm.

I stop in my tracks, halted by the confusion of why she's with him and not me. Zeke's head pops up and when he sees me, he sends the client to the front, telling her he'll be there in a minute.

"What's going on?" I ask when he walks closer to me. "Why's my client with you?"

"She called earlier and needed to get an earlier appointment. Some kind of conflict. You weren't due in for a bit, so I tattooed her."

"You took my design?"

"I made an adjustment or two."

I don't think I realized just how much of a dick Zeke truly is until I stopped getting his dick on the regular.

I blame it on bad judgment, loneliness, and tequila.

Either way, the guy is a jackass. Adjusting or not, it's still my artwork.

"I hope that's okay," he adds in a condescending tone.

"Not really, but as long as she knew the base design wasn't yours, it's already done now," I say sternly. "It was a small design anyway. I'll just do some work in my free time before my next client."

It's easy to brush it off rather than argue with him. The stick up Zeke's ass is so far that it's pressing on the cells in his very small brain.

One day, I'd love to be out of here. It's not the environment it was when Zeke's father brought me into the business—his son making it toxic. But that's not possible yet as I still have my own finances to worry about, and I'm saving for something I really want.

Something I've dreamed about.

When I feel risky enough to dream, that is.

After breaking away from Zeke, I find my way to my station and continue doing my normal routine: cleaning, prepping, sterilizing, and stocking.

Once I'm finished, I decide to take the extra time I have to work on the horror piece I've been working on periodically for the past year, and the last session to finish this piece is coming up in a little under two months.

I email back and forth with the client repeatedly, fine-tuning details and colors and making any necessary changes. And while I hate missing out on the earlier commission, I'm excited to sit down and work on this horror piece some more.

It's a piece that I'm ridiculously proud of, and it's a combination of hard work, blood, and my client's equally twisted mind.

But the more I try to work, the more my mind travels back to what Blake said about forgetting the strength I possess and how I left and came into work to let Zeke slide by with stealing my art.

I should have never done that. Change only comes by force of will; no one has more force than me to make this change happen.

After realizing I can't focus like I wanted on the horror piece, I decide to prepare for the rest of the day. But that irritation leads me through to the end of the day. Grabbing my things, I find myself walking to the front of the shop to find Zeke packing up for the day, thankful that everyone has cleared out but us.

"I think we should talk," I say, causing Zeke to stop whatever he's doing.

He drops the rag and leans back against the counter, crossing his arms over his chest. The way he already seems so disinterested in what I'm about to say has me apprehensive, but I'm gonna try not to let him bother me anymore.

"And why is that?"

"For starters, you took my artwork."

"I told you that I made adjustments," he defends, but I cut him off.

"Maybe you did, but that doesn't make it okay, Zeke," I yell. "Art is sacred to an artist, and for you to come in and just take it over, regardless of the changes you made, it was a personal hit to my creative spirit. My art is *my* art, and that's it. Why did you take my client to begin with?"

"Like I told you. She called in, needed to come earlier, and that's that," he deadpans, and I want to slap the shit out of him, but I can't.

Unfortunately, he's still my boss for the foreseeable future.

"You should really find a better way to lie, because you called and texted me on and off for three years whenever you wanted to hook up," I scold. "So, I know damn well that you could have picked up the phone and called to tell me. This is my job; I would have come in."

Zeke stands up straight, trying to make himself appear bigger even though he's built like a green bean.

"Listen, I'm not gonna beg somebody to come to work. You're never here, so I took the liberty of satisfying a customer. I have a business to uphold."

And that's the moment that my world turns *red*.

"I'm sorry," I say, eerily calm. "Repeat that."

"You're barely ever here. You're lucky that you still have a job with how absent you've been."

Briefly, my body goes stiff as a statue. My head tilts slightly in slow motion, my brows furrowing the more I move. My mouth goes agape the more that his words fully register.

I've been holding back a lot of things when it comes to Zeke. The way he runs the shop, the way he treats employees. His father would be ashamed of him for turning everything he built upside down.

But that isn't the issue right now.

No, right now… my issue is only *him*.

"You've got to be fucking kidding me," I say.

"Excuse me?" he responds, taking a—attempted—threatening step forward.

"You heard me, Zeke. First, you raise my chair fee. And even if mine is lower than the rest, which is bullshit for the other hard workers in here, you're taking more than you need. Things never would have been this way with your father.

"Second, you start taking away my scheduled workdays, and for no other reason than "you're not needed today." It's wrong and unprofessional. Tattooing is not only my passion, but it's my freaking livelihood too."

"Like you don't have a second job," he huffs.

"Whatever I do outside of this parlor is none of your business, and it shouldn't matter. I don't have to explain anything to you. You're out of line."

Zeke rolls his eyes, and that only rages me further.

"The icing on the cake was you stealing my artwork today. I checked it out online because you're stupid enough to post all of your shit, and the only addition you made was a fucking minuscule star. That's it. What the hell is your problem?"

Zeke tousles his fingers through his greasy black hair, appearing as if he didn't pay attention to anything I just said. "Are you on the rag or something?"

"The hell did you just ask me?"

"You must be on the rag because you're not normally like this. All dramatic and whiney and shit. You're quiet and meek."

"Not anymore," I grit.

"Well, as your boss, you're gonna take some time off and chill out because of this attitude," he says, pointing his finger up and down my body. "It's not cutting it."

"You can't just tell me what to do. I have clients," I tell him, my voice far beyond the normal level.

"Consider them mine until you've calmed down some. Acting out isn't a good look on you."

"God, you're such a dick." I grab my things and storm toward the front door, stopping with my hand on the handle. "Your father would be so ashamed of what you've turned his legacy into," I say deeply, my words pointed directly at him.

"Don't talk about my dad. And you used to love my dick," he yells as I push open the door.

"I was faking it," I quip, letting the so-called 'dramatics' end when the door slams, cutting off further conversation.

Let the unsatisfying little dick man stew on *that*.

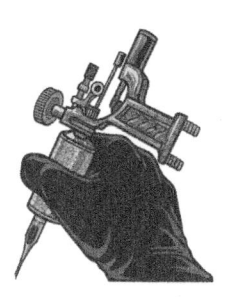

I try to let the frustration go as I drive home, blasting music to try and drown out all the thoughts in my head, but it doesn't work.

I'm too consumed with what happened at work. While I haven't been afraid to speak my mind in the past, that changed once my anxiety and depression got worse. I started overthinking every outcome, worried that I'd upset someone past the point of return, and someone would harm me because of it.

They're not rational thoughts—very few of them are regarding anxiety—but they're not like a light switch; you can't turn them off.

And while I'm so damn proud of myself for standing up to Zeke just now, the reality of the potential repercussions is crashing down on me.

If I lose this job, how will I pay my bills? How will I have any emergency cash in case something goes wrong? Like the crappy car I have that breaks down on me all too often.

There's no way in hell I can ask anyone for help if my finances take a hit. I've never really had anyone to turn to, and even though I do have that in Blake and Miles, I'd never ask them for something monetary.

Because then I'd owe them, and owing people eats away at

my insides until the only thing left is the ulcer I've worried myself to death with.

The thoughts in my head are in full chatter mode as I pull up to the house, wishing that Miles was home to vent to but realizing he's not when I see that his truck isn't here.

The world feels like it's crashing down with each step I take toward the house. My head is spinning, my vision is blurred, and air comes out of me in short puffs as I try to catch my breath.

The anxiety that was mostly at bay has now fully surfaced, and I fall against the wall in the foyer as thoughts flood my mind.

Why would Zeke really steal my art? Is my art so generic and unoriginal that anyone can pull it off? Why was the client so apt to change artists? Should art be something I'm passionate about if no one cares that it's me who created it?

Chief's bark breaks through the muffled noise, and I stumble through to the back of the house, opening the door for him to run out. Instead of following him, I stand by the pool, wishing that fresh air will calm me down.

It's not ready yet because it hasn't been shocked, but Miles had it refilled with new water a week or so ago. Nothing seems to have grown in there yet, and a thought occurs to me—the potential algae-infested waters be damned.

What would it feel like to be in there? Submerged under the water with nothing to worry about but holding your breath. No thoughts, no noise, no distractions. Just you and the density of the water, no ability to feel the world's weight on your shoulders as the liquid relieves the pressure.

The wind gently moves the water, the ripples that float through calling to me like a siren. Begging me to jump into a place that's cut off from the outside world.

As the thoughts run through my head, beating down at my sanity, my self-confidence, and my self-accomplishment, I make the risky decision to cut it all out of my thoughts, handing it over to a being much more powerful than me.

I give into the siren calls of the water, to the temptation, and I jump in, letting the coolness of the liquid infiltrate my entire body to calm the simmering rage that travels through my veins.

Immediately succumbing to the silent waters, I hand over every component of my being as I let the water take control.

If only to calm my mind for just a minute.

And when my ass hits the bottom of the pool, I close my eyes, shutting out the noise and the demeaning voices I've lived with for far too long. Relishing in the surrender.

And for however long I'm down here, I feel so damn free.

That is, until I feel the disruption of the surrounding water, and arms wrap themselves around me, yanking me to the surface.

Away from my freedom.

CHAPTER 31
MILES

When I pull up at the house from practice, I find that Riley has beat me home, and selfishly, I wanted to get here first. I had plans to order takeout and have the TV ready to watch so we could wrap up with each other and talk about our day.

It's my favorite part of the day.

Coming home to her. And waking up beside her.

Anything that involves her, honestly.

Walking into the house, I drop my duffel bag in the foyer and listen to see where Riley is. I don't hear the TV playing, and Chief hasn't attacked me by the door yet, so I take off through the house.

Barking near the back door has my body pulling in that direction. Looking outside, I see Chief by the pool but not Riley. I pull my phone out to text her to find out where she is as I walk over to him, and it's when I close in that I see a dark shadow in the pool.

Riley.

I don't think. I don't process. I just act.

My phone goes flying as I take a running jump into the water, the icy temperature of the water causing my body to lock up on impact.

When I'm within reach, I wrap my arms around Riley and tug her body to the surface. She doesn't fight me until we hit the surface, and I immediately spin her around in my arms.

Riley starts coughing, and my hands go for the hair matted to her face, pushing it away as she gathers her bearings.

I can't even comprehend what the hell is going on right now. All I know is that my heart is rattling uncontrollably in my chest, and my pulse is bounding so intensely that I'm afraid a vein will rupture. Adrenaline is the only thing keeping me standing at the moment.

"Are you okay?" I ask frantically. "Are you hurt?"

"Not physically," she says, and when her eyes finally open, what I find in them hits me like a knife to the chest.

There's so much pain in her eyes that I feel it myself. It's dulling the color of her eyes to a shade of blue I've never seen before.

The longer she looks at me, the more tears well in her eyes. They build until they finally spill over, and that's when Riley cracks.

She collapses into my arms, and I sweep my arms under her legs and pull her to my chest. Now that we're above the water, we're both trembling, and our skin is ice cold.

I carry Riley out of the pool and straight up to the bedroom, going even further to the ensuite. I won't let her down until the warm bath water has run, and I need to strip her of the wet clothes.

Once she's naked and settled in the water, I do the same and slide in behind her. Her head collapses against my chest, and she wraps my arms across her, hugging them tightly.

Her trembles go on for a few minutes, and when she quits, I quickly wash over us both and drain the water.

I wrap Riley as tight as I can into a towel and take her to the bed, her body feeling heavy as she lies limp in my arms.

After gently laying her on the bed, I find a pair of boxers and a shirt to dress her in. She stays eerily still until I get her dressed, and when I do, she robotically crawls under the covers, like she's checking off a list—bath, new clothes, get under covers.

I do the same and crawl behind her, pulling her to my body. She sinks against me, and we stay there until Riley is no longer shaking.

"Do you want to talk about why I found you in the pool?" I whisper.

"Everything got to be too much, and I needed it all to just… stop." Her tone is so dejected that my senses jump to alert.

"Tell me what happened," I demand gently, praying she doesn't shut down this time—especially since we've come so far.

"My boss is a dick," she says with a sigh.

"The Billie Joe Armstrong wannabe?"

Her defeated nature breaks for a moment as she laughs. "I've never heard that one, but oh my god, is it accurate.

"He's been an ass at work since I broke it off with him. Taking away scheduled workdays, taking more money from my commissions, and today…" she says, shaking her head.

"What about today?" I ask, mild panic in my tone.

I swear if that fucker touched her…

Riley turns to face me, placing both hands under her head as she connects her eyes with mine. They're a tad lighter, but they're still not the level of beautiful blue that I'm used to.

"I had this client on the schedule, and it got rescheduled for before I went in, and he stole my artwork to do the piece for her. He said he made changes, but he didn't. Not really. We had a confrontation before I left, and it didn't… it's hard to explain."

"Try…" I plead. "For me."

"I stood up for myself. Told him that it was unprofessional and inappropriate, and unethical. He brushed it off, then blamed it on my not being there. The asshole is in charge of my schedule mostly, and yet he blames me for not being there."

"What a dick."

"Extremely," she agrees. "But I spoke up and told him how it felt. He got extra dickish, and I said some intense but well-called-for words right as I left."

"I'm proud of you for standing up for yourself and your work. So, what led to the dip in potentially infested waters?"

A smile cracks the straight line of her lips. "You know how my finances are. You know my struggle and that I need every cent I get paid between my two jobs.

"It started with the worry that I may lose my job. That his huge ego would take a hit, and he'd fire me out of spite. That shifted into the worry that if I lost half my income, how would I be able to pay for things I need."

I want so badly to tell her that I'll cover anything she needs, but she's too independent for that. She'd take it as pity, and that's a fast way to anger her.

"It only got worse from there. Drawing has been a part of me since the minute I picked up my first pencil. It's been my escape, my safe space, and maybe even my lifesaver. And the way that he just took it... it made me feel like my art wasn't worth it. That it wasn't good enough, and anyone could assume it as their own because it's unoriginal."

"I've seen your art, and I can guarantee that's not true. Your creative mind is only yours; no one can recreate it, no matter how hard they try. You're not unoriginal. You're extraordinary."

"Thank you," she says, acting sheepishly. "But in that moment, the voices were too much. The worry, the fear, the anxiety, the self-doubt... I needed to drown it out, and that's how I found myself in the pool."

"You really scared me, you know. I thought..." I close my eyes, pained at the thought of speaking the words aloud. "I thought that you were trying to hurt yourself," I admit, letting the fear and vulnerability shine through my voice.

"Oh baby, no. I know that I have struggles, but it's never been to the point of self-harm. I promise."

Riley raises her arm, letting her hand rest gently against my cheek. "I'm sorry that I scared you. I didn't mean to do that."

"This isn't about me," I say, turning the conversation back around. This moment is about her weakness, and I won't be the selfish asshole that makes it about his own worry. "I just want you to be okay," I add, my voice lower than before.

"I will be," she says with certainty, but I'm not sure either of us believes the words fully. "I've been thinking about speaking to my doctor again."

"How long has it been?"

"Too long," she responds. "But that's on me. Out-of-pocket costs are… hefty, especially when your insurance isn't the best. I've been putting it off, and if I want to manage this better—since these meds aren't doing enough—then I need to go see her again."

"That's really brave of you. It takes courage to be vulnerable the way you have, the way you're going to be."

"I know," she says, briefly closing her eyes. "But I want to be better. I don't want to live with this burden to its extent for my entire life. I want to find ways to cope because I don't want to drag myself, or you, down a dark hole."

"You don't worry about me." My thumb brushes over her bottom lip, tugging it down slightly. "I'll be okay.'"

"I know you will." Riley smiles slightly, nuzzling further into me but keeping our eyes connected.

"Do you want me to go with you to the doctor when you go?" I offer. I want to support her in every way that I can, but I don't want to suffocate her with it either.

"No, the playoffs are starting in a couple of weeks, and it can take forever to get an appointment. You don't have to."

"But I want to, if you want me."

"You'd really make time for it?" she asks, and I hate the doubt that settles there. She worries that she won't be chosen when I'd choose her every day, over and over again.

"Do you not know the lengths I'd go to support you?" Her eyes peer into mine, an inscrutable look behind those alluring blue eyes. "Riley, I don't have to make time for you when you're the priority in my life. When you need me, I'll be there. Because your health matters more. *You* matter more," I say directly with an earnest tone.

"Thank you. But I think I need to do this part on my own. Is that okay?"

"More than okay," I tell her. "I'm really proud of you for being brave. For doing what you need to do for your health."

"Thank you," she smiles, and this one is genuine.

"About your art," I begin.

"What about it?" she asks.

"I want you to tattoo me. Reclaim your creative freedom and uniqueness. I'll be your canvas any day if it means that I can show you how amazing your art is."

She rises up quickly, hovering over me. Her damp hair tickles the exposed skin of my chest.

"You'd really let me tattoo you?" she asks, excitement in her voice and radiant eyes.

"Haven't I told you once before that I want you to mark me?" I give her a coy wink, and she begins laughing.

"You're such a man," Riley giggles, then she's moving from the bed.

"What are you doing?" I ask.

"Going to start drawing your tattoo."

"Wait, you're doing it now?"

"Absolutely. I have all I need here." I hear her walk across the hall into her room. "Any hard no's for what I'm drawing?"

"Surprise me."

"Okay. One giant green dinosaur dick coming right up!" she yells, and the resounding laugh that follows warms my entire body after having felt cold for so long.

Riley disappeared for an entire hour, even taking it as far as locking the door to her bedroom where she assured me she was "working her magic."

When she finally came downstairs, she was in total focus mode. She stealthily preps her area to make sure everything is as it should be.

Once we're finally in the living room and ready to begin, Riley places everything within reaching distance.

"Okay, strip your shirt and sit on the couch," she instructs, snapping her glove with added dramatics.

"Someone is enjoying this," I smile, and I'm met by one of hers. "If you wanted me naked, baby, you could have just said so." I do as she asks, shedding my shirt.

"Later," she says with promise. "Do you want to see it first?"

"Keep it a surprise. I won't look during, but I want to watch you soar. I trust whatever you designed."

"Speak now or forever hold your peace," she taunts, gloving her other hand.

"As long as it isn't a dinosaur dick."

"Oh no, baby. You said to keep it a surprise. I can neither confirm nor deny whether I'm slapping a big dick permanently onto your skin."

"You amuse me," I deadpan.

Riley slides her things close by and straddles my legs. When she drops her weight on me, I feel the heat of her pressing against my cock, and it jumps to attention.

She starts by wiping down my peck area and then shaves it. She wipes it down for a final time and then applies the stencil.

The gun buzz begins, and Riley gives me a scolding look. "Once this touches your skin, you won't be able to move. So, get your situation under control," she teases, eyes glancing down at the space between us to my crotch.

"I'll be on my best behavior. Scout's honor."

"You're not even a scout." Riley rolls her eyes, and a laugh escapes us both just before the familiar buzz touches my skin, and she gets to work.

I've gone to artists who have a heavy hand when it comes to tattooing, but not Riley. You'd never know she was on you if you didn't feel the needles penetrating your skin.

Riley moves swiftly and gently across my skin, concentrating fiercely as she works the ink into my skin. It's cute as hell too because in her intense focus, she sticks the tip of her tongue out of her mouth.

As promised, I don't look down at what she's doing. I know that whatever it is will be phenomenal, and I needed her to see that at this moment. A moment where she doubts her abilities.

She's the most talented person I've ever met.

I don't see how she doesn't see it, though. As I'm sitting here watching her mark my skin, I see the light in her eyes. A light that shines brighter than any I've seen in her before—one full of happiness, creativity, and true, unwavering passion.

It takes her nearly three hours to finish, stopping every thirty minutes for us both to stretch. When she finishes, she wipes down my skin and gets closer to me, if that's even possible, to inspect her handiwork.

She goes back to a few spots and works on shading and linework, and when she finally approves of what she sees, she wipes my skin again and applies a salve-like protectant.

"Are you ready to see the final product?"

I nod, and Riley and I walk to the guest bathroom just off the kitchen to find a mirror. I keep my eyes closed upon walking in, and when she turns my body correctly, she says, "open."

When I open my eyes and look at my chest, any words I thought I would say go right out the window. I was planning to tell her that it's beautiful, and that no one else could recreate her vision. Not because I thought she couldn't but because I knew she would.

All those words fly out the window because what she drew and created for me transcends more than I ever could have imagined.

Dark black ink lines my chest, giving the illusion that my skin is ripped to shreds. But underneath those shreds, right above my heart, lies a basketball.

Not just any basketball, though. The lines that make up the ball have words intertwined in them. *Legacy. Honor. Worship. Ambition. Dedication. Family.*

But in the midst of them, all lies one word bigger than the others, holding the spotlight in the dead center.

Passion.

Little lines that look like arteries drip bits of blood from them, making the entire image more life-like. It's... it's goddamn stunning.

"I'm not sure if your silence is a good or bad thing," Riley says nervously, bringing me out of my frozen state.

"I'm not sure I've ever loved anything more," I say with absolute wonder in my voice.

Riley's face is stunned, her eyes wide and her smile breathtaking.

"You really love it?" she asks.

"I do. You took the sport I love most and combined it with everything that I am and made it look like this badass, under-the-skin, a three-dimensional piece that makes you lose your breath."

Her smile says everything, and I need her to know that while this tattoo is me, this tattoo is also *her*.

Her dream. Her passion. Her life.

I hope she sees that now.

"Come on. I've got one thing left to do."

Riley pulls me back to the living room, directing me to sit back on the couch. She pulls out the Saniderm patch—like a second skin—and places it gently over the area, all while instructing me of proper care.

"Can you see now that no one can ever recreate the magic you make? Riley, this is stunning. The work you do is unmatched. Do you want to know why?"

She stares at me with curiosity, waiting for my answer.

"It's because you're passionate about what you do. Tattooing, art, drawing... is to you what basketball is to me. It's what we know. It's who we are. And no guy that wears more eyeliner than you should ever be able to convince you otherwise."

Tears well in her eyes, but an undeniable sense of calm also settles in her.

"I know that now. I let my insecurities sweep me up in the moment and control me. But I'll try to be better about reminding myself of why I do it."

"Which is?"

"I love creating art that means something to people. Art that tells a story, that shares a memory, that honors something or someone they love. And the look on their face when they see the final product..." Riley pauses like she's reminiscing on the feeling. "It's like an electric shock that fills your entire body with pride, pleasure, and self-accomplishment. It's my favorite part, actually. Seeing how much they adore it."

"Sounds like how I feel when I win a game." Reaching my hand up, I grab Riley's chin and pull her face to mine, pressing our lips together in a slow, sensual kiss that sends tingles all the way down my spine.

"But on those days where your power of will is low, and those thoughts wiggle their way in, I'll be here to remind you just how amazing you are and how lucky I am to call you mine."

"I like the sound of that," she says, pressing her lips to mine again. Her kisses are tender and sweet, each one showing more appreciation than the last.

When she pulls back, her smile hits me square in the chest, like a direct injection of serotonin into my system.

Gone is the girl I found in the pool mere hours ago. The version of Riley with me now believes in herself and her work and is proud of herself for what she's accomplished.

I like this version of her.

Riley settles her head on my chest, tangled locks resting against my sensitive skin.

"Can I ask you something?" I say, my fingers running through her blond hair, pulling gentle knots out as I go from her hair drying wet.

"Of course," she whispers against me, her skin warming me like a furnace. I'd be happy to burn if it was her heat that I was engulfed in.

"What's your biggest dream?"

"My biggest dream?" she echoes.

"Yes. Of all the things in the world, what's the one thing you want most for yourself?"

Riley is silent for so long that I worry she won't answer me, but then she starts to trace the flesh around the newly covered tattoo.

"I want to own my own tattoo parlor one day. A place where I can create the art I want that's not at the mercy of someone else. A place where people can feel at home at. Somewhere that isn't toxic, like the place I am now. Woman-owned, employed by only women. We're automatically looked down upon because we were born with a vagina and not a dick, and I want to highlight the talented women of New Orleans. Overall, I just want a place to do what I love that's totally mine."

"And I have all the faith in that world that you'll have everything you've ever dreamed of, even if it takes a while to accomplish it."

"Thank you for believing in me," she says, resting her forehead against mine.

"I've always believed in every version of you, Riley. Thank you for allowing me to be in the position to believe in you." I pull her to me, wrapping my arms around her back and holding her tightly. "I promise you won't regret it."

CHAPTER 32
RILEY

My nerves have my body in a jittery mess as I make the trek to the doctor's office. I'm proud of myself for doing it, and for taking the necessary steps to try and get better. I just wish it wasn't so hard, you know?

Living.

Living with an illness like mine.

My stomach tumbles the entire car ride, causing waves of nausea to flow through me. I wish it weren't this way, but what if there's nothing she can do to help?

What if there's no way I can get better?

The thought of that is harder to handle than being diagnosed in the first place.

When I pull into the parking lot, my hands tremble as I turn off the ignition. Today can either start me on the uphill climb of life, or I can be stuck on the same damn path that I've been on for far too long.

Checking in physically hurts because while I have the money to cover my copay, I know the out-of-pocket costs will take a huge chunk out of my savings.

Labs, physical, and don't even get me started on the price of medications.

It's ridiculous.

As I sit in the waiting room, listening for my name to be called, I find myself browsing the walls, consumed by the multitude of pamphlets staring back at me.

Words in bold heading—diabetes, hypertension, heart disease, headaches, cancer—stand out, and while they're all serious diseases, I don't see one single pamphlet relating to mental health.

It's disheartening.

Looking around the waiting room, I note how each person here has someone with them. A part of me is sad but also equally courageous.

Miles wanted to be here today, but this is something I needed to do by myself, for myself. It's why I purposefully scheduled it on a day that I knew he'd be busy. And while I appreciate his support more than he will ever understand, just knowing how much he cares makes me feel like he's here with me.

When the nurse calls my name, she takes me back to get my weight—a number no one likes to look at—and vitals before placing me in a room. She asks a few questions about why I'm here and after verifying some information, informs me that the doctor will be in shortly.

I've never experienced quiet like when I'm in the doctor's office. It's the type of quiet that makes everything else louder—that drives you mad.

It lets those voices back in, wondering what the hell will happen here. If I'll be helped at all. If I'll be able to turn my life around.

Ten minutes of that eerie silence pass by before there's a knock on my door, and then my doctor walks in.

"Ms. Davis, it's nice to see you again. How are you feeling today?"

Doctor Gentry is a kind woman in her late forties, with sandy brown hair that waves to her shoulders and kind blue eyes that hold so much sympathy.

"I've been better, but today is okay."

"It's been a while since I've seen you," she says, gently but admonished.

"I know. I'm sorry. Things have been difficult lately, and prioritizing myself hasn't been at the top of the list. I want to do better."

"I'm really glad to hear that," she says, offering a supportive hand by placing it gently on my hand. "Tell me what's been on your mind lately."

I spend as long as I need recapping Dr. Gentry on the last year of my life. Being kicked out, financial struggles, the deep depressive episodes I've had, and even meeting Miles. I vent as much as I can so that she knows everything that's happened.

"I'm going to assume by what you've told me that your medication is no longer helping."

"You'd assume correctly."

"Can you tell me more about that? I'd like to know how your symptoms are now."

"Um…" I pick around at my fingers, willing myself to be vulnerable for the sake of my health. There's a part of this disease that no one talks about. No matter what you say, or how exposed you make yourself, people won't believe just how badly you're affected by this monster in your head.

I take a deep breath and make eye contact with Dr. Gentry.

"My life has drastically changed since I last saw you. For a while, I wasn't sure I'd make it out of rock bottom. But things changed, and I could see through it—mostly. But lately, even though I'm in a more positive environment, I'm more easily triggered. Something bad happens at work, or worry overwhelms me, and I want to shut down."

"Do you?" I look at her. "Shut down, that is."

"Sometimes. The other day, I jumped into the pool because the voices in my head were so loud. It felt like the only way I could quiet them. My boyfriend came in and found me, pulled me out of the water. I really scared him."

"Your boyfriend?" she questions.

"One of those life changes I mentioned."

"And how did you scare him?"

"He thought I wanted to harm myself," I answer regretfully. I never wanted to scare him like that.

"And did you?" she asks with the utmost concern.

"Not at all. It's never been that severe."

"I'm glad to hear that," Dr. Gentry says warmly. "This illness can be very crippling, but I'm glad you have someone to support you. It seems small, but it can make a world of difference."

"I can tell that it has already," I admit honestly. I haven't relied on him to change me but used his belief in me to drive me to strive for something better for myself.

Dr. Gentry looks over her notes for a few brief moments before placing them away and focusing her attention solely on me.

"Okay, I have a few options. We can try increasing the dosage of your medication, but we've done that once before. There's also the option of trying you on a different medication. One that's stronger than your current. We can also try therapies as well."

"Respectfully, I've tried therapies before. Groups, one-on-one sessions, cognitive-behavioral therapy. None have been effective, so I'd be willing to try the new medication."

She spends a few minutes explaining the medication to me and its possible side effects along with some other potentially harmful things to look out for.

"Since we've reviewed the necessary information, I'll put the order in at your pharmacy. If you don't see a difference within a month, please reach out. I'm really glad that you decided to come in. Do you have any other questions for me before you leave today?"

There's only one, and it's about the cost of the medication. After explaining that there should only be a small cost for the new medicine, she sent me to checkout. It's a relief to finally sit down in my car.

I want to say that this visit fixed everything, but I can't. I'm not sure what will happen now that I'll be starting a new medication, but I'm hoping that new meds and my recent change in mindset will team up and help me deal with this better.

Because this illness can be daunting, and the last thing I want is to wear Miles down with it. I'm so afraid that he'll wake up one day and realize that I'm too much to handle, like many of my foster families, and I don't want that burden on him.

I know he supports me. He's made that crystal clear. But expressing that support and living through it are totally different things.

I'm most afraid that this happiness I feel around him—this all-consuming, total obsession and burning desire I have—will only be fleeting, and I'll lose him before we ever have a chance to love each other out in the open—

Oh my god.

Oh my god, oh my god, oh my god...

Do I love Miles? Is that what this is?

I mean, I've never known the true meaning of love. I've never experienced it. The only people I've seen that are truly in love are Blake and Kyler, and that wasn't an easy journey for either of them.

But if love is the way he makes me feel... like my entire body could explode into thousands of love-filled fireworks whenever he looks at me. Or he's the first person I want to speak to in the morning and the last one I want to speak to at night.

How he's the first person to ever make me want to be better —not for anyone else but for myself.

How he's made a more positive impact on my life in the last seven months of living with him than anyone else in the entire twenty-eight years I've been alive.

Or how the thought of us ever being separated again, our

tethered hearts shredding into halves, makes me sick to my damn stomach...

So, if that's love... then yeah.

I'm in love with Miles.

Every damaged but evolving part of me.

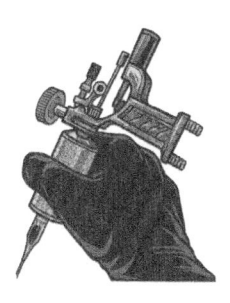

The drive home doesn't feel nearly as long as the drive there. Probably because my spirits are infinitely higher than when I first walked in.

I'm beginning a new regimen for my anxiety and depression, and I finally admitted to myself that I love Miles. But although I've admitted it to myself, I'm not ready to admit it to him.

I don't have a rational explanation for why, but there's just a feeling I have deep in the pit of my stomach that says now is not the right time.

Reaching out to turn the dial-up, the radio plays a popular song that I sing along to, but that doesn't last long as I catch the car in front of me swerving over the middle line. My foot automatically hits the brakes, wondering what the hell is going on when I see the reason why.

I push the brake all the way to the floor, thanking the Gods above that no one is behind me. Because sitting in the middle of the road are two small kittens, terrified for their life.

Parking off the road's edge and throwing my blinkers on, I step out of the car and take cautious steps toward the kittens.

"It's okay, babies," I coo to them, one solid black and the other solid yellow. "You're gonna be okay. I've got you."

The black one hisses when I get closer but doesn't try to move. Putting my hand down, I give them a second to check me out. When no more hissing occurs, I pick both babies up from the road, and I've just returned to my car when a vehicle comes speeding past.

Grabbing a sweater from the backseat, I pile it beside me and wrap the babies in it. They immediately find each other's warmth, cuddling up and looking at me with scared but hopeful eyes.

Something about this moment feels destined. I was in a situation remarkably similar to theirs. Alone, scared, unbeknownst to what was next.

I've always wanted animals of my own. I love them so much. I volunteered at a shelter during college the one day a week I had free, and I've practically claimed Chief as half mine.

But these kittens… these sweet, innocent kittens are so much like me, and I want to do for them what was never done for me.

I want to give them a home. Somewhere where they can be happy, nurtured, and loved. And I know I can provide that place for them.

But there's still one thing left to do…

I've got to convince Miles that he should let me keep these babies.

Maybe I should butter him up first. That may give me an advantage when I spring it on him.

I could cook for him again, but I'm positive he could never look at spaghetti again and be okay, even though he'd never say it. I may have cooked too much of it over the last month or so.

I know he likes steak. If I watch enough videos, I'm sure I could pull it off along with some sides.

I can pick up the medication later. I'm more determined to go home and do this. It brings me more happiness than anything else at the moment.

I mean… what could go wrong?

CHAPTER 33
MILES

Eager to get home to Riley, I defy a few driving laws and make it home ten minutes earlier than I normally would.

I wanted so badly to be with her today at her appointment, but I feel she purposefully scheduled it on a day when I couldn't be there.

I hate that I couldn't be present for her, but I'm so damn proud of her for doing it on her own and not because anyone else made her feel like she needed to.

Change can never truly happen for yourself until you're the one that implements it instead of obligation doing so.

Excited that Riley is already home, I hurry inside the house and drop my things in the foyer. But as I hang up my keys, an unfamiliar, slightly off smell invades my senses. An instinct has me following the smell.

When I hit the archway to the kitchen, I notice the smell is harsher in there. It smells like burnt... something. I can't place what it is, though.

Riley moves frantically around the kitchen, utensils in hand, something in her hair, and wet spots on her hoodie from who knows what.

The hoodie in question—it's blue, and it's mine. Upon

coming home and seeing her wearing my clothes, a feral feeling moves through me, and my dick jumps to attention with the blood coursing straight to my groin.

A filthy thought crosses my mind.

"What's going on here?" I speak up, and Riley jumps.

"You need to stop scaring me," she scolds, hand pressed against her chest. "I don't have time to pass out right now because you scared me to death."

She goes back to stirring something on the stove, but the amount of smoke from the pan is alarming enough that I decide to step in.

"Okay. That's it." Stepping over, I turn off the eye to the stove and move the pan with the unknown substance to the sink. "What did you think you were doing?"

"I was trying to cook for you," she states.

"And what were you trying to cook?"

"Steak, peppers, and then I have potatoes in the—Fuck!"

Riley runs to the oven and opens it, only for even more smoke to flood the kitchen.

Yeah, no. I'm calling this.

"That's it. Drop all utensils and step away from the kitchen appliances," I say sternly, although most of me just wants to laugh.

Riley backs away like she's been caught, throwing her hands in there. "You don't have to convince me."

Once I've checked to make sure all appliances are off and all food is thrown away, I join Riley at the island and grab her hands, rubbing my thumbs gently over the back of them.

"Are you okay?"

"Cooking sucks. I'm overwhelmed."

"How about this..." I move Riley's hands to her chest, splaying her palms flat against the material. "Take a deep breath in, then exhale. Feel your chest expand with each breath. Do it three times."

Riley does as I ask, and I breathe with her so she isn't alone. When she finishes, her body visibly relaxes.

"Feeling better?" I ask.

"Yeah, I do."

"Good. Now tell me why you were trying to cook for me."

"You mean trying and failing," she half-laughs. "You've done so much for me since I moved in, and I can't even fathom repaying you. I just wanted to do something nice, and I was banking on my new skills, which I've realized tonight are the Walmart version of Gordon Ramsay—" We both laugh. "It was small, but it was something I could do. Or so I thought."

"It's okay, baby. I appreciate the effort. I can order takeout for us both," I say with a gentle smile.

"I know, it's just… I wanted to do this. So badly."

"I know you did. I saw how hard you were trying. But I hope you know you don't have to do anything for me. I do things for you because I care about you so much."

"I'm really happy to hear you say that," she says, and a knowing smile graces her. But whatever she knows, whatever she's thinking, I don't know what it is.

"I'll remember to say it more often then."

"I'm looking forward to it," she says. "So, if you're ordering food, what are we having?"

The way she looks right now, so innocently beautiful and ethereal, and the fact that she wanted to conquer another fear of hers to do something for me… it creates a surge of desire through me, and only she can help it.

That filthy thought from before re-enters my mind, and it's because of it that my response is so heated and cliché.

"We can have whatever you want, but I'm planning to eat you instead."

"Oh, really?" she asks, a flash of heat in her eyes.

"Of course, baby. You *are* one of my favorite meals, and you're already ready to eat."

"And you're so sure about that?" Riley taunts.

"So sure," I respond in a husky whisper. "Ass on the counter, baby. I'm about to find out."

Redness starts at Riley's chest and quickly spreads to her cheeks, but she does as I ask, lifting herself onto the counter and spreading her legs just enough that I can slide in between them.

Letting my hand trace that redness, I stop at her neck, gripping it with a firmness that forces her eyes to mine. I can feel her swallow under the tightness of my hand.

"You're fucking irresistible. Do you know that?"

"I do when you look at me," she responds, a shininess coating her pretty blue eyes.

The feeling I only get when I'm near her settles deep in my chest, flooding my body with intense warmth. That desire and infatuation drive my lips toward hers, claiming them in an intense kiss.

The minute she gives, my tongue slips past her lips, tangling with her own in a heated kiss full of teeth and tongue, wandering hands, and hair pulling.

My hand settles on her bare thigh, wondering underneath my hoodie that she's wearing. Goosebumps form along every inch. As I ghost over her stomach, it contracts, pulling away from me while the place she craves pressure the most seeks me out.

My palm finds the space between her braless breasts, and I push back enough to break our kiss.

"Come here," I instruct, wanting her in a different way than I'd originally planned.

Riley slides off the island, and after her feet hit the floor, I spin her around and push her stomach down to the countertop, pinning her there.

Her legs tremble as my hands run up the sides. I hook my thumbs in the band of her panties and gently pull them down her thighs. When I'm on my knees, I push the end of the hoodie over her ass, exposing her to me.

Her legs shake more as my thumbs near her pussy, and when

I spread her lips, baring her clit to me, she gasps. Leaning forward, I swipe my tongue over the wetness coating her, barely touching her. The moan that follows shoots a blast of heat straight to my dick.

"Mmm," I say, swiping my tongue again. "Best fucking meal ever."

Riley pushes back against my face, and I take that as the invitation that it is.

My lips find her clit, wrapping around it. Then I suck, and she presses her hips further into my face, searching for more.

I push my fingers into her entrance, feeling her pussy stretch around my fingers. Hooking them downward, I apply pressure to that little spot that makes women go cross-eyed, and Riley's knees buckle.

"Hold on, baby. I'm not finished," I tell her, my teeth nipping at her ass cheek before finding her again.

Riley's legs stiffen as she leans forward against the counter more, allowing it to support her better. Then I waste no time.

I lift her leg onto the counter, spreading her out further for me, and dive in. My tongue swirls around her clit, nipping and tugging and pulling until arousal drips down Riley's thighs.

I swipe her arousal up with my tongue as my thumb applies pressure to her clit, and the little whimpers that escape her have me driving my fingers inside her.

Standing up, I hover over her back and sweep her hair out of the way. My lips find her neck, nipping and kissing at the skin there, and Riley arches further into me.

"As much as I want to see you come on my fingers, I'd rather see you come on something else. Strip that hoodie for me, baby, but don't move this leg."

Riley stays balanced, and the hoodie hits the floor moments later. My clothes follow them, and I step back to Riley. Swiping my hand through her arousal, I coat my shaft with it and press against her entrance.

"Ready, baby?"

"That's a stupid question. Just fuck me already!" she demands in a huff.

In one swift motion, I bury myself to the hilt. Riley's hands grip the edge of the counter on the opposite side, her knuckles turning white when she does.

It never fails, though. I'm as close to Riley as I can possibly get, yet this obsessive, consuming feeling I have for her makes me want to get even closer.

"I need more from you, usdi danuwaanalihi. So much more."

My hand hooks around her knee, and I lift it to the counter to mimic the other, her body splayed in half before me. I continue thrusting, feeling myself go even further than before.

"Fuck! You feel so good," she praises with a moan. "You're so deep," Riley adds breathlessly.

My hips piston forward, burying myself inside her with all my strength. The carnal desire to feel her clenching around me, to see the way she takes me, has the animalistic side of me trailing my hand up her spine to her neck, wrapping those gorgeous blonde locks around my fist.

"Shit," she hisses, feeling the pull.

I direct her head to the side, falling over her again. Her body, slick with perspiration, slides against the countertop. My free hand grips her shoulder, holding her in place.

"Are you gonna come for me, baby?" My lips press against the pulse point on her neck, feeling the way it bounds against me. Her mouth hangs open, and I can see the heat of her breath casting a light fog on the countertop.

"Yes," she whines, chasing the feeling that's slowly building around her—the one I can feel as she contracts around me.

"That's what I like to hear." I brush a piece of hair behind her ear, then lean down to whisper. "Because I want to feel this sweet pussy drench my cock with cum, feel it drip off me."

Trailing kisses down her jaw, I free my hand and tilt her face to mine, capturing her lips with my own. Our tongues tangle together as I pick up the pace, and Riley's arm tries to wiggle between herself and the counter, but she comes up short.

"I've got you," I soothe.

Pulling out, I flip Riley over to where her ass is at the edge, and I slip back in. My thrusts are deep and intense as our skin slaps together, and Riley's back squeaks against the laminate.

My thumb finds her clit as I trace kisses up her body, stopping to take equal care of the metal-clad peaks before me. My lips wrap around her nipple, sucking and tugging until I feel her tighten around me.

"I'm close, baby. I need you to be too. I need you to come."

I switch to the other side, sucking and tugging harder as my thumb works deftly at her clit. That familiar feeling starts racing up my spine, and I increase my pace.

"Come on, baby. Get there," I encourage her.

My thrusts are getting sloppy, but I don't let up. I'm moving so fast that she seems dizzy, her head falling forward as she captures her bottom lip between her teeth.

Lifting her hips, changing the angle, I thrust mercilessly until her abdomen begins to contract, and her head falls back with an exhaled "Fuck."

"I'm coming. I'm coming," Riley chants, and the minute I feel her body explode around mine, I let myself go, releasing inside her.

Once we've both come down from our high, Riley wraps herself around me, hugging me tightly.

"Do you know how well you fuck?" she asks with a smile.

"Being reminded is nice," I respond with a coy grin. "So, you want to tell me why you were really cooking?"

"What?" she squeaks. "I've already told you. I wanted to do something nice for you."

"And I appreciate that, but you have no idea how to cook steak, and yet you were trying."

Her jaw drops, and she's rendered speechless.

A loud crash sounds from the other side of the house, and I

throw my boxers on. Instinct has me following the sound immediately.

By the time I'm in the living room, two small kittens come running straight toward me with Chief hot on their tails.

"What the—"

"Shit," Riley yells. She threw the hoodie back on at some point. The kittens stop at her feet, and Chief does as well, licking at their backs. She picks them both up, and they cuddle further into her.

"Hey, little babies," she coos to them, petting their heads and smiling.

"Why are there kittens in the house?" I ask, staring at the little black and yellow balls of fluff.

"Listen, before you get mad, I found them in the middle of the road on the way home from the doctor, and they nearly got hit by a truck. I saved them. They just want a place to call home and to be loved and cared for. That's what we all want, right?" she rambles.

"If you're gonna be mad, be mad at me. But look at them. I couldn't leave them there. I had to bring them home. I had to."

There's fear in her eyes, and that breaks my heart a bit. Was she worried I'd be mad? That I wouldn't let her keep them?

Not that I would care, but the minute I saw her smile at them, I was convinced. She'd have them. Hell, I'll fix a dedicated room if that's what she wants.

If you've got love to give, I say give it.

"What're their names?"

"Names?" she stammers. "I didn't want to give them any in case…"

"Nope. No 'in case.' They're new members of the family. They need names."

"We can keep them?" she beams, and her smile stretches further than I think I've ever seen it.

"Of course. I'm a Rainwater. We bring in all the strays."

I'm able to hold my smile until Riley starts laughing, and then I can't anymore.

"Touché," she says. "I'm not sure yet. I'll figure it out soon, and I'm open to suggestions. But I have to get ready for work." She puts the kittens down reluctantly and heads back to the kitchen, starting to clean up. I follow.

"Speaking of your doctor's appointment. How did that go?"

"Better than I expected. I'm gonna try some new meds to see if they'll help. I was supposed to pick them up today, but I found the kittens and came straight home."

"I can go pick them up for you if you'd like. And I can get some things for the kittens as well. Things they'll need," I offer.

"Really?" She lights up. "That would be amazing."

Riley walks over to her purse in the foyer, digging out her wallet.

"I can get your medicine."

"Yes, you can. But I'm not gonna let you. My illness, I'm paying. The doctor said the copay shouldn't be much."

She hands me a twenty, and I start plotting how I'll sneak this back into her wallet. I don't want her money. I just want her to be healthy. And if these meds do it, I'll buy a damn truckload if I can.

"Fine," I surrender. "But let me get the stuff for the kittens. They're about to be half mine anyway," I wink.

"Deal."

Riley turns to step away but then turns around and runs toward me, jumping my body and wrapping herself around me. My arms fall under her for support.

"What's this for?" I ask.

She pulls back and kisses me so damn hard I think I'll buckle, but I welcome it.

"I'm so thankful for you," she tells me. The amount of sincerity and contentment, and honesty in her eyes has the organ in my chest picking up speed, rattling around like a caged butterfly. "You're so much more than I could have ever dreamed of."

"The feeling is mutual, baby."

Once Riley is off to work, I do as I said and grab things for the kittens before picking up her meds. It turns out that the copay is more than she initially thought, but I'll never tell her. Even if I'm the one to get her meds every month.

The simple act has me going over every moment I've had with her, and it's because of that I find myself at the hardware store instead of going home.

Hoping like hell she likes what I have in mind.

CHAPTER 34
RILEY

Work passed by slow as freaking molasses tonight, and all I wanted was to get my shift over and head back home to Miles and my extremely cuddly new fur babies.

But some drunk asshole tried to assault my friend, Aurora, so none of us could leave until we'd all given a statement. After checking on her and assuring that she didn't need anything, I was able to leave.

If people could keep their damn hands to themselves, things would be a lot different in the world.

When I get in the car, I check my phone and see that Miles texted a while ago to let me know that he got my medication and way too many things for the kittens.

Seeing how he's turned his life around for me, how he's done anything to make me happy—even turning his home into a mini-rescue just to see me smile…

It heals a massive part of my inner child.

The part that just wanted someone to see what makes me happy and do that because they wanted to nothing more than to see me smile.

I shoot him a text to let him know that I'm on the way, but he doesn't reply.

I find out the reason when I get home.

When Chief doesn't immediately greet me at the door, I follow the TV's sound to the living room, where my soul is blasted with a ray of blazing sunshine.

Miles is splayed out on the couch, shirtless and in cotton shorts that sport the V underneath those stacked abs of his. And on that sculpted chest of his sits the unnamed kittens.

The yellow one is stretched across Miles' abdomen, his little paw and precious toe beans resting lightly over his mouth. The black one is curled around his neck like a necklace, his little pink tongue peeking out to ghost Miles' cheek.

I want to capture the moment. I want to look back at it and remember how content and elated and full of bliss I feel right now, watching Miles embrace the animals that I brought into this home without his knowledge.

Another reminder of how far he'll go to make me happy.

I take more pictures than I need, but I stumble with the phone when he groans.

"I hope you got your picture because my neck is cricked so bad, and I need to move." He smiles, his eyes still closed.

"How long have you been in that position?"

His eyes open, and he moves each of his hands to a kitten, stroking their fur slightly. They stretch beneath his touch, releasing a small whimper.

"Too long," he responds.

"You look sexy as hell right now," I admit. "There's something about a masculine man holding a tiny animal. And cuddling, too? Damn." I whistle.

"Now you know how I feel when you send me pictures of you and Chief while I'm on the road." He moves the babies gently, placing them on the couch as he sits up. They stretch and find each other, staying asleep. My heart does a flippy flip.

"Something about a feminine woman with a large dog," he adds, winking.

"I've missed you," I confess with a sigh. Miles stands, and I meet him, wrapping my arms around his middle.

"It's only been a few hours," he reminds me.

"I know. But when you feel the way I feel about you, even a minute feels like an eternity."

He squeezes me tighter, and his warm breath hits the top of my head, coasting down my entire body and wrapping us in our own little bubble.

"I have something to show you," he says after a few minutes of holding each other.

"Lead the way."

Miles takes me down the hallway off the living room, coming to one of the first rooms on the right. He opens the door, and my heart swells.

There's a room made up for the kittens. There are two little boxes, and two different towers that are smaller in size. Tunnels, stuffed mice, interactive toys, and feather teasers. It's the carnival for cats, essentially.

"This is amazing."

I can tell how much work went into this, and he did it in just a few short hours.

"I plan on adding more," he says. "I've got even taller cat towers coming, more toys I found online, and I saw this video online of people building planks on the walls for their cats to run around. I want to do that as well."

"I fall for you more every day," I admit, and he smiles. But as I look around the room, I note that something is missing. "Miles, where are their beds?"

"In my room, of course. You sleep there every night, and I know that you'll want them in there with you. But I fully plan on building one of those pet beds that attach to the actual bed so that they can sleep even more so with us."

I… have no words.

"Have you shown them?"

"Not yet. I wanted you to be with me."

"Let's go get them," I say excitedly, turning to head out of the room. But Miles's hand reaches out to grip my wrist, stopping me.

"I have something else I want to show you first."

Miles leads us back into the hall, moving further down to the last door on the left. He pulls a key from the pocket of his shorts and unlocks the door but doesn't open it.

"Can you close your eyes?" he asks, turning to me.

"Uh, okay. But if it's another cat room, I can manage."

"Nope." He glares at me, and when I finally give in to his demands, he guides me into the room.

Nothing jumps out of me at first. There's no distinct smell, and I can tell that the light is off without opening my eyes. There is a slight chill in the room, but I can't tell from what.

There's something eerily familiar about the feel of this room, and I can't quite place it. The brightness flickers before my eyes, alerting me to the fact that Miles turned on the light.

My body buzzes with electricity in anticipation, wondering what the hell is so important that he locked the door to keep others out.

Miles props his head on my shoulder, leaning in toward my ear. "Open your eyes," he whispers.

I don't know what I was expecting, but it definitely wasn't this.

Tears prick my eyes, and a lump forms in my throat before I can even begin to process the sight in front of me.

Black bookshelves line the wall in front of me, all my books now stacked on them. An upgrade considering they were stacked on my dresser upstairs.

The walls are painted solid black, with a crimson trim highlighting the runners and surrounding space. The only thing there is a signed poster of my favorite band hanging on the wall. But the sentiment of him remembering that small fact about me is enough to make the walls feel overflowing.

Against the far wall, right beside the glass swing doors that are open to the night air—explains the chill I felt—sits a desk. I walk over to it, running my fingers over the smooth wood. It's filled with sketch pads and journals, expensive drawing pencils, pens, sharpies, and watercolor supplies.

It looks like every art store in existence threw up here, but I've never felt so settled.

I follow the chill to the opening in the room. An easel is perched right in front of the swing doors, leading out to the small patio. It's total darkness outside, but I know just from standing here that we're facing the backside of the property, a perfect view of the pond and the greenhouse Miles has built there.

I have no green thumb. You'll never catch me in there.

There's still so much potential for this room, but the meaning behind it...

It's everything.

"Is this all for me?" I manage through croaky words.

"All for you."

"How? Why?" I can't get anything further out. I'm too stunned.

"After I ran the errands, I went to the hardware store and got what I needed, then found a craft store. I plan to fill it more, but this is what I could do on a whim."

Miles takes slow, deliberate steps toward me until he's leaning against the swing door frame. His hands find my hips, pulling me to stand between his legs.

"As for why? You deserve a space that's your own. A safe space. For me, that's the court. This room can be your version of that. A place you can come to and create, cry, scream, dream, and express. A place that makes you feel more at home than anything else," he says earnestly. So much so that the room spins.

"I can't explain how much this means to me, Miles."

"You never have to. A wise man once told me to look past the eyes, and all the answers I looked for would lie there. I can see it in your eyes, how you looked at the room, how you looked at me… I know exactly what it means. And it means everything to me to see you like this."

"Like what?" I peer up, connecting with the brutal honesty in his eyes.

"Like you're at home."

I've thought about it so many times, about what home is. I've never experienced it. Never had the luxury.

But right here, right now, in the arms of a man I once only dreamed of having…

I feel more at home than I ever have, and I know that I'll always have one here.

This is my home.

Our home.

Together.

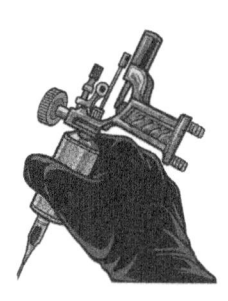

I feel like a brand-new person walking into work on my next scheduled day, even if working for Zeke is the last thing I want to be doing.

But until I can afford a place of my own, this is the paycheck I need.

After the last few days though, I feel like nothing can shatter the happiness I've begun to feel. The kind that's everlasting.

I've settled into my chair for the day when Zeke comes around the corner, his brows pulled tight and his angry green eyes on mine.

"What are you doing here?" he glowers.

"What does it look like?" I ask, my tone heavy with sarcasm. "I'm working."

"You can't be here today. You're not on the schedule."

"Yes, I am."

Zeke pulls out his phone, frantically pulling up the work schedule. His anger intensifies when he realizes that I *am* on there, and his hand tightens around his phone.

"Well, this is me sending you home."

"You can't just do that," I say, my voice rising higher.

"I can. That's what being the boss entails. Bossing people around. And I'm telling you to leave."

Zeke puffs his chest out, but it does nothing for him. I've been around intimidating people, and he falls so low on the list of people that I would consider to be it.

He's a Chihuahua trying to act like a Saint Bernard.

It's just sad.

"I'm not leaving."

"Yes, you are." Zeke reaches for my arm, but I step back.

"Don't you fucking think about it," I growl.

"Then get out!" he yells, gaining the attention of the other employees.

The bell rings on the front door, catching my attention. Billy, the guy I've been working on the horror sleeve with, strolls into the parlor, catching sight of me. My demeanor changes instantly.

"Billy," I beam. "I wasn't expecting you today. Did I mix up our appointments?"

"Uh…"

"He's here for me," Zeke answers.

"Why?" I ask, anticipating the answer I don't want to hear but feel in my gut is what's about to happen.

"I'm finishing his sleeve today. The one you started."

"Like hell you are!" I scream, not once stopping to think about my reaction or how it'll affect others. For once, I'm doing exactly what I want and standing up for myself without the potential repercussions.

"I am."

"What the hell did you say to him?"

"Only the truth. But you're not privy to that information anymore," he says in a cocky tone.

"Fuck you," I hiss. "Fuck you and this damn establishment."

Turning around, I immediately start grabbing my things. I'm not staying here.

"Come back when you've cooled down!" he practically screams.

"Not likely," I fire back.

Once I've grabbed everything of mine, I head toward the exit. But not before I stop in front of Billy. It may be petty, but I'm too pissed to care right now.

"I hope you know that my style and his don't mix well, so good luck with the jacked-up final product."

I leave, and I don't turn back.

It's time to focus on what's best for me, and that's achieving my own dreams.

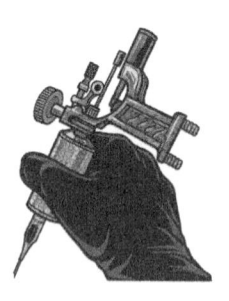

"That guy is a total dick. I've never liked him," Blake says, taking a sip of beer.

The minute I left, I called Blake. She came straight over, leaving the practice to the assistant coach. Even though the championship is a few weeks away, she still set aside her life to come be with me.

The guilt that follows rattles me as I think about the secret we're keeping from her.

"I should have never gotten involved with him. Or at least switched employers when his dad passed. He was a good man. I don't know what happened to his son."

"Probably dropped on his head too many times as a baby."

We both laugh, and a familiar feeling settles back inside me. The feeling that I had with Blake, my best friend, before Miles and I ever became a thing.

The feeling of true friendship, sisterhood; loyalty, and family. Each minute that goes by that I don't tell her feels like I'm betraying everything that she means to me.

"You okay?" she asks.

"Just thinking."

"What are you thinking about?"

About how I'm in love with your brother but still feel like I can't tell you and I don't know why.

"I'm thinking about the future. I want a place of my own. A business that's mine. But I'm nowhere near financially stable enough for that."

"If you wait until you're stable, you may never reach it. Sometimes you just have to take the leap, and know that if you fall, you have people who care about you to catch you and lift you back up," she says, placing a supportive hand on my arm.

"When did you get so wise?"

"I keep telling everyone I'm the wiser sibling and no one believes me," she laughs, but I know how deadly serious she is.

"Let me grab us some more beers," I offer.

I'm halfway to the kitchen when a clattering sound comes down the hallway. The next thing I know, Simba and Salem—previously unnamed kitties that I finally named—come running through the living room. Their paws are covered in paint, and an alarm sets off in me.

"Shit!" I scream, racing down the hallway to my art room.

Blake follows me in as I pick up the spilled paint that I stupidly left uncapped with the door open. It's my own fault.

"You have kittens?"

"Yeah, I found them a few days ago. I was waiting for them to come out and introduce themselves since they're skittish with people at first. Way to make an entrance," I laugh.

"You can say that again," she agrees.

As I'm cleaning up the paint, Blake walks around the room. Analyzing everything she comes across.

"What's all this?" she asks.

"All what?"

"This room. This looks like it was made just for you. Did you do it yourself?"

"Um." *Fuck.* "No, Miles built it for me."

The room is silent, nearly mute save for Blake's audible breathing. My hands begin to tremble.

"I'm sorry. Miles built this for you?" she questions.

"Yes." I'm finally able to look at her, but the emotions I see in her eyes are those of disbelief, worry, panic, and a tiny bit of anger.

"Why would my brother build you this entire room if you're not planning to stay here forever?" She takes a step forward, and the height difference between us—while always severe—feels belittling with me kneeling on the floor, pretending to wipe up paint.

"Is there something going on with you and Miles that I don't know about?" Another step. "Why would he do this?"

She looks so angry, and that anger has me crawling back into my shell.

It's infuriating. How you can feel like you make so much progress, then turn around and cower down like it never happened.

But I can't tell her. Not now. Not like this. Not without Miles.

So, I do the best I can.

"We've grown really close since I've been here. My finances haven't changed, and he wanted somewhere for me to feel safe and protected. He put this together for my well-being."

Blake walks over to the patio doors and opens them, and

steps out. She leans against the railing, staring out at the view. Finally, she turns around.

"He's never been like this before with anyone but his siblings," she voices out loud, and a gut-deep feeling has me believing that she's not talking directly to me. Her hands ghost over her face, settling into the dark black strands of hair at the root.

"I'm not sure I even know my brother anymore," she adds with a whisper.

A part of me is happy with that revelation because it's what we've been wanting for so long. For Blake to see how much Miles has changed, how we've changed together for the better.

But the other part of me, the part that cares so deeply for my best friend, is pained beyond belief when I look into her eyes and see the conflict there.

Without trying, I've created a rift in the relationship that Blake thought she had with Miles, that bond between twins, and I can't stand for that to go on too much longer.

I don't want that special tether they share to break.

It's then that I make a decision I've been too scared to make since the beginning.

It's time to tell Blake about me and Miles. Rather sooner than later. Because if not…

The damage may be irreparable.

CHAPTER 35
RILEY

I've been thinking about all the ways I could tell Blake about me and Miles. In private, so she knows how serious it is. In public, there's a crowd and she may not hit me as hard. None of it seems like the right way to do it.

I still have to talk to Miles though. Things have been so busy as the playoffs come to an end and the championship nears that I haven't been able to express my concerns to him about our near catch the other week.

And today, we'll have to continue to just be friends in public since there's a fundraiser to attend.

Kyler's organization, the one that helps children going through grief, has organized a charity event to raise funds for the facility. They're looking to afford a few new therapists, a new outside playground, and other necessities.

It's an amazing cause. They didn't have anything like this when I was growing up. I'm still angry with the way I was abandoned, I think I always will be. But when I was a kid, I was grieving the loss of the only parent I knew.

This place... it makes a difference.

I know it would have with me.

"What do I wear to a formal, non-formal event?" I yell across the hall, hoping Miles hears me from his room.

"Wear whatever you want. It's formal but not in the way of dress."

What I normally wear may scare a child.

Oh well.

I'm proud of who I am now. I'm not hiding that.

Thirty minutes later, we pull up to the facility. I'm thankful that the players were able to get private parking because there's no free space open within half a mile of the building.

There's the press, players, Warhawks staff, and referees.

When Miles first told me about this, I thought it was so cool.

The Warhawks players are participating in a charity game on the outside paved court, bringing it back to street-ball days. The cool thing about it is that each player is playing with a kid, giving them a chance to play in the big leagues.

For one day, they're not grieving kids.

They're just kids living their dreams and being how kids should be.

The minute we're inside, Miles is pulled away to do press with Kyler and Blake, so I decide to check out the place.

Vendors are set up all over the premises. Cotton candy, po boys, jambalaya, snow cones, and crawfish. Clothing boutiques and small businesses are set up as well, with a portion of the proceeds set to go to the facility.

There are also carnival-style games as well, where the kids play for free, and the adults pay. Anything that's won has been covered by the Warhawks organization.

It's an amazing thing Kyler has organized. Although all the Warhawks players have had a hand in it. While it's personal for Kyler, ever since the rest of the team learned about it, it immediately became their organization as well.

Grabbing a bag of popcorn, I find my way to the team and family area on the sideline of the court. The referees stand to the side speaking with reporters while the guys are warming up on the court with the kids.

It's fun as hell to watch the guys run around with these little kids on their shoulders, letting them make all the shots. Hearing them laugh, seeing the joy in their eyes as they use every bit of their strength to shoot the ball. It really brings everything full circle.

I was the kid grieving, thinking I'd never get out of the system or out of the hell hole I was living in inside myself.

But I stand here now, a woman in progress. With a prognosis that's better than I could have ever imagined when I was lonely and in the system.

I'm proof that you can turn your mindset around, and I think that's a beautiful thing to represent.

The game ends with a tie, making everyone the winner. The kids are over the moon, enjoying spending time with such esteemed people. Even after the game is done, the guys walk around holding the hands of little girls and boys as they pull them from game to game.

How anyone could come here today and not smile or donate beats me. It's the purest form of charity.

Needing to find a drink, I walk over to a lemonade stand and place an order. Out of the corner of my eye, I spy on one of the kids from the center sitting by herself, picking at the grass by her feet.

With her light brown hair, freckles, and oversized clothes, she reminds me of me when I was younger. She can't be more than eight or nine. Something pulls me to her, and I find myself ordering an extra lemonade and taking it over to her.

She lifts her head to look at me, and I offer her a smile. When she doesn't immediately run, I take that as it is and sit down beside her on the timber that splits the pavement from the grass.

"Hi." I wait for a reply, but one doesn't come. "My name is Riley. I brought lemonade for you. I thought you might need it in this heat. What's your name?"

She must see something trustworthy in me when she looks at me again because she reaches for the lemonade and finally speaks, "my name is Annie."

"It's nice to meet you, Annie. I love your name."

"I don't like it. The kids at school tease me and call me 'Orphan Annie.'"

"Screw the kids at school," I say, and she laughs. "I think it's cute. Reminds me of that Zac Brown Band song."

"You know country music?"

"I know a bit."

Annie eyes me up and down, analyzing all the exposed tattoos. "You don't look like you listen to country."

"Hey, don't judge a book by its cover," I say, nudging her elbow with a smile.

We fall silent again.

"So. Sweet Annie." She rolls her eyes at the nickname. "What brought you here?"

"My parents died. They had no family. This was my only option."

"I'm sorry about your parents." Annie nods. "You know, I was in your position once too. I grew up in foster care from the time I was five."

"Did you lose your parents too?"

"No. I never knew my father, and my mother didn't want me."

"I'm sorry that your mommy didn't want you."

Annie speaks so softly, and it's funny. My entire life, anytime I told someone my story, they'd simply say that if my mother couldn't see how special I was, she didn't deserve my time. But no one actually apologized to me.

"Thank you for that. But I think I'm better off because of it."

"You do?" I nod. "How did you make it through it?" Her voice is so sad when she says it, and my heart hurts that she even has to ask the question.

"You know... I found a really amazing friend. And whenever

I was sad, she cheered me up. Her family became mine. But that doesn't mean that I didn't have hard times because I did. I still do."

"How did you get through them?"

"I think the key is to focus on all the things that could be. All the happy and successful things you can achieve for yourself. If you can focus on that, it can navigate you through the hard times. Plus, it's those tough times that shape you into the person that you'll become."

I face Annie and stare at her with an expression full of sincerity and conviction. "I have a feeling that you're gonna be just fine, Sweet Annie."

Patting her on the shoulder, I stand and begin to walk away when her words cut through me.

"How do you know I'll be okay?" she asks.

I smile. "Because you remind me of me."

"And you're okay?" she adds.

Looking around, I find Miles and Blake in the crowd. Miles is playing hoops with a kid, and Blake is purposefully messing him up so the little boy can win. I know how lucky I am to have both of them.

I turn back to Annie. "Yeah. I'm okay."

And for the first time in my life, I say that with all the confidence and truth in the world.

"It was nice to meet you, Sweet Annie."

"It was nice to meet you too, Miss Riley."

As I walk through the crowd toward Miles and Blake, I realize how much of a full-circle moment it was to meet someone so much like myself.

Back then, I didn't think I'd ever be okay. I thought I'd be sad and angry for the rest of my life.

But now, having lived through it and being able to reflect on it...

I know that no matter what happens, I'll be able to get through it.

No matter how difficult the situation may be.

I barely slept at all last night. My mind was consumed by thoughts of Annie. How her story is so similar to my own.

It sparked the creative side of me, one I haven't explored since Zeke stole my most valued client.

That spark is the reason I slipped out of bed just after six this morning, rising with the sun. I found myself in the art room Miles built me, draped in only a sheet from the night before. I didn't even make time for dressing myself.

With the easel set up in front of the open doors, watching the sun continue to rise, I paint. My soul is still stuck on how much progress I've made, and how seeing Annie reminded me of that.

Laying out all my paints, I get to work drawing her.

A reminder to myself that even though I didn't have the greatest start to life, that doesn't dictate the way it'll end.

I'm so inspired by my work that it only takes an hour to complete, and then all I can do is marvel at it.

"You're so beautiful," Miles grumbles behind me, in that sleepy voice of his.

"You're cute when you wake up."

"Seriously. The morning light is hitting you in this way that makes you look angelic."

"Are you sleepwalking?" I place the painting down and turn around. "Because I look more like the devil than I do an angel."

"It doesn't matter if you look like the devil. You're my angel," he says with a sleepy smile, crossing the room to wrap me in his arms.

Miles doesn't let up, only hugging me tighter.

"You're very cuddly this morning," I mumble into his shirt.

"You deprived me of waking up next to you. What did you expect?"

He's so damn cute that it physically hurts.

"I'm sorry. But the creative juices were flowing, and I needed to express them."

"I can tell." He pulls away, looking at the painting on the floor. "It's beautiful."

"Thank you."

"Come here," he demands, pulling me to the small patio. "Let's watch the world wake up."

Miles presses me against the railing, wrapping his arms around me from behind. There's a chill in the air so early in the morning, but the warmth of his body keeps it from being unbearable.

After no certain amount of time, I relax further into Miles, and he props his chin on my bare shoulder. His breaths ghost over my skin, on the sweet spot of my neck, and tingles run through my entire body. I slide back closer to him, feeling a bulge press against my lower back.

"Riley Davis," he whispers huskily. "Are you trying to start something?"

"I am."

"Thank god," he sighs. "Because you look sexy as hell under the morning light wrapped in this sheet."

A rush of pleasure runs through me at the compliment, driving me to drop the fabric to the ground. "What sheet?"

"Fuck me," Miles says under his breath, and then he's on me.

His mouth descends on my neck, kissing up and down between my neck, my collarbone, and my shoulders. He moves each hand around me, one going straight for the piercing in my nipple and the other immediately finding my clit.

My body instinctively presses into Miles, rubbing against his still-covered shaft in those boxers of his. Wrapping my arm around my back, I find the lining of his boxers and pull down enough so that I can wrap my hand around him.

I run my hand down his shaft, swiping my thumb over the tip. The wetness pooled there lightly coats my hand, making the slide and twist of my hand smoother.

Miles' length grows in my hand, and he presses his fingers harder at my clit, running down my slit to gather the wetness pooled there.

There's something that feels different about this moment. The desire we feel for each other is no different, but we're not rushed this time. We're not racing to reach the goal, but more so enjoying the intimacy that comes with a moment like this one.

It feels a lot like making love.

Miles' hand continues to twist and tug at my nipple while the other retreats. The loss I feel isn't long because he immediately moves to swipe the tip of his cock through my slit, coating it with the pleasure that drips down my thighs.

Without warning, Miles presses the tip of his cock against my entrance and slides in slowly, prolonging the stretch that occurs when he enters.

His hands grip my hips, and he lifts me onto my tip toes. The change in angle has the tip of him pressing against that most sensitive spot inside me, and I clench my eyes closed as he continues to hit it at a speed that's both too much and not enough.

Miles lifts my hips even higher, the grip on my hips tightening. His slower thrusts increase in pace, causing my hip bones to hit the railing each time he moves forward. It's slightly painful, but the pleasure trumps it.

"You feel so good wrapped around me, baby."

My body screams internally every time he talks to me like that. Because when he does that, the words are like gasoline and my pleasure is the flame.

That tightening coils up in my abdomen, moving rapidly downward to the place that calls for it most. Miles reads my body language, increasing his pace so that you can hear our skin slapping together with each thrust.

Once that pleasure reaches its intended area, I whimper.

"Oh my god," I say breathlessly, unable to speak with how deep and hard his thrusts are.

That feeling detonates, a bright light flashing in front of my eyes. Miles follows right behind me.

I've realized since being with Miles that you don't always need hot, rough, dirty sex to feel pleasure. Sometimes, all you need is a slow love, the kind that comes after some work, where the sheer intimacy that you share is just as electric as any other type of pleasure.

Once our breathing has settled, Miles slips out of me. He bends down, picks up the discarded sheet, and wraps it around me.

"That's my kind of wake-up call," he says, spinning me around to kiss me. His lips are dry, but soft all the same.

"Yeah, I could get used to that too."

"Mhmm," he moans, kissing me again. "Any requests for breakfast?"

"Omelets," I smile.

For someone who hates their food to touch, I sure do like it when the food comes already together.

"Okay. You go get dressed or don't, and I'll have it ready in about twenty minutes."

Miles places a kiss on my forehead and then pulls away from me. But I grab his arm before he can get away.

"What's up?"

"We need to tell, Blake. I can't do the lying anymore."

"I agree. I want to be able to show you off. I'm tired of hiding it too. My sister's thoughts about us be damned," he says with complete honesty.

"But we need to wait until after the championship," he adds.

"I don't want whatever will happen to affect the outcome of that. We both need clear heads."

"I agree. After the championship."

"Okay."

"Okay."

"We're gonna be fine," he says.

"Yeah. We will."

And I believe that. Regardless of the outcome.

CHAPTER 36
MILES

No one really knows what it's like to be a professional athlete, not unless you are one. The mental game that comes along with it is nearly as tough as the game itself.

There's an immense amount of pressure when you're playing. Not only for yourself but for others as well. Our performance on the court affects not only us, our sponsorships, and our funding, but it impacts our coach also.

This is Blake's first season as Head Coach. If things don't go as planned today, that could impact her future in the organization. And as the point guard, it's my job to lead the team. So, if my leadership is skewed, it could mess up everything.

I'm confident in my skills. I don't doubt them. But you never know what you'll be walking into until you're already there.

I wish Riley was here to calm my nerves. She agreed to cover part of a shift for her friend at the last minute, so I'm not sure when she'll be here.

And I'm not about to be that needy boyfriend who distracts her while she's working.

Thoughts of Riley aside, I switch my mindset to game mode. Making sure that I follow my ritual step by step, including carrying the lucky deer antler that my ududu—*my grandfather*—gifted to me as a young boy.

Everything I need to feel secure for this game is on my person, and once my bag is packed, I leave the hotel and make my way to the arena we're playing at.

The minute I'm through the facility's doors, the only thing that's on my mind is securing the win for the Warhawks.

From the locker room, I can hear the arena filling up with fans. Thousands of them if we're being specific. You'd think the number would affect me, but when you're on the court, everything is tuned out.

You know the support is there, but it's not the main focus. If you focus on everything that goes on in the stands, you may as well not even be playing.

"Is your head in the game?" Blake asks as she approaches me.

I've changed into full game gear, and all I'm doing is letting the electricity build in my system so that when the game begins, that energy can be put to good use.

"As much as it always is. I know what's at stake." Blake nods, keeping her posture tight. "What about you, Coach? Is *your* head in the game?"

"I know what's at stake as well," she deadpans. Blake is the kind of person that when she's in the zone, nothing can break her from it.

"Has Riley texted you? My phone is put away and I want to know if she's here yet."

"I haven't heard from her, but I'm sure she'll be here soon." Blake checks the watch on her wrist and adjusts it absentmindedly. "Press wants a few words with the starters before the game. Make sure you see to that."

Blake pulls the polo away from her neck, putting some space between it and her throat as if it's suffocating her. I know that Blake would never admit it, but I know she's nervous. This game, and its outcome, will show a lot about how the team has performed under her leadership.

And considering how long Riley and I have been lying to her about us, I can at least ensure that she has this win.

***

The floor vibrates beneath me as we stand on the sidelines before tip-off. The air is filled with electricity, coming off the fans in droves to fuel our drive to win.

Some would believe that standing here would be the most nerve-wracking, but the truth is, I'm eerily calm. The stakes are higher, yes, but underneath all the titles and press and status, it's still the game we love. And that's why this game is like any other.

"I don't need to explain to you all what the win here would mean for us. You've heard me bitch and gripe about our shortcomings as a team and what we can do to get better. But aside from all that, don't forget what got you here in the first place—talent, hard work, and a coach that isn't afraid to run your ass until you figure out your fuckups."

Blake puts a fist to the group, a signal for the starters and surrounding players to join in.

"We go out there today, and we play our best. That's all I ask from you. Time to show the state of Louisiana what the Warhawks are all about. On three."

After we bump our fists, the referees blow the whistle, and we filter out onto the court. This is the moment that all the electricity that's built up transfers to pure fire and the intense need to dominate. It's an adrenaline high for any athlete, the moment you step onto your respective turf and set out to remind everyone why the hell you're here and why you deserve to win.

With a guy as tall as Dmitry, it's easy for us to win the tip. The ball finds my hands, bumping shoulders with the now defense as we come down from the jump.

By the time I've settled, my team has set up on our side of the court, their hands itching to touch the leather I now possess.

The first quarter is played neck and neck. Whenever we put up points, so does the opposing team. I have a few stupid turnovers, something I never do, and Blake is sure to remind me of that once I'm back on the sideline. The guys are grabbing water when she pulls me aside.

"What's going on in your head? You're not playing at your full potential."

"I'm good. Just shaking off the nerves," I say, but it's a lie.

I haven't seen Riley in the stands, and she has no reason to be late, so the alarms set off in my head, pulling my focus from the game. I'm hoping that she's here and I just don't see her, but I don't like the way it unsettles me.

"Shake the nerves off. You play better than this. Block out whatever is in your head and focus on the court, yeah? When you're out there, you're the leader. A team can't play to its full potential if the leader is only half present," she tells me, her voice full of conviction and quiet intensity.

"I hear you," I tell her, trying my best to compartmentalize.

Before now, I'd never had anything to worry about while on the court. But ever since Riley has come back into my life and flipped everything around, I didn't know what it was like to have something outside of the game that consumed all my focus.

And I'm worried.

So fucking worried that I haven't seen her.

"Consider the first quarter a trial period. I need to see more effort out there," Blake says. "The defense is reading y'all as easy as a damn picture book."

A circle wide 'yes, Coach,' goes around, and the refs blow the whistle to pull us back onto the court.

The second quarter flows much better. I put aside my worry, diverting my focus to what's happening right now instead of picturing all the bad situations that Riley could possibly be in.

If this is what anxiety is like… that constant deep worry that something is wrong or that situations will play out a certain way just because you don't have all the information, then Riley is even stronger than I could ever imagine. She lives with this daily.

We pull ahead in the second, taking better and more calculated shots. Concealing our plays better. Overall, just playing more as a team. And that's because the leader—me—is more focused now.

At least, that's what I'm telling myself.

People don't realize how hard it is being the point guard. We're responsible for reading the court while simultaneously protecting the ball, seeing the set-up of the defense, and watching for players who try to sneak the defense. We have to read the game like a book without knowing the premise of the story.

When the buzzer goes off at halftime, my stomach is eaten away by guilt. I know that I can play better than I am, and while we have a decent lead on the opposing team, that's all due to my teammates. I've not made half as many points as I normally do by this point of the game.

I'm more of a burden at this point than anything.

The guys lead us back to the locker room for the half, but before I can walk through the door, the familiar grip of my sister's arm yanks me back, keeping me from entering with the rest of the staff and team.

"What's going on with you? You're not you out there, Miles. What the hell has you so bent up that you can't play the very game you've dedicated your life to at your full potential?"

"I'm worried about Riley," I admit. "Has she contacted you? She should be here by now."

"I haven't heard from her. But Riley is a big girl, Miles. If something was wrong, we'd know. You gotta stop worrying about her right now. I need two more quarters from you."

"I can't help but feel like something's wrong," I admit, voicing the thoughts of the unnerving feeling inside that's clawing to get out.

"You can't focus on it. Not right now. Even Riley would tell you that. She knows what the game means to you, to us."

"This game doesn't trump her safety," I manage through gritted teeth, my voice angry.

Blake's brows furrow and her posture goes rigid. Her head tilts slightly to the side. "Is there something you want to talk to me about, Miles?"

"No," I answer immediately. "Let's focus on winning."

I push through to the locker room, ready to endure a verbal beat down from Coach and disappointed looks from my teammates.

"You good?" Kyler asks as we walk back to the court.

"No, man. I'm not. Riley isn't here and I haven't heard from her. I'm freaking out a bit. She wouldn't miss this."

I checked my phone during halftime, even though I shouldn't have, and other than the text I received earlier from her that she'd arrived at work, I've gotten nothing new from her.

"I know. I would feel the same way if it were Blake. But I

need you to focus for the next bit, okay? I promise, as soon as the game is over, we'll help you track her down." He places a supportive hand on my shoulder. "Okay?"

It doesn't make me feel better, but I nod in acceptance. "Thank you."

"We're family. It's what we do. Just give us the rest of the game, okay?"

"I'll do my best," I say reluctantly.

I don't like brushing it aside, not with the little itch that's scratching in the pit of my gut that something's off. But I don't have a choice. All I can do is try to help us win and secure the future for our team.

Once we're back on the court, we get another quick word of encouragement from Coach and the assistants, and we spend the rest of the time rehydrating.

Until Blake answers her phone.

Alarm bells don't just go off in my head, they fucking blare. So loudly that it's all I can focus on.

I make my way over to her, only catching the tail end of the conversation.

"Are you sure?" A pause. "If that's what you want." Another pause and the pit in my stomach triples in size. "Okay. We'll be there after the game. I love you."

Once Blake hangs up the phone, I jump on her.

"What was that?"

"Nothing. Just focus on the game."

"Tla," I growl. *No.* Because there's no way she's dodging this. "You never answer your phone during practice or a game which means that it's serious. I won't walk back onto that court until you tell me what's going on."

Blake steps to me, our noses nearly touching if it weren't for the minimal height difference. "You do realize that I have plenty of guys on the bench just itching for you to fuck up. Right? Just because I'm your sister doesn't mean that you can speak to me like that. I'm still your coach."

"Blake." My voice is still angry, but there's a pleading tone laced within that she senses.

"It was Riley. There was an accident. She's in the emergency room right now."

At Blake's admission, my entire body locks up. My blood feels like sludge under my skin, unable to pump my heart as needed. It's moving so slowly that for a minute, I feel pulseless.

That feeling... that fucking feeling I had was there for a reason. I'm so damn entwined with her now that we're connected on a level deeper than any other that I can feel when something is wrong.

"What?" I finally manage, the lump in my throat causing the word to come out broken.

"Riley said that it's fine. She's fine. She's a little bruised, sore and her arm is most likely broken, but she's okay. Riley told me that she'd be a while and the only thing we needed to focus on was winning this game. I told her we'd come as soon as it was over."

Anger rushes through my veins.

"I can't believe you're expecting me to go back out on the court knowing she's hurt," I nearly choke.

"Calm down, Miles. She said she's fine. It's no big deal."

"No big deal?" My voice rises. "Blake, respectfully, you clearly don't know your best friend. Because if she's saying it's fine, it's not. She's so used to being a burden to others that she won't admit it when she's actually hurting. Not to you. That's why I know she's lying about her pain."

"And what makes you think you know her better than me?" she asks genuinely.

There's something behind her eyes, a look that's familiar. It's the look I saw when Dmitry and Kyler called me out on my feelings for Riley. And at this moment, I know we're screwed.

The only thought on my mind is Riley. How badly she's hurt, how scared she must be, how alone she must feel.

It only leaves me with one decision.

I know that if I do this, I could jeopardize my future with the Warhawks. But I couldn't give a shit right now when all that matters, all that's *ever* mattered, is sitting in a hospital bed right now, scared and alone.

I also know that if I do this, I'm outing my and Riley's relationship to Blake without her permission.

But she's worth more than any consequence.

When I let the world back in around me, I notice that Kyler and Dmitry are so close that they heard everything. There's a knowing look in their eyes, and when the tears prick mine, Kyler places a hand on my shoulder.

"Go. We've got this." Dmitry nods at his side.

When I look back at Blake, her posture isn't rigid anymore. Her hand is propped on a chair, and she's barely holding herself upright.

And when I look at her eyes, they're filled with so many emotions that I don't know which one stands out the most.

Pain, disbelief, shock, self-doubt, anger, and most of all, betrayal. My sister's eyes crack right before me, the pupil going completely dark so you can't even distinguish the brown anymore.

The guilt is there under my skin, but it's not the prominent feeling.

The only thing I'm feeling is that I need to get to my girl.

"I'm sorry," I manage to whisper, then I run off the court.

And I don't look back.

I don't need to.

CHAPTER 37
RILEY

I can't explain how hard it was to call Blake during the middle of the most important game of the season. But I also knew that if I didn't, I'd get my ass kicked. By both Blake and Miles. And I hate that I'm missing this moment for them.

But I can't help that some drunk jackass tried to get handsy while Lux, Aurora, and I were onstage. Lux was near the stage and one of the guys tried cupping between her legs. Aurora stepped in and the guy's friend grabbed her, ripping her top off. Our security hadn't made it to them yet, and I couldn't stand watching it, so I stepped in as well.

Big mistake.

The guy's friend hit me and pulled my arm painfully hard, causing me to fall off the stage.

It could have been worse. I have bruises from where he grabbed me, where my face hit the floor, and most likely a broken arm. At least, that's what the doctor said after I cried when he touched it. I'm just waiting for the nurse to come take me for an x-ray.

It's been thirty minutes since she last came by, stating that radiology would call when they were available. Thankfully, I was given something for the pain so waiting isn't too unbearable.

Twenty minutes after I'm off the call with Blake, there's a knock at the door. It has to be the nurse, and I can't say that I'm not glad she's here. The sooner I get this done, the sooner I can get out of here.

I'm halfway off the bed when the door opens, but it's not the nurse.

"Miles," I squeak in disbelief. Hell, he's still in his jersey.

The game.

"Baby," he says with a sigh, his eyes filled with relief like seeing me okay settles something inside him.

"I'm okay," I tell him, but he's not convinced until his hands are on me.

His hands ghost over the bruises on my face, then moves to trace each and every bruise from the guy's hand like he's memorizing the exact number and for each one, he'll break a bone on the person that hurt me.

Once Miles finishes checking me over, he pulls me to him, wrapping his arms around me and pressing me so close to his body that you couldn't fit a sheet of paper between us right now.

He squeezes tightly, but with my body sore, beaten, and bruised, I let out a painful moan. Miles notices immediately, adjusting his hold on me. He guides me back into the bed with ease, pulling a chair to the side of the bed and taking my hand in his.

"Miles, what the hell are you doing here? You're supposed to be playing one of the biggest games of your life right now. Not sitting here with me."

"Why would I be anywhere else?"

"Because it's your life, your job, your career. You're putting all of that in jeopardy," I remind him.

"I do *not* care," he says with conviction. "You're more important than the game."

"No," I say in panic. "You can't jeopardize it. I won't let you."

"Things are gonna be okay, Riley."

Alarm bells flare in my head. "Miles, if you're here then Blake knows."

Miles gives me a knowing look, squeezing my hand tighter. "She does."

My fingers pick at the sheets, my heart beats faster. A tightness forms in my chest—I'm not sure if it's out of fear, or if it's because this moment, this single moment in time, makes everything the most real it's ever been.

"We were gonna tell her after the game. We decided on that together," I remind him.

"I remember," he says. "But when I heard, I didn't care about anything but getting to you. I didn't care that I was walking out on my team, and I didn't care that I was exposing our relationship to Blake. All I wanted was you," Miles says with conviction. "You're all I've ever wanted. When I first met you at eleven, when my feelings developed at fifteen, and even when you stormed back into my life at twenty-seven. I've wanted you in all the phases of our lives, and nothing was gonna stop me from being here for you."

There's a rawness to his tone that has my heart aching. We've danced around the realness of our feelings for so long... I mean, we felt them, we knew we did, but never had the voice to say it out loud.

I guess a frightening experience is the way to force things out in the open, but it doesn't escape the fact that he walked out of the damn championship game to be here.

"I want you too, Miles, but why the hell did you risk blowing up your life to come here when I told Blake that I was fine? Why?"

The question comes out broken, and I wish I knew why. This is a declaration of love if I've ever seen one—well, at least one that's not in a movie—and it solidifies everything that we are. Everything that we mean to each other.

I've known for a while that I love Miles, and I had a feeling that he felt the same way. But I feel like I'm about to hear it out loud, and I need that.

I need verbal confirmation to know that this all hasn't been in my head and that it's real.

That my illness hasn't somehow misconstrued what I believe that we are to each other.

Miles stands, sitting on the edge of the bed now. He props himself on his left arm, using the right to swipe across my lip and settle on my cheek.

His eyes are filled with so many emotions right now that I can't pick them all apart. But there's one that I recognize without question. It's what I see in Kyler's eyes when he looks at Blake, and it's what I see in my own whenever I think of Miles.

"Don't you understand by now? You're my everything, Riley. I'm so helplessly in love with you that when it came down to the game and you, there was no question. You have to know that."

Hearing the words from his mouth, they do things to me. Butterflies flip around in my stomach, my heart rattles around my chest, and my body buzzes with an energy that's begging to be unleashed but only with him.

"I am so happy to hear you say that," I beam, preparing to repeat the words back.

"What happened?" he asks instead.

"Some guys assaulted us at the club. I caught the brunt of it because I was pulled off stage. Our security stepped in thankfully, and I've already given a statement to the police, but it fucking scared me."

"Baby, I'm so sorry," Miles says, laying his hand on my thigh with a firm yet soft grip. "Don't be mad at me for asking, but why do you continue to work somewhere that's so dangerous?"

"I..."

My first instinct is to say that I need the money. It isn't a lie, but I've been able to save more than normal since living with Miles. I could probably do without this job, but what if things change and I need it again?

"If it's still about money, Riley... you're not gonna have to worry about that anymore. You haven't since you moved in with me. I know you're independent, and I know you want to do things for yourself, but you don't need to work somewhere dangerous when you don't need to anymore."

Miles leans forward, moving his hand from my leg to my cheek. He makes sure to avoid the bruises there.

"Your struggles are my struggles, baby," he continues. "I'll do what I can to keep you safe. I make millions of dollars per year, and money is no issue when it comes to someone you love. You could take everything I have that's mine and I wouldn't give a shit as long as you have my heart, which you always will."

Tears well in my eyes and Miles leans his forehead against mine. "Lean on me baby. Ayv uha ugisv nihi." *I have got you.*

"Okay, baby. Okay," I respond, giving in. If I'm being honest, I don't want to be somewhere dangerous either, no matter how much I love the people I work with.

I'm ready to tell him I love him, but then the door opens, interrupting our moment, and it's actually the nurse this time.

"Miss Davis. Radiology is ready for you now."

I open my mouth to speak, but Miles reaches to help me out of bed. "Go get your x-ray. We'll pick this back up when you get back," he speaks softly, his lips tilting in a smile.

I hate that this is the moment that gets interrupted. Of all the things they walk in on, they walk in as we're declaring our love for each other.

You couldn't just give me this one thing, life?

Either way, I'm so glad that he told me.

I just need to tell him in return.

Because there's nothing more blissful and fulfilling than hearing the person you love say it back to you and mean it.

"Are you really going with black?" Miles asks from across the room.

After my x-ray, where it's confirmed that I have a spiral fracture in my radius from being jerked, I'm immediately taken to have a cast put on.

It isn't until I'm back in the emergency room that I get to pick my color.

"Of course, I am. You know it matches my soul," I joke, but Miles simply laughs.

"How am I gonna sign a cast that's black?" he questions, looking genuinely hurt that he won't get to sign it. Like we're in middle school or something.

"Oh honey, don't you worry about that," the nurse cuts in. "They make all color sharpies now that show on black. White, silver, gold."

"Good." I can see him silently gloating. "I was thinking of making the base white, covering it in green. Maybe adding a dinosaur there. I hear they're all the rage."

There's an evil gleam in his eyes. He's picking at me the same way I did when I suggested tattooing a green dinosaur dick on him. The reminisce makes me laugh, and he joins in as we share that memory together.

"My grandson loves dinosaurs," the nurse, a woman who looks to be in her fifties, adds.

It only makes me and Miles laugh more.

The door opens, and the doctor I saw before, an older man in his sixties I assume, enters the room.

"Miss Davis. I see that your arm is all taken care of."

"It is."

"Good. How's your pain?" he asks, taking a seat on the rolling stool, coming closer.

"It's manageable. The pain meds help, but now it's just a… discomfort."

"It'll be that way for a bit. I've sent a prescription for hydrocodone to the pharmacy that you provided earlier. As for the cast, make sure to keep it dry. If you need to shower, double-wrap it in plastic or just keep it out of the water. If it gets itchy, please don't try to shove anything down the cast. Ask me how I know," he says, pointing his pen at me with a gentle grin.

"You can use the cool setting on a hair dryer and aim it under the cast. No powders or lotions. You'll wear this for six to eight weeks, and I've reached out to your primary care physician to get you scheduled there for a check-up then."

The doctor places my chart to the side, leaning forward on the stool. "Do you have any questions for me?"

"Can the cast hurt her?" Miles asks, stepping in to sit beside me on the bed.

"Not necessarily, but there are things to look for when it comes to casts and cast care."

"Which are?" Miles asks, bringing his phone from his pocket. I see him open the notes app out of the corner of my eye.

"You need to watch for increased pain in the limb, numbness or tingling in your hand or fingers, burning, stinging, and excessive swelling below the cast. You also need to watch for blueness and coldness in the digits, if the cast feels too tight, if the skin becomes red or raw around the cast, and make sure that you can't smell anything foul coming from it."

Miles continues to type, hanging on to his every word.

"Did you get all that?" the doctor asks.

"Almost done," Miles answers, typing away on his phone.

I look at the doctor, only to be met with a genuine smile, his eyes peering toward Miles in adoration. I return the expression his way.

"What else?" the doctor asks, but he isn't looking at me. He's looking at Miles.

"Does she need to elevate it or anything? I know that's common in injuries."

"Yes," the doctor answers. "I'd keep it elevated a fair amount over the next three days to reduce swelling. You can ice it as well, just make sure that the ice is wrapped so that the cast stays dry."

Miles continues to ask questions, and the doctor answers every single one with patience and knowledge.

Once Miles is done badgering him with questions, the doctor signs off on my discharge. The nurse comes in and recovers a few things, then she hands me my papers and tells me I'm free to leave.

Although I only have my work clothes, I put them back on with the help of Miles since I'm functioning with one arm.

"Ready to go?" Miles asks.

"Not yet." I step forward, wrapping my arms around Miles' midsection. "We need to finish the conversation you started earlier."

"We can do that once we get out of here," he suggests.

"No," I say, my voice stern. "No. I need to say this now. If there's anything I've learned in the last few hours, it's that you need to tell people how you feel because tomorrow—hell, even the next minute—isn't guaranteed."

Miles' grip tightens on my back, pulling me closer.

It's crazy how much a simple touch from the person you love can settle the most chaotic parts of you.

"Miles."

"Riley."

"I love you too."

A smile tries to peek through, but Miles holds back.

"I'm sorry. I didn't quite hear you. Can you repeat that?"

My jaw drops at the stunt he's trying to pull.

"Stubborn ass," I laugh, reaching up to pinch at his cheek. Miles finally folds, laughter escaping him. He shrugs, a smirk appearing.

I stand taller, lifting as far as I can on my tippy toes. My hand rests on Miles's cheek, holding his gaze with my own.

"I love you too," I say with a heavy, serious tone. "I loved you when we were kids. I loved you when we got older and became friends who were always more than friends, though we never admitted it. I loved you when I broke your heart. And I love you even more now that you've become the amazing man I always knew you would be.

"I love you, Miles Rainwater. I love you more than I'll ever be able to convey with words or actions." My hand traces the smile line on Miles' face. "If I could pull my heart out of my chest right now, the only thing you'd find is a tattoo of your name. I'm consumed in you, Miles. Every broken piece of me fits perfectly with every piece of you."

His eyes glass over, his smile growing. "I love you so much, Riley Davis."

Our lips connect in a heated kiss, one that's full of joy and yearning and undeniable love. It's intense but gentle, the way he holds me.

He holds me like we're free-falling, and the only way to keep us safe is to not let go of each other. Telling me in more than just words that with each other, we can get through anything.

"I'm so happy," I admit, breaking our kiss. It's the first time I've ever admitted the feeling and haven't been afraid that it would only be fleeting.

"I'm happy to see you so happy. If anyone deserves it, it's you, baby." Miles tucks a hair behind my ear, his hand lingering behind to trace all the soft features of my face.

"Are we ready to get out of here?"

"More than ready," I respond.

Miles grabs my purse in his hand and wraps his arm around

me with the other. Waking up today, I never thought this is where I'd end up.

But in a weird way, I'm also glad. Face planting the floor literally knocked the sense into me, forcing me to put my feelings out in the open and to stop hiding behind them in fear that they wouldn't be reciprocated.

Self-preservation, it is.

But I'm tired of listening to that fear, and I won't do it anymore.

Miles and I walk through the waiting room and out the exit, pausing briefly to let an ambulance pull through.

My head is leaning against Miles's shoulder, watching the ground as we walk through the parking lot. The medicine they gave me is starting to make me feel a bit loopy, and I nearly trip when Miles comes to a stop.

I see why when I raise my head.

Blake and Sam are walking through the parking lot in our direction, their bodies stiff and gait calculated.

Sam is as intimidating as ever, sporting a look on his face that screams *I told you so* mixed with *anger*.

And Blake...

The look that resides on hers makes me sick to my stomach, causing it to flip on itself and send waves of nausea through me.

I see anger, concern, and confusion.

But most of all, I see betrayal.

Betrayal that I caused.

They stop in front of us, no one offering to speak a word.

That fear that I've felt since the moment I decided to keep this secret comes back full force, and I know that I'm about to experience the most difficult thing in my entire life.

Because while I once thought the hard things I had to experience would make or break me, they didn't.

But this...

This just might.

CHAPTER 38
MILES

THERE'S A NEGATIVE ENERGY THAT FLOWS THROUGH THE AIR AS WE stand in front of my father and sister. One that causes the air to become stagnant and our bodies to stand rigid.

I look at Riley, and she's staring directly at Blake. Her face is sheet white, and her hand trembles slightly where it's wrapped around my arm.

Blake takes a deep breath. "Are you okay?" she asks Riley, nothing but concern evident in her voice.

"I'm okay," she manages through a whisper, clearing her throat once she speaks. "Sore and bruised. A broken arm. Some general pain. I'm in one piece though."

"I'm glad that you're okay."

The atmosphere returns to an unnerving kind of quiet. We're all looking at each other, but no one says anything. That is until my dad opens his mouth.

"Is anyone planning to address what's really going on here?" he butts in.

"Edoda," Blake growls. "This doesn't concern you."

"It concerns me when my son is trying to throw his damn life away for some temporary fixture."

I open my mouth to step in, but Blake beats me to it first.

"You don't speak about her that way," she says, turning to get in my father's face. Things may have been tense with our dad over the years, but never once has one of his kids stepped up to challenge him like that.

"Riley is a part of our family, Dad. She doesn't deserve the way you've treated her or the things you've said. Which I've heard, by the way. None of what's happening here concerns you, so wait your damn turn and keep the disrespect of her out of my ear. Got it?"

Our father doesn't respond, stunning the hell out of me. Maybe because it's Blake that's pressing him, he doesn't push back. Because if it were me or any of my brothers, we'd be met with a firm backhand.

Blake rights herself, pushing our father out of focus, and instead, places her intense gaze on ours.

"How long has this been going on?"

"Since Christmas," I answer.

"Christmas?" she huffs. "You've been keeping this a secret from me for six damn months?" I nod. "Whose idea was it to keep it a secret?"

"Mine," Riley answers immediately, triggering an angry response from me.

"No, don't let her lie to you. It was as much my idea as it was hers. No single person here gets the blame. It was mutual."

Blake looks at the ground, capturing her bottom lip between her teeth. I can see the way she swallows nervously, and although we haven't been as close lately, she's still my twin sister.

Which means I know how hard she's trying to hold back her pain. And guessing from how long she stays silent, she's feeling a lot of it right now.

When she finally raises her head, her eyes are shining with tears but she's keeping her expression neutral. She's hiding, trying to make sense of the situation without digging the knife deeper into the wound we've caused her to find answers.

"Why did you keep it from me?" she asks, her voice weaker than I've ever heard it.

"I couldn't risk—" Riley attempts to say, but the consistent flow of tears that stream down her face prevents her from getting any more words out.

"Neither of us wanted to hurt you, Blake," I say, stepping in. "We've both tried to bring it up subtly before, and your blatant disagreement of anything happening between us only added to the reasons we had for not telling you."

"Are you saying it's my fault that you kept it a secret?"

"No, I'm not," I counter quickly. "You just didn't make the decision any easier. Nobody likes conflict, Blake. Not when there's so much at stake."

Blake shakes her head, the kind that you do when your mind is overwhelmed and you're moving to settle the boggling thoughts.

Riley visibly shakes beside me, and if I weren't standing beside her, I have no doubt that her body would collapse.

"I didn't want to lose you," Riley manages in a meek tone. "You're my best friend."

Blake's expression floods with anguish, and for the first time in a year, a single tear rolls down her cheek. She doesn't blink, and another follows.

"I just... I can't believe you didn't trust me enough to tell me, regardless of how I was acting. I'm not justifying my actions but... we tell each other everything, Ri. Or so I thought."

Riley blubbers tears, and Blake discreetly swipes at the ones in her eyes.

Something familiar prickles at me. I find my father and a look I know too well grows more intense. It's the one he has when he's about to throw his two cents into the mix.

And his two cents aren't even worth that.

"Can't you see what she's doing to your life, son? She's shifted your priorities, caused you to walk out on the biggest game of the season, and she's tearing you and your sister apart."

"Who says we're tearing apart?" Blake speaks for me.

"I shifted my own priorities, Dad. Unlike you when you were my age, I can see past the sport, and I know that I won't always have it. I won't let it become my life like you did and ruin the best and most important things."

"You're already more like me than you think," Dad spits.

"And how's that?"

"Because you're with someone like *her* who only aims to cause pain in your life."

"Someone like who?" I question further.

"Someone like your ungrateful, cheating, bitch of a mother."

Fuck.

It makes so much sense now.

Our mother is a subject that we don't discuss often—hell, at all, even.

I don't have many memories of my mom. We were younger when she left, and even when I can remember back that far, she was never really present.

She walked out on our family to run off with some guy she met at an event. I'm not even sure where she went. Other than explaining what happened and that she wasn't coming back, Dad never discussed her with us any further, and we were okay with that.

I look at Riley to check on her, but her only focus right now is Blake. And my sister...

Her brows are intensely furrowed, her jaw set tight. Redness climbs up her neck and settles onto her face. And if it were a thing humans could do, she'd be steaming out of her eyes and pointing laser beams through our father right now.

"The fact that you can say that just makes you more of a jackass than I originally thought," I say, shaking my head. "Riley is nothing like her. She only caused pain because you made her choose to sacrifice her own feelings to save my image. Since she's come back into my life, she's only made it better.

"And I'm sorry that you can't see that, Dad. But don't force your life's failures onto me because you're so damn miserable."

"I'm not miserable," he argues.

Blake shifts around, coming to stand beside Riley. Drawing a distinct line between us and our father, showing whose side she's really on.

"Yeah, you are, Dad." She takes a protective step forward. "I didn't think about things in the moment, but once Miles pointed out how badly you've treated Riley, I've started to see it."

Blake steps forward until there's only a few inches between her and Dad. "You know, I thought you were starting to change. You were really supportive when I came to you with my trauma last year, and I thought that things would be different going forward. And it really makes me sad to see that I was wrong."

Dad looks like he's been hit, disappointment washing over his features. It's so unlike him but I can't feel bad for him at the moment. Not with how he's treated everyone.

"I'm not sure what your issue is, Dad," Blake continues. "But Riley is one of the best people I know. She's endured more pain and loneliness in a lifetime than anyone else I know, and she doesn't deserve to be belittled and degraded because of situations that were out of her control.

"She's not our mother, Edoda. She never has and she never will be. Is this unwarranted issue you have with her really worth losing all of your kids? Because we're all a close-knit family, my brothers and I, and she's a part of it. More so than you right now, even considering the current situation. And if you can't get your shit together, you *will* lose them."

Our father stands unmoving in front of us. I can't be sure he's even taken a breath since Blake began talking.

The entire time we've been keeping this secret, I thought our biggest issue would be Blake, but I was sorely mistaken.

Because if this doesn't show how much she still cares about us, nothing will. And that gives me more hope than I'll ever admit out loud that we'll be able to repair our twin bond and her relationship with Riley.

Anything that I wanted to say to my father, Blake has already said. I wrap my arm tighter around Riley, pulling her closer to me. Then I lay a supportive hand to Blake, a gesture to back down.

"I think it's time for you to leave, Dad." I say it with an austere tone and a set jaw, telling him without words that this isn't a suggestion.

Dad doesn't move, continuing to stand there with a clenched jaw and arms crossed over his broad chest.

"Now," Blake adds through gritted teeth.

When our father begins to retreat, Riley shakes my arm off and takes a tentative step forward.

"Mr. Rainwater."

Dad stops, turning just enough to look back in this direction.

"I'm sorry that I remind you of your own pain, but don't be so blinded by it that you push away the only people you have left in your corner. As someone who has lost family before, nothing can help the kind of loneliness that accompanies it." He turns away, but Riley keeps going. "And I look forward to proving your thoughts about me wrong."

Dad keeps walking through the parking lot until he's out of sight, and Blake turns around to grab hold of Riley's hands.

"Are you okay? You know that you have no reason to apologize to him, right?"

"I know. But as someone who was blinded by their own pain in the past, I see why he is the way he is. He just needs some guidance, like I did, to see through to the other side of it."

"You're being awfully nice to a man who has been nothing but cruel and hateful to you," Blake states.

"I've learned that some people are cruel to be cruel, but others, like I suspect your dad to be, do it out of misguided love and protection."

"Maybe. It doesn't excuse it though," I add.

Quiet grows between the three of us, the weight that was there before my dad stepped in settling back on our shoulders.

"Blake, I'm really sorry," Riley whispers sincerely, tears immediately finding her again.

Because even though my dad interrupted the bigger issue here, it didn't go away. The betrayal we caused Blake is as present as ever.

"I know you are," Blake murmurs, rubbing her hands up and down Riley's arms, settling with a comforting grip on her forearms. "But I just need some time to wrap my head around this, okay?"

"Blake..." Riley croaks saying her name.

"Just give me some time," she responds, backing away, giving me an apologetic look. One that I was expecting. One that stings but that I honor and reciprocate.

Once Blake is in her car, Riley turns into me and lets the floodgates open, apologizing profusely for the conflict our relationship has caused.

"It was both of us, baby," I say in a soothing tone. "It'll be okay. It'll be okay."

I held a crying Riley all night, only grabbing a couple of hours of solid sleep.

Ever since we've been home, she's been curled up on the couch, surrounded by Simba, Salem, and Chief while staring at her phone, willing Blake to reach out.

"Riley, can I get you anything?" I offer.

"Yes," she speaks clearly but softly. "I need you to go talk to your sister. She told me to give her time, but not you. Don't let your relationship fracture like mine and hers. You're twins, and there's something even more special in a bond like that."

"I can't leave you alone," I counter.

"Yes, you can. Because I'm telling you to." I don't want to, but then she stares at me with pleading eyes. "Please," she adds.

And because I'd do anything for her, I find myself heading over to my sister's to try and straighten things out. I need to offer perspective and try to explain why we made the choices we made.

I can't stand seeing them hurt the way that they are.

Knocking on the door, I wait for just a few seconds until it opens with Kyler on the other side.

"Oh, thank god," he says, and I tilt my head to the side in surprise. "She's been mopey, and Blake isn't a mopey woman. Fix it."

Kyler leads me into the living room where Blake is watching a game tape from the championship. Turns out that the Warhawks won, but it was a fight. I still love my team, but not more than I love Riley.

"Blake, someone's here to see you," Kyler announces.

"Miles," she says without looking my way, but she does pause the game tape.

"I think we should talk."

"I think so too," she responds.

"That's my cue," Kyler says, but Blake isn't having it.

"Absolutely not," she yells, and Kyler goes stiff. "Let's not forget that I saw the way you looked at him when he made the choice to leave the game like you knew what I didn't. Which you did. So, no, you're not leaving."

Kyler and I take seats around Blake, and she wastes no time jumping straight to it.

"I need to know why you lied."

"You do know that I'm about to be brutally honest with you,

right? Because we agreed to always call each other on our bullshit."

"I do. And I encourage it."

"Okay." Here goes nothing. "At first, neither of us knew how to bring it up to you. It's a difficult situation all around. So, I started dropping hints—Riley too—and do you remember how you responded?"

"I don't."

"You said that we would never be good together. In fact, you said that I wasn't serious enough to handle Riley's demons. And in case you weren't aware, Riley told me all about her struggle with anxiety and depression, and her strength through it all only makes me love her more."

Blake seems stunned that I know about Riley's struggle with her mental health, but she also looks... relieved.

"Also, if you haven't noticed, things have changed this year. I don't party as I used to, and instead of spending extra time at the gym, I go home to *her*. To spend time with her. I walked out of the biggest game of the season because she means more to me than basketball, and if that doesn't convince you how serious I am about Riley, then I don't know what will."

Blake turns to Kyler, and she looks at him with disbelief. Not with our relationship, but with herself.

"How did you see it and I didn't?"

"This year has been a lot for you, Blake. It's hard for us at times to see things when we're not looking for them specifically," Kyler responds.

"Oh my god," she sighs, placing her hands over her face. She drags them down, pulling at her skin. "I'm such an asshole."

"You're not an asshole."

"No, I am," she says with confidence. "Listen, I'm not ghosting over the fact that part of your distrust in telling me is my fault. Because it is. This entire year, I've been so focused on my new role with the Warhawks that I've pushed everything that mattered before aside. And that's on me."

"Blake, I'm not gonna lie. When you said we weren't right for each other, that I wasn't serious enough for her… that hurt. It made me feel like you didn't see me, or see who I could be…"

"I'm really sorry, Miles. I don't know how I'll ever make up for that. But I know that starting now, I'm gonna try to be better."

"Thank you," I say. "But is that the only reason you couldn't see us together?"

"Maybe. Riley's my best friend. And now that you're with her, I'm sure that you know as much, maybe more than I do about how she grew up. It's no secret that when we were teenagers you were a playboy. And I thought that if something ever happened between you and you broke up with her—because you weren't known for commitment back then, even a few months ago too—that she wouldn't feel comfortable there. She had a home with us, and I didn't want her to leave it because of that."

"You never gave us the chance to prove you wrong, but I understand now why you've responded the way you did."

"Because I love you both and I would never be able to choose if things went awry."

"You wanted to protect us both because you love us."

She nods, and silence falls over us both.

"Seems we have some things to work on," Blake suggests.

"I look forward to it."

Blake turns to Kyler, who's wearing a proud smile.

I thought this would be much worse, confronting Blake. But I think she can see the change in me, and I can see why she acted the way she did.

It sucks how difficult things can be when a conversation could have solved everything before it all began. But even though things happened the way they did, I really do think this was the best way for it to happen.

"You really love her, don't you?" she asks.

"More than you'll ever know."

When Blake's lips stretch into a gentle smile, her eyes nail me with something I once only hoped I'd see in my sister's eyes.

Acceptance.

Blake leans forward, and I meet her in the middle, wrapping my arms around her. I've felt an emptiness with my sister since the season started, and with things happening between Riley and me, we drifted apart.

But right now, I feel like the part of us that separated is slowly beginning to stitch itself back together, and that partial wholeness is enough for me to be okay right now.

"There's one more thing," I tell her, disconnecting our hug. "You need to talk to Riley soon. She's terrified that she's lost you and that you'll be mad at her forever."

"I'm not mad at her or you, Miles. Hurt, yes. Mad, no. But I will, I promise. I owe her that for not being there for her the way I should have been this year."

"And we'll be okay?"

"More than okay," she answers. "But if you hurt her, brother or not, I'll kick your ass for breaking her heart and being an idiot for letting her go."

"That won't be necessary."

"Good."

"Great."

Once things are a bit more settled, I begin to head out, stopping once more to say something to Blake.

"Hey, BOGO."

"Yeah?"

"When you reach out… please go easy on her," I plead.

"There's no reason for me to go hard on her."

I leave there more optimistic than I've ever been, and even more eager to get home to Riley to hopefully provide some relief in that internal war she's got going on with herself by telling her what happened here today.

I can only hope the result is the same for them.

CHAPTER 39
RILEY

Ever since Miles returned home last night and told me that Blake would be reaching out, I've been staring at my phone like an obsessed teenage girl waiting for her crush to message back.

I've been making myself sick over what has happened. I didn't like that she found out the way she did, but according to Miles, it was easier that way because his leaving the game was irrefutable proof that he loves me. Which made talking to Blake easier.

But that's him and Blake. Not her and I. Things may not work that way when we have a conversation.

She hasn't reached out though, and that scares the hell out of me. What if she changed her mind about reaching out? She could have easily made peace with Miles because he's her brother but has no interest in doing so with me. Best friend or not.

I know that's my anxiety talking, but the silence as I sit here and wait is deafening. It does nothing for that insecure voice in my head.

And while the new medication I've been taking has been working better than the previous one, I still have these moments. And I'm learning that they'll never disappear, but the way I handle them can change.

Pulling myself out of my insecure daze, I refocus my thoughts on the positive. Blake and Miles made up and even made progress with repairing what went wrong in the relationship.

If it can happen for them, it can happen for us too.

I won't settle for less.

Coming to peace with the fact that I may be waiting a while to hear from Blake, I head out back and down to the garden where Miles is working.

He looks damn good out here shirtless. Smears of dirt across his abdomen, sweat dripping down every ridge and cut of muscle that's placed throughout his body.

Damn, I'm lucky. Not only does he look good, but the man can grow food that he can cook like no other.

It's domestic, and it's hot.

"Hey, baby," he says, noticing me approach.

"What are you doing?"

"Just suckering the tomato plants and working dirt up around them."

"What the hell is suckering?" I laugh. The term just sounds funny.

"Look here. Do you see this stem? How there's another one growing out of it. That's a sucker. It steals from the actual stem and can keep it from growing."

"Like a leech."

"Kind of, yeah." Miles smiles. "What about you? What are you doing out here? Other than ogling me, of course."

"You know how much I appreciate art," I say with a sly smile. "Honestly though, I'm going crazy in the silence of the house. I needed a distraction."

"I take it she hasn't reached out yet," he guesses.

"No. I've been holding my breath, but I'm not going to anymore. When she's ready, I'll be ready."

Miles nods, continuing to sucker the tomato plants. After he's done a few more, my phone dings in my back pocket and I freeze.

"Maybe she's ready now," Miles suggests. He leans back on his feet, gazing optimistically at me as I reach back and grab the phone from my pocket.

My heart sinks when I see the name written across the front.

> Asshole Ex-Boss: I need you to come in today. We have some things to discuss.

"It's not Blake," I say, dispirited.
"Who is it then?"
"Fucking Zeke," I grumble.
"What the hell does he want?"
"Wants me to come in."
"He's a self-righteous dick. He stole not one, but two clients, then told you to come in when you've calmed down like your anger wasn't warranted," Miles states in a defensive tone.

"You're right about that. But I need to go in anyway. If anything, just to grab the things I left behind and to tell him exactly what you said. I haven't been happy there in a while. There's no need to leave any ties."

"I'll go with you."
"What? Why? To punch him?"
"Your arm is broken, remember? I'll be there to help with your things," he answers. "But if the opportunity arises, then maybe," Miles adds.

"Okay."
"Let me grab a shower and then we'll go. I can finish this later."

"No, don't take a shower. You're all stinky and sweaty now. Maybe your odor will keep him away from me," I joke.

"I'll remember that next time you want to shower together."
"Oh, I'm so scared," I mock, heading toward the house.

"You should be," Miles says, his voice closer than before. He smacks my ass on the way by, and I chase after him.

Stupid idea on my part.

Now I'm tired.

And tired plus angry—an emotion that Zeke summons from me well—is not going to be ideal for him.

Oops.

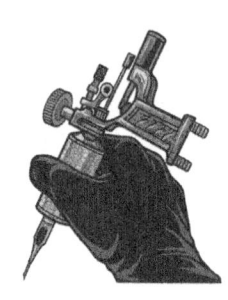

"If you get angry, no punching," Miles tells me. "That cast may be plaster, but you'll still feel the pain."

"Says the guy who literally threatened to punch him," I laugh.

But as we near the door to the parlor, my sunny disposition changes, and I channel the dark, angry side of me. Because I'm not here to be nice to someone who disregards and mistreats me the way that he has.

The receptionist gives me a sympathetic look as I walk past, and as if he sensed me coming, Zeke's waiting at my chair when Miles and I approach.

"Nice of you to show," he says.

"You're right. I am nice."

He glowers at my sarcasm.

"You wanted to discuss something."

"Yes. I'm filling your position here, effective immediately. You're fired."

I laugh. "Did you miss our last conversation where you told me to come back when I was calmer, and I said not likely?

Because if it wasn't clear then, I quit. Can't exactly fire me when I'm not an employee here."

"You're such an ungrateful bitch," he spits.

Miles takes a defensive step forward, but I keep him from going at Zeke by placing my non-injured hand on his chest.

"Months ago, those words would have bothered me. But I've learned over the last year that only miserable people try to make others as miserable as they are. And I'm better than that now. Better than this place too."

"You won't succeed without this place."

I begin packing up the things I left behind, taking everything that I paid for and contributed and not a single thing more.

"Your father made this place a safe environment. He wanted to inspire people. How he ended up with a manipulative, lazy, thieving son like you, I'll never know."

I gesture at Miles, and he picks up the box of my things for me. I step toward Zeke, standing tall with my head held high.

"You stole my work, but I'm gonna forgive it this time. Not because it'll happen again, but because you'll do it to someone else in the future since you lack true talent. And that person may not be as *nice* as I'm being. Karma's a bitch that keeps on giving, Zeke. I hope you two have a wonderful life."

Miles leads the way, box in hand. He tucks it under his arm and takes my hand in his, interlacing his fingers with mine. When I look at him, he mouths *"I'm proud of you,"* and I respond with a smile.

I'm proud of myself too.

It's an unusual but extremely welcoming feeling.

Right before I'm out of the door, Zeke yells, "Fuck you!"

"Right back at you, Zeke!" And with a middle finger to the air, we're out of the door.

I breathe a sigh of relief, releasing the tension I gained from working here and opening the door for new possibilities.

When Miles and I get to his truck, he slides the box of my

things into the back seat. Then he places his hands on my face, planting a quick, pride-filled kiss on me.

"What's next, baby?"

"Career-wise, I want to know what it would take to open my own place. I'm talented, and I don't doubt that anymore." He smiles, his eyes filled with delight. "But right now, I want you to take me to see Blake."

"I thought you were gonna wait for her to reach out?"

"Yeah… I thought about it, and I don't want that anymore. I don't want to sit with this feeling. I'm sorry for how it happened, but not why. Take me to see her."

Miles does exactly that, and I'm mentally preparing for how this is going to go. I don't think anything could prepare me for this conversation though. All I can do is be honest.

I don't even knock once we get there. She walks into Miles' place all the time without doing it, so I'm not either.

Kyler's in the kitchen working on dinner when we walk in.

"You're here," he says, looking directly at me.

"I'm here."

"She's out back shooting hoops," he offers up.

I leave Miles in there with Kyler and continue through the house. Once I'm outside, Blake looks up and stops dribbling.

"Riley."

"Blake."

"You're here."

"I am." I walk onto the court out back and stop a few feet from her. "I know you wanted time, but I was tired of waiting around. And I'm okay if you need more time to come to terms with it, but I came here to talk and to clear the air, and I'm not leaving until I do. You can just listen if that's what you want."

Blake nods, and I take that as the green light I was looking for.

"I'm sorry for hurting you the way that I did, and I'm sorry for betraying you. I went about it in all the wrong ways, and it was basically a slap to everything you mean to me. You're my best friend, my soul sister, and the first family I ever had. You took me in and showed me what genuine care for someone looked like. You dried my tears, listened to me whine about my problems, and that's just to start.

"Things with Miles started a long time ago, but it never went past more than friendship. I always had that feeling there, the one that longed for him, but I never acted on it. We knew there was something beyond friendship, but by the time we were ready to act on it, that guy filed charges against him."

"He told me what you did," she interjects.

"Yeah. I paid him off with the one nice thing my piece of shit mom left me. The situation was misconstrued, he said some things, and we didn't see each other again until you moved back here, but we didn't interact. Not until you sent me there when I needed a place to live."

Standing here, explaining this to her, is the most vulnerable that I've felt in a while. But the more I speak about it, the lighter I feel.

"Not gonna lie, things weren't great at first. We were both exercising our anger with each other. That happened for... a while. It was tense and uncomfortable, and one day, things just started to shift. Our anger lessened, his resentment drifted away, and then he found out about what I did. From Sam, no less. It forced us to admit a lot of things.

"And then Christmas happened. It put a lot into perspective, and that's when things became official. It was my idea at first to hide it from you. Then I heard the things you said to Miles, and the decision to tell you only got harder. You mean so much to me, and I was afraid to lose you forever. My only family—you and Miles," I say, the words croaking out of me.

I look to the sky to keep the tears from welling, not even realizing the emotions building inside me or the tightness in my chest.

"I'm sorry for the way I hurt you. I'm sorry for keeping it a secret for so long. I'm sorry for the conflict I've caused. I'm sorry for everything I've done, Blake. And I understand if you hate me; I wouldn't be surprised," I rush out, desperate for air.

Long-winded conversations aren't for me, and neither are speeches.

"I don't hate you, Riley. I could *never* hate you," she throws in, dropping the ball to come closer.

"But there's one thing I won't apologize for. I won't apologize for falling in love with your brother. He's everything I never thought I deserved, and so much more than I thought I'd end up with. He's kind, generous, funny, and extremely supportive of my mental health, which he understands better than I expected him to. He's attentive, and loving, and makes me a better person. I'm my best self with him, Blake. And I love this version of me."

"I love it too," she says, stopping in front of me.

Hold up.

What?

"Repeat that."

"I love it too."

I have no words.

"What, are you surprised? Did you think I was gonna slap you or something?"

"I've seen you do worse."

"True," she says with a laugh. "I'd never do that to you though. I know that I've been absent since I got the Head Coach job, and I haven't been around to be there for you. That's my fault and something I explained to Miles also. I promise to do better for you too.

"But in those times that I did see you, I saw how much your confidence had grown. I saw the way you began to see yourself differently." She bends down, getting eye level with me. "I saw you bloom, Riley. And if Miles helped you get there, then I have something to thank him for."

The tears flow, but this time they're accompanied by a burst of relieving laughter. Like the frozen ice that had consumed my body since she found out about us thawed, letting the warmth and hope back into my soul.

"Oh, babe," she sighs, wrapping her arms around me. "Please stop crying. You don't need to cry. Everything is okay."

"No, it's not. I've spent the last two days thinking that you hated me and now that I know you don't, I'm feeling everything at once."

"Get it all out, girl. Get it all out."

Blake holds me tight, letting me cry it out. These are far from sad tears though. They're like rainbow, sunshine, unicorn happy tears. Whatever the happiest thing in the universe is, that's how I'd describe them and this feeling.

When I've finally settled down, I pull back from Blake and stare up at her and her freakishly tall self.

"I love you. I hope you know that."

"I do know that, and I love you too, Riley."

"Is he the reason you like to cook now?" she asks, stepping back to pick up the ball.

She passes it to me, and I pass it back one-handed for her to shoot. With one simple conversation though... everything is resolved, and Blake and I are back to exactly how we were before.

"He taught me how. Said he wanted me to be okay and fed while he was on the road."

"How cute," she says, shooting and making the shot.

"Oh my god. The hot tub," she states with surprise. I immediately blush, knowing exactly what she's referring to. "I don't want to ask about the boxers, do I?"

I shake my head. "Probably not."

"Ugh," she gags, and we both fall into a fit of laughter. After helping Blake shoot around some more, we head back into the house. I stop her one more time.

"I'll be honest with you from now on."

"Please don't be too honest," she jokes. "There are some things I *don't* need to know about."

We're still laughing when we enter the house, my gaze finding Miles immediately. And when he returns my smile, watching Blake and I walk in with our arms locked, I get a rush.

A rush of bliss, of content. That rush fills the hole that's been inside me since I was a scared five-year-old, the one that grew when I parted with Miles all those years ago.

But now, I feel fuller than I ever have.

And it's all because my roommate kicked me out and my best friend forced me to live with her twin brother.

Not your average, normal, happily ever after story...

But when have I ever been normal?

That shit is overrated anyway.

CHAPTER 40
RILEY

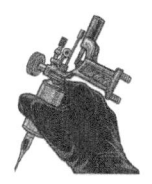

"What time is everyone getting here?" I ask.

"I told them to be here at six. I should have everything ready by then. It'd be easier if you helped," Miles says, his eyes lifting.

"Absolutely not. The whole Rainwater sibling clan will be here tonight and I'm not risking any aspect of this meal being messed up. I'm great at setting the table."

"As long as you don't trip," he adds, smirking as he flips ribs on the grill.

"Now why would you say that?" I mock fake hurt, heading back in the house. His laughter follows me inside.

I've never felt as much love and care as I have in the last few weeks. Now that we're no longer hiding it—at least with Blake—things have been better than ever.

And tonight, the rest of the siblings come over for us to tell them, but there's no worry in that department. I'll probably get a lot of shit for it, but that's just how Caleb, Asher and Hunter are.

I always vibed with Asher's grumpiness better, but I love the other nuts the same.

Just before six, Miles enters the dining room with the last bit of the food he prepared, all wrapped in tin foil to stay warm. He walks up behind me as I finish setting the table, sliding his hands around my waist to hook into the front belt loops of my shorts.

"How excited are you?"

"Pretty excited. It'll be nice for everyone to know that we're together. I just hope it isn't weird."

"Why would it be weird?" he questions.

Turning in his hold, I wrap my arms around his neck. "Miles, I've been around for a long time. And for many of those years, I was like the little sister. We'll basically be telling them that their so-called little sister is dating their little brother."

"Thank god we're not actually related," he says instead, ignoring the awkwardness that was what came out of my mouth. "Don't worry about them though. They'll be good."

"Good. Because I've been here too long to run off like some of the others." I pat Miles on the shoulder and head back to the kitchen to grab silverware for the side dishes and plates.

"That was one time," he yells. "And she was a gold digger after the Rainwater fame! We did Hunter a favor."

I'll give him that. She was an awful person.

Ten minutes later, all the Rainwaters crowd the foyer of our home. As if they're on some internal sibling clock that allows them to show up everywhere at the same time. It definitely isn't the first time.

The boys head straight to the kitchen for beers before beelining to the dining room. I exchange a hug with Blake and Hunter's girlfriend, Lanie.

Once we're settled in the dining room, everyone digs in like they've been starved at sea for months, bumping elbows and slewing expletives all around as they battle to get food.

"What's in this sauce?" Caleb asks.

"Chef's secret, man. You'll never know," Miles responds.

The guys congratulate Kyler and Miles on their championship game, apologizing for missing it. That's not all they manage to talk about.

"Why'd you run out halfway through the game?" Asher asks.

I'm mid-bite of slaw, but I can feel all eyes on Miles, and me.

"Riley was in an accident. I needed to be with her."

"And why's that?" Asher asks, a knowing glint in his eye.

Forever the perceptive one, that brother.

"Because Riley and I are together now. We're a couple."

Asher finishes his beer and stands from his chair. I'm not sure why, but it's definitely not what I expected as he walks over to the space between Caleb and Hunter, holding out his palms.

"Pay up, asshats," he demands in that gravelly tone of his.

"You fucking suck, I hope you know that," Hunter grumbles.

"You play pro baseball and Caleb is an agent. You can both spare a hundred bucks."

"No one likes giving away their money to their own siblings," Caleb offers up.

"Then don't make stupid bets," Asher quips.

He returns to his seat, and I lean forward to gain a better visual of him.

"I'm sorry. What bet?" I ask.

"I bet Caleb and Hunter before we walked in that you two would be together by now and that you'd tell us tonight at dinner," Asher answers. "They're stupid, and I'm two hundred dollars richer."

"Like you need money," Blake huffs. "You manage the damn Warhawks."

"True. But it's not about winning, usdi ulv." *Little sister.* "It's about bragging rights," he responds, adding, "you'd do a lot better for yourselves if you just paid attention to things. Not to mention, they were living under the same roof with all that pent-up sexual tension. It was bound to happen sometime. I figured it'd be back in high school but… semantics."

"Nope," Blake interrupts. "That's where the conversation stops. I don't need the risk of visuals."

"Were we that obvious?" I ask Miles, my voice low as the others pick up a different conversation.

"Apparently so. But it's also Asher we're talking about. The man is freakishly perceptive when it comes to people."

When everyone is through with eating, Blake places her napkin on the table and turns toward me and Miles.

"The food was good as always, Miles. Did you make anything this time?" she asks me.

"Not this time."

"Riley can't cook though," Caleb adds, finishing off his beer. "Unless you count burnt noodles as a meal."

Here we go.

"Hey, she's learned to cook now," Blake defends.

"I'm so confused," Lanie says with wide eyes. She looks so uncomfortable right now. But this family does take some getting used to.

"Oh baby, I'm sorry," Hunter soothes, grabbing her hand. "Let me fill you in. So, this one time when we were younger..." I roll my eyes.

Yeah, it's official.

I'm never *ever* living that down.

"What are you doing sitting all by yourself?" Asher asks, sitting down on the swing beside me.

The rest of the guys are busy putting together a bonfire while the girls are inside getting smores ingredients ready.

"I'm just enjoying the view." The view is Miles and Caleb joking around as they see who can pick up the biggest log for the fire. I don't think the competition ever ends in this family.

"You look good like that."

"Like what?"

"Happy."

"Yeah... I think I do too."

"I heard you quit your job too," he says.

"I did. My boss was a total dick anyway. I've been looking for potential places of my own, and I'm going to check them out next week. I'm hoping that I'll find a place."

"You're talented as hell, that's for sure. You'll find a place that's right for you."

"I know I will."

"But," he continues, "if that doesn't work out, you can always come be my assistant."

"You don't have an assistant. You work better alone."

"The organization is making me get one next season. I'm not looking forward to it. I don't have the time to train someone who will never get anything I ask right."

"Maybe you wouldn't be so particular if you pulled out one of the sticks up your ass."

He shoves me playfully. "I like things how I like them. I can't be faulted for that."

"Maybe so, but don't scare them to death whenever you meet them."

"I make no promises," he says, and I instantly feel sorry for someone that I don't even know.

His poor new assistant...

"Come on," he says, standing. "Let's go and see what kind of shit they're getting into."

"As long as they're not trying to push each other into the fire once it's lit, I don't care what they get into."

"Let's hope not."

"If they do, I'm not cleaning up the mess," I add.

"Hey, you chose this family. You knew what you were getting into from the start."

"Your sister coerced me into coming home with her the first time. I had no idea what would happen to me."

"Yeah, but you chose to stay," Asher reminds me, and I let it settle in for the first time since I was five years old.

I have a family now, and not one that makes me feel like a burden. Not like the family I was born into.

I guess the saying is right though.

You really can choose your family.

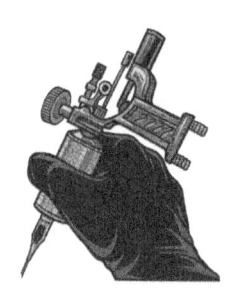

Once everyone has gone for the night and we've finished cleaning up, Miles and I pile into bed, the dog and cats piling in with us.

"Have you talked to your dad?" I ask Miles, deciding to address the absence in the room tonight.

"Not since we saw him at the hospital. I'm not gonna entertain the thought of him until he shows up with an apology in hand—for you and for me."

"You have every right to do that," I tell him. "But it's okay to miss him too. Regardless of how he's treated me, he's still your dad. You've only got one parent."

"And I'd be okay with having none if he doesn't pull it together and apologize to you. He's got a problem."

"We all know that, but when it's you, you can't begin to solve the problem until you recognize that there is one. All I ask is that when he reaches out, and I know he will, don't just blow him off. Be willing to hear him out. However misplaced his efforts are, he only did it because he loves you."

"You're a better person than I am, baby." Miles pulls me to him, my head falling to his chest. "But I'll think about it."

"Thank you."

"Can we talk about how great tonight was now?" he asks.

"Of course."

"I can't believe my brothers bet on us," he shakes his head.

"I can. But I'd never get in on one if Asher is the one setting it up. He's got a wicked sixth sense for reading people."

"So true," he says. "But I'm talking about how amazing it was to be able to love you out in the open. No hiding small touches and quick gazes, kissing in secluded corners, or dragging you away for stress-relieving orgasms. We were finally able to be just us."

"Yeah. It was really nice."

Miles's fingers run through my golden strands, pushing them out of my eyes. "Are you happy, Riley?"

"I'm happier than I've ever been in my entire life, and I owe it all to you." I press a kiss under his jaw.

"No, I don't get all the credit for this one. The majority of it goes to you because you finally allowed yourself to feel what you thought you'd never have, and no one is more deserving than you."

Pride and love and gratification shine in Miles's deep brown eyes, luring me in.

"I love you so much."

"And I love you," he responds, kissing the tip of my nose, causing a blush to appear on my cheeks. I can feel the heat in them. "What's next?"

"First, I need some sleep. Dealing with your family is exhausting," I say with a playful smile and a roll of my eyes. "And then I want to look around for more spots to add to the potential real estate list for the parlor. I'm tired of waiting for life to happen to me. This time, I'm gonna make it happen."

"Yeah, so… about that."

EPILOGUE
MILES

Today is a day that Riley has been looking forward to longer than she'll ever admit she has. It's been nothing but a labor of love over the past couple of months, but I can't be prouder of her.

It's pretty perfect honestly. I'd had a guy looking into real estate for her, and he was able to find the perfect place off-market and it became the parlor of Riley's dreams.

She was upset at first because I went behind her back to help find it, and even more upset when I didn't let her get a loan through a bank. I make millions of dollars per year. This was barely a drop in the bucket for me, but you can bet your ass she argued and settled on a compromise with me for the money.

I want none of it back. Absolutely zero. So, she'll be having a walk-in day each month where all the proceeds go to the grief and foster organization that Kyler works with.

I didn't need anything, but I'm proud of her choice.

We arrived here early this morning, making sure that everything was exactly as Riley wanted it. The decorative front lobby —full of trinkets, goddess statues, homemade art and all the items to make the waiting area homey—stocked supplies and clean equipment.

The place is perfectly Riley, and also perfectly anyone who needs a safe place.

Just before people start to arrive, Riley finds me in the front. Her arms wrap around me just before her head falls to my chest.

"I'm so tired," she sighs.

"You've worked really hard to make this grand opening a success. And I know that people will see that hard work and appreciate it. This will become everyone's favorite place to hang out."

"I hope so," she mumbles into my shirt.

"You did get it catered though, right? I'd hate for people to give you a bad review because you made the food."

She pulls back from me, her gaze nothing short of murderous.

"Not funny. Please remember that I can still make that green dinosaur dick happen."

"You're so cute."

"Sure, I am," she says.

"Before this all gets started, I just want you to know how proud I am of you for chasing your dreams, and not stopping until you had it in your hands."

"I couldn't have done it without you."

"Are you ready for this?"

"More than ready."

An hour later, the building is full of people grabbing food and talking amongst others. The sketchbooks that Riley and her employees have left lying around have been thoroughly looked through, and she's booked solid for the next two months.

Fairly sure the entire first month is players from the team and their significant others.

Riley gathers in the front lobby, standing on a footstool to gather the people's attention.

"Thank you all for coming out today," she begins. "I'm not good at long-winded speeches, something I've learned recently.

So, I'll be sure to make this as quick and as painless as possible… for me." The room erupts in laughter.

"Owning my own parlor has been a dream of mine for as long as I can remember, and I wouldn't have been able to do it without the support of my family and friends. I want this place to be a safe haven for anyone who needs it, and a place to express oneself without fear of judgment.

"Everyone here today will get a voucher for twenty percent off services for your first one, and if you book while you're here today, you'll receive free aftercare at your appointment. Feel free to ask questions, mingle, and eat all this food so I don't have to take any home.

"I hope it brings you a sense of home that way that it has brought me. We all deserve a place in our life where we can be authentically ourselves, and that's what I want this to be. Welcome to Wayward Souls Ink."

"I'm so happy to see her like this," Blake says, taking a seat beside me.

I've been sitting just outside Riley's room for the past two hours, watching people come in and out with fresh ink. Seeing her work is one thing but seeing her in her element is an experience all on its own.

"Like what?"

"Happy," Blake answers. "She's spent so many years watching us live out our dreams, only admiring from the sidelines. But it's her time to shine now, and I couldn't be more grateful to be here to watch her finally get her dream."

"I feel the same way."

Blake stares in awe at Riley, her eyes mirroring that of reminiscence. "I remember when we were kids and Riley used to doodle all over me like her own personal canvas. I always knew she was talented, but damn. This is something else."

"She's one of the best I've ever seen."

"That she is," Blake says with pride.

Blake and I continue to watch Riley in her element, lost in the world of creativity and imagination. Until Blake's eyes cut to the door.

"You invited Dad?" she asks with surprise.

"No. But Riley did."

"Why?"

"Because she's a better person than I am. And she thinks that we should mend fences."

"Do you want to?"

"I don't want to hate Dad forever, but I can't condone a relationship with him where he constantly belittles the woman I'm in love with."

"I'm still getting used to hearing that," Blake shakes her head. "But I'm glad you two found each other, my reluctance aside. You're pretty perfect together." A smile stretches over our faces. "And if you want to mend it with Dad, I'll help you. But don't expect immediate change. Because anyone *that* set in their way won't change overnight."

"I'm not expecting it to. But the door is open. It's on him if he wants to walk through it."

"Seems like he just took the first step." Blake reaches a hand over, gripping my own with a gentle force.

"Thank you for protecting her and standing up for her. She deserves to have as many people in her corner as possible."

"Always, Blake," I say with a squeeze of her hand. "For as long as she'll have me."

A few minutes later, Blake leaves to find Kyler in the crowd. I stay and watch as Riley finishes up with her current client. Once she's done, she walks out to me with a beaming smile stretched across her jaw-droppingly beautiful face.

"I have so much adrenaline right now," she laughs.

"That's how it feels when I'm on the court doing what I love. And you look so good doing what you love too."

"It feels good," she says, leaning down to rest her hands on my shoulders.

She presses her lips to mine, unable to keep the smile from spreading. It's barely even a kiss when I think about it. She's too damn happy to keep her lips pressed to mine. It makes me laugh.

Riley's laughter entangles with mine, and I pull her down so she's sitting on my lap. Her arms wrap around my neck, and I embrace the momentary reprieve from having her away from me all night.

She's warm and loyal and kind. Just her presence alone fills with me everything I thought I was missing. Turns out those parts of me were just missing her, and now I'm finally whole.

Riley pulls away and she sets her gaze on the crowd around us.

"There's so many people here," she acknowledges.

"All for you."

"And your dad came," she states, her voice laced with both shock and hope.

"Seems that way."

"Let's go say hello," she rushes out. She lifts from my lap, but my hand wraps around her wrist, keeping her still.

"Do we have to?" I ask.

"Miles, I know that you're still angry with Sam for the way he's treated me as of late. I'm not condoning it, but he's acted the way he has because of his own demons. And as someone who has struggled with many of them, sometimes we act rashly when we feel we don't have control."

I hate to admit it, but she makes sense.

"And I think there's something you need to consider," she adds.

"Which is?"

"He took the first step by showing up tonight. Now it's your turn to show up too."

It pains me to hear, but I know she's right. I think I'm just worried that I'll be disappointed again. I idolized my father growing up, aspired to be like him, and felt gutted when I realized he wasn't the man I thought he was.

What if I give him this second chance and he doesn't change?

"Okay," I sigh.

Riley grabs my hand, interlacing our fingers together. She begins to pull me in the direction of my dad, and my first few steps are slow like my feet are caked in cement, unable to move.

When we finally sidle up beside my dad, my hand grips Riley's tighter, and she squeezes back in a comforting manner.

"Sam," Riley says, grabbing his attention.

When my father turns around, I notice a difference in him. The hardened expression that's usually permanently etched on his face is no longer there. It's still tense, but not in an intimidating, closed-off way. And his uncaring eyes are no longer that way as he looks between Riley and me to see our hands molded together.

"It's nice to see you. It's, uh… a great turnout."

"Thank you for coming," she says, but Dad simply nods.

He finally looks at me, and there's a vulnerability to his eyes that I haven't seen before.

"Son," he says, his voice unsure.

"Dad."

The air grows stagnant around us, and you'd never know the room was bustling around us. It's never been this awkward with my dad, so the moment is extremely uncomfortable.

Riley must grow tired of the unnerving silence because she steps forward and lays a gentle hand on my father's forearm.

"Thank you again for coming. It means a lot." She pauses. "To us both."

He nods again. At least he's saying something even if it isn't with words. When I turn to pull Riley away to go back to her guests, my father's voice halts me.

"Son."

"Yes?"

"Would you like to come over for dinner one evening? To talk."

"Only if I can bring my girlfriend with me," I say with a firmness that's weighted with stone.

"I'd actually prefer it," he responds, shocking me with his agreeability.

"Then we'll reach out."

"I look forward to it," he replies, then he nods politely and walks away.

"I think things went really well today," Riley says, flipping through the books.

"Well? Riley, you killed it tonight. You set yourself up for success with this opening and tattooed as many people as you could."

"I hope so," she says with a sigh.

Closing the schedule book, I twist Riley around and place her on the reception desk, stepping between her thighs.

Her eyes are tired, slightly sunken, and purple underneath.

She's barely slept the last few days, worried about the opening. But it's the kind of exhaustion that's deserved.

"So, how does it feel?" I ask.

"How does what feel?"

"Getting everything you've ever wanted."

A sleepy smile stretches across her impossibly gorgeous face.

"It doesn't feel real yet. I can't explain how full I feel, but I know that I could have never dreamed how proud I would be of myself. It's everything and more."

"And no one deserves it more," I tell her, drawing her lips to mine.

The kiss is slow and sweet, full of yearning and fulfillment and so much love. Her lips are soft, molding with mine perfectly. The kiss turns lazy quickly, but Riley's hands begin to lift the hem of my shirt.

"What's my sleepy girl doing?"

"Trying to convince you to christen this new space with me."

"Aren't you tired?"

"Never," she answers.

Riley drags me to her room, placing me in the chair. She wastes no time dragging my jeans down my hips, discarding them on the floor beside her. She drops to her knees.

"What are you doing? This is your day. I should be the one on my knees."

"I've caught sight of you all day and couldn't stop thinking about all the ways you've helped me. And as much as I'm happy with myself, I'm in the mood to celebrate and reward you for helping me see my potential and helping me get here."

"If you insist."

"Oh, I very much do," she answers in a sultry voice.

Riley takes my shaft in her hand, dropping to kiss the tip of it. It's a quick tease as she repeats that a few times, and when I start to breathe heavier, she finally wraps her lips around me and takes me as far as she can. A hiss escapes my lips.

"Damn," I exhale in pleasure.

Riley uses her mouth and hand in tandem, swirling her tongue and alternating the intensity of her grip with each swipe. My legs tighten with each light graze of her teeth.

My hands find their way into Riley's hair, gripping it in my fist. It allows me to slow her pace, prolonging the pleasure and slowing the build of my release.

"Gotta admit, baby… you look sexy as hell taking my cock down your throat, stretching it just for me."

Dragging her off me, she looks even better this way. Her lips puffed and red, saliva dripping down her chin, eyes watery.

I can't stand it anymore. I need to be inside her.

Releasing her hair, I begin to rid Riley of her clothes until we're both as naked as the day we were born. Then I pull her to hover over me, straddling the chair, where she slides her slickness up and down my shaft.

"What's that?" she asks, pointing to the wrap on my forearm.

"I may have gotten a tattoo today."

"Let me see," she says, eyes lighting up.

Unwrapping the covered dressing to expose the Saniderm, Riley inspects the ink at the female warrior freshly tattooed on my skin.

"It's beautiful. What is it?"

"Do you remember the name I like to call you?"

"Yes, but don't ask me to pronounce it."

I laugh. "Usdi danuwaanalihi. It means little warrior."

"Why little warrior?"

"Because no one has fought in their life as much as you have. You never back down from a fight, Ri, and you never stop fighting, even when you feel like there's no way out. Your strength is unmatched, baby." My hand finds her cheek, the lightest of touches. "My little warrior," I whisper with a voice full of gratification and content.

Riley seals her lips with mine, slipping her hand between us to grab hold of me and press the tip to her entrance. In a quick movement, she's seated on top of me, filled to the hilt.

My hands find her hips on instinct. Riley slings her hair behind her back, her hands find my shoulders. She begins to swivel her hips, tilting forward to grind her clit against my pelvic bone.

I try to help out, adding pressure and pulling her down, but this is clearly her show, and I'm only here to enjoy the ride.

Riley works herself tired, giving out as she leans into my body, her hips slowing.

"I can't believe we get to do this forever," she says sleepily, joyously.

"I can."

My hands shift around her thighs, my fingers digging into the meat of her ass.

"Hips up, baby."

When Riley lifts, I hold her there with my arms, wasting no time in thrusting upward into her rapidly. Her hips shift into the right position, and I know I've hit that spot that makes her go hazy when she screams out.

I don't stop, not until she buries her breasts in my face and clenches around my cock, her response practically pulling the orgasm straight out of me.

I'm still seated inside Riley, the mixture of our cum dripping down our legs, when I feel the teardrop on my chest.

"What's wrong?" I ask, gripping her chin to bring her face level with mine.

"Absolutely nothing," she smiles. "Everything is exactly as it should be in my life, and I can't wait for what's gonna happen next."

"And what happens next?" I ask.

"Anything we want," she answers, with more glee than I've ever heard in her voice.

"I like the sound of that. We've played the game long enough. Had some losses, had some wins. And even if we struggle or lose things in the future, you need to know that I won the minute I met you. Okay?"

"We both won." She smiles, accentuating her words with a kiss. "And I wouldn't have wanted to play the long game with anyone else."

"Although…" she trails off. "We wouldn't have had to play for so long if you would have just took your shot a lot earlier."

"No," I shake my head. "Because then we may not be where we are now, and I think it's pretty perfect."

"We're pretty perfect," she says.

That may be true, but she's more perfect than I'll ever be.

And we have the rest of our lives for me to prove that.

THE END

WANT TO READ MORE MILES AND RILEY?

GET THE EXCLUSIVE BONUS SCENE HERE:

https://dl.bookfunnel.com/f04jpjk3me

GLOSSARY

A translation for the Cherokee language shared throughout the book.

Gvsgasdagi – rude
Usdi danuwaanalihi – little warrior
Wado – thank you
Alewisdodi – Stop
Uwoduhi – Beautiful
Ududu – Grandfather
Ulisi – Grandmother
Ulihelisdi udetiyisgv – Happy birthday
Sagonige – Blue
Nahnai winiduyugodvna – There's no way
Usdi ulv – Little sister
Tla – No
Ayv uha ugisv nihi – I have got you

THANK YOU FOR READING!

If you loved reading about Miles and Riley and enjoyed their story, please consider leaving a review!

Crescent City Book 3 will be coming soon and if you didn't figure it out in the epilogue, Asher is the MMC! But his heroine is someone you've never met before. Can anyone guess the tropes?

To be the first to know about book related things and get access to exclusive content:

Join My Reader Group on Facebook
Or
Sign Up For My Newsletter

CONNECT WITH ME

Want to stay in the know and be my friend?

Instagram: @authorcassieflinchum
Join My Facebook Reader Group:
Cassie's Cliterature Squad
TikTok: @authorcassieflinchum

ACKNOWLEDGMENTS

As with every book I write, there are a multitude of people that I want to thank for helping me bring this book to life.

To my Alpha readers: Katie, Nikki, Isa, Frances, Shani, and Jeri - I never know where to begin here because I can never truly express how thankful and blessed I am to have you. Thank you for giving me honest feedback in a kind, constructive way, and thank you for helping keep my vision for Miles and Riley clear. You play a huge part in turning my OG pile of crap into something I can honestly say I'm proud of, and for that I am forever grateful. I couldn't be more blessed to have you on my team.

To my cover designers: Jo and Aliyah - Thank you both so much for absolutely crushing my ideas for both the spicy and discreet covers and for not being annoyed every time I wanted to make another change. I give you the bare minimum, and you turn those ideas into something spectacular. The final products are stunning and I can't wait to have them on my shelf.

To my editor, Jenn - This is my first time working with you but I can say for certain it won't be my last. Thank you for taking a deeper look into Miles and Riley's story and for pointing out potential flaws in their overall arc. Without your feedback, this book wouldn't be half of what it is. Thank you so much for being my editor.

To my proofreader, Sophie - Thank you for being such a light to work with and for putting the final polish on all my manuscripts. Your endless support and excitement for my writing means so much to me.

To my best friend, June - Words will never describe how thankful I am to have you in my life. My twisted sister from another mister, the person whose mind is as dark as mine, and the person who never fails to make me smile even when we both feel like shit. Thank you for always being there for me whenever I need it. I appreciate you, and I love you.

To my author best friend who is more like my IRL best friend, Avery - I don't know what I'd do without you. Personally, I can't imagine my life without you in it. Thank you for your knowledge, for your advice, and for your help. But thank you the most for always being there to hear my rants, and for always being down to shit talk for hours. I cherish those conversations more than you know. I'm so thankful to have you. Thank you for being my friend.

To my personal cheerleader, Katie - Thank you for being the light in my darkest days. You send me daily sunshine's every single day without fail because they really do bring light to my day, especially when I'm feeling down. You're my alpha and my personal cheerleader, but most importantly, you're my friend, and I am so thankful to have met you. Please never change.

To my voice of reason, sounding board and copy/line editor, Isa - Thank you for always expressing your belief in me, especially on my worst days when I have no confidence in myself. Thank you for letting me bounce ideas off you, giving me your honest opinion, and for being my official, unofficial copy/line editor because without you, I'd have too many commas, misplaced em-dashes and who knows what else. You are still one of the kindest, sweetest, and most giving people I've ever met, and I'm thankful to have met you. Thank you for being my friend.

To my ARC readers and everyone else who reads my book - Thank you! ARC readers, your early interest in the book and posting reviews, teasers, etc. helps me more than you know. I can't tell you how grateful I am that you took a chance on this book, and on me, especially for those of you taking a chance on a new author. To all the other readers who get this upon its release, thank you for taking the time to read this book and for supporting me. Your interest, your support, and your recommendations are what drives me to continue on this writing journey, and without you, I wouldn't be here. Thank you from the bottom of my heart.

ABOUT THE AUTHOR

Cassie Flinchum is a part time steamy romance author, full-time procrastinator, self-proclaimed comedian, and considers profanity her first language. Her goal in writing is to provide you with your next book boyfriend, teach you how to read one-handed, and give you a heart-grabbing happily ever after that will have you smiling until your face hurts while keeping it real.

When she's not writing and immediately hating what she wrote, you can find her binging TV, working on her family's farmland, using her nursing degree, or being the resident crazy cat lady. She lives in the middle of nowhere, USA—seriously, you can't find it on a map—okay, it's just North Carolina but in the backwoods—with her support system and her many cats.

Cassie wouldn't be here without the support of her friends and readers, and she can't wait to grow with you on this journey as she continues to write contemporary romance of all sub-genres, and one day, hopefully, dark romance.

- facebook.com/authorcassieflinchum
- instagram.com/authorcassieflinchum
- tiktok.com/@authorcassieflinchum
- amazon.com/stores/Cassie-Flinchum
- goodreads.com/Cassie_Flinchum

ALSO BY CASSIE FLINCHUM

Standalones

Worth Fighting For

Crescent City Series

Calling the Shots (Book 1)

The Long Game (Book 2)

Printed in Great Britain
by Amazon